KALYX

KAREN LYNCH

ALSO BY KAREN LYNCH

Relentless Series

Relentless

Refuge

Rogue

Warrior

Haven

Fated

Hellion

Tempest

Fae Games Series

Pawn

Knight

Queen

For April

Every writer should have a friend like you.

ACKNOWLEDGMENTS

Thank you to my family and friends for your love and support, my beta readers (Anne-Marie, Irina, April, Sarah, and Eva), my editor, Kelly, my cover designer, Melissa, and all the readers who make this possible.

1

I crouched behind the gnarled maple tree, my eyes fixed on the stately brick house. It was dark except for the soft glow from a second-floor window. He always left that light on when he wasn't at home.

A ping sounded in my ear, and I pulled up my sleeve to check the timer on my phone. It counted down from ten, and the second it hit zero, my ears picked up a whirring sound that grew steadily closer.

Flattening myself against the tree, I listened as the security drone did its slow sweep of the backyard.

After a minute, the surveillance device disappeared around the side of the house. I restarted the timer on my phone as I rounded the tree and ran silently across the yard, mentally rehearsing my next steps. I had only three minutes until the drone came around for another pass.

Mrrroww.

"Gah!" I slapped a hand over my mouth and dropped to the ground. Rolling onto my side, I glared at the gray Persian cat two feet away. "Winston, you jerk," I hissed, though I was more annoyed at myself for letting him sneak up on me.

Winston sat and began to wash his face as if he hadn't made me nearly jump out of my skin.

I moved to sit up and heard a faint whirring from somewhere off to the left that quickly grew louder. *Crap!*

I looked around for cover and dived beneath a large Rhododendron shrub. Through the thick canopy of leaves, I watched the flickering lights of the security drone zooming toward me. The drone, which resembled a big metal bug, stopped to hover directly above my hiding place.

Home security drones were programmed to search within a set of parameters, and they didn't deviate unless they picked up a noise or movement that was out of place. The standard models took video of anything suspicious. The more expensive ones could also digitally tag you and follow you right to your door.

This one was expensive. Its camera eye swiveled in its socket, scanning the area like it could sense my fear. I held my breath as it slowly rotated in a full circle looking for the cause of the disturbance.

Winston hissed up at the drone and caterwauled as if the thing offended him. It didn't react to him because it was programmed to ignore small animals. It did another three-hundred-and-sixty-degree sweep of the area and flew off to resume its normal security routine.

I exhaled slowly, pulse hammering. Resetting my watch timer, I emerged from beneath the shrub. I skirted around the cat, ran across the yard to the patio, and tapped the back door's keypad with my gloved hand. The display lit up, and I entered the eight-digit code.

Nothing happened.

My heart missed a beat. The code had to be right. Finley never got it wrong.

I tried it again. The display flashed green, and there was a soft click.

Easing the door open, I listened for sounds inside. All I could hear was the beeping of the security panel near the door telling me I had less than thirty seconds before the alarm went off. I slipped inside and used a different code to disarm the system.

The light overhead flicked on, and a female voice came from the speaker on the panel. "Welcome home, Stephen."

I flipped off the light, throwing the interior back into darkness. I'd been here before, so I knew my way around. Crossing the spacious living room, I walked down a short hallway to the office at the end of the house. I closed the door and shined my penlight around the room. It was richly decorated with antique furniture and two abstract oil paintings Mr. Palmer had paid five figures for. I studied the angry slashes of color on the canvases and shook my head. I didn't get it, but to each their own.

I leaned down to pull back the Oriental rug in the center of the room, revealing a twelve-inch wooden square set into the hardwood floor. Kneeling, I lifted the piece of wood and smiled at the keypad and digital display beneath. There must have been a sale on these safes because it was the third time I'd seen this model in the last three months.

Shrugging off my small backpack, I took out my code reader and placed it over the keypad. The digital readout on the device lit up, and within ten seconds, it had the first number locked in. I sat back on my heels and watched it cycle through digits before it quickly found the second one. This thing was worth every one of the two thousand credits I'd paid for it.

It took less than a minute for the code reader to crack the six-digit code. I lifted the door and looked down at a file folder, a sheet of notepaper, and a small crystal disc. I paused to admire the disc. It was one of the newer drives, which could hold a petabyte of data and required a ten-digit code and biometrics to unlock it. It was the most secure drive on the market and serious hardware for someone who used a mediocre safe to store it in. It was also not what I was here for.

I lifted the papers and drive to reveal the real prize, and I whistled softly at the stacks of credit chips. There had to be over eighty thousand dollars here.

Thank you, Mr. Palmer, for your generous donation.

Smiling, I grabbed one stack and stuffed it in my backpack along with my code reader. My number one rule was never get greedy. If you took a small amount, it was less likely to be noticed right away, if at all.

I picked up the folder to return it to the safe and glanced at the notepaper on top. On the paper was a list of six random sequences of numbers, letters, and special characters, which looked like passwords. All but the last one had been crossed off.

Shaking my head, I placed the paper in the safe along with the folder and drive. At least he wasn't dumb enough to keep them on a sticky note in his desk drawer like some people did.

I locked the safe and let the rug fall back into place. Even when no one else was around, I tried to make as little noise as possible. It was good to keep that skill sharp in case I ever needed it. I donned my pack, did a last visual sweep of the room, and turned off my flashlight before I went to the door.

My hand had barely touched the doorknob when a man's voice drifted down the hall toward me.

I froze. He was supposed to be out of town tonight. What was he doing home?

His voice grew louder, and I jerked back from the door. He was coming toward me.

I looked around frantically, but there was nowhere to hide in here. My eyes went to the window behind the desk, and I hurried toward it. If I went out this way, there was a high probability of being spotted by the security drone. If I stayed, I'd be caught for sure.

I had the window open when Mr. Palmer's voice came from right outside the office door. "I must have left the drive in my safe. This damn project has me running in circles half the time. I even forgot to set the alarm when I left this morning."

There was a pause, and he spoke in a raised voice. "I know what Dev will do if he finds out I brought it home with me. I'll bring it back, and he never has to know."

I threw a leg over the window sill. The doorknob turned, and I froze like a deer in the headlights of an oncoming truck.

"Hold on, Jake." The knob stopped moving. "I think Winston might have gotten out." There was a pause followed by a laugh. "I'll call you back in a few minutes."

I pulled my leg in and closed the window as his footsteps receded. Hurrying to the door, I cracked it open and listened to him walk to the back door. This was my only chance.

I slipped out of the office and quietly shut the door. Moving with all the stealth I possessed, I sped across the living room to the foyer where a laptop bag sat on the floor.

I cracked the front door open half an inch and checked my phone. The security drone was due to pass by the front of the house in fifteen seconds. I was trapped.

The back door closed, and footsteps entered the kitchen.

Shit.

I pressed my back to the foyer wall, but he'd be able to see me if he entered the living room.

My heart pounded in my ears. I was wearing a mask, and I could outrun him, but there was no way I'd outrun his security drone.

Winston let out a demanding meow. Mr. Palmer muttered something and opened a cabinet door. The sounds from the kitchen almost drowned out the whir of the security drone as it passed by the door.

I silently counted down the seconds until the drone finished its sweep. The kitchen recycle bin opened, and a can was dropped inside. Water ran in the sink as he washed his hands.

A glass shattered on the tile floor, and the man swore loudly. "Winston!"

I widened the door just enough to slip through and eased it shut behind me. I flew down the steps and across the lawn to the street. The house across the street was dark, and I hoped there was no one at home to see me.

Yanking off my mask and gloves, I stuffed them in my pocket as I started down the sidewalk. My breath came out in harsh pants like I'd run a five-minute mile. That had been too close.

Five minutes later, I came to another house. It was one of the biggest in the neighborhood, but there was no security drone patrolling the property. Like Mr. Palmer's house, it was dark inside, and I shook my head as I walked to the front door and punched in the code. Inside, I flicked on a light and disarmed the security panel.

"Welcome home, Charlotte," said the system.

I scowled at the display before I walked to the kitchen where a note lay on the island. *Charlotte, don't forget to fill out your college applications tonight. Mom*

I crumpled the note and tossed it in the garbage.

Dropping my backpack on the stone countertop, I went to the refrigerator and pulled out a cooked chicken breast, a bottle of salad dressing, and some chopped vegetables.

As I assembled the salad, my thoughts kept circling back to the Palmer house. I replayed every step while I ate at the kitchen island, one eye on the news.

I clicked through the channels: catastrophic flooding in Myanmar, a deadly heatwave in the Middle East that had already killed hundreds, Hurricane Thelma gaining strength in the Gulf, and riots in Beijing, Paris, and Moscow.

The food in my gut soured at the footage of endless lines outside food distribution centers in Lisbon and Paris. People wore masks or scraps of cloth to filter the dirty haze choking the cities. Soldiers tried to hold the lines as desperate people surged forward. There just wasn't enough for everyone.

So far, North America had avoided the worst of it. The U.S., Mexico, and Canada had worked together aggressively to protect our food production when extreme droughts began to impact the global food supply. Huge hydro-farms designed to grow crops in drought conditions now stretched across the Great Plains, southern Canada, and northern Mexico. Dozens of coastal desalination plants had also come online in the past decade, converting seawater into just enough drinkable water to keep major cities going.

We were okay for now, but at the rate things were deteriorating, it was only a matter of time.

I flipped again and landed on a wide shot of the international space dock, and the shell of a massive ship under construction there.

"The North American Coalition currently leads in the race to Alcea, though the EU and China report significant progress," said a smooth male voice. *"Critics of the program call it a fool's mission, arguing that governments should focus on saving the planet we have, instead of putting all this money and effort into trying to colonize one light-years away."*

Nothing new. I clicked again and stopped on a science panel show where three guys with messy hair were animatedly discussing the history of the FTL drive.

Nineteen years ago, the invention of the faster-than-light drive led to the launch of the Centauri probe. The probe had traveled to Alpha Centauri and returned ten years later with data confirming the existence of a habitable Earth-like planet in that system.

Everyone over the age of ten understood the implications of such a discovery, and the race to colonize the planet, named Alpha-C-A1, had begun. Someone had shortened it to Alcea, and the name had stuck.

I wasn't against the space program. What angered me was how fast the people in power had given up on Earth. They weren't even pretending to fix it anymore. They were pinning all their hopes on a distant planet we might never be able to reach.

"*Technology has come a long way since the probe,*" one of the panelists said, "*but it's been seven years, and we're still nowhere near sending people to Alcea in our lifetime.*"

"*One of the major obstacles,*" the third chimed in, "*is adapting the FTL drive to a manned ship. You're talking about g-forces strong enough to turn a person to paste and radiation that'd fry you before you left orbit.*"

I turned off the TV. No longer hungry, I put the rest of my salad in the fridge, grabbed my pack, and headed upstairs to my bedroom. I laid the credits on my desk where my mother's list of college applications lay. The one for Caltech was at the top of the list, no surprise since it was my parents' alma mater. They had been talking about me going there for years.

Below that was Stanford, Georgia Tech, and MIT. Opening my desk drawer, I stuffed the paper inside. I'd already applied to my top choices: Carnegie Mellon, UW, and – yes – MIT. I just hadn't told my parents yet.

I retrieved the credit reader and extra laptop I kept hidden at the back of my walk-in closet and carried them to the desk. Firing up the laptop, I scanned the credit chips. It was amazing what you could find online if you knew where to look for it. Or you had a friend who knew her way around the dark web.

After the scanner had removed the digital tag from each chip, I looked at the total on my screen and smiled. Five thousand dollars. This was my best take yet.

I deposited the credits into the secret account I shared with Finley and logged into the encrypted messenger app she'd created for us. It was one-thirty in the morning in London, but she always stayed up to wait for me.

Charlie: Special delivery.

As expected, my best friend responded immediately.

Finley: Wow! Nice haul. Any trouble?

Charlie: Nope. The security codes you gave me worked great.

Finley: Of course!

Charlie: We really need to do something about your lack of self-esteem.

Finley: Har har. What was your time?

I made a face.

Charlie: Two minutes slower than last time. He came home while I was in the office.

Finley: What?! You said there was no trouble.

Charlie: There wasn't. He had no idea I was there.

Finley: I think I'm having a heart attack.

Charlie: You are not. How did yours go?

Finley: I only scored £700. Mum came in and I had to abort.

I chuckled, picturing her sitting at her computer, deep in some server on the other side of the world with her mom standing in the doorway.

To the people who knew her, Finley was a tech whiz destined to create the next *Microsoft*. On the darknet, she was Nightshade, an elite hacker who'd slipped past secure firewalls that intelligence agencies couldn't breach. Most people thought Nightshade was a man. Others were sure it was a collective.

No one would ever guess the truth: their idol was a seventeen-year-old girl with a curfew and a weekly allowance.

Charlie: You'll catch up to me someday.

Finley: You're wearing that smug smile again, aren't you?

Charlie: Me? Never!

Finley: Tonight's haul gives us enough to feed the shelter for 3 more days.

Charlie: Only 3?

Finley: Cost of food went up again.

Charlie: We need a new source of revenue. Almost tapped out here.

Finley: Let's brainstorm when I get back from the wilds of Scotland.

Charlie: Are you really going off grid for a whole week?

Finley: 6 days. Might as well be 6 years. Save me!

Charlie: I wish I could.

Finley: Gotta go. Mum's yelling at me to go to bed.

Charlie: I miss being in the same time zone with you.

Finley: Hopefully soon. Fingers crossed.

Standing, I stripped off my black pants and coat and tucked them away in my closet along with my pack, laptop, and chip reader. I pulled on a pair of sleep pants and my favorite old T-shirt, and opened the window a few inches to let in the October air. My room faced the woods, and I liked listening to the forest sounds until it got too cold to sleep with the window open.

I detached my phone from its wristband, and it flattened out smoothly, the display adjusting to the larger surface area. Placing it on the nightstand, I climbed into bed and curled up on my side, thinking about Finley and her parents.

Things in Europe had been bad for a while, but until two years ago, the UK had managed to keep the unrest outside its borders. Now there were protests almost every day and violent crimes had been rising steadily. The country was a powder keg waiting for a spark to ignite it.

Finley's family lived in a safe neighborhood, but it was only a matter of time before nowhere in the country was safe. Her parents had applied for Canadian and U.S. visas a year and a half ago. The only people granted entry were those in highly skilled occupations, but it was a long process. It could take another year or two for them to get their visas.

My mind was finally slowing down when the house shuddered, and the windows rattled in their frames. I bolted upright as something roared overhead so low it felt like the ceiling might come down.

I ran to the window in time to catch a dark shape slicing through the night sky, barely clearing the treetops as it flew over the forest.

It wasn't unusual to hear Sutton's test planes, but they never flew this low or directly over town.

For a second, I thought I saw flames licking along one wing before the thing dipped over the hill and vanished toward Alder Ravine. If that was one of Sutton's prototypes, someone had just crashed a thirty-million-dollar aircraft.

Climbing back into bed, I got comfortable again. Less than five minutes later, two helicopters flew overhead going in the same direction as the plane. I thought about the pilot of the downed plane and hoped he was okay.

I jerked awake with a start. My heart thudded, and I looked around the dark room in confusion. The house was quiet, and a glance at my phone told me it was almost 3:00 a.m. I heard an engine in the distance and realized Sutton must be out there in the ravine cleaning up the crash.

I closed my eyes and drifted off again. I was on the edge of sleep when a new sound tugged at my awareness. It was the scrape of metal mingled with a low, guttural sound.

Weird, I thought, but the pull of sleep was too strong, and I gave myself up to it.

"Charlotte, why haven't you submitted your college application to Caltech?"

I signed off the virtual school portal and swung my chair around to face my mother, who stood in the doorway to the den.

"How do you know I haven't submitted it?" I asked even though I already knew the answer.

Her mouth turned down. At forty-seven, Evelyn Ross was an attractive woman, thanks in part to a rigid diet and a lifelong abhorrence of the sun. Her pale blonde hair had no hint of gray, and her five-foot-nine figure was as slender as it had been when she was in college.

Today, she wore jeans, a black long-sleeved tee, a cap, and hiking boots. It was a far cry from the pants, shirt, heels, and lab coat that made up her normal work attire. She was an astrophysicist, and she worked for the aero-space division of Sutton Technologies along with my father, who was a nuclear physicist.

The American Coalition, which consisted of the U.S., Canada, and Mexico, had contracted companies around the globe to work on various sections and systems of their colony ship. Together, my parents were leading the development of the FTL drive and its power source – two of the most vital pieces of the entire project.

The test plane that had gone down in Alder Ravine four days ago was crucial to her project, and she had been personally overseeing the cleanup of the crash site. It was probably the only thing that could get her out of the lab during daylight hours.

"I spoke to Marian Edwards today," she said. "She told me Caltech has not received your application. I called the admissions offices at Stanford and Georgia Tech, and they don't have one from you either. Explain that."

"The explanation is simple. I didn't apply because I don't want to go to any of those schools. I've told you that a hundred times."

She tightened her grip on the paper. "Do you know how many people would kill to get into one of these colleges?"

"Then one of them will be very happy to take my spot." I stood and stretched my back, stiff from sitting too long.

Her eyes narrowed. "These schools all have excellent engineering and science programs, and you can have your pick of them. What more could you want?"

"What I want is to decide for myself where and what I'll study." I suppressed a sigh. "You love your work, and that's great, but I want to do my own thing."

"You're being ridiculous," she snapped. "We're entering a new age for science and technology, and the possibilities are endless for those who make the right career choices."

"And what about the people who don't have a choice?"

She huffed. "Life is not fair, Charlotte. You cannot hold yourself back because you have opportunities others do not. And there are always choices for people who work for them. Your father and I didn't get where we are without dedication and hard work."

I could remind her that she and Dad came from money, which had put them ahead of the game before they'd even thought about what career they wanted. Instead, I said, "Just because I don't want a job like yours, it doesn't mean I'm holding myself back."

Her spine went rigid. "Vanguard is more than a *job*. It's the most important and significant undertaking in the history of mankind. This project could be the key to ensuring our survival as a species."

"But not the whole species," I said before she could launch into one of her lectures extolling the greatness of their precious colony ship. She always conveniently left out the billions of people who would never get to travel on that ship. "Wouldn't all the funding and that collective brainpower be better served trying to save the planet we have?"

A furrow appeared in her smooth forehead. "I think that collective brainpower knows better than an eighteen-year-old what is best for us all."

I walked past her into the kitchen, feeling her eyes on me as I opened the refrigerator and took out a bottle of orange juice. I poured a glass and drank half of it before my mother spoke again.

"Charlotte, juice is full of sugar." Her critical gaze dropped to my waist. "Drink water instead."

I finished the juice and rinsed my glass, choosing not to respond. Ever since I hit puberty, she'd been pushing me to eat healthier. She refused to consider that not everyone could be pencil-thin like her.

She placed the paper on the countertop. "I have to get back to work. We'll continue this discussion later."

I waited for the sound of the door closing to turn away from the sink. As far as arguments with my mother went, this one had been mild, but it left me with the same feelings of resentment she always stirred in me. She and I were polar opposites, and she would never accept me as I was. The more she tried to change me, the harder my resolve grew not to be like her.

I headed for the stairs and paused at one of the artfully arranged pictures in the downstairs hallway. It was one of my parents and me from two years ago. My mother's Nordic heritage was obvious in her blonde hair, fair skin, and pale green eyes. It was a striking contrast to the dark hair, warm olive skin, and blue eyes my father and I had inherited from his Italian roots.

I studied the portrait. We were all smiling, but mine didn't reach my eyes.

It was taken a month after we left London, when I could barely pretend to be okay. I was devastated when my parents announced we were moving back to the U.S. so they could head up the Vanguard project.

I looked younger, even though it was only two years ago. It was probably the hair. I'd worn it long back then. Six months after we got here, I found a stylist to chop it into messy layers that fell just past my chin. My mother had a meltdown. She'd been trying ever since to get me to grow it out again.

Running upstairs, I changed into leggings, a long-sleeved top, and hiking boots. I grabbed my small hiking backpack and left the house by the back door.

The stone patio, with its outdoor kitchen and table for twelve, was a leftover from the previous owners, who had apparently loved to entertain. Steps led down to the yard that had more shrubs and flower beds than grass and was meticulously tended by a landscaping company.

The sky had its usual grayish haze, not thick enough to block the sun, but enough to dull it, and the air smelled stale. We were lucky here. In the larger metro areas, the air quality was a lot worse and most people wore masks outside all the time. We had days like that, but mostly it was tolerable like this.

I entered the woods. The deeper I went, the better the air got until I could almost pretend the whole world was like this. We should be feeling the first bite of fall, but the air was warm, and the leaves had barely begun to change color. Winter would be here soon enough, so I'd enjoy the warm weather as long as I could.

The military had ordered the town to stay out of the woods while Sutton searched for pieces of the engine that had fallen off before the crash. I figured they'd had more than enough time to clean up their mess.

I set off along a winding trail that ran past our neighborhood and went on for several miles toward the ravine. Tree roots and jutting rocks made the trail a little treacherous for joggers, which meant more solitude for hikers like me.

A pair of squirrels chattered and chased each other through the branches above my head as a chickadee sang cheerfully. In the underbrush, a small creature scurried past.

I smiled to myself and remembered how alien the woods had felt to me when we'd moved to Hudson Ridge. For the first week after we got here, I'd stayed in my room, feeling sorry for myself. Eventually, boredom drove me out of the house. I'd always been a city girl, but it didn't take long for me to fall in love with the Hudson Valley.

I followed the trail for half a mile, before I veered left and started uphill. There was no trail to follow, and it was a bit of a hike, but at the top was an overlook that provided a breathtaking panoramic view of the town and surrounding area.

Thirty minutes into my brisk climb, I stopped to sit on a downed tree and drink from my water bottle. I took a few minutes to catch my breath and enjoy the quiet before I continued my trek. I still had another twenty minutes to go to reach the top, but it was worth the effort.

My fingers toyed with the small charm dangling from my backpack zipper, and a smile tugged at my lips. It was a silver padlock, part of a set Finley and I had found at a street market in Notting Hill. Her charm was a key that fit perfectly into the lock's keyhole, a design clearly meant for a couple, but we'd bought them on a whim.

I stood, stuffing my water bottle into the pack, when it struck me how quiet the woods had become. No, not quiet – they were dead silent. I frowned up at the trees where no birds or squirrels stirred. How long had it been like this? Since I left the main trail or had it just started?

A chill skittered down my spine. Something about this silence felt... wrong.

A sound came from somewhere to my right, and I jumped, almost falling off the tree. I cocked my head and listened. There it was again, the scrape of metal on rock. It definitely was not an animal.

I stared in that direction, but I couldn't see anything through the trees and thick underbrush. I indecisively twisted the strap of my backpack. My curious side wanted me to go investigate, while my pragmatic side told me to get the hell out of there.

I took a step back to retreat down the hill and froze when the scraping sound came again. What if someone was hurt and unable to call for help? If I left, it could be days or weeks before another person came along.

Reaching back, I pulled out the multi-purpose tool I kept in a side pocket of my pack. The two-and-a-half-inch blade wasn't much protection, but it was better than nothing. I sent up a small prayer that I didn't have to use it as I ducked under a low branch and moved in the direction of the sound.

A dozen yards in, I stopped to examine a spot where the leaves and dirt had been churned up and partially smoothed out by rain. It had rained three days ago, which meant whomever or whatever had come through here had done it before then. I also noticed a few freshly broken twigs and a splotch of purple on a rock. Some idiot boys had spray-painted graffiti on the overlook this summer on a dare. It was possible they had come this way.

Bending, I touched the rock and rubbed the purple substance between my fingers. It didn't have the consistency of paint. I lifted my hand to my nose and sniffed it. It had a strangely metallic scent I couldn't identify. Some kind of machine lubricant maybe.

I wiped it off with some leaves and resumed walking, trying not to let the eerie absence of animal sounds creep me out. A hush had fallen over the woods as if every living thing here was waiting for something. Afraid to be the one to break the silence, I walked as quietly as I could, avoiding dead twigs on the ground and carefully sidestepping branches instead of pushing through them.

I came to a large tree that had fallen over and was resting at an angle against another tree, leaving its massive roots exposed. I started to go around it when something glinted in the hollow beneath the tree.

Creeping closer, I squinted into the darkness. A yellow light appeared and blinked out. Movement came from inside, and suddenly there were two lights, like pieces of amber swirling with fire.

The hair lifted on the back of my neck.

If I didn't know better, I'd almost think they were eyes.

2

A shape exploded from the darkness, all fur and claws and metal. I screamed and stumbled back, tripping over a rock and landing hard on my ass.

The creature was wedged halfway out of the hole, only its head and front limbs visible. It looked like a panther at first, but the resemblance ended at the fur. The top of its head was partly covered by black metal that had a jagged tear on one side, and its once amber eyes, now burned red.

It growled and lunged, a massive paw slashing through the air just short of my face. I scrambled backward, heart racing. I caught a glimpse of long, black claws before the thing let out a pained sound that was half snarl, half scream and fell back into the hole.

Over the roaring in my ears, I heard the creature thrashing in the hole, struggling to climb out again.

Get up, shouted a voice in my head.

I sprang to my feet and ran, branches whipping at my face, roots tripping me. I slipped once, hit the ground, and pushed myself up again, racing down the hill as if a pack of demons were on my heels.

I hit the main trail, scraped and breathless but still in one piece. Barely pausing to catch my breath, I started for home at a brisk pace. I knew the trail so well I could manage a light run without risking a twisted ankle. Every sound made me jump, and I expected the creature to leap out at me at any second.

I screamed as a figure stepped out of the woods, directly into my path. I slammed into him at full speed, and he caught my arms to steady me.

I tried to back away, but his grip clamped down, bruising and unrelenting.

"Let go of me." I twisted and kicked at his knee, but it was as solid as a tree trunk.

"Who are you?" he demanded. "What are you doing out here?"

He was tall, in his late thirties, and dressed in camo, with close-cropped blond hair and a hard, angular face. There were always military people stationed at Sutton because of the FTL project, and they were a common sight in town. This was the first time I'd been accosted by one of them.

I glared at him. "I live here. Who the hell are you?"

His pale blue eyes were like chips of ice. "I'm asking the questions here."

"On whose authority?" I shot back.

"Mine," he said before another voice interrupted us.

"What is going on here, Colonel Mason?"

We both turned. My mother was striding toward us, her expression unreadable.

"Charlotte, what are you doing here?" she asked as if I were the problem, not the man restraining me.

He spoke before I could. "You know this girl, Mrs. Ross?"

My mother eyed me like I was the one in the wrong. "She's my daughter. You can release her."

He let me go but kept his hard stare on me. "I caught her running through the woods, and she refuses to explain her presence here."

"There's no law against running in the woods." I glowered at him as I rubbed my aching arms. "And I don't need to explain my presence to you."

He crossed his arms. "You were scared. Did something frighten you?"

An image of the creature flashed through my mind, but I said nothing.

"Answer him, Charlotte," my mother said. "You're a mess. What have you been up to?"

"I was hiking, and I fell," I said tightly. "And you'd be scared, too, if a strange man grabbed you in the woods."

Her gaze narrowed, but she didn't argue. "Go home, and clean yourself up. And don't come back into the woods until I say you can."

I adjusted the straps of my pack. "I'm fine by the way. Thanks for asking." She didn't respond as I turned away from them and headed toward home.

At the bend in the trail, I glanced back. My mother was talking, gesturing with her hands. But Colonel Mason wasn't looking at her. He was still watching me, his expression unreadable.

A shiver went through me. I rounded the bend and broke into a run. By the time I emerged from the woods onto our property, I was panting, sweaty, and feeling like my heart was going to burst through my ribcage. I didn't stop running until I was inside the house with the door bolted behind me.

I lay on my side in bed the next morning, watching the sky lighten through my window. I couldn't stop thinking about the creature in the woods. What was it? Where had it come from? No animal had eyes like those. And that metal plate covering its head had looked like armor. But who would put armor on an animal? And why?

The only high-security lab nearby was at Sutton Aerospace, but as far as I knew, it was strictly aerospace research and development. Then again, Sutton had other facilities in Canada and Europe. Was it possible one of their projects involved animals?

Lab testing on animals had been outlawed nearly ten years ago, not just here, but globally. If Sutton was using animals, they weren't just crossing ethical lines, they were breaking international law.

Did my parents know? They were obsessed with their work, but animal testing? I didn't want to believe they would condone that.

I reached for my phone to call Finley and remembered she was still on holiday. I adored her parents, but they couldn't have chosen a worse time to go on an "unplugged" camping trip in the Scottish Highlands. Poor Finley had to be going out of her mind by now.

My parents' voices came from down the hall, low and muffled. A moment later, there was a soft knock at my door, and my father peeked in.

He stepped into the doorway, already dressed in dark blue slacks, a white shirt, and a tie. "Morning," he said in his quiet, serious way. "I heard you had some excitement in the woods yesterday."

I rolled onto my back and propped my hand behind my head. "That Colonel Mason seriously needs to chill out."

The corners of his eyes crinkled with a small smile. "Colonel Mason can be a bit overbearing, but he's right to be cautious. They haven't found all the plane debris yet and some of it could be dangerous. You should probably steer clear until the cleanup's finished."

I studied his face for any sign of a lie. I didn't see one. Either he had suddenly become the world's best liar, or he didn't know anything about the creature in the woods.

He leaned into the hall, listening to something my mother said. Nodding, he returned his gaze to me. "Your mom told me about the college applications. We'll talk about it tonight."

"We have Dev's dinner party tonight," my mother said from the hallway. "Senator Bradley's coming specifically to speak with us."

Dev Malik was the CEO of Sutton Aerospace and my parents' boss. She wouldn't miss one of his parties if the house were on fire.

My dad grimaced as she walked past him. I almost pitied him. He hated those events, but he never said no to her.

"Then we'll talk tomorrow." He gave me a small, apologetic smile before following her.

They talked as they descended the stairs, but I paid no attention to their conversation. My mind was already back on the animal. Before the front door closed behind my parents, I knew what I was going to do.

I got out of bed and dressed, telling myself over and over that this was a terrible idea. But every time I wavered, I heard that awful, pained cry again, and my resolve grew.

It's probably gone already, I told myself, grabbing my hiking pack.

Downstairs, I filled my water bottle and pulled three vacuum-sealed synth steaks from the fridge. They were the closest thing to real beef unless you wanted to shell out a fortune. Dad said they didn't taste the same, but I'd grown up on them. They tasted fine to me. I stuffed them in my pack and headed out.

I was extra vigilant on the main trail because running into Mason again was the last thing I needed. I veered off at a different spot than yesterday and began the steep climb toward the overlook.

The higher I got, the quieter the woods became. When I reached the downed tree where I'd rested yesterday, I stopped. *This is insane.* I should go back and tell someone. If that thing came from Sutton, they were better equipped to help it.

I remembered Mason's grip on my arms, the cold in his voice. If that was how he treated me, what would he do to an animal?

No. I couldn't turn it over to Sutton.

I'd check if it was still here, then call someone else. The ASPCA, a wildlife rescue – anyone but them.

I stood for a moment, listening. The uprooted tree wasn't visible yet, but there was no birdsong or squirrel chatter, only stillness. I wanted to believe it was gone and I could stop worrying, but the silence said otherwise.

"Damn it," I muttered. If I didn't go check, I'd drive myself nuts later wondering about it.

I found the tree easily this time. As I neared it, a low growl came from the hollow beneath it.

"I'm not coming closer," I said quietly, trying to sound calm. I eased off my pack and pulled out a steak, slicing it open with my knife. I tossed it at the hole and winced when it landed a foot short.

I jumped when a paw shot out, hooked the steak with long claws, and dragged it into the shadows. Wet gnawing followed.

I quickly opened the second steak and threw it. It landed at the edge of the hollow and vanished a second later. More chewing sounds.

My hands trembled as I opened the last steak. He sounded ravenous. *Please don't decide I'm the next course.* I tossed the steak, and it went straight into the hole. There was a soft *clunk* followed by a growl.

I cringed and backed up a few steps. "Sorry."

When the chewing stopped, there was a heavy silence. I was afraid to move, not sure what he'd do when no more food came. Time stretched until I realized I wasn't breathing, and I gulped in air.

I nearly jumped out of my skin when its head appeared deeper in the shadows, and two glowing amber eyes stared at me.

"Uh... that's all I have," I squeaked. I cleared my throat. "I'll bring more tomorrow." *Just, please don't eat me.*

He slowly sank back into the darkness as if he understood me. I exhaled shakily and grabbed my pack. I was out of my mind. There was no way I was coming back here again.

Instead of returning the way I'd come, I cut across the hill until I reached a brook. I followed it downstream toward a larger stream. This route added twenty minutes to my hike, but it would throw off anyone I might run into.

I was crossing a narrow section of the stream when voices carried over the water. Ducking behind a thick clump of brush, I listened as the voices drew closer.

"We've gone over the ravine twice," a male voice said. "If it came down with the pilot, there's no sign of it."

"Then it survived the crash," Colonel Mason snarled. "How far have you expanded the search?"

"We've got teams covering the river and moving west. If it's alive, it'll need water and food."

I was right. The animal was on that test plane. Sutton *was* experimenting on animals.

The two men passed less than fifteen feet away. Mason wore the same fatigues as yesterday. The other man wore a navy-blue jacket with a Sutton Aerospace logo on it.

"I want people out here day and night," Mason barked. "I don't care what it takes. Find it."

"Yes, sir," the other man said.

I stayed hidden until their voices faded. I was tempted to follow them, to see what else I could learn, but common sense kicked in. If Mason caught me, I didn't want to find out what he'd do.

I needed to be smart about this and figure out how to help that animal without getting caught. I had no clue what to do, but right now, the animal in the hole didn't scare me nearly as much as the one walking on two legs.

Right on time.

As the security drone flew past, I reset the timer on my phone and settled deeper behind the stone fence. I'd been here nearly an hour. The drone flew by every three minutes like clockwork. One more pass, and I'd test how fast it responded to a disturbance.

Pulling my knees up to my chest, I rested my back against the fence and thought about the animal for what felt like the millionth time. I'd spent the whole day trying to figure out how to help it without getting eaten by it or caught by Mason and Sutton's people.

I'd ruled out telling my parents. Even if they'd had no knowledge of it, I didn't trust them to not turn around and tell Sutton everything. And the more I thought about the conversation I'd overheard between Mason and the other man, the more determined I became to keep Sutton from ever getting their hands on the animal.

There was only one person I could trust completely. I wasn't sure how much help Finley could be from halfway across the world, but she was one of the smartest people I knew. As far as allies went, there was no one else I'd rather have in my corner.

The crunch of feet on dry leaves snapped me out of my thoughts. I caught a blur of movement – a black-clad figure running low toward the fence. He hadn't seen me, but he was about to come face-to-face with that security drone.

I launched from my hiding spot and tackled him, one hand clamping over his mouth. He let out a muffled grunt when we hit the ground with me on top of him. After a moment of stunned silence, he tried to push me off, but lucky for both of us, he was a scrawny thing and I was stronger. He yelled against my palm, and I pressed my hand tighter to his mouth.

"Quiet," I hissed. "The security drone will be here any second."

That got his attention. He stilled as a soft whir signaled the approaching drone, and we stared at each other as it passed by. When I knew it was safe, I let him go.

The boy scrambled to his feet. I guessed him to be around thirteen, five foot five and thin, dressed in black jeans and a black hoodie that was at least two sizes too big for him. His hood had fallen off, revealing a thin face and unruly black hair. I recognized him. He was one of a group of boys that liked to hang around the skate park, the same boys who'd had the brilliant idea to paint the overlook.

He swiped angrily at the leaves and dirt clinging to his jeans. "You always hide in the dark and jump people?"

"You always in such a hurry to get arrested?" I retorted in a whisper. "Because you will if you don't keep it down."

He looked around furtively and dropped into a crouch. "What do you care if I get arrested?"

"I don't, but I'd rather not go to jail with you."

He took in my black outfit and pointed an accusing finger at me. "You just want to break in here yourself."

I checked my phone. "If I did, I certainly wouldn't be stupid about it. You don't just walk into a house like this."

"Oh, yeah?" He folded his arms across his narrow chest. "What would you do then?"

"Shhhh." I put my finger to my lips, and neither of us moved as the drone flew by again. When enough time had lapsed, I said, "Watch."

I picked up a small rock and stood. Finding my target, I threw the rock, and it struck a metal planter on the other side of the kidney-shaped pool with a clang.

"Nice shot," the boy said.

Security lights came on around the pool as I grabbed his arm and dragged him out of sight with me. We pressed our backs to the fence and didn't have to wait long before we heard not one but two drones arrive. The boy tried to stand and peek over the fence, but I held him fast until the drones had scanned the yard and left.

Quietly, I got up and snuck into the small park behind the house. I heard the boy following me, but he had the sense to not say anything until we emerged on a street on the other side of the park.

"So, that's it. You're leaving?" he asked.

"Yep."

He caught up to me. "Then what was the point of all that?"

"That was fun." The last thing I was going to do was admit I'd been scoping out the place for my own job. Finley was the only person who knew about my extra-curricular activities, and I planned to keep it that way.

"Fun?" he echoed.

"Yeah. I like setting off the security drones in those big houses." I shrugged. "What else is there to do in this town?"

"But you live in one of those houses."

I turned my head to stare at him. "How do you know where I live?"

He snickered. "This town isn't that big. There are two groups of kids here: those that go to the public school, and those who live on this side of town. And you definitely don't go to my school."

"If it was up to me, I'd go to school instead of doing the virtual classes," I said. "The last place we lived I went to a school with all my friends."

I left out the fact that my old school had been a private academy in London where three quarters of the student body were the children of celebrities or diplomats. The others were rich or had scholarships. By most people's standards, my parents were rich, but it was their connections that had gotten me into the exclusive school. Finley was there on a full scholarship.

"Why don't you go to school here then?" my nosy companion asked. "You one of those geniuses who takes special classes?"

I snorted a laugh. "My mother wouldn't be caught dead sending her daughter to a public school. There's no private school here up to her standards, so I'm stuck with virtual classes."

He grimaced. "That sucks."

"Yeah, but it's not all bad. They don't care if you skip a few classes here and there as long as you keep up with the material and do all the assignments and tests." We approached the spot where I'd left my scooter. "Why were you going to break into that house? Was it another dare from your friends?"

It was his turn to stare at me. "How do you know about my friends?"

"This town isn't that big," I said, mimicking his earlier words. "I've seen your little gang around."

He kicked a rock and sent it skidding across the pavement. "I just needed some money is all."

"Fair enough." We reached my scooter, and I unlocked my helmet. Straddling the machine, I looked at him. "You need a lift?"

"On that thing?" He curled his lip at the electric scooter. "Not if I want to show my face at school again."

Laughing, I donned my helmet. "Suit yourself." I started the engine that purred so quietly you couldn't hear it unless you were within ten feet of it.

"Wait," the boy called when I eased away from the curb.

I stopped, and he climbed onto the seat behind me. "Just as far as the bridge. I can walk from there."

Grinning, I pulled back the throttle and drove us out of the neighborhood. "I'm Charlie, by the way."

"Xander." He didn't speak again until we were traveling on the main road at a blistering thirty-five miles an hour. "Can't this go any faster?"

"Don't worry. If we see someone you know, you can hide behind me."

He muttered indignantly, and I held back a laugh.

We crossed over the river that dissected the town, and I pulled into a convenience store parking lot just past the bridge. Xander hopped off the scooter before I brought it to a full stop. He pulled up his hood, which had fallen off during the ride, and stuck his hands in his pockets. "Uh... thanks."

Before I could reply, a white pickup swung into the parking lot. The faded letters on the door read COLE ELECTRONICS.

"Shit," Xander said as the truck pulled up beside us.

The window rolled down. Expecting someone my parents' age, I was surprised to see a young man barely older than I was with a dark crew cut, dark eyes, and a jaw set like stone. The resemblance to Xander was obvious.

"Get in," the man said.

Xander shuffled his feet. "Ethan –"

"I just spent an hour driving around looking for you, and I'm late for work," Ethan said in a hard voice.

"You could have gone to work." Xander pushed his shoulders back and lifted his chin. "I don't need you to drive me home."

Ethan's gaze flicked to my scooter without even a passing glance at me. "I'm here now, so let's go."

His tone brooked no argument. Xander muttered angrily and stalked around the front of the truck. At the passenger door, he stopped abruptly and looked at me. "Thanks for the lift."

I raised a hand. "No problem."

I watched the truck disappear down the road before pulling out of the parking lot. I started toward home, but the idea of being alone in that big, silent house was suddenly unappealing. At the next light, I made a U-turn and rode aimlessly around the town that seemed quiet for a Friday night.

Hudson Ridge had seventy thousand people, but after five years in London, it felt small. Its downtown was a mix of historic and newer buildings with quaint cafés, boutique shops, and places that looked like they belonged in a Hallmark movie.

Thanks to Sutton and two manufacturing plants on the outskirts, our economy was stable, and the region's hiking, fishing, and river access drew in nature lovers year-round.

Tucked into the Upper Hudson Valley, we were sheltered from the worst of the climate collapse. Our summers had grown hotter, and we had bad air days whenever smog or wildfire smoke reached us, but we fared a lot better than most of the country. If you didn't watch the news, you could almost pretend the rest of the world wasn't falling apart.

Over the last decade, people had flowed into the Northern states from the parts of the country hit the hardest by extreme weather and coastal flooding. The population in many towns and cities swelled until some states had to put a cap on how many people could move there each year. Hudson Ridge's population had doubled in size before New York started limiting new residents.

I turned onto a road and saw a sign for Sutton Aerospace. My thoughts went to the creature in the woods. I was planning to bring it more food tomorrow... but then what?

What did you do with an injured armored panther... thing that had escaped from a lab?

I made a face. It sounded crazy even in my head.

It wasn't until I saw another sign that I realized I'd turned onto the two-lane road that led to the Sutton facility on the edge of town. There was nothing along this route except a few businesses, and I had no interest in them or Sutton.

I slowed the scooter to turn around and stopped in the middle of the road. There were lights moving in the woods about a hundred yards away.

I lifted my visor, squinting. Were they flashlights? It was hard to tell through the trees. A week ago, I would have found it strange, but my definition of that word had changed in the last two days.

I turned the scooter to head back toward town. Just as I opened the throttle, a figure burst out of the woods and into the road directly in front of me.

I jerked the handlebars hard to the side. The back wheel hit loose gravel on the shoulder, and the scooter started to skid.

And then everything went sideways.

3

I swore through clenched teeth, fighting to control the scooter that was determined to throw me into the ditch. Turning slightly into the skid, I managed to straighten the bike and get it back onto the pavement.

I came to a stop and looked back, afraid I might have clipped the man. The road was empty. I swung the scooter around to point the headlight back the way I'd come, but the man was nowhere to be seen.

"What the hell?" I scanned the woods, but he was gone.

"Halt," called a male voice behind me.

I whipped my head around so fast I nearly gave myself whiplash. A flashlight beam blinded me, and I threw up my arm to cover my eyes.

Armed men poured from the trees. Most wore fatigues, but at least four wore the black Sutton security uniform. Two of them shined their lights on me and one spoke into a radio. The rest stared at me down the sights of their guns. I gulped and didn't move.

"Get off the bike and remove your helmet," said the same voice.

I did as he said, and he barked, "Show me some identification."

I wanted to ask why, but I wasn't stupid enough to argue with a group of armed men. I pulled my driver's license from my back pocket and held it out.

A tall sandy-haired man in fatigues stepped forward and took it. His nametag read PETERSON. He studied my license for several seconds. "State your business here."

"I don't have any business. I was just riding my scooter."

"Out here? At this time of night?" His voice dripped suspicion. "Why were you stopped when we found you?"

I shielded my eyes. "Do you mind pointing those lights somewhere else?"

The flashlights lowered.

"Answer my question," he said.

I blinked to clear the spots from my vision. "Someone ran out in front of me, and I nearly wiped out."

"You saw him?" Peterson's tone sharpened as the men around him stirred. "Where did he go?"

I pointed to the woods on the other side of the road. "I think he ran that way."

Everyone except Peterson and one Sutton security guard took off into the trees. I turned back to the two remaining men and found the burly security guy still holding his gun. At least, it was no longer aimed at my head.

"Are you aware this area is off-limits?" the guard asked me.

"Since when? This is a public road."

Headlights rounded a bend in the road. None of us spoke as a black Jeep pulled up in front of us.

Peterson wrapped a hand around my upper arm. I yanked away, but he grabbed me again.

"Hey! Let me go," I yelled.

He pulled me toward the Jeep. "Not until after you answer some questions."

"Questions about what?" He didn't answer, and fear coiled in my gut. "You have no right to take me anywhere. This is kidnapping."

He opened the back door and shoved me inside. I slid across the seat and tried the other door. Locked. A woman in her late twenties sat in the front passenger seat, her dark ponytail pulled through the back of a Sutton uniform cap. She watched me coolly. I glared back.

"Where are you taking me?" I demanded as Peterson climbed in beside me.

He snapped his seat belt in place. "Calm down. We're taking you to Sutton."

My fear gave way to anger. "First, you hold me at gunpoint and now this. Don't tell me to calm down."

No one answered me. I looked out at the man who had stayed behind. "What about my scooter?"

"Nico will follow us with it." Peterson held out his hand. "Give me your key."

I opened my mouth to refuse but only sighed and shoved the fob at him. He tossed it to Nico and shut the door.

I slumped against the seat and buckled in as the Jeep headed back to Sutton. A few minutes later, we stopped at a metal gate set in a twelve-foot chain-link fence topped with concertina wire and cameras. The guard in the shack opened the gate, and the row of steel bollards on the other side lowered.

If not for the fencing, security drones, and armed security, the Sutton complex could pass for any high-tech campus. The main building was six stories of glass with the company name in big letters at the top. Behind it was a sprawling three-story building that spanned almost two acres, and beyond that were three huge hangars and a runway.

Sutton had more security than a military base. After seeing what they'd done to that poor animal in the woods, it wasn't hard to guess why. What else were they hiding in here?

We pulled into an underground garage beneath the main building. Peterson opened my door and led me to a locked entrance. He scanned a card and typed a code, disabling an alarm inside. We climbed three flights of stairs and walked down a hallway to a closed door.

I expected a holding cell or an interrogation room like the ones in the movies. What I got was a small conference room with a ten-person table and a coffee cart.

"Sit." He pointed at a chair.

"Listen," I began. "If you'll just call my parents, they'll clear this up. They are David –"

"You can call them after we're done here." He left and locked the door behind him.

I tried the knob. "What the hell?"

I pulled up my sleeve and touched my phone. A tiny red bar blinked at the top of the screen. No signal.

I began pacing. This couldn't be legal. You weren't allowed to snatch people off a public road so you could "ask questions." Peterson hadn't told me what they wanted to question me about.

Twenty minutes later, the door opened, and I spun as a woman in a severe dark gray suit entered the room. She looked fortyish and wore her red hair in a bun. A younger Black man in a blue suit followed her.

"Take a seat, Miss Ross," the woman said as she pulled out a chair for herself.

I crossed my arms. "Not until you tell me who you are and why I'm here."

She sat and laid my license on the table. She knew my name, so she had to know who my parents were. She clearly didn't care how they would react to me being dragged in here like a criminal.

She smiled, but irritation flickered in her eyes. "My name is Lydia Warren, and I'm head of security here. This is Anthony Brooks."

They looked at me expectantly, but I didn't move.

I met Warren's stare silently until she said, "You are here to answer questions about the incident on the road."

"You mean the one where your men pointed guns at me?" I retorted. "Or the part where I was forced into a Jeep and brought here against my will?"

Warren's smile thinned. "That was unfortunate but necessary. They were in pursuit of someone who broke into our facility. He's armed and very dangerous."

"What does that have to do with me?" I demanded.

Brooks leaned forward. "You stopped your scooter at the exact spot and time he crossed the road. That's a little too coincidental."

I put my hands on my hips. "I stopped because I nearly ran the guy down. Didn't Peterson tell you that?"

Brooks nodded slowly. "He did, but it's a little hard to believe you just happened to be there."

Warren reached over and laid a hand on her partner's arm. "Let Charlotte tell us her side of the story."

I looked from one to the other as the utter ridiculousness of the situation hit me. I was being interrogated for riding on a public road, and these two wanted to play good cop/bad cop with me?

"There is no story," I bit out. "I don't know anything about that man."

"I believe you," Warren said in a conciliatory tone. "If you almost hit him, you must have gotten a good look at him."

"All I saw was his outline."

Brooks scoffed. "You got that close to him, and you didn't see his face?"

I shot him a scathing look. "I was a little too busy trying not to wipe out."

"How do you know it was a man if you didn't see his face?" Brooks asked smugly.

"Maybe because you two keep referring to him as *he*." I clenched my jaw, and my gaze fell on the ceramic cups on the coffee cart. Was it assault if you hurled cups at the people holding you against your will?

"You seem very defensive," Warren said. "Why?"

I shook my head. "Oh, I don't know. Maybe because I was kidnapped at gunpoint and asked a bunch of stupid questions."

Her pleasant façade slipped.

Brooks stood and planted his hands on the table. "You'll be here all night if you don't start cooperating with us."

I almost laughed at him. I'd spent half my life butting heads with my mother, and he wasn't even in her league. Yanking out the chair across from Warren, I sat. "Then the least you can do is bring me some water. And I want to call my parents."

Warren gave me a tight smile. "Your mother already knows you're here. She gave us permission to question you."

The words hit me like a slap. Mom knew, and she let them do this to me? She hadn't even come to see if I was okay?

Warren stood. "Colonel Mason will be in to question you when he returns. I suggest you take this time to search your memory for something you might have forgotten." She paused at the door. "I'll see about getting you that water."

I stared after them. She had to be lying. My mother would never win any parenting awards, but she wouldn't do this. Would she?

It took a minute for Warren's parting words about Colonel Mason to register. I shivered. She and her partner didn't scare me, but there was something about Mason that unnerved me.

When the door opened ten minutes later, I jumped, but it was a young security guard carrying a bottle of water. He left without saying a word.

I checked the seal on the cap before I opened it. Maybe I was being paranoid, but who could blame me?

I snatched my license off the table and slid it into my back pocket as I walked to the window. All I could see was the other building lit with office lights and a lone figure at a desk. My parents weren't the only workaholics here.

The window was one of those with a crank, and it didn't open wide. Not that it would make a difference. I was three stories up, and I wasn't desperate enough yet to attempt that climb even if I could.

Another hour passed before the door swung open again. I looked up from my useless phone and a blast of relief hit me when my father walked in. He wore the blazer and shirt he'd dressed in for the cocktail party, and the worry on his face made my throat tighten.

"Charlie, are you okay?" he asked, hurrying toward me.

I shot up from my chair and threw my arms around him. He hesitated and hugged me back.

He pulled away to look at me. "Are you hurt? What were you doing alone out there in the middle of the night?"

I let out an aggravated breath. "I was riding my scooter. That's not a crime, is it?"

"Of course, not. I'm just glad you're okay." He put a hand on my back. "Let's go."

"Are you breaking me out?" I quipped as we turned toward the door. Warren stood outside in the hallway.

He steered me out of the room. "I told Lydia you couldn't possibly be involved in the break-in."

"Oh. You mean all I had to do was explain my innocence?" I met Warren's eyes as we passed her. "Why didn't I think of that?"

We took an elevator to a lobby with a polished white tile floor and double glass doors. At the reception desk sat a security guard, who inclined his head at my father as we passed him. Outside, Dad's silver Mercedes was parked in front of the building.

"I need to get my scooter," I said when he started for the car. "They took it from me."

He opened his door. "Someone will bring it to the house for you tomorrow."

"Why can't I get it now?" I pressed.

"Because they have more important things to do trying to catch whoever broke in here tonight," he answered with a note of exasperation in his voice.

I slid into the passenger seat, fuming. He started the engine, and soft jazz music filled the car. Neither of us spoke until we drove through the gate.

"Are you sure you're okay?" he asked as he turned onto the road.

"Peachy." I stared out my window. "How was your party?"

"The party was good, but I want to talk about you," he said. "You have no idea how worried I was when I heard what happened."

I turned my head toward him. "Really? Then why did it take you two hours to get me out of there?"

He took his eyes off the road to frown at me. "I came as soon as my assistant called to tell me where you were."

Even in the dim light I saw enough of his expression to know he was telling the truth. Mom hadn't told him about the call from Warren. Her actions shouldn't hurt me by now, but they did.

"Then you and your wife need to work on your communication skills." I didn't try to disguise the bitterness in my voice.

"What are you talking about? And don't refer to your mother that way."

My fingers clenched the shoulder strap of my seat belt. "Lydia Warren said they called Mom. She gave them permission to hold me and question me."

"What?" Dad's voice rose, and the car gave a little jerk. "You misunderstood Lydia."

"I'm not stupid, and she was pretty clear about it."

He didn't respond right away. "I'm sorry, Charlie. Sutton's security is tight because of the Vanguard project, but they should have known you couldn't be involved."

"Tell that to Mom," I muttered, turning away.

We didn't speak for the rest of the drive. As we crossed the bridge, I caught sight of bobbing lights along the river. Sutton's security people were still searching for their fugitive. Part of me hoped he got away.

It was after midnight when we got home to a dark house. Mom must have already gone to bed. That was fine by me because she was the last person I wanted to see tonight.

Dad's phone buzzed as the garage door opened. He read the message and sighed. "They need me to go in. Your mom is on her way there now."

"Duty calls." I opened my door and got out. "I won't wait up."

"Charlie..." he called after me, but he didn't finish the sentence.

I reached the door to the kitchen as his car pulled away.

I checked my phone for the hundredth time. It was almost noon, and neither of my parents had come home from the lab. As much as I wanted to confront my mother about what she'd done, I had a more pressing need. Sutton still had my scooter, and with both cars gone, I was stranded. That meant I couldn't go buy more meat for the animal, who had to be hungry by now.

In the kitchen, the refrigerator screen lit up when it sensed me. I hesitated before pressing the order button. A list of options popped up, and I hovered over the meat category. Maybe if I ordered only three or four chicken breasts or synth steaks, neither of my parents would notice. It wasn't like they ate at home enough to track what was in the freezer.

The doorbell rang, and I startled. I hadn't even heard a vehicle pull up. At the living room window, I spotted a white cargo van with the Sutton Aerospace logo pulling away. Opening the door, I found my scooter parked in front of the garage, the helmet and key fob resting on the seat.

"It's about time." I walked to it, noting the gleam of clean metal and the water droplets clinging to the odometer. Someone had washed it recently. Even my helmet had been wiped down. Why would Sutton wash my scooter? An apology for being insufferable jerks, maybe?

I ran inside, grabbed my coat, keys, and backpack, and headed out. Last night, I'd read that large cats needed four to six pounds of meat a day. That was a lot of meat. How I was going to manage that, I had no idea.

Normally, I shopped at the market a mile away, but people would notice if I was in there buying meat every other day. It was better to spread my purchases across different stores. Today, I headed to Valley Foods, a big supermarket chain I'd only been to a couple of times. As I approached the entrance, I weighed the merits of whole chickens versus synth roasts. Whole chickens were cheaper than pieces, and the panther would probably enjoy chewing on the bones.

"Oof!" I cried as I collided with someone. I flailed and landed hard on the pavement. Something squished beneath me, and I silently begged the universe that it wasn't dog poop.

A man swore. I looked up at a pair of work boots and jeans splashed with coffee. Scrambling to my feet, I blurted, "I'm so sorry! I wasn't paying attention."

"Clearly," he snapped as I looked for what I'd landed on. I grimaced when I saw what had once been a chicken salad sandwich.

I lifted my head and was surprised to meet the dark gaze of the man who had picked up Xander last night. He didn't recognize me, which made sense. I'd been wearing a helmet and a different jacket.

I checked my clothes and found a couple of coffee splotches on my jeans. He'd taken the worst of our collision.

"I'm sorry about your lunch," I said. "Can I buy you a new sandwich?"

"You can watch where you're going next time." He tossed his half-empty coffee cup into a nearby garbage can.

My smile fell away. "I said I was sorry. And you couldn't have been watching where you were going either, or you would have avoided me."

"I don't usually have to worry about some kid barreling into me." He picked up the flattened sandwich and threw it away.

"I just turned eighteen," I shot back.

His eyebrows rose in mockery, and heat crept up my neck. Why was I defending myself to him?

I moved to walk past him, but he turned at the same time, and our shoulders brushed. I jumped back like I'd touched a live wire. He muttered something under his breath.

I met his glower with my own. "Ever consider switching to decaf?"

His phone rang. He checked the screen, swore again, and walked off without another word. He crossed the parking lot to the strip mall and disappeared into a store on the end with the name Cole Electronics above the door.

Jerk. It was no wonder Xander was on the fast track to juvenile detention with someone like that as a role model.

I grabbed a basket and headed to the meat department, passing the deli where a man was ordering a sandwich. I paused in front of the premade sandwiches. Despite his rudeness, I felt a flicker of guilt. It *had* been partly my fault that his food was ruined.

Before I could second-guess myself, I grabbed a chicken salad sandwich and ordered a large coffee.

Steam wafted from the cup as I carried it to the checkout, and I marveled at how much it smelled like the real thing. Real coffee had become a luxury as global crops dwindled. Seven years ago, someone had invented a synthetic version. It was cheap, and it even had caffeine. My mother and I didn't drink coffee, but my father loved it, so we always had the good stuff at home.

I paid for the coffee and sandwich and crossed the lot to the electronics store. It was one I hadn't been to before, and I saw no one when I entered. The front counter was cluttered with unopened boxes and papers, and the older cash register looked out of place next to a digital card and chip reader.

Voices drew me past crowded isles to the fourth one where Ethan was cleaning up shattered light bulbs while a ruddy-faced man ranted over him. The middle-aged man wore a wrinkled shirt, and his hair stuck out like he'd just woken up.

"This is still my store, and I won't have you telling me what I can do." The man swayed and grabbed a shelf for balance. His bloodshot eyes found me. "Who are you?"

Ethan looked over his shoulder. When he saw me, his expression darkened. "What do you want?"

"Wow. With a greeting like that, I'm shocked this place isn't packed with customers," I retorted.

The older man glared at Ethan. "I won't have the girls coming around here like they did when you were in school. You hear me?"

"Dad, stop," Ethan said sharply.

I looked between them but couldn't find a resemblance. Then again, my mother and I looked nothing alike.

Ethan's father stomped toward the back, muttering to himself. Ethan watched him go, and I thought I heard a sigh as he straightened his shoulders and turned to face me. My opinion of him softened a fraction. He didn't get a pass for being rude, but I'd be in a bad mood, too, if I had to deal with that man.

I held up the coffee and sandwich and set them down on a shelf with some sugar packets and creamers. "I brought you decaf."

Before he could reply, I turned and left. Back at the supermarket, I filled my basket with just enough meat to feed the animal for two days. The display cases looked sparse.

"Did you have a sale?" I asked an employee tidying the display.

He straightened to look at me. "Nah. I heard there was a power outage at a processing plant in Pennsylvania. The trucks are running a few days behind."

A woman beside us added more meat to her cart. At this rate, the shelves would be empty by tomorrow.

Images from the news flashed in my mind of empty store shelves and food riots. Unlike here, many places didn't have trucks coming regularly to restock.

At the self-checkout, an older woman shot me a disapproving look. I avoided her eyes as I stuffed the meat into my backpack.

Outside, I spotted Ethan standing in front of his store, eating the sandwich. He frowned, and this time, recognition flickered in his eyes as I climbed onto my scooter. I gave him a little wave before driving off.

As soon as I pulled onto the street, my thoughts returned to the animal. I'd feed him until he healed – but then what? Someone was bound to discover an armored panther running wild in the woods. The moment Sutton found out, they'd swoop in and lock him up again.

At the entrance to our neighborhood, I came to a stop when the gates didn't open automatically. I waved my key fob at the sensor, but nothing happened.

I kicked down my stand and walked to the small terminal. I held my fob over the sensor. Still nothing. Grumbling, I entered the code manually to open the gate.

Two minutes later, I pulled into our driveway and tapped the garage button on my phone. The door didn't move.

"Does anything work right today?" I grumbled, climbing off the scooter again. The door started to rise as soon as I was within two feet of it.

I scowled at the sky. "Really?"

And that was when I saw the drone.

4

I froze, staring at the object hovering a hundred feet above the house. It was a camouflage drone, designed to blend into the background, but it couldn't disappear against the sky. From here, it looked like a weird distortion of the light, and I might have dismissed it as a trick of the eye if not for my encounter with Sutton last night.

The garage door stopped moving, snapping me back to my senses. I wheeled the scooter inside, my mind racing. That wasn't just any drone. I recognized a military-grade surveillance drone when I saw one.

And it was following *me*.

Security was one thing, but Sutton was taking it too far. How could they possibly think I was involved in the break-in just because I'd almost run into the guy?

My hands trembled as I transferred the meat from my backpack to the fridge. I'd planned to head straight to the woods, but I couldn't risk leading that drone to the creature. I might've already been tagged and not known it.

I ran down to my workshop in the basement. The workbench was covered by an anti-static mat and cluttered with tools and electronic parts. The pegboard above the bench held an assortment of pliers, wire cutters, screwdrivers, soldering irons, and other tools. I loved working with electronics, a pastime my parents fully supported and encouraged.

I dug through a cabinet for the scanner I'd built last year, which could detect RF, GPS, and microwave signals. I ran it up and down my body and exhaled when the only signal it picked up was from my phone.

A darker thought struck me. My scooter had been at Sutton all night, and they could easily have hidden a tracker on it. At this point, I wouldn't put anything past them.

Back in the garage, I scanned every inch of the scooter. Just when I was starting to feel paranoid, the scanner beeped. My gut tightened as I moved the device slowly toward the headlight. The beeps escalated into a long, piercing tone.

Fury surged through me. I grabbed my tools, removed the headlight, and found a tiny black tracker no bigger than my thumbnail attached to the frame. That explained the gate and garage door malfunctions. The transmitter must have interfered with the signals.

I held the tracker between my fingers. Surveillance was illegal unless you were law enforcement, but Sutton clearly thought they were above the law. If they had no issue spying on the daughter of their top employees, what else were they capable of?

I fired off a text to Finley, who was supposed to be home from vacation today. **Urgent. Call me the second you get this.**

Two hours later, I was pacing my room when the garage door rumbled open. I ran downstairs and was waiting in the kitchen when my mother entered the house.

She took in my folded arms and tense stance but said nothing as she set down her satchel and draped her coat over the back of a chair. She didn't hang it in the closet, which meant she was heading back out soon.

I gritted my teeth. "How was your party last night? Did they serve the imported caviar you love? Did Senator Bradley promise you a spot at the next White House dinner?"

She walked past me and took a glass from the cabinet. "I didn't realize you were interested in our social events," she said, filling it with water.

"I can't help but wonder what I'm missing out on. It must have been quite the party for you to be unable to tear yourself away when your daughter is dragged into a vehicle, interrogated, and locked in a room for hours." There was no hiding the resentment that crept into my voice.

She sipped from her glass. "Don't be so dramatic, Charlotte. We have critical projects in progress at the lab. Lydia was understandably concerned about what you might've witnessed, so I gave her permission to question you."

"Without any inconvenience to you," I ground out. "They didn't treat me like a witness, Mom. They acted like I was working with that guy, and they threatened to keep me locked up until I 'cooperated.'" I added air quotes.

She waved a hand. "That's just a tactic they use, and they wouldn't have followed through with it. You were never in any danger."

"Do you hear yourself?" My hands gripped the edge of the countertop. "They pointed *guns* at me, Mom. Do you have any idea how scary it is to have armed men come out of the woods and surround you? Do you even care?"

"Of course, I care."

"Then act like it," I shouted.

"Guns?" Dad said from behind me. I turned to see him standing in the doorway to the garage.

"You didn't tell me they had guns." He looked at my mother. "Evelyn, did you know about this?"

"No," she admitted, clearly caught off guard.

I spun back to her. "Lydia Warren didn't mention that part, huh? What else could she be keeping from you? Maybe the fact that Sutton is following your daughter."

"Following you?" Dad burst out.

Mom scoffed. "Don't be ridiculous. Why would Sutton want to –?"

I slapped the tracker down on the counter so hard my mother flinched. "That was hidden on my scooter when Sutton dropped it off this morning."

Dad walked over and picked up the tracker to examine it. He handed it to Mom, who for once, seemed to be at a loss for words. He lifted shocked eyes to meet mine. "This was on your scooter?"

"Behind the headlight."

"You just happened to search your scooter for tracking devices?" Mom asked, her voice laced with skepticism.

I swallowed the anger rising in my throat. "No. I searched it *after* I saw the military surveillance drone following me home from the store."

Dad's eyes widened. "What?"

I nodded. "It's probably still out there. It's camouflaged, but you can see it if you look hard enough."

He stared at me for a beat and headed to the front door in quick strides. A few seconds later, Mom followed him. I stayed where I was.

Several minutes passed before I heard them coming back, their voices raised.

"I'll speak to Lydia," Mom said, sounding flustered.

"No, I will handle this," Dad replied sharply. "They held her at gunpoint, and now they're doing surveillance on her. I'm putting an end to this right now."

She murmured something, and he said, "I don't care what her reasons are. I'm calling Dev."

My jaw went slack at hearing him speak to her this way. I couldn't remember the last time I'd heard him argue with her, especially about me.

They entered the kitchen, and he came over to me. His face was tight with anger, but his hands were gentle when he rested them on my shoulders. "I'm so sorry, Charlie. Your mom and I had no idea how far Lydia's people went with this. I'll make sure it never happens again."

I gave a small nod, but I had a bad feeling Lydia Warren wouldn't let this go just because he told her to.

He pulled his phone from his pocket and strode from the room. My mother stared after him for a few seconds before she followed him without another word.

I checked my phone, but there was no reply from Finley. I climbed the stairs and paused at the top when I heard my father's raised voice coming from the office.

"I don't care how thorough they are. They crossed the line," he said. "They pointed guns at my teenage daughter, Dev."

A door closed, muffling the rest, and I continued to my room.

Ten minutes later, my father knocked and stepped inside. He surprised me by sitting on the foot of my bed.

"I'm so sorry about all of this. If I'd known last night how bad it was, I wouldn't have left you here alone." His expression hardened. "You don't have to worry about Sutton or their drones anymore."

"Thanks, Dad." My voice cracked. It had been a long time since he'd shown this much concern.

He touched my foot. "Your mom and I are supposed to fly to DC tonight for two days, but I'll stay home if you want me to."

"No, I'm okay," I said, surprised by the gesture.

His eyes searched mine. "Are you sure? It's just meetings."

I smiled. "I'm sure."

For a moment, he looked like he wanted to say more. He gave my foot a light squeeze and stood. "We're leaving in a few hours. If you change your mind, let me know."

"I will."

He left, closing the door behind him, and I lay staring at the ceiling. If there ever was a time I needed to talk to Finley, it was now. She wasn't going to believe it when I told her about all of this. I could hardly believe it myself.

All this weirdness had started the day I found the animal, and I had a feeling it was only going to get worse. The smart thing to do would be to stay far away from it. What was I going to do with an armored panther anyway?

"That's it then," I said to the ceiling. "I'm done with it."

"What am I going to do with you?" I murmured, unwrapping a frozen chicken breast. Dropping the wrapper on top of the others at my feet, I tossed the meat toward the hole beneath the tree. It landed a few inches from the edge.

I held my breath as his head appeared. I stepped forward for a better look, but a low growl stopped me in my tracks.

"Okay, we'll take it slow," I said gently, retreating until the growling stopped.

He snatched the chicken, and I caught a glimpse of long, double fangs before he slipped back into the shadows. I frowned. None of the big cats I'd studied had double fangs. Had they engineered him like that?

I tossed in another piece of meat. "I don't blame you for not trusting me after what those people did to you. I don't know what happened in that lab, but you're free now."

He moved again, and my heart thudded when I found those amber eyes watching me from the shadows. He came into the light, and I caught sight of a wet patch beneath the tear in his armor.

"You're bleeding," I started to take a step and stopped myself.

He let out a pained whine, and it twisted something in my chest.

I threw the last chicken breast. "I wish I could do more than feed you. You've probably never known kindness, have you?"

I expected him to take the meat and disappear, but he stayed where he was, watching me.

"That's all I have. I'll bring more tomorrow." Thank God my parents never checked the freezer. There was no way I could explain going through this much meat.

He rested his chin on the ground and continued to watch me. It was the most relaxed I'd seen him, and for a second, I thought I saw flecks of blue in his eyes.

I picked up the wrappers and stuffed them into my backpack. "I have to go, but I'll be back tomorrow."

He slid back into the darkness just as I heard the distant *whomp-whomp-whomp* of helicopter blades. There had been choppers out here every day since the crash, but until now, they'd stuck to the area around the ravine. How long would it take for them to expand their search this far?

The helicopter came within half a mile of us and veered off. I let out a breath, but it didn't ease my worry. If he stayed here much longer, Mason was going to find him.

There were caves and old mines a few miles from here where he could hide, but I had no idea how to get him there or if he could walk that far. He could have other injuries I hadn't seen.

"You stay out of sight," I said as I shrugged on my backpack. "I'll try to figure out something tonight."

I was almost home when Finley's text came. **I'm here. Can you talk? Give me 5.**

I ran the rest of the way, burst into the empty house, and flew up to my room.

After Finley had created our encrypted messaging app, she didn't stop there. She went one step further and built a custom encryption program for our phones. With it installed on both ends, it scrambled calls and texts into gibberish for anyone without the code. I'd never been more grateful for it than I was right now.

My anxiety eased the moment her face filled the screen. Finley's warm brown skin glowed in the soft light of her desk lamp, and her dark curls framed her delicate features. Her brown eyes searched mine, wide with alarm.

"What's wrong?" she asked before I could speak. "Did they catch you?"

"No." I blew out a breath. "It's not about that."

She visibly relaxed. "Then what?"

"It's big." I propped my phone in the stand on my desk. "Really big."

She leaned forward. "Tell me."

I started from the beginning. "The night of the last job, one of Sutton's test planes went down in Alder Ravine. You remember. I took you hiking there when you were here in June."

Her hand flew to her mouth. "Was anyone hurt?"

"The pilot ejected, and he's okay." I paused. "But he wasn't the only one on the plane."

I told her about the panther. And about Colonel Mason.

Finley's eyebrows practically hit her hairline. "A panther? With armor? Are you sure you didn't fall and hit your head out there?"

I rolled my eyes. "I told you it was weird. And you haven't even heard the half of it."

She sat back, listening as I laid it all out – the men with guns, being interrogated, the drone, the tracker, my parents' reactions. By the time I finished, her jaw was slack.

"First of all, your mum is a queen biatch, but you already know that." She pushed her hands through her curls. "Second... this is insane. I don't even have a word for this."

39

"I told you it was big."

"No wonder they're desperate to get that thing back," she said. "If people find out they're experimenting on animals, Sutton's finished. Every animal rights group on the planet will sue them into oblivion."

"It's not just Sutton," I reminded her. "The military is involved, which means the government knows what they're up to."

She got up and started pacing. "If they find out what you know..." She stopped walking to stare at me. "What if they bugged your house?"

The thought made my blood run cold. I hadn't even considered that.

Finley sat again. "Let's not panic. Get your scanner and start with your bedroom. If they did bug your house, your room is the most likely place."

I ran to get the scanner. Little did I know when I built the thing that I'd be using it to check for hidden bugs in my house. I ran it over every inch of my room. When I declared it clean, she exhaled with a dramatic sigh.

"You're probably safe, but you should check downstairs to be certain," she said.

I was already moving. I left my phone on the kitchen island and scanned the main level. "All clear," I said, picking up the phone again.

She wiped her brow theatrically. "That's a relief." She paused, listening. "Hold on. Mum's calling me."

She left her room, and I headed back upstairs. While I waited, I stretched out on my bed, listening to faint laughter on her end. I'd always envied her relationship with her parents. Her mom was a pulmonologist and her dad a math professor, and despite their busy careers, they put family above everything else.

Finley returned and dropped down in her chair. "Mum says hi."

"Tell her hi back."

Her face turned serious. "Do you think your parents are involved in this?"

I hesitated. "Honestly, I don't know. They work on the Vanguard project, and my mother has been overseeing the crash site cleanup. Dad would never be okay with experimenting on animals. I don't know about Mom. I hope not."

"I thought that facility was just for aerospace," Finley said. "Why would they do animal experiments there?"

"Maybe they engineered him somewhere else and brought him here. But why put a panther on a test plane."

She frowned. "Forget the plane. Why make an armored panther at all?"

I thought about him out there alone and injured. "How do I move him so they don't find him?"

She stared at me like I'd lost my mind. "You can't go back out there. You have no idea what they did to that thing or what it's capable of. And if the military catches you..."

"I have to help him, Finn," I said firmly. "I can't let them take him back to that lab."

"Then call PETA, and let them take care of it. They'll have it on every news site before Sutton knows what hit them."

She was right. PETA could be a bit extreme in their methods, but they had been instrumental in instituting the global laws banning lab animals. They were powerful, and if anyone could protect him, it was them. The last thing I wanted was for him to end up at the center of a media circus, but that had to be better than being experimented on in a lab.

I opened the PETA website on my laptop. "They have an office in New York. I just hope they take me seriously."

"Don't mention the armor," she said. "Just say it looks like it escaped from a lab. That'll be enough to get them interested."

"Good idea." I walked to the window, mentally rehearsing what to say.

A flicker of movement near the shed at the back of the yard caught my eye. A few seconds later, something moved near the back corner.

"I think there's someone in my yard."

Finley gasped. "Who? Is it one of the soldiers?"

"I don't know. They went behind the shed." I pulled on a pair of sneakers.

Alarm filled her voice. "You're not going out there?"

"It's broad daylight. I'll be fine," I said, tying my laces. "I bet it's the same kid I saw near the Martin house last night."

"Or it could be a trigger-happy soldier with a gun."

I looked at her. "I'll take the phone with me, and if anything goes wrong, you can call the police."

"A lot of good that will do if you bleed out before they get there," she said.

I stood. "If that happens, you can do my eulogy. Try to make me sound cool."

"I don't like this," she said as I descended the stairs.

"Don't worry. I'll be careful." I reached the back door and paused. "I'm going outside now. Radio silence."

I stepped onto the patio and listened. Nothing. I stopped again when I reached the grass. Still nothing.

If someone was back there, they were probably watching me. I gave up all attempts at stealth and jogged to the shed.

"Xander, is that you back there?" I called.

There was no answer, but there was a soft rustle as if someone had shifted their feet.

"Don't make me tackle you again," I said playfully and rounded the corner.

And found myself staring into a pair of amber eyes.

5

The sound that came out of me was something between a squawk and a scream. My heart slammed against my ribs as I gaped at the creature standing before me.

He was smaller than I'd thought, but big enough to terrify me. Built like a panther, he was more the size of a Great Dane. Glossy black fur covered his body, but over half of it was fused with a black metal that seemed to grow out of his skin. The metal started at the crown of his head and flowed down his spine and halfway down his sides. A ridge of sharp, blade-like spikes bristled along his back.

The weak sunlight revealed more details I'd missed in the shadow of the trees. His muzzle was longer than a panther's, his ears short and pointed. His long whiskers twitched, and his eyes flickered between red and amber as we stared at each other.

I knew one thing for certain. This was no cat.

"What the hell is that?" Finley shouted.

The animal growled, and I fumbled to mute the phone.

I spoke in a soothing voice. "It's okay. You remember me, don't you?"

He made a rumbling noise that wasn't quite a growl, but it didn't sound friendly either. I backed up a step, and the spikes lowered a fraction. Encouraged, I took another step backward. The spikes lowered again until they were almost flush with his armor.

I released a shaky breath. "Are you hungry? Do you want more food?"

He cocked his head slightly, and his eyes turned solid amber. It made him appear a little less threatening.

"I'm going to get you something to eat," I said softly. When I turned to go, it moved a paw forward as if to follow. I raised my hands. "No, you stay here."

He pulled his paw back like he understood me. I shivered at the intelligence in his eyes.

I backed away slowly. Once I was past the shed, I sprinted to the house and entered on rubbery legs. I was taking packages of chicken from the freezer when I noticed Finley waving wildly on my phone. I unmuted her and was hit with a barrage of shrieking until she had to stop and take a few puffs from her asthma inhaler. She got like this every time she was overly excited.

"You said it was a panther," she wheezed. "I don't know what the hell that is, but it's not a panther."

"Yeah, I figured that out." I tossed chicken onto the counter. "It was darker in the woods, and I only saw its head and paw."

"Did you see those fangs...?" she trailed off. "Wait. You're going out there again?"

"Yes." I laid the chicken on the island.

"Are you insane? That thing will rip your throat out and eat you instead."

I opened the packages and filled a reusable shopping bag with the meat. "I don't think it will."

"Since when are you an expert on... whatever that thing is?" she asked. "You've never even had a dog... or a cat."

"I think he followed me home because he knows I'll feed him." I eyed the meat and hoped it was enough.

"Or he followed you because you smell like chicken to him," she retorted. "Just call PETA, and let them deal with it."

I hefted the bag of meat. "You saw him. PETA is no longer an option."

"Then call the Department of Wildlife. They know how to handle dangerous animals."

"They'll take one look at him and ship him off to another lab to be studied. Or the government will give him back to Sutton and cover it all up." I felt a surge of protectiveness for the animal. "I won't do that to him."

Her voice turned pleading. "Please, don't go out there, Charlie."

I met her eyes. Of the two of us, I was the daring one. She was more comfortable with her computers where she could control her environment.

"I can't explain it, but I really don't believe he wants to hurt me," I said. "I was with him in the woods an hour ago, and he didn't attack me, even though he clearly could have." I walked to the door and opened it.

She shook her head. "I still don't like it."

"Do you want to stay on the call, or should I call you back?" I asked in a low voice as I stepped outside.

"I'll stay, and I'll be quiet this time."

He was standing exactly where I'd left him. "Here you go." I approached him carefully, dumped the meat onto the ground, and backed away.

He devoured it in less than a minute and lifted his head to look at me. I couldn't tell if he was asking for more or sizing me up for the second course.

"That's all I have. I'll get some more tonight."

He watched me for half a minute longer and sat.

I got a better look at the tear in his armor. Beneath it, the fur appeared to be matted with dark blood, but I couldn't tell how serious the wound was.

A dog barked in the distance, and he jerked his head toward the sound. On the back of his head, there were strange glyphs I didn't recognize etched into the metal.

I lifted my phone and snapped two photos. I zoomed in, cropped them, and sent them to Finley. If they were part of any written language, she would find it.

"What are these?" she asked when I switched back to the call.

"I don't know," I whispered. "Can you search?"

"Yeah."

The animal looked almost relaxed, except for his eyes, which remained alert. Now that we had established he wasn't going to eat me, I had to figure out what to do with him. He was too exposed here. It was only a matter of time before a helicopter or drone spotted him.

I tilted my head back, scouring the sky. Sutton had told my father they would stop following me, but after everything that had happened, I wasn't ready to take them at their word.

"If you stay out here, they're going to find you," I said. "We need a better place to hide you."

I looked around me. The shed was too obvious. Mason might start searching nearby yards if he hadn't already. My eyes fell on the basement door on one side of the patio, and I paused. Was I seriously contemplating that?

The more I thought about it, the more it made sense. My parents never went down to the basement. What better place to hide him than in the home of Sutton's top employees?

"Wait here," I told him and ran back to the house.

"I can't believe that just happened," Finley said. "What now?"

I hurried down to the basement and stopped in the main room, which

45

contained two couches, a large flat screen TV, and a small bar. Past it was a bathroom, a storage room, my workshop, and the utility room.

"*Hello,*" Finley called. "Am I on mute again?"

"I'm here." I opened the door to my workshop. "There's plenty of room in here."

"For what?"

I went inside. "The panther."

"I thought we agreed it isn't a panther." She let out a choked laugh. "You're joking, right?"

I looked at her. "He can't stay in the backyard. Mom and Dad are gone to DC for two days and, it'll only be until I can figure out what to do next."

She shook her head slowly. "I knew it would happen eventually. Living with your mum has finally made you crack."

I laughed at her sorrowful expression. "I'll have to wait until dark. That gives me time to go out and buy more meat."

"Won't people notice you buying that much meat every day?" she asked as I started back upstairs.

"I'm spreading out my purchases." I grabbed my backpack and scooter key from my room. "Any luck with those symbols?"

"Not yet, but I'll keep looking. And I'll poke around Sutton to see what I can find."

I smiled at the phone. "Thanks. I'll message you when I'm back."

Thirty seconds later, my phone buzzed. **Try not to die. Finding a new best friend is too much work.**

I'll do my best.

Before I left, I checked on the animal again. He was still behind the shed, lying with his chin on his paws.

"I'm going out to buy food," I said. "You need to stay here until I get back. If anyone sees you, it's game over."

He didn't move.

"I'll be back as soon as I can," I promised and left.

I kept checking the sky for drones as I rode across town to a grocery store I hadn't been to before. I bought two whole chickens and a large beef bone, which was all I could fit in my backpack.

It was dark by the time I got home. He was exactly where I'd left him, and he lifted his head when he saw me.

"Do you want to come inside?" I motioned for him to follow me.

He stood and limped toward me, favoring his back leg. It was eerie how he seemed to understand everything I said. Before animal testing was banned, scientists had begun experimenting with implanting AI chips in animal brains. I'd bet anything he had one.

He walked without making a sound. An intelligent, armored animal that moved with stealth and looked deadly enough to take down a bear – what the hell was Sutton doing in that lab?

"You'll be safe in here," I said entering the basement. He hesitated for a moment before he followed me inside.

He immediately went to the pot of water I'd placed in the workshop and drank deeply. After he had his fill, he lay down facing the door.

I sat on the floor with my back against the wall and sighed. "I don't know about you, but this has been the craziest twenty-four hours of my life. The only thing that could top it is aliens landing on the lawn."

My gaze went to the tear in his armor and the matted fur beneath it. "I wish I could look at your wound. I'm no vet, but I can clean it so it doesn't get infected."

He blinked, and I caught a flash of blue in his eyes. What did it mean?

Gathering my courage, I got to my knees and crawled slowly toward him. When he lifted his head, I paused. "I won't hurt you. I just want to help."

He lowered his head again, and I inched forward until I was within reach of his powerful jaws.

A few minutes passed before I was brave enough to lean in for a closer look at his head. I did a double-take when I saw what lay beneath the armor.

I'd taken apart a lot of electronic devices, but I had never seen anything like this. Instead of circuits and traces there were glowing crystalline nodes connected by a network of shimmering crystalline pathways. Dispersed among them were beads of what looked like liquid mercury and strange fibers with specks of light pulsing through them continuously. Two of the crystalline nodes were dark.

I sat back on my heels. "Wow. I don't think I can help you there. I'm going to look at your leg now."

I moved to his hind legs. He was resting his weight partially on his uninjured side, making it possible to see a wet patch of fur and a nasty gash on his thigh. I stared at it for a long moment, trying to make sense of what I was seeing.

I turned on my phone's flashlight and shined it on his thigh. Shock rippled through me again. His exposed flesh looked normal but his blood was... purple.

I sat back heavily on the floor, my mind racing. What kind of Frankenstein genetic modifications had they done on him to change the color of his blood?

My phone vibrated, startling me. I glanced down at a text from Finley. **Symbols not in any known database.** It was followed by a bunch of laughing emojis. **Maybe he's an alien.**

Chuckling, I met his amber gaze. Something clicked in my brain, and all the heat drained from my body.

"It wasn't a plane," I whispered.

My eyes trailed over the seamless fusion of flesh and the strange metal unlike anything I'd ever seen. A light winked at me from the circuitry beneath the tear in the metal, circuitry so advanced it looked futuristic.

"You're an alien."

The room swayed, and I took in several slow, deep breaths.

It all made sense now – the orders to stay out of the woods, the military involvement, and their relentless search for the creature. They weren't after an escaped lab animal.

My mind whirled. *His spaceship crashed. Sutton has the pilot. Did he die in the crash, or is he...?*

The memory of the man I'd almost run down on my scooter came rushing back. Lydia Warren said he was an intruder, but what if he hadn't been breaking in? What if he had broken out? What if he wasn't a man at all?

The rest of the pieces clicked into place. The alien had escaped, and I'd nearly run him down. They thought I'd seen him.

Where was he now? Had they caught him, or was he out there somewhere?

I put my head in my hands. This was bigger than anything I could have imagined.

The animal... alien... made a sound, and I looked up to find him watching me. If I was overwhelmed, what was he feeling? He was hurt and alone on an alien planet with no idea what had happened to his... companion.

I reached out and laid my hand on his side, the fur soft and warm to the touch. "You're safe now."

His eyes went to the hand touching him, and I realized what I'd done. Fear gripped me when he shifted his body so he was facing me. Less than a foot separated us, and his head was almost level with mine. One snap of his jaws was all it would take to end my life.

Blue bled into his eyes until they were a deep cobalt that seemed to glow from within. I was afraid to move as he sniffed me, his hot breath washing over my face. The tip of his nose brushed against my jaw, and I squeezed my eyes shut.

I couldn't hold back a gasp when a weight settled on my lap. My eyes shot open, and I looked at the big head resting there. I raised a tentative hand and touched his forehead. When he didn't react, I lightly stroked the fur there, and he let out a long sigh.

My chest squeezed. "I don't know if I can find your friend, but I promise I'll do what I can to help you."

What could I do other than hide him? If Sutton caught the alien pilot, he'd be under heavy security. Even if I could somehow get to him, they were stranded here without their spaceship.

"I wish you could talk to me and tell me more about you and your friend. That might help me figure out how to help you." I stroked the part of its forehead not covered by armor. "I don't even know what to call you."

I moved my hand up to touch the armor. I expected cold metal, and I was surprised to find a warm surface, which felt more like carbon fiber. I pressed my palm against it and detected a steady, almost imperceptible vibration.

A wave of dizziness slammed into me. I swayed as the room spun and the static sound of white noise filled my ears. The noise grew louder inside my head, and grainy images rapidly played across my mind. It was like watching a snowy TV screen, only this one caused pressure behind my eyes that increased the longer I looked at it.

The images began to come into focus – an instrument panel with alien symbols, a ravine, the alien creature. The images changed to a bright white room with medical equipment, people in white biohazard suits, and finally, a helmeted figure behind the beam of a headlight. Was that... me?

The static and images abruptly disappeared, leaving a headache in their wake. I rubbed my temples until the pain subsided enough to think straight.

"What the hell was that?"

My first thought was that the images had come from the creature, but he hadn't been there when I almost hit the person on my scooter. It had to be the pilot. He must share a connection with the creature, and intentionally or not, he'd somehow sent me images of things he had seen.

It *was* him on the road last night.

I touched the armor again. "Can you show me where you are?"

He either couldn't hear me or he wasn't able to send more because no new images came from him. I sighed heavily. "You have to give me something."

A string of gibberish, which might have been an alien language, flowed into my mind. I waited for it to stop before I said, "I don't know what you're saying."

Another word came, and I turned it over in my mind a few times before I tested it on my tongue. "KAL-icks," I murmured tentatively, sounding out the syllables.

The creature's head shot up.

"Kalyx," I said with more confidence.

He whined.

"Is that your name?" I asked, and he cocked his head.

I scooted backward a few feet and said the word again. He belly-crawled toward me. It was such an animal-like behavior I forgot for a moment I was sitting here talking to an alien.

The room seemed to take on a dreamlike quality, and I put a trembling hand to my forehead. This could not be real. Hesitantly, I touched the armor again. The word Kalyx repeated in my head along with a series of images and the knowledge my new friend was a *she*. I had no idea how I knew that; I just did.

Before I could process this new information, another alien word came to me easier than the first one. *Ta-RUTH*. It had to be the name of the alien talking to me.

"Taruth," I said out loud. "How are you doing this?"

No answer came. Maybe images and single words were the only way he could communicate. I lowered my hand and looked at the creature in front of me. Taruth was the pilot, and Kalyx was his pet, the alien equivalent of a feline. Until I knew otherwise, she was a cat.

"My name is Charlie," I said. I had no idea if Taruth could understand me.

There was no response, and after a minute, I assumed the connection with him was broken.

"At least, we know he's alive." I pursed my lips. That knowledge did not put us any closer to finding him. He was at Sutton, I was sure of it, but he might as well be on the other side of the country.

My phone vibrated with another text from Finley. **Are you still there? Do I need to send in the National Guard?**

I'm here, I wrote back. **There's been a new development.**

Let me guess. I was right and he's an alien.

I laughed. **Yes**

My phone rang.

It took five minutes to calm Finley down enough to listen to me, and another thirty to fill her in on everything that had happened since I got home.

"Charlie, do you realize how huge this is?" Her eyes were wild. "This is bigger than the FTL drive, bigger than Alcea."

"I know."

She blew out a breath. "What are we going to do?"

"The first thing is figure out where Sutton is keeping Taruth."

"Then what?" she asked.

I shrugged. "And then we'll figure out the next step."

She frowned. "And what are you going to do about your new pet? If you keep her in your house, someone is bound to find her."

"I know." We had a cleaning lady who came once a week, and Kalyx was too big to hide from her.

The thought of what would happen if my parents found Kalyx made my stomach twist. My mother would sell her soul for a chance to study alien technology. My father wasn't as bad, but I didn't believe he would pass on the opportunity either. No scientist would.

"I'll look for somewhere else to stash her before Mom and Dad get back," I said.

Finley looked up from typing. "I can't believe how calm you are. I'm freaking out inside."

I rubbed the back of my neck. "Honestly, it all happened so fast I haven't had time to really process it. Until an hour ago, I thought I was harboring a cybernetic panther created in a lab. Is an alien cat that much more of a stretch?"

"Yes!" Finley's laugh was a little hysterical. "It's an *alien...* from another *planet!* And you talked to the other one." Her eyes went so round the whites showed. "Charlie, you made first contact."

My gaze flicked to Kalyx. "Sutton found Taruth first, so technically they made first contact."

"Nope. First contact means the first communication with an alien. Do you think your friend Taruth is talking to the people holding him captive?" She pressed her hands to her cheeks. "Gah! My best friend talked to an alien."

"If you help me rescue Taruth, I'll introduce you to him." I held my phone away so it was facing Kalyx. "Finley, meet Kalyx. Kalyx meet Finley."

"Hi, Kalyx," she called with barely-contained excitement.

Kalyx tilted her head to one side and then the other as she looked at the phone.

"Can you give me a closer look at those circuits?" Finley asked.

"Hold on." I snapped a few closeups and sent them to her. When I switched back to her, she was studying them with a gleam in her eyes – the same one she got when she was about to tackle a tricky piece of code.

She tapped a finger against her lips. "I wonder if those damaged circuits caused the bad connection with Taruth."

"It was a telepathic link, not a phone call."

"Yes, but it only happened when you touched the metal," she said. "I bet you could talk to him again if you fixed the circuits."

I snorted. "Are you telling me you know how to repair alien technology now?"

She rolled her eyes. "Show me the rest of her, smartass."

I angled the phone for her to see the dark metal that covered the top half of Kalyx's body. I ran my hand lightly along the alien metal and down to where it met the skin. The metal moved with her breaths as if it was living tissue.

"What does it feel like?" Finley asked breathless.

"It's hard to describe. I've never felt anything like it."

She sighed wistfully. "I'm going to be the first person in history to die from envy."

My fingertips moved over a slight indentation in the metal between Kalyx's shoulders. I felt around it and applied a tiny bit of pressure.

There was a barely audible hiss. I jerked my hand back when a four-inch panel opened to reveal a small screen with alien symbols along the bottom.

"Holy crap," we said in unison.

"It must be a control panel, but for what?" Finley asked.

I studied it. "For maintenance maybe."

"Or it could trigger a self-destruct weapon," she said as I reached toward it again.

My hand paused over the screen. "I don't think so. They wouldn't make that so easy to trigger."

I touched the screen. It lit up, and a blue light rose from it, forming a 3D holographic projection of Kalyx's body. I passed my hand through the hologram, and it began to rotate slowly.

I touched one side of the holographic cat, and it zoomed, showing a network of electronics and mechanical parts interfused with organic tissue.

"Wow." I'd seen holographic displays before, but they showed static images. This was a live interactive 3D schematic of Kalyx's entire body.

A spot on the head was outlined in orange. I zoomed in and saw the two dark crystalline nodes from her injury.

"I won't be running out to buy replacement parts. That's for sure," I said as I studied the hologram.

Finley's voice dropped. "Charlie, this is light-years ahead of our technology. Can you imagine what's in the ship?"

I nodded. "It must have an FTL drive. If Sutton can figure out how to replicate that technology, they'll be able to build a drive for the colony ship."

"And North America will win the race to colonize Alcea." Her voice was grim. "They'll do everything in their power to keep the world from learning what they have."

"Which is why they need to find Kalyx, "I said. "I have to keep her safe from them and find Taruth."

"*We* will find Taruth," she said. "Just as soon as I get into Sutton's system."

I smiled. "You do your thing, and I'll look for a place to hide Kalyx."

She cracked her knuckles. "If they're hiding something, I'll find it."

"Just don't forget to sleep." She often got so wrapped up in her work she'd stay up all night.

She grew serious. "You need to be careful. If they find out you have her, who knows what they'll do to keep you quiet. Your parents might not be able to protect you."

Goose bumps rose on my arms. "We need a contingency plan. Insurance if things go bad."

"Do a video," she said. "I'll set it up to go online if anything happens to you."

"A video won't be enough. They can say it's fake." I thought for a moment. "The cut on Kalyx's leg is still bleeding. What if I take a sample and send it to you? They can't say I faked alien blood."

"Perfect."

I got to my feet. "Okay. I'll do it right away."

"Sounds like a plan."

We ended the call, and I grabbed a tissue and a small storage bag from the kitchen. I gently dabbed the wound until I got enough of the purple blood for a good sample. I sealed the tissue in the bag, tucked it between the pages of a book, and put the book in a padded envelope to send to Finley tomorrow. Then I sat beside Kalyx to make the video and uploaded it to the hidden cloud account I shared with Finley.

"I hope it's enough," I said to Kalyx.

For the next few hours, I researched places in town to hide her. It was almost midnight when I found one that had potential. It was an old mechanic's shop on the outskirts of town that had closed five years ago. I'd check it out tomorrow.

Yawning, I stood and stretched. "Time for bed, Kalyx. Do you need to go out first?"

I walked around the back yard with her for fifteen minutes, but she seemed more interested in following me than doing her business. Maybe being only half organic meant it took longer for her species to digest their food.

"We'll try again in the morning," I said when we returned to the work-shop. "I'll see you in a few hours."

I walked to the stairs and jumped when I found her behind me. "No, Kalyx. You need to stay here so my parents won't see you."

She didn't move as she watched me climb the stairs. I felt bad when I closed the door and saw her still standing there, but what else could I do?

In my room, I moved on autopilot as I got ready for bed. My mind spun with everything that had happened today, and the fact that I had an alien in my basement.

I walked out of the bathroom and almost screamed. Kalyx stood in the middle of my bedroom.

I put a hand over my racing heart. "How did you get out of the base-ment?" I glanced at the closed bedroom door. "You can open doors?"

We stared at each other, and I sighed. "You can sleep up here, but only for tonight."

She padded over and settled down beneath the window as if she slept there every night.

I got into bed thinking I wouldn't be able to sleep with her in the room, but I was out in minutes. My dreams were full of aliens, spaceships, and people in biohazard suits. One pulled off their respirator to reveal my moth-er's face.

"You can't hide her from us forever, Charlotte," she said as she walked toward me holding up a bone saw like a mad scientist.

I jerked awake, heart racing. Rubbing my tired eyes, I sat up and swung my legs over the side of the bed. The room was dark except for a pair of glowing blue eyes. A week ago, that sight would have terrified me. This morn-ing, it was a relief.

I looked at my phone and groaned. It was just after 5:00 a.m., and I was wide awake.

"You want to go out?" I asked Kalyx, who lifted her head.

Standing, I glanced out the window and froze. Was that a light in the woods behind our neighbor's house?

I moved to the window. A minute passed before the bobbing light reap-peared. Someone was out there with a flashlight. I shivered, watching the light blink in and out of view. Maybe the neighbor's cat got out, and she was looking for him.

And maybe my mother was going to start baking for the PTA.

Kalyx stood, and I placed a hand on her back, not sure if I meant to comfort her or me. The light moved closer, sweeping in a circular pattern behind our property. Unease crept over me. Had they found footprints? A drop of blood?

The light vanished. I stayed by the window until dawn, but I saw no one. I hurriedly changed, took Kalyx back to the basement, and hopped on my scooter. I couldn't shake the fear that time was running out for us.

My heart sank when I reached the mechanic's shop and found a demolition crane in front of it. I rode around the area searching for another place, but I found nothing. By the time I got back to my neighborhood, desperation had set in.

Then I saw them.

Two military vehicles were parked near my neighbor's house. A uniformed man spoke to Cathy while others walked around the property. I kept my pace casual and pulled up at the house across from mine. Mr. and Mrs. Oakly, a retired couple in their sixties, stood on their porch watching with interest.

Pushing up my visor, I asked, "What's going on?" I hoped I sounded calmer than I felt.

"They're looking for a fugitive," Mrs. Oakly said, her face flushed with excitement. "They think he might have come through the woods."

I let my jaw drop. "A fugitive? Is he dangerous?"

She blinked like she hadn't considered that. "They didn't say."

I followed her gaze to the man talking to Cathy. Another soldier said something to him, and he turned.

Colonel Mason.

Panic threatened, but I forced myself to breathe. He had to suspect Kalyx was nearby. An escaped fugitive was the perfect excuse to search the neighborhood.

Stay calm. I pulled into my driveway. There was no evidence Kalyx had been in the yard. Even if they found something, there was no reason to search the house.

"Miss Ross," Mason called before I could open the garage.

I removed my helmet and turned to him. He stood at the base of the driveway, his face as hostile as that day in the woods. Did he look at everyone that way?

He approached. "We're searching the neighborhood for a man who escaped police custody yesterday. Have you seen anything suspicious?"

"Yes," I said, catching the way he said *anything*, not *anyone*.

His eyebrows lifted in surprise. "What?"

I pointed at the woods. "Around five this morning there was a light in the woods behind Cathy's house. I figured maybe her cat got out, but it could've been someone else."

"Are you always up at 5:00 a.m.?" he asked.

"No. Why does it matter when I wake up?"

"It doesn't." He waved two men forward. "My people are going to do a quick search of your yard and shed."

I didn't think they could do that without permission, but objecting would make me look suspicious. "There's not many places a person can hide in our yard."

The men walked past, guns drawn. I moved to follow, but Mason held up a hand. "Stay here. We'll move faster if we don't have to worry about your safety."

I shoved my hands into my coat pockets to hide how tightly they were clenched. The soldiers headed straight for the shed, and I held my breath as they disappeared behind it.

"Does the military normally help the police track fugitives?" I asked.

He looked annoyed. "Sometimes, when asked."

His men reappeared and went inside the shed, where they'd find nothing. They came out and walked around the shed again, and a cold sweat broke out between my shoulders.

"Wait here," Mason ordered and joined them.

They spoke, and he did his own walk around the shed. When he returned, his eyes gleamed with something that made my mouth go dry. I scrambled to think of what I could have missed. A hair, a speck of blood?

"We believe he was in your yard," he said. "We'll need to search the house."

"No," I said sharply. "I think I'd know if there was a man hiding in my house."

Mason's mouth thinned. "You just got home. How do you know he didn't enter while you were out?"

"We have a Solis system," I said, naming one of the best residential security systems in the country. "Unless your fugitive's a professional burglar, he didn't get into my house."

"Is there a reason you don't want us to search the house?" Mason pressed.

I crossed my arms. "Would you want strangers going through your house?"

"I'd want to know it was safe, just as I'm sure your parents would." He pulled out his phone and walked a few steps away. After a moment, he returned and held it out on speaker.

"Go ahead," he said.

My mother's voice came through the phone. "Charlotte, Colonel Mason explained the situation. I gave him permission to enter and look around."

"But –"

"Do not argue with me," she said briskly. "Let them do their job so they can move on."

A sick weight settled in my stomach. They were going to find Kalyx, and there was nothing I could do to stop it. I promised to keep her safe, and I failed her.

My mother said something else I didn't hear and hung up, leaving me with Mason who wore a satisfied smile.

I unlocked the front door with shaking fingers. As I reached for the knob, his arm shot out to block me.

"You stay out here," he said. "We'll move faster if we don't have to worry about your safety."

"I need to disarm the alarm."

"Give me your code."

I reluctantly gave it to him. He entered with three soldiers while a fourth stayed with me. I watched helplessly as the door closed behind them.

6

The minutes ticked by like hours.

I pictured the soldiers finding Kalyx in the basement. What would she do if she was cornered? I didn't want her captured, but I didn't want anyone getting hurt either.

I'm sorry, Kalyx, I thought miserably. What would they do to her? What would they do to me? Mason wasn't an idiot. He'd know she didn't end up in the basement without help.

Thank God I'd made that video and sent it to Finley. At least we had that and the –

Oh no.

I thought about the padded envelope on my desk, addressed to Finley. The one with the tissue soaked in Kalyx's blood.

Once they found Kalyx, they'd bring in a team and go through the house. They'd find the tissue. They'd know Finley was in on this.

Red alert, I texted. **We might need that video sooner than we thought.**

Her reply was instant. **What???**

They're searching my house.

OMG!!

If you don't hear from me in an hour, send it out, I said.

I cast a glance at the soldier standing six feet away. Would he try to stop me if I ran? And where would I even go?

My phone rang. My pulse jumped when I saw my father's name. Mason must have found Kalyx and called them already.

"Your mom told me what's going on," Dad said. "I wanted to make sure you're okay."

"I'm... fine."

"You don't sound fine." His voice was gentle, concerned. "I know this must be upsetting, but you have nothing to worry about."

Not until they find her, I thought, inching toward my scooter. "It just caught me off guard. Mason's not exactly Mr. Congeniality."

Dad chuckled. "That he isn't, but you're safe with him. I'm sorry this happened, especially after everything with Sutton."

I glanced at the door. Any second now, it would open, and I had to get out of here before it did. "Finley's calling," I lied. "Can we talk later?"

"Of course. You know you can call me anytime."

"I know." I hung up and walked toward the scooter.

"You were told to stay put," the soldier said in a clipped voice, though he didn't raise his weapon.

I faced him. "I'm not a dog, and Mason isn't my commanding officer."

He scowled. "It's *Colonel* Mason."

"*Colonel* Mason has no authority over me." I raised my voice so the neighbors could hear. "Since when does the military detain citizens on their own property? Are you going to shoot me if I try to leave?"

The soldier shifted. "No one's detaining you. The colonel's just making sure you're safe while they search."

"How long does it take four trained soldiers to search one house for a man?" My eyes flicked toward the front door. "It's been over ten minutes."

"They're being thorough," he replied.

"There are only so many places a man could hide –"

The door opened. Mason stepped out, the three other soldiers behind him. His expression was pinched and his stride brisk. He looked at me like I was personally responsible for ruining his day.

I stared back, confused. They hadn't found her. How?

"The house is clear," he said flatly.

I almost said *told you so,* but kept it to myself. No need to poke the bear.

I waited until Mason and his men reached the street before I bolted for the front door. As soon as it shut behind me, I ran for the basement. It was empty.

Panic flared. I searched the whole house. All the doors were locked, the windows secure. Nothing was out of place.

How the hell had she gotten out and locked the doors behind her?

All good. Will explain, I texted Finley when I found her envelope on my desk, untouched.

From an upstairs window, I watched Mason talking on his phone beside the vehicles while the other soldiers searched the next yard. I couldn't go out to search for Kalyx until they were gone.

I went back to my room and scoured the woods from my window. She had to be out there somewhere. What made her leave?

Turning, I let out a yelp when Kalyx materialized in the middle of my bed. My heart galloped like a prized racehorse. Before I could speak, she vanished again.

I stared at the empty bed. "Kalyx?"

The air distorted as parts of her flickered in and out, first her hind legs, and then her head appeared and vanished again. It lasted thirty seconds before she fully reappeared and stayed.

I sat beside her and reached out, needing to be sure she was real. "You can cloak?"

I dropped back on the mattress, nearly limp with relief. No wonder they hadn't found her.

Her cloaking device must have been damaged in the crash, but by some miracle, it had worked long enough to hide her during the search.

"If we could fix that, we wouldn't need a place to hide you."

I sat up and activated her hologram. Zooming in on the two dark crystalline nodes, I studied them alongside the glowing ones. After switching back and forth several times, I saw that both dark nodes were slightly misaligned, off by just a few millimeters.

A tiny thrill went through me. If I could realign them, would that be enough?

"I have to try." I stood. "Come with me."

We went to my workshop. I opened a case of precision pliers, tools you wouldn't find in any electronics store. These were the kind used in research labs, a Christmas gift from my parents.

I selected a mid-sized pair, grabbed my magnifying glasses, and sat cross-legged beside Kalyx. She had her head on her paws, eyes closed. When I settled in front of her, she opened them briefly and closed them again.

Holding up the pliers, I said, "It's a tool. I'm going to try to fix the damage." I didn't know if she understood, but she made no move to stop me.

I leaned in, the built-in light in my glasses illuminating the tear in her armor. Everything was just as I'd seen on the hologram. My hand stayed steady as I eased the pliers in toward one of the crystalline nodes.

I paused a millimeter away. These weren't ordinary electronics. For all I knew, one wrong move could fry me.

Before I could talk myself out of it, I touched the tip to the node. Nothing happened.

I aligned the tips on either side and gently nudged it into place. It looked right, but it stayed dark. I moved on to the second one and did the same. Still no change.

Trying not to feel defeated, I looked closer. Two of the tiny glasslike fibers connected to one of the nodes had no moving lights. The fibers looked bent, not broken.

I sat up and grabbed the micro-tip pliers. I'd never used them before. Painstakingly, I isolated one fiber and applied the slightest pressure to straighten it.

A stream of lights raced along it.

Yes!

I focused on the second fiber. It was harder to reach, but I managed to adjust it. Seconds later, it pulsed with light.

I studied my work. The nodes were still dark, but at least, I'd fixed something.

"I gave it my best shot," I told her, removing the glasses.

I picked up the largest pair of pliers and started straightening the jagged edge of the tear in the armor. The metal was surprisingly pliable, and it only took a minute to do one side.

"Almost there," I told her.

I started on the other side, and my hand stilled.

One of the dark nodes had lit up. A second later, the other flickered on.

"It worked." I activated the hologram. The damage was no longer outlined in orange.

I sat back, hands on my head, grinning. "It worked!"

Kalyx raised her head, giving me a puzzled look. I impulsively threw my arms around her neck.

She let out a low rumble, and I pulled back, alarmed. Then she laid her head on my legs and began to make a deep, resonant sound.

She was purring.

I stroked her face. She was safe. If her cloak was working again, it would make hiding her a lot easier.

"I need to tell Finley."

"I think I'm getting an ulcer," Finley groaned after I filled her in about Mason. "I'm not built for this much stress."

Laughing, I said, "Maybe this will make you feel better." I told her about the repair.

"No wayyyy," she wailed. "You did it without me?"

"What were you going to do? Supervise?"

She huffed. "I could have watched."

I held up the pliers. "Want to watch me finish fixing her armor?"

Grumbling under her breath, she watched as I smoothed the torn metal. When I was done, it looked more like a crack than a gaping wound, and the internal circuitry was no longer visible.

"Not bad," Finley said grudgingly. "I can't believe you get to play with alien tech while I'm hacking corporate servers."

I got up to put the tools away. "How's that going?"

"Their surface network was a joke," she said. "But the secure system is locked down tight. I wouldn't be surprised if the NSA helped build it. The Kremlin's security is easier to crack."

I stopped what I was doing to look at her. "I'm not going to ask why you hacked into the Kremlin."

Her face broke into an impish grin.

"How are you going to find out if the cloaking works?" she asked.

"I guess I could ask her." Finley laughed as I said, "Kalyx, hide."

She vanished.

I reached out cautiously until my fingertips brushed against her warm fur. "Kalyx, show."

She reappeared.

"She understands you," Finley breathed. "How?"

I pulled my hand away. "Maybe she has a built-in translator."

"This is amazing. I wonder what else she can do," Finley leaned in closer to her screen. "Do you think her cloaking hides her electronic signature, too? She must have one."

I stared at her in dismay. "I didn't think of that."

Finley's face was serious. "I bet Sutton has, or they will."

Scrambling to my feet, I picked up the scanner. It was unlikely the device could pick up an alien signal, but it was all I had.

I held it above Kalyx. Nothing. I lowered it.

It let out a small beep, and the digital meter jumped erratically. I held it away from her and brought it back. It went haywire again.

"Charlie, hello?" Finley called in a singsong voice.

I grabbed my phone from the workbench. "I used my scanner on Kalyx. It picks up something when it's close to her."

"How close?" she asked.

"Within two feet."

She pursed her lips. "Was Kalyx cloaked?"

"No." I asked Kalyx to hide and used the scanner again with the same result.

Finley's mouth fell. "So much for that. The good thing is a scanner would have to be within two feet of her to detect the signal."

"This is Sutton we're talking about," I said. "How long do you think it'll take them to build something strong enough to find her?"

She thought for a moment. "You need a signal dampener. Small enough for her to carry."

"Sure. I'll just run out and pick one up."

"You could make one." She began typing, and a minute later she said, "Got it."

My phone vibrated with an incoming message. I opened the attachment and scrolled through pages and pages of instructions and diagrams.

"There's a parts list on the second page," she said. "You should be able to buy all of this at electronic stores or scavenge it from a salvage place."

I skimmed the diagrams. "I need to read through it first."

She cocked her head, and someone called to her in the background. "Coming," she called back. Making a face, she said, "It's been raining since we got home and guess whose week it is to walk Milo."

I laughed. Milo was their West Highland Terrier, whom she adored. She would walk through a blizzard for that dog.

We ended the call, and I went to the den to print the instructions. I sat at my desk to read through them while Kalyx made herself comfortable on the bed.

The instructions were clear, nothing I couldn't do. If I could scrounge up all the components I needed, I could build it in a day or two, easy.

"I have to run out to buy this stuff," I told Kalyx, grabbing my backpack. "You stay in here and hide if anyone comes in."

She got up to follow me, and I put up a hand. "You can't come with me. I'll be back as soon as I can."

I left her on my bed and headed out. Three stores later, I had everything but one part. There was one place left to try.

As I pulled up to Cole Electronics, I replayed yesterday's run-in with Ethan. I wasn't eager for a repeat, but I needed the part.

His father stood behind the counter, tidier and more sober than last time. There was no sign of recognition when he looked at me.

"Excuse me. Where's your salvage section?" I asked.

"Back corner," he said, pointing.

I turned down the nearest aisle and spotted the bins. As I passed the storage area, Ethan walked toward the open loading door, carrying two boxes.

I couldn't help but admire his athletic build and the way his black T-shirt stretched across his broad shoulders. Too bad he was a jerk.

He let out a grunt of pain and stopped to rest the boxes against some shelving, visibly straining.

I jogged over. "Hey, let me help with that."

"I don't need help," he snarled. Then he saw me. "What the hell are you doing here?"

"You really need to work on your store greeting," I said.

The boxes wobbled, and his left hand trembled as he tried to adjust his grip. I placed my hands under the bottom box to take some of the weight, and it only made him angrier.

"I said I don't need your help." He tried to pull away, but I moved with him.

"Too bad. You're getting it anyway." Ignoring his glare, I grabbed the top box and lifted it. I wasn't expecting it to be so heavy, and I nearly dropped it. I set it carefully on the floor and turned back to him.

Freed from the extra weight, the strain on his face eased, but his left hand still couldn't get a good grip on the remaining box. Bracing myself for the backlash, I took it from him. He resisted, but I held firm.

He swore as I laid the box on top of the first one. "I had it."

A stocky man walked through the loading door. "Everything okay?"

"Yeah," Ethan said between clenched teeth.

"Just a minor disagreement over lifting technique," I said. The man shook his head and headed back outside.

I nudged the bottom box with my foot. "What's in these, gold bricks?"

He glared at me. "Nothing you would understand."

"Try me."

"Graphene-based supercapacitors," he said, rubbing his elbow. "Do you need me to explain what they are?"

It was a struggle not to roll my eyes. "They're high-energy storage devices." At his raised eyebrows, I said, "All the cool kids know that."

"Why is she back here?" his father demanded from behind me.

Ethan's scowl returned. "She's one of Xander's friends, and she was just leaving."

"Yes, I can only take so much of your sunny personality," I said, heading for the salvage bins.

A shelf held an assortment of old surveillance drones – the kind you could only buy new with your home security system. I picked up one to examine it, returned it, and selected the next one.

"What are you doing now?" Ethan asked.

"Browsing for shoes. Am I in the wrong aisle?"

He took a slow, measured breath. "Don't you have something better to do?"

"Yes." I resumed looking over the drones.

"None of those work," he said. "The new and refurbished drones are in aisle three."

"Thanks for pointing that out." I turned the drone over in my hands. It was a newer model and exactly what I needed. It was also dirt cheap.

Footsteps approached. "That's only good for parts. It won't fly without the security code."

"I know. I need its wideband frequency oscillator." I tucked the drone under my arm. "Do you need me to explain what that is?"

Surprise flickered in his eyes, followed by a look of grudging respect. His expression soon settled back into the surly one, which seemed to be his default. I wondered if he was always in a bad mood. It had to be exhausting.

"Hey, Charlie." Xander popped around the corner of an aisle and gave me a big smile. His eyes widened with curiosity when he saw the drone. "No one ever buys those old drones. What are you working on?"

"School project."

"Cool." He stuck his hands into his pockets. "I wish we got to work on stuff like that at my school."

"You can always take it up as a hobby. That's what I did."

"Yeah?" Interest sparked in his eyes. "Where do I start?"

"There are tons of beginner projects online. You can also take apart old stuff to see how it works." I waved at the aisles behind him. "You have everything you need right here."

Xander's hopeful gaze shifted to Ethan. I wondered if his older brother and father would support his new interest. Neither of them struck me as the nurturing type.

I smiled at Xander. "I need to get home to work on my project. See you around."

I walked to the front of the store and laid the drone on the counter. Ethan followed me and rang me up without comment.

"Thanks for your help," I said sweetly and left.

Kalyx and I spent all day and most of the night in the workshop. The next day, I skipped half my classes so I could finish the dampener before Mom and Dad got home. By midafternoon it was done.

It wasn't much to look at, a small black box with a stubby antenna. There were no lights, but its faint hum told me it was on. I didn't know if it would hide her from a powerful scanner, but it blocked mine.

I attached the device to a thick leather dog collar and held it up to show Kalyx, who did not look impressed. She pulled her head away when I tried to put the collar on her, and it took several attempts before she allowed me to fasten it around her neck.

I leaned back to admire my work and frowned. My fingers touched the place on her armor where the crack had been. It looked like it had never been damaged.

After I cleaned up my work bench, I opened a DIY security system I'd bought yesterday. I needed to know if Mason or anyone else came back when I wasn't here. The four tiny motion-sensitive cameras were easy to hide. I placed them in the basement, garage, living room, and my bedroom, and I hid the hub in my room. With the pet setting enabled, Kalyx wouldn't trigger alerts. My parents were rarely home anyway.

I caught up on homework until I heard the garage door open. "Closet," I said to Kalyx, who lay on my bed.

Instead of going into the closet, she cloaked herself.

"No. You have to go to the closet," I whispered as the murmur of voices came from downstairs.

She didn't move.

Footsteps started up the stairs.

I tried to look casual when my father came to stand in my doorway, holding his carry-on.

"I wanted to make sure you were okay after all the excitement yesterday," he said. "It must have been frightening to have those soldiers show up at the house."

"They didn't scare me. Like you said, I was safe with them." I glanced at my comforter, which had flattened under Kalyx's weight. "How was the trip?"

"Meetings," he said tiredly.

My mother appeared behind him. "Charlotte, have you bought your dress for the company party?"

I blinked. "Uh..."

Her head tilted slightly. "It's this Friday night. I told you about it three weeks ago."

Every year, Sutton held a party at the country club. It was a boring five-course meal, followed by drinks in the private lounge. I'd pass on it if she didn't insist on me being there.

I caught a flicker of movement from the bed. Was the cloak malfunctioning? The thought of Kalyx suddenly appearing in front of my parents made my mouth go dry.

"Did you hear me?" my mother asked.

I blinked. "Yes. I'm just thinking of the best places to buy one."

She rattled off the names of a few boutique stores downtown. The only time I'd been to any of them was to shop for the dress for last year's party. It still hung in my closet, but wearing the same outfit two years in a row was unheard of.

"I'll go tomorrow." I'd agree to anything to get my parents to leave my room.

"Good." She glanced down at her phone. "I need to change and get to the office."

She went to their room, but my father lingered in the doorway. "Are you sure you're alright?"

I smiled. "I promise I'm fine. I just didn't like the idea of them going through the house. But they weren't here long."

"Okay." He started to leave and paused. "I'll leave my car here for you tomorrow so you don't have to carry a dress on the scooter."

"That'd be great. Thanks."

He left, and I hurried to close the door. When I turned, Kalyx was uncloaked on the bed with her head resting on her paws like she didn't have a care in the world.

"Bad alien," I scolded in a whisper. "What if they'd seen you?"

Her answer was to roll onto her side and go to sleep.

I groaned and dropped into my chair.

I adjusted the garment bag draped over my arm as I walked to the silver Mercedes. The savory aroma of baked dough, melted cheese, and tomato sauce from the pizzeria across the street reminded me it was almost dinnertime. I tried to remember the last time I'd had pizza as I hung the bag in the back of the car.

"Sweet ride," said Xander, sauntering toward me.

I closed the door and hit the button to lock the car. "It's my father's."

There was a moment of awkward silence before he said, "Did you finish your project?"

I smiled at him. "Yes. Did you decide to give it a try?"

"Not yet."

"You should," I said. "It's a lot of fun, and there are all kinds of contests online you can enter."

He perked up. "Contests? Can you win money?"

I nodded. "Some give away stuff like tools and electronics, but most of them have money prizes."

"Cool." He stuck his hands into his hoodie pocket. "You know a lot about this stuff, huh?"

I thought about working on Kalyx's alien technology and held back a grin. "You could say that."

A light breeze carried a fresh wave of heavenly smells from the pizzeria, and my stomach growled. "I'm going to grab a slice of pizza. If you want to join me, I can tell you more about the contests."

Longing filled his eyes, and he shook his head.

I smiled. "It's on me. I hate eating pizza alone."

"Okay," he said eagerly.

Instead of getting us each a slice, I ordered a small pizza, and we sat on the covered patio to wait for our food. When it came, he took his first bite and moaned blissfully.

"Oh, man, this tastes like real pepperoni and cheese, not that stuff on the pizza at school," he said around a mouthful of food.

I plucked a piece off mine and ate it. "It's synth meat, but it's close." The cheese was vegan, but I didn't ruin his pleasure by telling him.

He dug in like he was half starved. I wasn't sure what to make of him and his family. They had their own store, so they must be doing okay financially. But Xander dressed and acted like a street kid. He was easygoing, while his brother and father were angry and unpleasant, at least during the times I'd seen them.

As if my thoughts had conjured him, a white truck drove by with Ethan behind the wheel. His face was set into the same hard lines, making me wonder again if he ever lightened up.

"He wasn't always like that," Xander said.

"Who?" I asked, barely listening to him.

"Ethan."

I swung my gaze back to Xander and found him watching me with sad eyes. He put down his pizza and took a long drink of soda. "I remember when Ethan used to laugh a lot. He doesn't do that anymore since he came home."

"Where was he?" I asked.

"Asia." Xander drew a line in the condensation on his glass. "Ethan and his buddy Colin were in the marines."

"What happened?" I suspected this story didn't have a happy ending.

He sighed. "They were in South Korea when fighting broke out. Two people in their unit were killed, and a bunch were injured. Ethan was shot in his shoulder and leg. His leg was okay, but his shoulder was too messed up, so they sent him home."

I remembered his struggle to carry the boxes. It was no wonder he was so testy about it.

"What happened to Colin," I asked, almost afraid to learn his fate.

"He recovered, and he went back to his unit. Ethan's been in a bad mood since he came home in June." Xander picked up his pizza. "I guess I can't blame him. Everything sucks here now."

I wanted to ask what he meant by that, but I didn't. I doubted Ethan would be happy about his little brother sharing as much as he had with me.

"So, you must be pretty rich to live up by the country club," Xander said. Subtlety clearly wasn't in his vocabulary.

I chuckled. "My mom and dad work for Sutton Aerospace on the FTL project."

"Cool! My class is going there on a field trip next month. Maybe we'll get to see it."

"Maybe." I didn't have the heart to tell him the project was so classified I hadn't even seen it.

"Oh, no," said a distraught female voice.

I looked around and saw the other diners staring at the television mounted in the corner. On the screen was a picture of a polar bear with a headline at the bottom that read QANNIK HAS DIED.

The patio fell silent. Qannik was the last surviving polar bear. She and her brother Amaruq were born in captivity and raised at Wapusk National Park in northern Canada. Amaruq died two years ago at the age of seventeen, and Qannik's health had declined since then.

My throat tightened. Polar bears weren't the first species to go extinct in the last decade, but it was hard to believe such majestic animals were gone from the world forever.

"My biology teacher told us there's polar bear DNA in the World DNA Vault," Xander said as if he had read my mind. "So, they're not really gone."

The World DNA Vault contained eggs and DNA for over one hundred thousand species of mammals, reptiles, birds, fish, and amphibians. It also held insect DNA. I applauded the global effort to preserve the DNA, but at this rate, there wouldn't be a planet left to repopulate.

A message from Finley lit up my phone screen. **Did you hear about Qannik?**

Yes, I wrote back, and we exchanged a bunch of crying emojis.

I have more bad news, she said. **Can you talk?**

Give me 5. I looked at Xander, who was about to start his third slice of pizza. "I need to go. Do you want the rest of this?"

He stared at me like he couldn't believe his good fortune. "Really?"

"Yes." I waved over the waitress and paid for our meal.

"Thanks," he said when I stood.

I hurried to the car and called Finley, who picked up immediately. I knew it wasn't good the second I saw her face.

"The only way to access Sutton's hidden segment is from a computer inside the building," she said.

I dropped my head back. "Damn it."

"I can create a backdoor to gain access to an authorized computer, but their intrusion detection is one of the best." She typed on her keyboard. "I tested it, and they caught my dropper in less than three minutes. If I was doing this for fun that would be more than enough time to get in and out. But it's going to take longer than that to find what we're looking for."

My heart sank. "That's it then."

"Not quite," she said slowly. "I'm working on a new piece of code that will –"

I raised a hand. "Layman's terms, please."

She rolled her eyes. "The code will lie dormant on a computer until the user is logged in. It'll allow me to piggyback on their session to access the protected segment when they do. I just need a couple of days to perfect it."

I smiled broadly. "That's brilliant."

"There's one problem. I can't insert the code remotely without setting off their security." She gave me a pointed look. "The only safe way is to load it directly onto one of their computers when it's not connected to the network."

I shook my head. "If you mean Mom or Dad's laptops, forget it. They're hardly at home anymore, and even if I could get time alone with one of their laptops, I don't know their passwords."

She pursed her lips. "That's our only option. Unless you happen to know of another Sutton employee with access to that protected segment who leaves their laptop lying around."

"No."

A memory surfaced of a piece of paper containing a list of random passwords. My pulse quickened as an idea began to take shape in my mind. "Mr. Palmer."

"Mr. Palmer from the last job?"

"I think he keeps his password in his safe." I told her about the sheet of notepaper I'd seen there. "And he brings his laptop home with him. At least, he did that night."

Finley stared at me. "You want to break into his house while he's at home? Are you nuts?"

"No." I laughed at her slack-jawed expression. "You should see your face right now."

She attempted a scowl, but it came across as more of a pout.

"If those were passwords, I can go in when he's not at work or at home," I said. "As long as he hasn't changed his security code, I could be in and out of there in no time."

Her expression turned thoughtful. "But how will you know when he's out? You'll have to stake out his house."

"Nope." I grinned at her. "I already know when and where he'll be on Friday night. Sutton is having their annual party at the country club, and everyone who's anyone at Sutton will be there."

"That changes things." She tapped a finger against her chin. "I can take care of the security code, but the rest is going to depend on sheer luck. *If* that was a list of passwords, and *if* it's still there, and *if* he leaves his laptop at home, it could work."

"And *if* you can get the code written by then," I added.

She made a *tsk* sound. "Oh, it'll be done."

I glanced in the rearview mirror at the dress bag hanging in the back. "There's just one tiny wrinkle I need to work out."

"What?"

"I'll be at the party, too. Mom's orders," I said.

Her eyebrows rose. "So, you'll need to sneak out of the party, do your thing, and sneak back in without anyone noticing you were gone."

"And I'll be in a dress and heels."

She sputtered a laugh. "Anything else?"

"I think that's it." I placed my phone in the dash mount and started the car. "We have some planning to do."

7

The Hudson Ridge Country Club was a sprawling two-story building with ivy climbing halfway up the brick exterior, and a covered entrance flanked by two stone columns. Warm light glowed behind the tall windows and through the open doors at the entrance where a valet hurried to a white Land Rover ahead of us.

Dad pulled his car up to the entrance, and a valet opened Mom's door for her. I picked up a small clutch and reached for my door, but the valet was already there to do it for me. Sliding out of the car, I straightened and smoothed out the skirt of my knee-length cocktail dress.

I looked up to thank the valet and startled. It was Ethan.

I took a step back, my heel catching. He grabbed my arms to steady me, sending a warm tingle through them.

He let go, and I gave him a wry smile. "Thanks. I guess that makes us even."

The slight tightening of his mouth was his only acknowledgement before he walked around the car to my father, who handed him the keys and a fifty. Ethan thanked him and slid behind the wheel without a glance in my direction.

Inside, the marble-floored lobby gleamed with chandeliers and framed landscapes. Standing behind my parents, I examined my reflection in a tall mirror. I wore a dark blue dress paired with silver heels and a matching clutch, and silver clips pinning back my hair. Overall, it was a look of simple elegance. Even my mother had approved.

We followed the music to the ballroom, where tables glittered with crystal and candlelight. I scanned the room, but there was no sign of Mr. Palmer yet.

Dad found our table near the front, where Dev Malik sat with his wife Indira, their son Ari, and another couple. My parents' boss stood when we arrived, greeting us warmly. Tall, broad-shouldered, and always impeccably dressed, Sutton's CEO gave off the vibe of someone who saw straight through people and didn't miss a thing. When his gaze met mine, I had the unnerving feeling he could read all of my secrets.

"Charlotte, you remember my son Ari," he said as we sat. "He's home from MIT for the weekend."

"Hi," I told the nineteen-year-old beside me, who looked like a younger, softer version of his father. We'd met at his family's holiday party last year, where our mothers had tried to play matchmaker with us.

As the room filled, I surreptitiously searched for Mr. Palmer. Still no sign of him. My fingers clenched the purse on my lap.

A large dark-haired man in a black suit stood nearby, his eyes sweeping the room in a slow, practiced pattern. Even if I hadn't noticed his earpiece, I knew security when I saw it. Why would Sutton need security at a company dinner?

The meal was Sutton-level over-the-top: wild mushroom tartlets, filet mignon, and rich desserts. When the meal was over, Dev took the podium to praise everyone's work and hint at a coming breakthrough. As everyone applauded, all I could think about was Taruth and his alien technology, and what they might be doing to him to achieve that breakthrough.

Dev concluded by inviting us to join him in the club lounge for cocktails. The security guy positioned himself behind Dev and Indira as they went through the connecting door.

"Come on," Ari said to me when we entered the lounge.

We walked over to a group our age. Savannah and Serena were nineteen and in their second year at Yale. Damian, a quiet boy my age, attended a private boarding school in Connecticut.

"What's with the bodyguard?" Savannah asked Ari.

Ari gave a little shrug. "Dad got hate mail from one of those anti-space program crazies, and Sutton insisted on hiring personal security for him. The guy is ex-Special Forces, and you'd think he was a Secret Service agent protecting the president."

Serena huffed. "I don't get people. The space program could save us. Why would anyone be against that?"

"They'll change their tune when the first colony ship launches," Savannah said.

They jumped into a discussion about the Vanguard project and life on Alcea. Our families would be among the first to go, and my companions had all chosen their career paths to prepare them for that. Savannah and Serena were going to medical school, Ari was studying engineering, and Damian planned to go into robotics.

I pretended to listen as I searched for Mr. Palmer. Relief filled me when I spotted a slender Black man in his late thirties near the bar with his partner Jake.

Excusing myself, I went to the bar and ordered a glass of sparkling water. I lingered close enough to the two men to hear their conversation.

"We should be on our flight, sipping martinis," Jake said glumly.

"We can't control the weather." Mr. Palmer replied. "How about Christmas in London instead? You don't want to be stuck in a hotel for a few days when that storm hits."

Storm? I did a quick search on my phone. Storm Felix was heading toward the UK, bringing wind and flooding.

I texted Finley. **Storm Felix?**

Mostly going to hit the coast, she said. **We'll get some rain here but nothing bad.**

I replied with a happy emoji.

How's the party? she asked.

Boring.

Jake's voice grabbed my attention again. "How long do you want to stay?"

Mr. Palmer checked his watch. "These things usually end around ten. We should stick around until then so I can make the rounds."

My pulse kicked. That would give me ninety minutes. It should be more than enough time, but I needed to leave soon.

Gotta go. I texted. **Time to plan my exit.**

I rejoined the others, who were now debating living quarters on the colony ship. I wished I could share their excitement, but my expectations were more realistic. If we did succeed in building the ships, the five of us would probably be too old to take the trip.

Ari's mother came over to us. Indira Malik was elegant in her red embroidered salwar kameez, her smile soft and friendly.

"Excuse me." She placed a hand on Ari's arm. "I need to steal my son."

The moment they walked away, I gave the others a resigned smile. "I guess I should check in with my parents, too."

I walked over to stand beside my parents, who were talking to two women I didn't know. Mom introduced me to them, and they resumed their conversation. I listened for a few minutes and slipped away through a door that led to the restrooms.

I headed for the locker rooms at the rear of the building. The club had a fitness center, pool, tennis courts, and riding stables, which were available to members and their families. Yesterday, I'd used the gym, and I had been assigned a locker where I'd left my backpack. I retrieved it and changed into black leggings and a thin hooded jacket.

Cracking the door, I spotted an employee pushing a wine cart. I waited until he disappeared to exit the building through a door that led to the empty pool and tennis courts. Conscious of the security cameras, I kept my hood up and my head down as I passed the courts and crossed the lawn toward the stable. I felt exposed out in the open, but it was the fastest way off the grounds.

I made it to the cover of the trees and found the riding trail that encircled part of my neighborhood. I broke into a jog, and in less than five minutes, I was standing behind the big maple tree at the edge of Mr. Palmer's yard.

I texted Finley. **I'm here. You're sure the security code is still good?**

Yes.

Ok. I'm going in, I said.

I put in my earpiece and donned my gloves while I waited for the security drone to make its appearance. When it passed, I started the timer and sprinted to the back door.

Winston met me when I entered, rubbing against my legs as I disarmed the system. I bent to scratch his head, and he purred loudly.

In the office, I took out my penlight and swept it around the room. I gave a little fist pump when I spied the laptop bag sitting upright on the chair.

I pulled back the rug and opened the safe. There was no folder or notepaper, just stacks of credits.

Disappointment hit hard. I searched the desk drawers, careful not to disturb anything. Nothing.

My phone vibrated. **Are you in?**

Yes. I went back to the safe, reluctant to tell her the plan had failed. Crouching, I grasped the door handle and gave one last look inside as I closed the door.

Wait.

I yanked it open again. Reaching inside, I shoved two stacks of credits out of the way and grasped the edge of a piece of paper. I withdrew my hand and stared at a folded sheet of notepaper.

What's going on? Finley asked. **You're making me nervous.**

I unfolded the paper. The list had grown by one, and the previous one was crossed out. My fingers shook a little when I texted back. **I have the list.**

And the laptop?

Yes.

I removed the slim silver laptop from the bag and opened it. I flexed my fingers nervously and typed the last sequence on the list into the password box. My hand hovered above the keyboard for several seconds, and then I pressed the key.

The home screen appeared.

I stared at it, a little stunned it had actually worked. I texted Finley. **I'm in.**

I removed a data tag from my backpack. It was a new tag that held nothing but the code Finley had sent me that afternoon. I connected it to the laptop's Bluetooth and opened the file explorer to drill down deep into the system files until I found the one I was looking for.

Are you sure they won't detect this? I asked Finley.

I'm 99.8% sure, she replied.

I paused. **Not 100%?**

I don't like to be too cocky.

I snorted and copied her code to the system file. The computer kept a history of connected Bluetooth devices, but no one would look at that without good reason. If they did, they would only see an unknown device.

It's done. I returned the laptop to the case, placed the paper back in the safe, and made sure the office was as I'd found it.

Winston was waiting when I opened the door, and he tried to sneak past me into the room. I caught him and received a playful scratch for my efforts. Luckily, the glove protected my hand. It would have been hard to explain how I got cat scratches at the country club.

I cracked the back door to watch for the drone. Then I reset the security system and slipped out, locking the door behind me. Back in the cover of the trees, I checked the time, surprised to discover only thirty-five minutes had passed since I left the country club. This was going much better than I had expected.

I'm out. OMW to the club now, I texted.

Finley replied with a thumbs-up.

In no time, I was in the woods behind the stable, which was no longer quiet. The lights were on, and a woman was walking a horse while two men watched. There was no way I'd get to the tennis courts without being spotted.

I had two options. I could wait until the coast was clear or go through the woods to the parking lot at the end of the building. There were more cameras over there, but if I stuck to the edge of the parking lot, there was less chance of being seen.

I set off for the parking lot. Stopping outside the ornate wrought iron fence, I surveyed the rows of expensive vehicles. The lot was quiet, and I didn't see any valets.

I grasped two of the bars, stuck my foot into one of the gaps in the metal design, and hoisted myself up. Finding a second foothold, I precariously straddled the top between two pointed finials. It was a little trickier to get off the fence without impaling myself, but I managed to reach the ground without injury.

Crouching low, I hurried along the fence to the gate that led to the fitness center. I didn't hear the footsteps until it was too late.

Someone tackled me into the fence. I twisted trying to break free, but a strong arm pinned me against the cold iron.

"You're not going anywhere," said a harsh male voice.

My hood was yanked down, and Ethan's shocked face loomed over me. "What the hell?"

His hold on me loosened, but I couldn't move. I didn't know what was worse – getting caught like this or getting caught by him.

"What are you doing here?" he demanded. Releasing me, he stepped back to take in my black clothes and sneakers.

"I... um..." My mind raced to come up with a plausible reason. "I was meeting someone."

His raised eyebrows told me I needed to do better than that.

"My parents don't like him because he's... not rich." My mother didn't approve of anyone not from our social sphere, so it wasn't a total lie.

"So, you snuck out in the middle of the party," he said, clearly still not buying it. "You two couldn't find a more convenient time to meet up?"

"No. Besides, these parties are so boring, and my parents are always too busy to notice I'm not there." I hoped that was true tonight.

He gave me another long look and stepped aside to let me pass. "Go on. I doubt someone like you is here to break into the cars."

I bristled at the words *someone like you* but bit my tongue. I walked to the gate and looked back at him. "I'd appreciate it if you didn't tell anyone about this."

He gave a curt nod.

"Thanks." Pulling up my hood, I hurried inside.

I cursed my bad luck as I changed back into my dress and shoes. *Everything was going so well. You just had to get caught.*

I headed back to the lounge and tried to slip into the room unnoticed, but my mother confronted me almost immediately.

"Charlotte, where have you been?" she asked in a sharp whisper. "I've been looking for you for the last twenty minutes."

"I wasn't feeling well. I think it was something I ate at dinner," I said.

She studied my face. "Are you feeling better now?"

"Yes."

Lydia Warren walked up to us before she could say anything else. She wore a dark green sheath dress, and her red hair was in a less severe bun, which gave her a softer appearance. She smiled, but I didn't return it.

"I'm sorry to interrupt, but something has come up that needs your attention," she said to my mother.

My mother looked at me, and I said, "I think I'll get some water."

She nodded, and they left the room together. What could be so important that the head of security needed to pull my mother aside at the party?

I was sipping water at the bar when my mother returned several minutes later. She went straight to Dev Malik and said something to him. I didn't miss the excitement that crossed his face. Something was up.

Mom left Dev and went to my father. Together, they walked over to me.

"Charlotte, we have to leave early," she said. "There's a project issue I need to see to."

"It must be serious for you to leave the party," I replied as we started for the door.

"It's crucial."

My parents didn't speak much on the short drive home. My father didn't even bother pulling into the garage. We entered via the front door and went to our rooms to change.

I closed my door and turned to the bed. Kalyx didn't appear.

"Kalyx," I whispered. I walked to the bed and felt around, but she wasn't there. She knew when to cloak herself, but the thought of her loose in the house with my parents here made me uneasy.

On silent feet, I hurried downstairs and went straight to the basement. "Kalyx," I whispered over and over, my voice growing frantic as I went from one room to the next. By the time I returned to the stairs, my stomach was in knots. Where was she?

I was halfway up the basement stairs when I heard my mother's voice coming from the garage. I crept closer until I could make out her words.

"The scanners are prototypes, and they have to be within two hundred yards," she said in her *we've already been through this* tone. "It was a stroke of luck we picked up the signal tonight."

Signal? I gripped the handrail. Was she talking about Kalyx?

"There's a lot of electronic interference in town." Pause. "We have our people, and Mason's on it. If it stays in town, we'll find it before the night is out."

I fought my rising panic. Kalyx was out there somewhere, and the signal dampener wasn't working.

Footsteps in the kitchen signaled my father's approach. I retreated to the basement and out of sight before he called my name.

"I'm in the workshop," I called back.

"We're heading out," he said.

"Okay."

The garage door opened, and Mom's car pulled out. I ran upstairs to change, and a few minutes later, I was on my scooter speeding away from home.

I had no idea how to find Kalyx, no plan except to ride around town and pray I reached her before they did. If she was cloaked, it wouldn't be easy, but that might also keep her hidden from Sutton. If she saw me, maybe she'd reveal herself.

The only times she left the house was when I took her into the woods for exercise. She'd never left on her own, and I couldn't figure out what had driven her to go into town. Had she gone looking for Taruth? He hadn't reached out to me again, and I had no idea if he was even still alive.

I rode around for thirty desperate minutes before I caught sight of a nondescript white cargo van moving along at a crawl. I might have overlooked it if not for the short, thick antenna protruding from its roof. It had to be one of theirs.

I pulled over, pretending to fiddle with my phone as the van passed, and fell in behind it at a cautious distance. At the next intersection, it turned right just as a black SUV passed, moving at the same speed. It didn't take long to realize they were working a grid.

I passed another van, a military Jeep, and a truck, all doing a slow sweep of the streets. I was sure there were more of them out there, closing in on Kalyx at this very moment.

I switched between tailing the van, the SUV, and the Jeep to avoid drawing attention. Without warning, the Jeep veered sharply to the left. I braked hard, heart pounding. Had they spotted me?

Before I could decide to make a run for it, one of the vans and the SUV drove past going in the same direction. They were on to something.

I hung back, giving them more space, waiting until they fanned out again to continue the sweep. We were now in a nonresidential area occupied by stores, restaurants, and other businesses. It was after ten, so most of the businesses were closed, and there wasn't a lot of traffic, making it harder for me to blend in.

Three more vehicles joined the search, spreading out to cover the area faster. At least, there were no helicopters. Sutton wouldn't want to attract too much attention to what they were doing.

Then I saw them, four men moving between two buildings with deliberate caution, almost in formation. One of the men held a device in front of him and another carried a gun. Kalyx had to be close.

I gripped the handlebars, desperate to do something… anything.

Raindrops splattered against my visor. "Not now," I groaned as it picked up, turning the men into a blur. Then the sky opened, and I couldn't see ten feet in front of me.

Headlights appeared in my mirror, nearly blinding me, and a horn honked angrily as a car swerved to avoid hitting me. I needed to get off the street. I had to open the visor to see the entrance to a parking lot, where I found cover beneath the overhang of a strip mall.

Lightning streaked across the sky, followed by the roll of thunder. Through the curtain of rain, I made out the hulking shape of Valley Foods, the supermarket where I'd first gone to buy meat for Kalyx. So much had happened since our first encounter in the woods. Had that really been less than two weeks ago?

Across the street, two vehicles were parked in front of a restaurant, their headlights glaring at me. I could almost feel the menace behind them. Were they waiting out the rain, too, or planning their next move?

Removing my helmet, I wiped my wet face and slumped on the seat. "Where are you, Kalyx?"

Another flash of lightning lit up the parking lot. In that split second, something moved near the supermarket.

I strained to see through the rain, but all I could make out was a semi parked on that side of the building. My mind was playing tricks on me.

"Kalyx?" I called, but my voice was drowned out by the rain.

The third flash came. A cry caught in my throat when the light illuminated a form standing between the truck and the building.

I started to climb off the scooter to run to her but held myself back. Any fast movement might get the attention of the people in those vehicles across the street. I rode the scooter slowly until I was out of sight of the road, and then I jumped off and ran to her.

Reaching Kalyx, I knelt and wrapped my arms around her thick neck. "You scared the hell out of me."

For a moment, her body was tense. She softened, leaning into me and resting her large head on my shoulder. I trembled with pent-up emotion as I clung to her, barely aware of the rain soaking through my clothes. I hadn't realized it was possible to care so much for an animal in such a short time.

Thunder boomed, snapping me back to reality and to the chilling reminder of the threat looming over us. I stood and leaned over her to feel for the dampener still attached to her neck. "Shit," I muttered when I couldn't feel the usual hum. A quick tap brought it to life for a few seconds before it faded again. That explained why Sutton's scanners kept losing her signal – the dampener was on the fritz.

I needed to fix it, but there was no way we were making it home without them following us. If they tracked the signal to my house, it was all over. I had to hide her somewhere until I could repair the dampener, which required tools I didn't have with me.

I pushed wet hair out of my face and peeked around the corner of the building. The rain had lessened enough to see past the parking lot, and I jerked back when I spotted four men standing beside the vehicles in front of the restaurant. Two of the men were facing this direction.

"Kalyx, hide." We had to get out of here, but I had no idea where to go. I looked around frantically as if the answer would suddenly appear to me. My gaze landed on the strip mall, and I remembered my mother talking to Dev about electronic interference in town.

"Come on." I jumped on the scooter and rode it around the back of the strip mall, passing a large dumpster and stopping in front of the loading door to Cole Electronics. The keypad lock taunted me with its flashing red light, and I thought about my code reader sitting in the locker at the club.

My gaze moved over the building and stopped on a small sliding window six feet above the ground. If I could reach it, I might be able to open it, or break it if it came to that. Guilt pricked me, and I pushed it back. We were desperate, and I'd pay anonymously for any damage I did.

The rain started coming down in sheets again, plastering my hair to my face and running into my eyes as I pushed the scooter over and stood it beneath the window. Climbing up to stand on the seat, I cast a fearful glance over my shoulder, half-expecting to see men pouring around the corner.

Seeing nothing, I turned to the window. It was wide enough for me to fit through, but as I suspected, it was locked. I scanned the ground and spied a two-foot length of board beside the dumpster. I jumped down and ran to pick it up.

Headlights swept around the end of the building.

I froze. They'd found us.

The dumpster stood between us and them, so they hadn't seen me yet. I went to stand beside my scooter. "Kalyx, stay hidden."

She brushed against me just as the headlights sliced across the slick pavement, the low rumble of an engine rising above the relentless rain drumming against the dumpster. Every muscle in my body tensed as the lights struck my face, blinding me.

8

I threw up my arm to shield my eyes as the vehicle stopped in front of me.

I imagined the discussion taking place inside. They'd expected an alien, not a teenage girl, and they were deciding what to do next.

Once they discovered my identity, I was going to be in a world of trouble. No one would believe it was a coincidence I'd shown up both times they were chasing an alien, especially not after Mason had tracked one to my house.

Kalyx growled as the driver's door opened, and someone stepped out. I grabbed her collar, even though I could never hold her back if she lunged.

The door closed, and I could barely make out the outline of a man behind the glare of the headlights. *Don't let it be Mason.*

The man stepped into the light, and I made a choked sound. Ethan.

Rain dripped from his hair and soaked his shirt, but he seemed unaware of it as his gaze shifted from the board in my hand to the scooter beneath the window. His face was stony. I wasn't talking my way out of this.

"Give me one reason I shouldn't call the police right now." His voice was colder than the rain running down my back.

"Ethan, I..." I swallowed, searching for words that wouldn't come.

He folded his arms. "I knew you were up to something when you snuck out of the party. Is this what bored little rich girls do for fun – breaking and entering?"

I scrambled for anything that might make him let me go. At this point, the truth might sound more believable.

"I don't need this bullshit. You can explain it to the police." He turned back to the truck.

"Ethan –" I faltered as headlights splayed across the parking lot. They were here.

"What?" he snapped, glancing back at me.

I had to do it. "We need your help."

He spun to face me. "We?"

"Kalyx, show yourself," I said, my eyes never leaving Ethan's face.

Nothing happened at first. Then his mouth dropped open, and his eyes went wide. "What –?"

"This is Kalyx. I'll explain everything, but first I need to hide her," I said quickly. "Sutton is after her, and they'll be here any second."

"Sutton?" He sounded dazed.

"I'll tell you everything. Just help us. Please."

Whatever he saw on my face must have convinced him. He shut off the truck and hurried over to unlock the door, pausing to disarm the security system, which I'd completely forgotten about.

I followed him inside, Kalyx on my heels. As soon as we were in, he locked the door and turned to stare at her.

Not long ago, I'd been in his shoes, so I knew how it felt, but there was no time for that now.

I checked the dampener. It had shut off again, and it took a few taps to get it working. How long before it died completely?

"Ethan." I had to say his name two more times before he looked at me. "I need something that can interfere with wireless signals."

He frowned, and for a second, I thought I'd have to repeat myself. Then his eyes widened in understanding.

He opened the door to a workshop much bigger than the one I had at home. Shelves lined the walls, crammed with half-finished projects and dusty devices. The workbench was barely visible under a mess of parts and tools.

Ethan pulled a large Universal Power Supply from a bottom shelf and plugged it in. He grabbed a second one and did the same. Next, he turned on a computer, a wireless router, four Bluetooth speakers in the corners, a Bluetooth printer, and a VR gaming headset.

He waved us inside. "Now tell me why I'm helping you hide Sutton's property from them."

"Kalyx doesn't belong to –"

A sharp buzz cut through the air. I jumped and turned toward the noise, my heart pounding. It was the doorbell.

Ethan strode to the security panel by the door and pressed a button. "Who is it?"

A male voice came over the speaker. "My name is Anthony Brooks, and I work for Sutton Aerospace. Who am I speaking to?"

I backed up a step, but there was nowhere to go. Kalyx growled, and I put a hand on her back. "Shhh."

"Ethan Cole. How can I help you, Mr. Brooks?"

"I'm looking for someone who stole sensitive technology from Sutton," Brooks said.

Ethan pinned me with a sharp look.

I shook my head vehemently and mouthed, *"No."*

Brooks continued. "We followed them as far as this shopping center and lost them. Have you seen anything suspicious in the last thirty minutes?"

"No."

"May I ask if you're here alone?" Brooks asked.

I gave Ethan a desperate look. *"Please."*

"I'm here with my girlfriend," he replied, his voiced edged with irritation. I couldn't tell if it was real or just convincing. "Anything else?"

"That's all. Thank you."

Ethan started to pull back and paused. "What do they look like? In case we do see someone hanging around."

There was a brief silence before Brooks answered. "We don't have a clear description of him. He was wearing a hood."

Ethan's suspicious gaze landed on my dark hoodie. "So, it was a man."

"Yes."

Ethan visibly relaxed. "We'll keep an eye out for him." He stepped away from the panel. "Xander lies better than that guy."

I managed a weak smile as a shiver ran through me. Now that the adrenaline was wearing off, it was impossible to ignore the cold in my drenched clothes.

Ethan adjusted the thermostat and disappeared for a minute. He came back with towels, handing all but one to me.

I peeled off my soaked hoodie and used one of the towels on my hair. It snagged on something, and I realized I still wore the clips in my hair. Pulling them free, I stuffed them in a pocket.

There was nothing I could do about my clothes, so I used the other towels to soak up what I could. I was still cold, but physical discomfort was the least of my worries.

"Here. This is all I could find."

I looked up to see him holding a pair of gray coveralls. I took them, and he left the room, closing the door behind him.

I changed quickly. The coveralls were too big, and the fabric was rough against my skin, but it was a lot better than wet clothes.

He knocked as I rolled up the pant legs, and I called for him to come in. Keeping his distance from Kalyx, he wheeled his work chair toward me. "Sit."

I obeyed. Kalyx sat beside me, resting her chin on my thigh. After I checked the dampener again, I stroked her head. "This is going to sound crazy."

He arched his eyebrows. "Crazier than a cyborg cat that can make itself invisible?"

"Kalyx isn't a cyborg." I took a breath. "She's an alien."

"An alien?" He narrowed his eyes at me. "I'm sticking my neck out for you, and that's your story?"

I shook my head. "I'm telling the truth. I said it would sound crazy."

"You got the last part right." He let out a short laugh. "Maybe I should call the psych ward along with the police."

"Wait," I pleaded. "Give me just five minutes."

He leaned against the door frame, hands in his pockets. If his wet clothes bothered him, he didn't show it.

I debated how much to tell him. I knew very little about him other than what Xander had told me. I had no idea if I could trust him, but I had no other choice.

I told him everything except Finley's hacking and my visit to Mr. Palmer's. He listened without interrupting as the story spilled from me. By the time I finished, at least twenty minutes had passed, and the room was warm.

Ethan raked his fingers through his damp hair. "I think I actually believe you. No one could make up a story like that."

I hadn't realized how tight my shoulders were until they started to relax. "You see now why I can't let Sutton or Mason find her."

"Yes, but you can't hide her forever," he said. "And if you figure out where they're keeping the other alien, what then? You'll never be able to get to him, let alone free him."

"I'm figuring things out as I go."

His eyes kept straying to Kalyx. "You really built a dampener to mask an alien signal?"

"Yes." I touched the device, "And now it's acting up. She must have damaged it somehow when she left the house tonight."

He looked around the workshop. "We should have everything you need to fix it here."

Relief flooded me. "I can do it, but I don't know how long it will take."

"If Sutton is as relentless as you say they are, we'll be here a while." He left and returned a minute later, wearing a grim expression. "They're still out there. I saw two vans in the parking lot and four people near Valley Foods. Are you sure they can't detect that signal?"

"If they could, I don't think Brooks would have bothered to knock," I said.

He pointed at Kalyx. "And when you turn the device off to fix it?"

"I don't know. I can risk it or wait until they're gone."

"Okay." He sat on a stack of boxes. "I guess we'll wait."

"You don't mind?" I hadn't expected him to help us, let alone hang around for hours.

He gave me the barest hint of a smile. "I planned to be here anyway. And it's not every day you meet an alien cyborg cat."

"You're handling this better than most people would," I said, thinking about Finley's freak-out.

His dark eyes studied my face. "How are you so calm about it? You found an alien, and you're hiding it under your parents' noses."

"Remember, I thought she was a lab experiment at first. I had a few days to get used to that idea before I realized what she really is." I stroked her head. "As for my parents, they're so caught up in their work, they barely notice what's happening at home."

"And you're sure they're involved in this?"

I nodded. "My mother is for sure. I don't know if my father is directly involved, but he has to know about it."

Ethan was quiet for a moment. "What would happen if they found out you've been hiding her?"

"Nothing good." I didn't want to dwell on that. "Why did you come here tonight?"

"Inventory," he said. "It's the only time I can work without interruptions."

"I can help. It's better than sitting around doing nothing while we wait." I looked down at my borrowed coveralls. "I'm already dressed for work."

Another faint smile played around his mouth, and his eyes, usually serious and guarded, were warm with amusement. I was surprised by a tiny flutter in my stomach.

"What about her?" he asked.

I stood and looked at Kalyx. "You stay in here, okay?"

She lay down with her head resting on her front paws.

Ethan tilted his head. "She understands you?"

"Yes, but she doesn't always listen." I followed him from the workshop to a small office. There was an ancient desk and chair, a computer, a metal filing cabinet, and a bulletin board covered in invoices and bills. Several of the bills had the word OVERDUE stamped on them in big red letters.

A security monitor in one corner cycled through three feeds – the front counter, the front exterior, and the back exterior. How had I forgotten the cameras?

"How long do you keep security footage?" I asked.

He reached for a tablet on the desk. "Two weeks, why?"

"Kalyx."

He logged in and pulled up the rear camera. We watched me arriving on my scooter, checking the window, and grabbing the board. Then he arrived. It was all there. Including the part where Kalyx appeared out of nowhere.

He hit pause. "What are the odds of Sutton asking to see this?"

I rubbed my forehead. "High. They'll probably check with every business in this lot."

"We can't delete it. They'll notice the gap," he said.

"I know." I blew out a breath. "There is something I can do. I can make it look like there was a glitch in the camera."

Ethan gave me a look, and I smiled. "I may have done it once or twice at home."

He stared at the frozen image on the screen. "It'll be suspicious if the camera glitches at that exact time."

"Not if I make it happen at other times throughout the day," I said. "It'll look like that camera has been acting up."

He got up from the chair. "Do it."

It took forty-five minutes to make the changes. When I was done, it appeared that the camera had started glitching two days ago. An expert might spot the tampering, but it was the best I could do.

"You can do this, and you were going to break the window to get in?" he asked in a teasing tone.

"Not one of my finer moments." I gave him a sheepish smile. "Now, how about that inventory?"

He nodded, opened the app on the tablet, and handed it to me. "I'll count, and you record it."

We got to work. Ethan was focused on the task, leaving little room for conversation, but it wasn't an uncomfortable silence. It was easy to be around him like this, and I found myself enjoying it.

He kept an eye on the parking lot, and I stayed out of sight, wary of Anthony Brooks seeing me.

"I think they're gone," he said at last. "It's stopped raining, too."

I took that as my cue to leave. "I'll get Kalyx."

He frowned. "Don't you need to fix the dampener first?"

"Yes... that's what I meant," I said, trying to cover my slip.

Kalyx raised her head when I entered the workshop, and I crouched to remove her collar. "Now let's see what's wrong with this."

I carried it to the workbench and used a screwdriver to open the box. I peered inside at the tangle of scavenged components I had pieced together. It wasn't pretty, but I was proud of it.

"You designed this?" Ethan asked over my shoulder, making me jump.

I bent my head for a closer look. "No. I found the instructions online. Anyone could do it with the right parts."

"Most people couldn't build that." He stood beside me. "This is why you needed the drone."

"Yes."

I couldn't see any damage, so I'd have to take it apart piece by piece. I hoped he was serious when he said he didn't mind staying here awhile.

I brought up the instructions on my phone. "Do you have a printer? These are too hard to read on a phone."

"Send them to me," he said. I did, and he opened them on the tablet. "How is this?"

"Perfect."

We didn't speak as I worked, except when I needed a tool or to consult the instructions. It was tedious work, and it took over an hour to find a broken wire connection. It was an easy fix. I reassembled the device and was rewarded with a reassuring hum.

I fastened the collar around Kalyx's neck. "Good as new."

Ethan took the chair I'd vacated. "Is she always this calm?"

"I don't know if this is normal behavior for her. I hope Taruth contacts me again so I can ask him." I lowered myself to the floor beside her and slumped against a stack of boxes.

"You want something to drink?" he asked. "We have water and soda in the cooler near the front."

I nodded, parched. "A soda would be perfect."

He left, and I began stroking Kalyx's soft fur. By the time he returned, she was purring with her head in my lap.

"You're good with her," he said, handing me a soda.

Warmth spread through me. "Thanks."

He sat on the floor across from us and took a long drink. "It's almost three. Won't your parents wonder where you are?"

"Do you hear my phone ringing?" I asked. "They won't be home tonight. When they are, I'm usually in bed."

A line creased his brow. "They leave you alone that much?"

I shrugged. "I'm used to it. My mother and I don't get along, so it's easier this way."

"And your father?" he asked.

I ignored the slight constriction in my chest. "We get along okay. We used to be closer."

His look of sympathy made me bristle. I wasn't a neglected child to be pitied.

"What about you?" I asked, deflecting.

"What about me?"

"You know something about me. Tell me something about you," I pressed.

He rubbed his jaw. "Not much to tell. It's just me, Xander, and our dad, and I spend most of my time here."

I considered asking about his mother, but his expression said he didn't want to discuss his family. "So, why did you help me?"

"Because you asked me to."

I tilted my head. "You took a big risk for someone you don't like."

"I never said I didn't like you."

A laugh escaped me. "You didn't have to say it. I've had friendlier run-ins with Colonel Mason."

Ethan scowled, and I pointed at him. "See? That's how you normally look at me. I didn't know you *could* smile until tonight, and I'm not sure it was a smile. The jury is still out."

His lips twitched. I didn't get the smile I was hoping for, but it was an improvement over his usual glare.

His gaze shifted to Kalyx. "Do you wonder why they're here?"

"It's probably for the same reason we sent the Centauri probe. They wanted to see what was here."

"Maybe they're looking for a new place to colonize, too," he said.

I scoffed. "Boy, did they choose the wrong planet."

He was quiet. "Have you considered that they might be hostile?"

"No," I admitted. "I can't explain it, but I didn't get a hostile vibe from Taruth when he tried to communicate with me."

"He's an alien," Ethan said. "You could be reading his emotions wrong."

"Maybe I'm biased because of Kalyx." I pushed some stray hairs behind my ear. "But he's the first alien – that we know of – to visit earth, and we imprisoned him in a lab. We're the villains here."

He set his bottle on the floor. "So, tell the world about him instead of trying to help him on your own."

"You think other countries won't want him and his technology for themselves?" I asked. "And I'm not on my own."

"You mean your friend on the other side of the ocean." His tone was flat but not mocking.

I scowled. "Finley could be on the moon, and I'd still choose her over anyone else."

He held up a hand. "I'm not dissing your friend. If you get into trouble, there's not much she can do for you from Europe."

"I'll just have to stay one step ahead of them," I said around a yawn.

"We should get you home." He stood and offered me a hand. "Come on. I'll drive."

"I have my scooter." I let him pull me to my feet. Kalyx stood too, looking at us expectantly.

"You're too tired to ride," he said. "And what about her?"

"I'm fine, and Kalyx can cloak herself." I picked up my wet clothes, grimacing at the thought of putting them on.

"Wear the coveralls home," he said.

I gave him a grateful smile. "Thanks. I'll bring them back." I looked around for my helmet before I remembered I'd left it on the scooter.

At the back door, I told Kalyx to cloak. She disappeared, and Ethan stared in wonder at the empty space.

"I see it, and I still don't believe it," he said, opening the door. He checked outside before he stood aside to let us pass.

I went to the scooter and picked up my helmet. I turned to thank Ethan, who was setting the security system.

"I'm following you home," he said, locking the door.

I got on the scooter. "You don't have to do that."

"It's the middle of the night, you're tired, and they could still be out there." He walked toward his truck. "It's not up for debate."

I didn't argue. I wouldn't admit it, but I *was* afraid of running into Mason or Sutton's people on the way home. I felt better knowing Ethan was with me.

"Kalyx, stay close," I said.

Ethan trailed me all the way home, keeping a safe distance between us. I didn't see any of Sutton's vehicles, but I knew they hadn't given up that easily.

At my house, I parked in front of the garage and walked to his truck.

"Thanks for everything," I said. "Can I ask you not to...?"

"I won't tell anyone," he promised. "But I think you're in way over your head."

I managed a tired smile. "You're probably right, but I'm all Kalyx has. I know it sounds crazy, but I think I was meant to find her."

"It's not the craziest thing you told me tonight," he said lightly. "For what it's worth, I think she's lucky it was you."

"Thanks." My eyes stung. I had to be a lot more tired than I thought.

A light came on next door.

"That's Cathy," I said. "She's a pilot, and she keeps weird hours."

He reached for the gearshift. "I should go."

"Thanks again," I said as he backed out.

He said something that sounded like *you're welcome* and drove away.

I couldn't open the garage door at this hour, so I wheeled the scooter behind the house and entered through the front door.

Kalyx didn't uncloak until we were in my room with the door closed. She immediately went to her spot near the window.

I was too exhausted for a shower. I pulled on a T-shirt and shorts and collapsed into bed. I barely managed a sleepy, "Night," before I was out cold.

I floated in a sea of white. Around me, objects began to come into focus – sterile white walls, a pale gray floor, and soft lights overhead. Cold metal pressed against my back, and there was a band of pressure across my chest. I tried to look down at my body, but my head wouldn't move. I was strapped to a wheeled upright stretcher, and I could hear the breathing of the person pushing me from behind.

Ahead loomed a pair of white doors. There was a sign on one of the doors, but I couldn't make out the writing. As we drew near, the doors slid open, and I glimpsed a robotic arm poised above a metal table before the room dissolved into white again.

The world came back into focus, and I was standing in a massive aircraft hangar where people in white coveralls moved around me. I turned, and before me stood a sleek, black spaceship, its metallic surface gleaming under the bright lights. The hull's contours were smooth and seamless, and there were no windows or doors. The ship looked completely alien, yet eerily familiar.

The scene vanished, and I drifted in a drowsy haze, not fully awake but no longer asleep. My room was dark, and I felt the weight of something pressed against my side. It took my groggy brain a few seconds to realize Kalyx was curled beside me on the bed.

Images flickered through my mind, and I couldn't tell if I was awake or dreaming again. They hit in a chaotic rush at first, too fast to follow, until they slowed just enough to make sense. I saw the spaceship from my dream, a planet with two moons, the inside of a cockpit, Kalyx, and a view of Earth from space.

I opened my eyes and blinked at the dark ceiling as I shook off sleep. "Taruth?"

A string of alien words played in my mind, and I cupped my head in my hands. "I don't know what you're trying to tell me."

The words and images stopped abruptly. I thought he was gone until another image of Kalyx appeared. It shifted, morphing into a hologram of her body, and zoomed in on her side. A panel opened, revealing four oblong devices inside. Whatever they were, Taruth wanted me to see them.

Fully awake now, I sat up and turned on my bedside lamp. Kalyx lay on her side, taking up three quarters of the bed. She opened her eyes and tilted her head slightly to look at me when I leaned over her.

I gave her head a quick scratch and pressed the place between her shoulders to reveal the hidden screen. Activating the hologram, I zoomed in until I located the right spot. I touched the hologram to open the compartment.

It slid open to reveal the four translucent objects, no bigger than a quarter. Nestled beside them was a small black device fitted snugly in a slot. Taruth hadn't shown me that, so I didn't touch it.

I studied the smaller objects for a long moment. Pinching one between two fingers, I picked it up. It felt like very soft silicone, and when I laid it on my palm, a tiny light blinked inside of it.

"What the heck do I do with this?" It had to be important if Taruth wanted me to find it, but there could be any one of a thousand possible uses for it.

Think, Charlie.

Taruth was trying to tell me something. There had to be a clue in what he had shown me. I replayed my strange dream, which I suspected was not a dream at all, but Taruth showing me what he saw.

I didn't know if the individual images were meaningful or a jumble of random thoughts he was projecting. This would be a lot easier if we could use words instead of images. He seemed to understand English, but he couldn't speak it. And I didn't speak whatever his language was.

I gaped at the object in my hand. If there had been a light bulb over my head it would have exploded.

It's a translator.

The revelation made me almost giddy with excitement. I held it up to the light. Inside was a lattice of fine green lines like the delicate veins of a leaf, which made it look almost organic. When I squished it gently, the lines shifted, adjusting like it was alive.

Goose bumps prickled my skin. Was it alive? Or were Taruth's people so advanced they could combine technology and biology at this level? And why did Kalyx have them? Had Taruth anticipated needing to communicate with humans?

Was I supposed to wear it? I chewed my lip. I had no idea what this thing could do to me.

I rolled it between my fingers. I was touching it with my bare hands, and it wasn't hurting me.

Before I could talk myself out of it, I pressed the device experimentally against the back of my hand. Nothing. I didn't know if I was disappointed or relieved.

A translator – if that's what it was – probably needed to go near the ear. My insides clenched at the thought of putting it near any of my body orifices. Being adventurous didn't make me *that* brave.

I got up and went into my bathroom. I stared at my wild hair and tired face in the mirror. My eyes were uncertain, but they also gleamed with curiosity.

If this worked, I could have a real conversation with Taruth. There was so much I wanted to know, and the only thing standing in my way was my fear.

"Ah, hell." I pressed the device to the soft skin behind my ear. Nothing.

I closed my eyes. There was one last thing to try, but a little voice in my head screamed that I was crazy to even consider it.

A whisper of sound drew my gaze to the doorway where Kalyx stood watching me, so trusting and completely dependent upon me.

Ethan was right. I couldn't hide her forever. The only way to keep her safe was to free Taruth. And to do that, I needed to understand him.

My hand trembled when I raised the device and touched it lightly to my earlobe.

9

The device latched onto my ear.

I yelped, clawing at it as horrific visions of alien parasites burrowing into my brain played in my mind. But it was stuck fast, and all I could do was watch as it reshaped itself, molding snugly to the shell of my ear like it had always been there.

When it stopped moving, it was nearly invisible against my skin. I leaned in closer to the mirror, and my fear subsided when I realized it was attached only to my outer ear. I touched it and noticed it was warm now. Did that mean it was working?

"Taruth, can you hear me?" I asked, expecting to hear his voice in my head. Nothing. I frowned at my reflection, hoping I hadn't just made a colossal mistake.

I went back to my bed, and Kalyx jumped up beside me. I reached out to scratch behind her ear, and the second my fingers touched her, a stream of alien words filled my mind. Of course. I had to be touching her to communicate with him.

"I'm sorry. I still can't understand you," I said, my voice heavy with disappointment.

The alien words stopped. Seconds later, I heard a voice as clearly as if they were standing beside me. *Hel-lo*, it said.

I almost jumped off the bed before I remembered I needed to keep contact with Kalyx. "Hello."

Hello, Char-lie, he said in a strange voice that sounded neither male nor female. *I am Taruth.*

I grinned so wide it hurt. "I'm so happy to meet you."

I am happy also, he replied in halting English as if he was unsure what words to use. *You wear the... transcriber.*

"The translator? Yes." I touched it again. "How did you know it would work for me?"

It functions for many species.

"Is this how you communicate – mind-to-mind?" I asked.

My people use spoken language, he said. *My bond with Kalyx allows me to... mind-speak with her.*

My mouth formed an O. "And that's why you can talk to me when I'm touching her."

It is.

I was bursting with questions, but I didn't know how long our connection would last. I started with the most important. "Can you tell me where you are? What are they doing to you?"

I do not know where I am. It is a place where they build space... ships. They want me to repair my ship. I comply because I must have it to go home.

"Where is your home?" I asked.

My planet is Kruran. It is... thirty-five trillion of your miles from here.

I knew Alcea was twenty-five trillion miles – over four light-years – away, which meant Kruran was closer to six.

I stared out my window at the dark sky. "Why did you come to earth?"

I came to look for my friend, Enoin. There was a subtle change in his tone. Sadness?

"Your friend?" I prodded softly.

Yes, he said. *My people believed there was no advanced species in this star system until we saw the scientific ship you sent to a system near ours. There was much debate about coming here. Enoin tired of waiting and left to explore this system alone. He did not return.*

"How long has he been gone?" I asked.

Many kels. Nine hundred solar days.

I did the math. "That's almost two and a half years ago. Are you sure he came here?"

There was no mistaking the pain in his voice. *Yes. His ship crashed on this planet. He does not live.*

"How do you know that? Did you find his ship?"

His ship is here in this place. It is broken beyond repair. He was quiet for a long moment, and I thought we'd lost the connection until he said, *I have not seen Enoin. I heard the humans speak of him.*

"I'm so sorry, Taruth." My chest tightened. Not only was he a prisoner, he was grieving over his friend.

Why do you apologize?

"It's not an apology," I said. "It's what we say to show sympathy when someone you care about dies."

I do not know sympathy.

Explaining human emotions to an alien was not something I expected to do this morning. "Sympathy is when you care that someone else is in pain."

Half a minute passed. *I understand. Thank you for the sympathy.*

I was about to ask him another question about his planet when something clicked. What were the odds of two spaceships crashing and both ending up at the same lab? Unless...

"Taruth, what caused your ship to crash?" I asked, though I already had a bad feeling.

I followed the signal from Enoin's ship to this location, and my ship was attacked.

The pieces fell into place. Sutton had his friend's ship for over two years, long enough to develop a warning system.

Another realization hit me like a punch. Two years ago, my parents had taken the job at Sutton. They'd been working with the alien technology this whole time. That made what they were doing even worse.

"Will your people come for you?" I pictured an alien fleet showing up in our orbit.

I disobeyed the leaders. I came here without permission, he said. *I do not know if they will come when I do not return.*

My heart ached for him. "What about your ship? Can you fix it so you can fly it home?"

I believe I can. I am using parts from Enoin's ship to make repairs.

"That's great." I fell onto my back, smiling at the ceiling. "You said they're making you fix the ship. You can talk to them?"

My translator lets me learn their words, but they do not know mine, he explained. *They use their hands to show me what they want.*

My face broke into a grin. Wait until I told Finley she was right about me making first contact. She was going to flip.

I must stop talking soon, Taruth said. *It is tiring me.*

Guilt stabbed me. I hadn't even asked if he was okay. "Were you hurt when your ship crashed? Is that why you're tired?"

No. The air is wrong. It is heavy in... He paused. *Oxygen. There is not enough sulvon.*

I sat up. "Sulvon? Is that a gas you have on your planet?"

Gas, yes. Humans expel it, but it is not enough. Breathing is more difficult here.

Understanding dawned. "You mean carbon dioxide?"

Yes. My flight suit helps regulate oxygen levels, but it is damaged, and it must be recharged often in my ship.

I hadn't considered how different his physiology must be. Did he eat and drink like we did, or did he get his nutrients another way? Could he consume the food here? Kalyx had no problem, but she was a cyborg. She'd probably been designed to adapt to her environment.

"What about food and water?" I asked.

My suit hydrates me. I have nourishment in my ship – He broke off. *They come to take me to my ship. I must go.*

"I'm going to find you and get you out of there," I said quickly. "Just hold on."

I will, he said faintly. And he was gone.

I rubbed my eyes. "That just happened, right? I'm not dreaming."

Kalyx lifted her head, and I laughed softly. I was sharing my room with an alien. At this point, nothing should surprise me.

My eyes grew heavy, reminding me I'd gone to bed only two hours ago. I wanted to call Finley, but I needed sleep. I wouldn't be able to help anyone if I was too tired to think straight.

I slipped under the covers, and my eyes had barely closed when I began to drift off. A thought tugged at the edges of consciousness. I'd forgotten to ask Taruth something, but the pull of sleep was too strong. I gave in and let it carry me way.

It was almost 11:00 a.m. when I opened my eyes again, and I stared at my phone in disbelief. I couldn't remember the last time I'd slept this late.

I dragged myself to the bathroom, and a laugh burst from me at the sight of my hair sticking out in every direction. I smoothed it and caught sight of the translator on my ear.

Goose bumps rose on my arms. In all the excitement earlier, I'd forgotten to ask Taruth how to remove the device. I let my hair fall into place and turned my head from side to side. It was hidden, but I didn't want alien tech permanently attached to me.

As I showered, the events of the night replayed in my head. It scared me every time I thought about how close I'd come to losing Kalyx.

Ethan had been right – I was in way over my head. But Kalyx and Taruth were relying on me, and I couldn't trust anyone else. Except Finley.

And maybe Ethan. He'd surprised me last night, and my gut told me he was someone who kept his word. If not, the military would have busted down the door by now and dragged me out of bed.

After I dressed, I noticed I had a missed call from Finley. Had she already gotten in Sutton's hidden segment? My heart sped up as I hit the button to call her back.

The second she answered, I said, "Did you get in?"

She laughed. "He hasn't connected to the network yet."

"Oh. I thought that was why you called."

She gave me a chiding look. "I called because I haven't heard from you since you left his house."

"Sorry, but I have a really good excuse." I propped myself up with pillows. "Wait until you hear what happened after the party."

"Oh, no. The last time you had that look you told me Kalyx is an alien." She eyed me expectantly. "Spill."

I grinned. "You better get comfortable."

It took twice as long as it should have to fill her in because she kept interrupting. She had more questions about Ethan than anything else. I didn't even get to my news about Taruth.

"He did all that for you *and* made sure you got home okay?" She did a fake swoon.

I shook my head. "*That's* what you took away from all of this?"

She lifted her head. "You're hiding an alien from your parents and the military. Nothing you say shocks me anymore. I want to hear more about Ethan. Do you have a picture of him?"

"No, I don't have a picture." I gave her a half-hearted scowl. "I've been a little busy with more important things."

She propped her phone in its desk mount and pulled up something on her computer. "Dang, girl."

She turned the phone toward her monitor, which displayed a picture of a slightly younger Ethan in his service uniform. He was clean-shaven with a buzzed haircut, and even with his serious expression, there was a light in his eyes I hadn't seen before.

"He looks different now." I searched for the right words. "He's usually in a bad mood. I think he's angry at the world."

Her face appeared on the screen again. "But he did help you last night."

"Yes, but I still don't know why he took such a risk for someone he barely knows." I hoped he didn't end up regretting it.

I pushed my hair behind my ear, and my fingers brushed the translator. I wished I hadn't forgotten to ask Taruth how to remove it.

"What's wrong?" Finley asked. "You have a weird expression."

"Yeah." I dragged out the word. "I have something else to tell you."

Her eyebrows shot up. "What more could there possibly be?"

"I don't know. Maybe the conversation I had with Taruth this morning."

"Shut up!" She gaped at me. "He contacted you again? What did he say? Did he show you more images?"

I grinned. "Yes, but only to show me where to find a translator in one of Kalyx's hidden compartments."

"No way."

I brought the phone in close to my ear. "Can you see it?"

"No..." She made a strangled sound. "Oh my God. Is that thing attached to your ear?" Her voice went shrill. "Charlie, are you out of your mind?"

I met her horrified gaze. "I was afraid to use it at first, but it was the only way to talk to Taruth. I took a leap of faith, and it worked."

She sputtered loudly. "You stuck an alien device in your ear without knowing what it would do to you."

"I'm okay, Finn," I said. "It didn't hurt me or turn me into some alien zombie."

"Not yet." She glared at me. "Why are you still wearing it?"

I smiled sheepishly. "I... um... forgot to ask him how to remove it."

She looked ready to hyperventilate. "It's stuck to you?"

"It's temporary," I assured her, hoping that was true. "Now, do you want to know what was said in the first ever human-alien conversation?"

Grudgingly, she said, "Of course, I do."

I told her everything Taruth had said to me. My voice trembled with anger when I got to what Sutton and the military had done to him. "They knew more aliens might come looking for the first one, but instead of trying to make contact, they shot him down."

"And now they're holding him prisoner to steal his ship's tech," she ground out.

"Now I know why we left London so suddenly," I said. "My parents knew about the first alien all along."

Finley's gasp was audible. "I didn't even think of that." She shook her head. "Honestly, I'd expect something like this from your mum, but not from your dad."

"Me either." Everything I'd learned the last few weeks made me question how well I knew either of them. My parents and I did have one thing in common – we were good at keeping secrets from each other.

"Do you know when Taruth is going to contact you again?" Finley asked.

"No." A chill crept in, and I rubbed my arms. "I've got to find him, Finn."

"We will." She cocked her head and said, "Hold on a sec." She got up to open the bedroom door. In the background, I heard her mother's voice. A minute later, she was back. "I'll call you back later."

I hung up and went downstairs for something to eat. Kalyx trailed silently after me, and I fed her a synth steak before I made a sandwich for myself.

Her appetite had decreased a lot over the past few days. At first, I thought she might be sick, but now I believed it was the opposite. She ate more when she was injured and didn't need as much once she healed. It was something else I'd forgotten to ask Taruth. I added it to my list for our next conversation.

I almost choked on a bite of food when the front door opened.

"Kalyx, hide," I whispered seconds before my mother came into view.

She wore the same outfit she'd left here in last night and carried her suit jacket over one arm. Her shirt was creased, and a few hairs had come loose from her bun. I wondered how long she and the others had been out searching for the elusive alien.

"Long night?" I asked, unable to keep a hint of mockery out of my voice. I usually avoided conversations with her, but last night had confirmed my suspicion she was involved in all of this. Considering her position at Sutton, she was most likely leading the team working on Taruth's ship.

Her tired eyes met mine. "Yes," was all she said before heading upstairs.

I wondered where my father was. He hadn't come home last night either, and it bothered me more than I wanted to admit. I was still clinging to the childish hope that the father I used to adore wasn't capable of the things they were doing to Taruth.

After lunch, I took Kalyx to my workshop to check on the dampener and recharge it. I wasn't taking any more chances with it. Since I couldn't risk bringing her upstairs with my mom home, I used the time to clean and reorganize the workshop.

It was late-afternoon when I heard the click of heels on the kitchen tile. After my mother left, Kalyx and I went upstairs.

I turned on the TV, but every channel seemed to be full of the same thing. If they weren't talking about the space program, there was always a storm, flood, drought, forest fire, or conflict to cover. I hated watching those stories. They made me feel helpless and angry I couldn't do anything about it, and that the people who could do something wouldn't.

I stopped channel surfing when the words STORM FELIX appeared on the screen. The storm had been upgraded to a *significant weather event* as it tracked eastward, and a red weather warning had been issued for the south-west coast of the UK. Red meant dangerous weather with a high risk to life.

They showed people in coastal towns boarding up windows and

preparing to ride out the storm, while others packed up and headed inland before landfall tomorrow.

When I learned an amber warning was in effect for London, I reached for my phone. Amber meant strong winds, possible power outages, and heavy rainfall and flooding.

"I was waiting for your call," Finley said when she answered. She was on the couch in their living room, the TV in the background talking about the weather.

"I just saw the update. How bad is it?"

She made a face. "It's nothing we haven't seen before. We'll probably lose power for a few hours, but we're all set. You know Mum and Dad, always prepared. I think my dad actually enjoys it."

"I heard that," her father said, and she laughed.

I relaxed a little. If Mr. Bennet wasn't worried, then I shouldn't be either.

"How will you live without your computer if the power goes out?" I teased.

She rolled her eyes. "Please. My portable power supply can charge my laptop and phone for forty-eight hours. As long as we don't lose cell service, I'm good."

She started typing, and a text popped up. **If our friend logs in tomorrow I'll have lots to keep me busy.**

"Fingers crossed," I said.

She gave me an impish grin and typed, **Soon we'll know all of Sutton's dirty little secrets. Then the real fun will begin.**

"Are you two texting and talking at the same time?" her father asked.

"Uh-huh," she said. "We're making plans."

He chuckled. "For what?"

"World domination," she answered with a straight face.

"Oh, okay," he said. "Just remember you two have school tomorrow."

We snickered, and she started to speak when her eyes went wide with excitement. Seconds later, she texted, **He logged in!**

My pulse jumped. It was happening. If her code could outsmart Sutton's security, she'd be inside the hidden segment the moment he accessed it.

She winked. "Speaking of school, I need to work on a project. Talk tomorrow."

I wandered aimlessly around the house, too restless to focus on anything. I checked my phone so often it felt like I was developing a tic.

Normally, I didn't mind being alone. I rarely got bored because there was always something to occupy my mind. But today, I was filled with nervous energy and the feeling that something big was coming.

Later, Kalyx and I went for our daily walk in the woods. We didn't go far, even though she was cloaked. I wished she could run free without the threat of capture, but that would never happen as long as she and Taruth were stranded here.

It was after eight when I accepted that I wouldn't hear from Finley tonight. I caught up on school reading and worked on a term paper. I had three pages of notes when my phone lit up with a text from Finley.

I frowned at the time on my phone. It was 2:00 a.m. in London.

Writing in case I lose service. Going to stay with the Barrows. Didn't want you to worry if you can't reach me tomorrow.

My breath caught. **Why are you driving to Highgate at this hour?**

A minute passed before she replied. **Felix got bigger. It's really bad on the coast. Flood and wind warnings here. Raining like crazy. Traffic is awful.**

Ten seconds later, another message appeared. **We're safe. Don't worry.**

I opened a news site on my laptop, and the headline jumped out at me.

UNITED KINGDOM BRACES FOR HISTORIC STORM

I clicked on it and stared at the words that followed.

Storm Felix to make landfall with winds exceeding 160 miles per hour. Mandatory evacuations underway for southern coast.

My gut twisted. Felix was now as strong as a category five hurricane, and it would devastate the southern coast. How had it gotten so strong since this morning? Could they evacuate everyone in time?

Red warnings had been issued for every town in its path, including London. In addition to the wind and torrential rain, a storm surge was building in the English Channel, and there was concern it could funnel into the Thames. The Thames Barrier would hold back a surge, but a flood warning was in effect for low-lying areas, and people were being urged to evacuate.

Finley lived in Chiswick, which was prone to flooding, so it made sense for them to go to Highgate. I'd been to the Barrows' sturdy Georgian home, and it would be a lot safer from the wind than her house. The worst they'd have to worry about was losing power for a few days. Even my tech-obsessed friend could deal with that.

I woke to the news that Storm Felix had made landfall just after 8:00 a.m. UK time. The images of the devastation to the southern coast were gut-wrenching.

Entire coastal towns were underwater, their buildings swept away or destroyed. Eastbourne looked like an angry giant hand had swiped its seafront, leaving only twisted wreckage behind. Many of Brighton's buildings had been reduced to rubble.

Felix was closing in on London, which was already being slammed by rain and winds over ninety miles per hour. Roofs had been ripped from buildings, windows shattered, and trees uprooted. The streets were clogged with unmoving vehicles, and the city looked eerily devoid of life as everyone took shelter from the storm.

I had one text from Finley, sent at 6:00 a.m. UK time. **Almost there. So tired. World domination will have to wait.**

It had taken them over four hours to drive from Chiswick to Highgate, a trip that should have taken less than one. It was noon there now, so they'd be hunkered down at the Barrows. Cell service had to be down, or she would have texted again. That was confirmed when I replied, and my message failed to deliver.

Two hours later, Felix hit London at one hundred and ten miles per hour. I completely zoned out in calculus, watching the limited news coverage.

The entire city was in blackout. Low-lying areas were flooded from the heavy rain, and there was widespread structural damage. Experts were already estimating the damage to the country in the billions. News anchors were saying it could take a week or longer to restore power in London.

"Poor Finley. She'll go bonkers without power that long," I said to Kalyx, who dozed nearby.

After school, I shut off the computer and forced myself to stop doom-scrolling. I ran upstairs to change and grabbed the laundered coveralls. I couldn't think of a better time to return them.

It felt strange walking into Cole Electronics after what had happened there two nights ago. Mr. Cole was behind the counter watching a muted TV screen, and the look he gave me said *You again.*

"Is Ethan here?" I asked politely.

"Yes," Ethan said from behind me before his father could answer.

I turned to see him walking down the aisle, carrying several small boxes. His expression gave nothing away, but he wasn't wearing his usual scowl. I took that as a good sign.

I lifted the rolled coveralls. "Do you have a minute to talk about that project I'm working on?"

He set the boxes on a shelf. "Yes. Come to the back."

I followed him to the office and waited for him to close the door. "I wanted to thank you again. I don't want to think about what would have happened if you hadn't helped me."

"I was starting to wonder if I dreamed the whole thing," he said.

"I feel like that a lot these days." I smiled tentatively and held out the coveralls. "I even washed them."

He took the coveralls, and his brow creased. Unrolling them, he stared at the bag of coffee beans. His questioning gaze met mine.

I couldn't tell if he was pleased or offended. Did he think I brought the beans because I thought he couldn't afford them?

"I know you can buy real coffee beans in town, but I wanted to give you something as a thank you. My father loves that brand."

"That wasn't necessary." He held the bag out to me. "You don't owe me anything."

I refused to take it. "I know. That's why they call it a thank you *gift*."

He placed the bag on the desk. "Is the dampener still working?"

"Yes, or I assume it is." I made a face. "The only way to know for sure is to get within range of Sutton's scanners, and I'm not that crazy."

"I'm still not sure about that," he said dryly, but one corner of his mouth twitched. "Where's your feline friend today?"

"At home."

"You're not worried she might leave again?" he asked.

"Always." I frowned. "But I can't stay with her twenty-four-seven. I just wish I knew why she came into town the other night."

Ethan considered that. "Could she be looking for the other alien?"

"Maybe. But she's smart, and I think she understands the danger." I hesitated. "Thanks for not telling anyone about her."

He leaned back against the desk with his arms crossed. "You need to stop thanking me. And I never go back on my word."

"Thank –" I caught myself. "Sorry. I'm not used to trusting anyone except Finley."

"You trusted me the other night."

The note of kindness in his voice surprised me, and I spoke without thinking. "I was desperate. I mean –"

"You don't have to explain," he said. "I saw how scared you were."

I thought about how close Sutton had come to catching us and shivered. "You have no idea."

His eyes didn't miss a thing. "They would have taken her, but they wouldn't do anything to you."

A bitter laugh escaped me. "They might not hurt me, but that doesn't mean they wouldn't disappear me for a while."

"Your parents wouldn't let that happen."

"My mother might let them hold me until they could move Taruth to a new secret location," I said. "My father would fight it, but in the end, she would convince him it's for the best."

"Jesus." Ethan shook his head. "And how long do you think you can stay ahead of them like this?"

"As long as I have to," I said with more confidence than I felt.

His expression said I wasn't fooling him.

"Are you any closer to –?" His eyes shifted to something behind me. I followed his gaze to the security monitor.

Four men in army camo entered the store. One of them walked to the counter to speak to Ethan's father.

I stared at the screen in dismay. "Mason."

Mr. Cole scowled. He reached under the counter for a small handheld radio and raised it to his mouth.

A beep came from Ethan's back pocket. He pressed the earpiece I hadn't noticed he was wearing. "Yeah?" His face darkened. "I'll be right there."

He looked at me. "Your Colonel Mason just asked to see Friday night's security footage."

My stomach twisted. I'd known this could happen, but doubt nagged at me now. Were the fake glitches good enough to fool them?

Ethan picked up his tablet and gave me a reassuring look. "We've got this."

"Mason's going to be suspicious when he sees me here." I thought about slipping out the back, but Mr. Cole knew I was here, and he might mention me.

Ethan thought for a moment. "Follow my lead."

We walked to the front of the store. As I'd predicted, Mason's eyes narrowed on me.

"Charlotte Ross, what a coincidence," he said.

"That one's been hanging around lately," Mr. Cole grumbled. "Always some girl sniffing around for Ethan."

"Dad," Ethan snapped.

I wanted to hug Mr. Cole for giving me the perfect cover.

Mason's shrewd gaze moved between Ethan and me. "So, you two were here together Friday night?"

"That's right," Ethan said.

I nearly jumped when his arm slid around my waist. Heat suffused me, and I didn't need to fake the blush that rose in my cheeks.

"What were you up to at the store that late?" Mason asked him.

"Inventory."

Mason smirked. "You spent your Friday night doing inventory?"

Ethan's jaw tensed. "You told my father you want to look at our security footage. I assume this has something to do with the man from Sutton who was here that night."

"What man?" Mr. Cole demanded. "What's going on, Ethan?"

"As I explained, someone stole a piece of equipment from Sutton," Mason said. "They were last seen near this shopping center."

Mr. Cole's frown deepened. "What does that have to do with Ethan?"

"It happened Friday night while Charlie and I were here," Ethan told him. "A Sutton employee came to the door and asked if we'd seen anyone suspicious."

Mason nodded slowly. "We're checking the security cameras of all the businesses in the area."

Ethan opened the security app on the tablet and handed it to Mason. "Go ahead."

Surprise flashed in the colonel's eyes. He hadn't expected that. He brought up the front exterior camera and scrolled through Friday night's footage. He paused it when a scooter went past.

"That's me," I said.

He watched me closely. "Do you always ride around in the rain?"

"It wasn't raining when I left my house," I replied.

He resumed the recording and paused briefly when Ethan's truck drove by. A few minutes later, a white van drove slowly past.

He switched to the rear camera and pointed at a red mark on the timeline. "What's that?"

Ethan leaned over. "No idea."

Mason tapped the mark, and a frozen static image appeared. He went back a few minutes, and I rode up on my scooter. The picture froze and didn't come back until Ethan drove up in his truck. It froze again until we were inside. Not long after, Anthony Brooks and two heavily armed men walked up to the door.

Mason looked sharply at Ethan. "Interesting time for your camera to malfunction?"

"I've never seen it do that before." He held out his hand for the tablet. Mason turned it over, and Ethan expanded the timeline to twenty-four and then forty-eight hours. A total of seven red marks were visible at uneven intervals. Each one revealed a similar frozen image.

"The camera must be going on the fritz," Ethan murmured.

"Of course, it is," his father said with a sneer. "Like everything else in this place."

Mason studied the screen. "How long does your security company keep a backup copy? I want to check theirs."

Ethan shook his head. "We don't have one anymore. All we have are the cameras and an alarm. That's the only copy."

"I see," Mason said clearly displeased.

"Why is the military searching for stolen Sutton property?" Ethan asked him. "Seems a bit like overkill."

"Sutton has several military contracts," Mason replied. "That is as much as I am at liberty to say."

I met Mason's gaze. "This guy managed to get past all of Sutton's security and steal something. Don't you think he's smart enough not to get caught on some store security camera?"

Mason didn't respond, and I was satisfied to see a muscle tic in his jaw.

"My God," Mr. Cole uttered behind us.

Ethan, Mason, and I turned at the same time to see him staring at the TV. My world tilted at the breaking news headline across the screen.

FELIX'S FURY. THAMES BARRIER FAILS AGAINST HISTORIC STORM SURGE.

10

Mr. Cole unmuted the TV, and the reporter's urgent voice filled the store.

"We can only describe it as catastrophic. The city, already crippled by the winds, had no defense against the massive storm surge when the Thames Barrier failed to hold it back."

The footage was from earlier that day, before Felix hit London. The winds were still too strong to send in helicopters or drones, leaving everyone blind to what was happening now.

I clutched my phone and texted Finley before I remembered it wouldn't get through. "Damn it," I choked out. *Please let them be okay.*

"Charlie," Ethan said. "What is it?"

"Finley."

Understanding lit his eyes. "Your friend in London."

"Yes." My voice cracked. I was aware of his father and Mason looking at me, but I didn't spare them a glance. "I have to go."

Ethan's hand closed around my wrist before I could bolt for the door. "You're too upset to drive."

"I'm fine." I tried to shake off his hand.

He refused to let go. "You're not fine, and I don't want it on my conscience if you crash your scooter. I'm driving you home."

"My scooter..."

"Don't worry about that. I'll take care of it." He steered me away toward the back of the store. "My truck is parked out back."

"Corporal Cole," Mason called.

We stopped and turned. "Yes, Colonel?" Ethan said.

"I have some questions I'd like to ask you? When can I expect you back?" he asked.

"I don't know."

Mason scowled. "This is a serious matter. I would expect more cooperation from you."

Ethan's voice turned to ice. "Did you not just see what is happening in London? There are things more important than your search."

He resumed walking. "I'm taking Charlie home. If you can't wait for me to return, give my father your number, and I'll call you."

He muttered something under his breath as we walked to his truck. We got in, and he started the engine. "Nice fellow."

I didn't respond as I buckled my seat belt. My chest felt like it was in a vise while I scrolled through news sites. The London flood was the only story on every site, but no one had new footage yet.

They're safe with the Barrows.

I didn't want to think about what would have happened if they hadn't left so early to drive to Highgate. How many people had stayed in their homes to ride out the storm, never imagining the unthinkable could happen? How many of them wouldn't make it?

We stopped at the gates to my neighborhood. I handed Ethan my key fob, and he held it up to the sensor. When the gates opened, he passed it back to me.

We pulled into the driveway, and I jumped out. I turned to thank him and found an empty driver's seat.

He was waiting for me when I rounded the front of the truck. Neither of us said anything as I let us into the house.

"Are your parents at work?" he asked.

I nodded and walked to the kitchen. "Do you want something to drink?"

"No. I'm good."

I checked my phone again as if a message from Finley would magically appear. Then I grabbed the TV remote and flipped through channel after channel. All of them were speculating about the Thames Barrier, but no one had fresh updates.

"Maybe you should call your parents," Ethan said, startling me. I'd forgotten he was there.

"Why?" I walked to the couch and sat, tucking my legs beneath me.

He followed me. "You're upset. Don't you think they'd want to be here with you?"

His furrowed brow and concerned eyes made a lump form in my throat. I was about to answer when my phone rang. It was my father.

"I just heard the news," he said. "Have you talked to Finley?"

My voice broke. "Not since last night. They left Chiswick to stay with the Barrows in Highgate." I relayed what Finley had told me.

"I'm sure they're safe." He paused. "Nobody can do anything until after the storm passes. I'll call the Sutton branch in Cambridge and have someone check on them. It might be a few days before they can get through, but we'll find them."

Tears pricked the backs of my eyes, and the weight on my chest eased a little. "Thanks, Dad."

"Try not to worry," he said. "I'll be home as soon as I make the call."

I hung up and looked at Ethan. "My dad's going to call some people to check on Finley and her parents when it's safe."

Ethan gave me a small smile. "That's good."

"You don't have to stay with me," I said. "He said he'll be home soon, and you probably need to get back to the store."

He sat on the other end of the couch. "I'm in no hurry to talk to Colonel Mason again. I'll stick around until your father gets here unless you want me to leave."

"No, stay." There was something comforting about his presence, and I didn't want to be alone.

"Your friend lives in Chiswick?" He asked. At my questioning look, he said, "You mentioned it when you were on the phone with your father."

"Yes." I lowered the TV volume. "Are you familiar with London?"

He nodded. "A little. I spent a month there last year. You?"

"I lived there for five years. That's how I met Finley. My family moved back to the U.S. two years ago when my parents started working for Sutton."

Surprise crossed his face. "You were what, eleven, when you moved to the UK? You don't have an accent."

I shrugged. "I just never picked up one. My parents are American, and my school had more foreign students than Brits. I did call the bathroom the loo for almost a year after we got here."

"Do you see Finley often?" he asked.

"We talk every day. She was here for two weeks in June, and I'm going there…" The words died on my tongue. I was supposed to spend Christmas break in London, but that wasn't going to happen now.

It would take months for the Bennets to clean up from this and repair their house, if it could be saved at all. They had the money to replace what they'd lost, but there was already a severe housing shortage in London, and this disaster could leave thousands of people homeless.

"You sound very close," Ethan said.

"She's more like a sister than a best friend." I held up my phone, which had a photo of us as the background.

Kalyx padded silently down the stairs. She paused at the bottom to give Ethan a long look and came over to sit in front of me.

Ethan stared at her as if he still couldn't believe she was real. "You let her have the run of the house? Aren't you afraid one of your parents will see her?"

I reached out to give her head a scratch. "I don't have much choice. She can unlock and open doors. But she's good at staying out of sight."

"She's so docile," he said.

I laughed softly. "She is now. She was kind of terrifying at first."

"And you still went back."

"Yes." I stroked her sleek fur, and she leaned against the couch as if she sensed my distress.

Affection swelled in my chest. I knew I shouldn't get attached because she had to go home, but she'd carved out a space in my heart I wasn't ready to give up.

I looked up to find Ethan watching me with a curious expression. "What?"

"I'm just trying to figure you out. There's a lot more to you than you let people see."

I tilted my head. "What do you see?"

One corner of his mouth lifted. "First, I thought you were a snarky friend of Xander's. Then a bored rich girl. Then a would-be thief." He motioned to Kalyx. "Then you laid that on me."

"I like to keep people guessing." I wondered what he'd think if I added professional burglar to that list. Better to keep that one to myself.

"It takes guts to do what you're doing," he said. "I still think you're in way over your head, but I'm impressed you've managed to stay one step ahead of Sutton so far."

I smiled at the praise. "And the military. Can't forget Colonel Mason."

Ethan grew serious. "No. We can't forget him."

"Do you think he suspects Kalyx was in the store, or he's just being thorough?" I asked.

He scrubbed his jaw. "I think they would have stormed the place that night if they believed she was there. They're being cautious because they aren't sure."

I pulled my knees up to my chest. "I'm sorry I got you mixed up in this."

He frowned. "I could have called the police or given you away when Brooks came to the door. I chose not to."

His eyes strayed to Kalyx. "Have you thought about what you'll do if you can't find the pilot? Or if you find him, and they're stranded here?"

"I'll find him," I said. "And he told me he's repairing his ship."

Ethan's gaze snapped back to me. "He *told* you?"

I nodded. "I was going to tell you about it today. Taruth contacted me yesterday, and we had an actual conversation."

"How?"

I lifted my hair to show him the translator and told him everything. He was stunned, but his reactions were nowhere as dramatic as Finley's had been.

He raked a hand through his hair. "They've known about these aliens for two years and didn't think the rest of the world should know?"

"They want the technology for themselves." I curled my lip. "All they care about is being the first to build their colony ships."

"I get that, but this is about more than getting to Alcea first," he said. "People need to know there are advanced civilizations out there before they start travelling across the universe. We don't know how they'll react to humans settling on one of their planets."

"About as well as people would react to an alien colony ship coming here," I said without humor. "If I was an alien, and I saw what humans did to this planet, I wouldn't want them anywhere near mine."

"Do you think Sutton can get the alien drive working with their ship?" he asked.

I shook my head. "I've seen some of Kalyx's technology, and it's so advanced. I think it would be like trying to fit a quantum processor into an old steam engine."

"Nice analogy," he said. "But everyone said FTL was impossible until it wasn't. And they have your alien friend to help them."

I set my jaw. "Not for long, if I have anything to say about it."

Kalyx lifted her head. A car door closed outside.

"It must be my father," I swung my feet off the couch. "Kalyx, go to my room."

She obeyed without hesitation, cloaking herself as she climbed the stairs.

The front door opened, and my father came in. He came up short when he saw Ethan. It was the first time I'd had someone other than Finley here.

"Dad, this is Ethan," I said.

My father smiled warmly. "Hello, Ethan."

Ethan rose. "It's nice to meet you, sir." He looked at me. "I should get going."

I stood, too, a little disappointed he was leaving. "Thanks for everything."

"Anytime," he replied.

After he left, my father turned to me. "Wasn't he our valet at the club the other night?"

"Yes." I didn't expand on it, and he left it at that.

He came over and pulled me into a warm hug, the kind that used to be a regular occurrence. I hugged him back tightly.

"Your mom is down in the lab with her team, running a test," he said when he let me go. "I left her a message. I doubt any of them has heard about London."

I didn't think it would matter if she had heard about London. She'd say there was nothing they could do, so they might as well finish the test.

My father and I sat together on the couch, and he put an arm around me. I couldn't remember the last time he'd held me like this. I hadn't realized how much I needed it.

"The Bennets are going to be okay," he said. "No hurricane is a match for the Barrows' old house."

His reassuring voice wrapped around me like a blanket. He wasn't the type to sugarcoat things. If he said they were safe, it was because he believed it. I had to believe it, too.

I leaned into him, letting my eyes drift shut. *Please, let him be right.*

Charlie.

"Mmm," I mumbled into my pillow.

I must speak with you.

"What?" I opened my eyes and blinked at the black shape inches from my face. It took a few seconds to recognize Kalyx's back. She lay curled beside me, and I had one arm thrown over her.

Charlie, do you hear me?

"I'm awake," I said groggily.

Please, I do not have much time. They will come for me soon.

"Who?" The fog of sleep cleared from my brain, and I was suddenly wide awake. "Taruth?"

Yes, it is I. I must speak with you about something of importance, he said, an urgent note in his voice.

I rolled onto my back, keeping one hand on Kalyx. *What is it?*

Kalyx's body rumbled with a low growl. I thought she might be dreaming until a knock came at my door.

"Hide," I whispered and called, "Come in."

I expected my father and was surprised when my mother opened the door. She was dressed for work, her hair pulled into a perfect bun and a suit jacket over one arm. I'd gone to bed early last night, so I hadn't seen her when she came home. She couldn't have picked a worse time to pop in for a chat.

"Your father told me about the Bennets," she said, her tone lacking its usual coolness. "Tom and Norah are very capable, and it was smart to leave when they did. I'm sure they are safe in Highgate."

I stared at her, unsure of how to respond to this show of empathy from her.

She took a step into the room. "He said there was a young man with you when he got home last night. You've never mentioned him."

"I wasn't aware you were interested in my social life," I said, reaching for my phone. I knew before I looked that Finley hadn't texted me.

"I'm interested when you're dating a twenty-one-year-old man, who moonlights as a valet," my mother replied. The slight emphasis she put on *valet* said she was more bothered by his job than his age.

I sat up. "How do you know how old he is?"

"Colonel Mason ran a background check on him."

Of course, he did. I should have known he would go running to her. And that there was more to her visit.

"At the club, you acted like you didn't know him," she continued. "Would you like to explain how you ended up at that store with him a few hours later?"

"I'm eighteen, and last time I checked, I didn't have a curfew."

Her mouth tightened. "You haven't answered my question. Why were you at the store on Friday night?"

I huffed. "Ethan had to work, and it was the only time we could see each other. Satisfied?"

"He had to work?" She arched an eyebrow. "*After* his valet shift when the store wasn't open."

"Yes, Mom." I said, annoyed on Ethan's behalf. "Believe it or not, some people work two or three jobs. He had to do inventory, and I helped him. Why does any of that matter?"

Her eyes sharpened. "It matters because you and he were the only people in that building when Sutton's security tracked a suspect to that shopping center."

"What exactly are you accusing us of, Mom?" I demanded.

"I'm not accusing you of anything."

"Really?" I retorted. "Because it sounds a lot like you're implying Ethan and I helped your suspect get away."

She shook her head. "I'm not saying that, but Colonel Mason is a suspicious person by nature. He's started to question the number of recent incidents connected to you."

"Me?" My voice rose. "What incidents?"

"First, you were near Sutton during the attempted break-in," she said. "Then a fugitive was tracked to our house. Now there's this situation at the store."

I threw off the covers and got out of bed. "I was a *mile* from Sutton on a public road when that guy ran out in front of me. And that fugitive Mason tracked to our neighborhood could have been hiding in anyone's yard. Mason searched our house and found nothing, remember?"

My anger surged. "Why would I help any of those people? Have you asked Mason that? And what's with all these break-ins at Sutton lately? Do they have anything to do with the plane that crashed?"

Her gaze narrowed. "Why would you ask that?"

"Because they all happened since the crash," I shot back. "Your plane came down a few miles from our house. Does Mason think I was involved in that, too?"

"Don't be absurd," she said, but it had less bite.

My father appeared in the doorway, his hair damp from the shower. The look on his face said he'd overheard some of our conversation.

"Evelyn, tell me I didn't just hear you suggest Charlie was involved in any of that," he said.

She adjusted the coat over her arm. "I didn't suggest anything. I told her Colonel Mason questioned her presence at Cole Electronics Friday night. It's near where they lost the... suspect."

I pretended not to notice her slip. Was she about to say signal or alien?

My father shot me a confused look. "You were at the store that night?"

"Do I have to go through this again?" I threw up my arms. "Yes, I was there with Ethan. No, we're not serious. We did inventory. We did *not* see or help a thief with stolen Sutton property." I glared at my mother. "Is that enough for you, or should I take a polygraph test?"

"No." My father's voice was tight, but the look he gave me was apologetic. "You have nothing to explain. As for Colonel Mason, if it walks and talks, he thinks it's guilty of something."

I felt a rush of warmth for Dad. He'd stood up for me again. It didn't make up for all the times he hadn't, but it was a start.

"I should get ready for school," I said even though my first class didn't start for two hours. What I really wanted to do was talk to Taruth. He'd gone silent when my mother came in, and I had no way to reach out to him.

My father smiled at me. "I'll try to get home early again tonight."

"Okay." I was surprised to realize I hoped he did.

They left, and he closed the door. I heard the murmur of their raised voices as they went back to their bedroom, and I waited for their door to close before climbing onto the bed next to Kalyx, who was visible again.

"Taruth," I whispered. "Are you there?"

Nothing.

I said his name a few more times, but he was gone. I bit my bottom lip, wondering what he'd wanted to talk about and how long it would be before he could contact me again. It had been two days since our first conversation, and I hoped it wouldn't be another two before he could do it again.

I slid off the bed and opened my laptop. Felix had moved on by now, and I was filled with dread as I opened a news site to see the aftermath.

I covered my mouth with a hand when the images loaded. The Thames had swallowed entire districts, its murky waters stretching far beyond the banks. Greenwich and Southwark were almost unrecognizable. Entire blocks were submerged, with only the tops of streetlights and traffic signals jutting above the surface. Boats moved through streets, navigating around over-turned buses, floating cars, and debris.

The view switched to Westminster Bridge, which was partially under water and choked with wreckage. Big Ben's clock face was cracked, and large sections of the Parliament roof were gone. Its lower levels and Parliament Square were engulfed by water.

The camera swept over a neighborhood I knew as well as my own. Chiswick was under water. Along the riverside, only the roofs of Georgian houses were visible. Farther from the river, floodwaters reached the second-floor windows shattered by the wind. Roofs had caved in or ripped off entirely, and from the upper floors, people waved frantically at helicopters.

I searched for Finley's house among the wreckage, but it was impossible to tell one ruin from another. Reality settled like a lead weight on my chest. The Bennets' warm, happy home was gone. Even if it still stood after the flood waters subsided, it would be unlivable, and everything inside was lost.

I was almost relieved when the camera panned out and away to show parts of London that had been spared from the water but not the wind. In Hampstead and Highgate, entire streets were buried by fallen trees, collapsed power lines, and pieces of roofs ripped from rows of terraced houses. Even the buildings that had withstood the storm had windows missing and trees uprooted.

Across London, billboards had been torn from their frames, scaffolding lay in tangled heaps, and glass and debris littered the streets. Not one building appeared unscathed. The scale of the devastation stole my breath. I couldn't imagine how they'd even begin to recover.

When the news anchors began discussing the Thames Barrier failure, I scrolled to other sites for glimpses of Highgate. I couldn't find the Barrows' house, but seeing similar homes still standing gave me hope.

I kept Kalyx close to me all day because I had to be touching her for Taruth to reach me. Her presence was comforting, especially whenever my thoughts drifted back to Finley and what was happening in London.

I skipped my last class and sat on the couch with Kalyx, watching for the latest news out of the UK. Experts were calling Felix the perfect storm, explaining the conditions that came together to cause the historic storm surge. The Thames Barrier had not been built to withstand something this massive, and a second barrier had been under construction for years. When the discussion turned to the bureaucracy that had held up the construction, I turned it off.

Kalyx shifted, resting her head on my lap. I stroked it absently, thinking about all the people waiting for news about their friends and loved ones. They were saying the death toll could be in the thousands, and it might take weeks to learn the fate of the missing.

Charlie.

I jumped when Taruth's voice filled my mind. "I'm here."

I do not have long. They will come for me again soon. His voice was clearer, more fluent than last time.

"What is it?"

My ship's repairs are near completion. Soon I must run system diagnostics.

"That's great!" I exclaimed. "You'll be able to fly it home."

Yes. He was quiet for several seconds. *When I start the ship, it will activate the beacon I placed on your moon. The beacon will detect that my ship was damaged and come to find it.*

My excitement dimmed. "And that's bad?"

It is. His tone was heavy. *The beacon sends a signal to nearby Kruran ships to alert them a vessel is in distress. The signal also helps the pilot locate the beacon, which contains emergency rations and tools.*

"Why is that a bad thing?" I asked.

The signal summons the pilot's vestra. It will call to Kalyx, and she cannot disobey it.

My stomach dropped. "Sutton will find it, and when they do, they'll find Kalyx."

Yes.

I put a hand to my throat. "There has to be a way to stop it. She must have a button or switch to disable it."

It can only be deactivated at the beacon, he replied.

"Then I'll need to get to it before Sutton does." My mind raced. They had helicopters. I'd never reach it before them. "Taruth, do you know where it will land?" If he said it would come to his ship, we were screwed.

The beacon will land where I crashed and scan for me and my ship.

My relief lasted two whole seconds until he added. *When it locates the ship, it will come here and begin to emit the distress signal.*

"Shit," I muttered. "How long will the beacon stay at the crash site? Will I have enough time to deactivate it before it leaves?"

It will remain there for sixty seconds.

"Sixty seconds!" I burst out. "It's impossible to do this in a minute."

My apologies. It is sixty minutes.

I slumped back. "Okay. How long does it take to deactivate it?"

Not long. I will show you how to do it. I thought I heard relief in his voice.

An image of a black sphere appeared in my mind. It was six feet in diameter and etched into its surface were glyphs like the ones on Kalyx's body. A second image arrived. In this one, the surface was slightly iridescent, and there was an opening that revealed a small control panel.

Every beacon is encoded for one vestra. You do not wear Kalyx's tether, so you will need her to open it for you. Have her press her paw to the lock, and it will open.

What followed was a series of images showing the buttons to push to turn off the signal and power down the beacon. Each button had a different glyph which he called forms. Krurans had no alphabet. The way he described it, each form had a meaning and when used in combinations they took on different meanings and formed words.

It was easier for me to think of them as glyphs so I stuck with that. We went through it half a dozen times, and I jotted down his instructions in my phone. Done correctly, the whole process would take less than a minute.

There is one more thing you must do, he said. *The core must be removed so the beacon cannot be reactivated.*

"The core?" Visions of a radioactive fusion reactor flashed through my mind.

He sent me another image of a large glyph a foot from the control panel. Kalyx had to unlock it. When she did, a circular opening would appear. The opening looked to be roughly four inches in diameter and there was a handle deep inside. I had to turn the handle to detach the core, a glowing cylinder approximately four inches long. It resembled one of the test tubes from the lab at my old school.

"Is it safe for me to touch the core?" I asked.

Yes.

I glanced down at the notes on my phone. "How will I know when you start up your ship? And how long will it take the beacon to get here?"

I have thought on this, Taruth said. *I will contact you before I am taken to my ship. When I activate the beacon, it will take one hundred and twenty-seven minutes to reach earth.*

That gave Kalyx and me enough time to get to the ravine. If all went according to plan, we'd be out of there before Sutton arrived.

"When do they take you to your ship?" I asked.

They come at the same times every day. I have learned your clock. The first time is seven-thirty. The second is three-thirty. I will run the test then.

"Okay. We'll be ready."

Thank you, Charlie, he said. *You do much for Kalyx and for me.*

I smiled. "What are friends for?"

You are a good friend.

"Hopefully soon we'll meet in person." I realized I still had no idea what he looked like.

Taruth's voice softened. *That is my hope, too.*

11

An hour later, I entered Cole Electronics. As soon as I'd lost contact with Taruth, I'd started planning for tomorrow, and it didn't take me long to admit I needed help. Ethan was the only person I could turn to, but I wasn't sure if he'd want to get involved again. Helping me had already brought Mason snooping around his store. I wouldn't blame Ethan if he said no.

Today, Xander was behind the counter. He looked up from his phone and grinned. "Hi, Charlie."

"Hey." I walked over to him. "Whatcha up to?"

"Nothing." He waved his phone. "Did you hear about London?"

"Yes."

His grin faded. "I never thought something like that could happen there."

"Me either."

There were terrible storms and floods all the time, but London had always felt... indestructible. Seeing it so broken was a brutal reminder that no place in the world was truly safe. And it would only get worse.

I wished I could believe this would be a wake-up call for governments. But more likely, it would push them to throw more resources at the space program.

"I'm always saying how boring it is here, but I guess it's not so bad, huh?" Xander said.

I nodded. "Is Ethan here?" Ignoring his sly look, I added, "I left my scooter here yesterday."

"Why'd you do that?"

"I... wasn't feeling well, and Ethan gave me a ride home," I said.

"That sucks." He glanced past me. "He's back there somewhere. Want me to get him for you?"

"I can find him. Thanks."

I headed toward the back of the store and found Ethan in the office poring over papers. I retreated, not wanting to interrupt him.

"Charlie," he called. "You can come in."

"Are you sure? I can come back."

"Yeah. I could use a break." He stuffed the papers into a manilla envelope and waved at the other chair. "Have a seat."

I stepped into the doorway. "Do you think we could talk outside?"

Surprised, he said, "Sure."

He pointed at my scooter as we walked to the back door. "We've had some thefts in the area, so I brought it inside."

"I wonder if it's the same person who broke into Sutton," I said with a smirk.

Ethan wore a secretive smile as he opened the door. "Could be."

Outside, I walked about a dozen feet from the building before turning to him. "I may be paranoid, but I wouldn't put it past Mason or Sutton to bug the store while you were out yesterday."

He gave me a skeptical look. "You think they'd go that far?"

"Sutton put a tracker on my scooter and followed me with a drone," I reminded him. "So, yes, I do."

He swore under his breath and rubbed his face.

I patted my backpack. "I brought my signal scanner to search for them."

"I'm not even going to ask why you own a signal scanner," he said.

"I built it. Bored rich girl, remember." I sobered. "I'm sorry I dragged you into this."

"Stop apologizing. It's not your fault," he said. "So, you came to get your scooter and to check my store for bugs?"

I hesitated. "I was going to ask for your help with something, but I don't think I can. It could be risky."

His lips parted slightly, interest sparking in his eyes. "Why don't you let me decide if it's too risky?"

"It might be dangerous, too," I added.

"I was a marine, Charlie." He gave me a small smile, but a flicker of pain crossed his face. "I think I can handle it."

I looked past him at the building, my thoughts racing. He was more qualified than I was by a mile to do this, but what if something happened to him? What if he got caught?

"I heard from Taruth again. He warned me about something that's going to happen tomorrow," I said. "If I can't stop it, Sutton's going to catch Kalyx."

"After an opening like that, there's no way you can't tell me now," he teased.

I laid it all out for him. Sharing it with someone helped ease the knot of anxiety in my gut.

Ethan gave me a wry smile. "You don't do anything halfway, do you?"

"Now you see why I was hesitant to tell you," I said. "If you just could listen to my plan and offer advice, that's all I'll ask from you."

"Hold on. You don't really expect me to stay here while you go off alone to sabotage an alien beacon." He shook his head. "That sounds even stranger when I say it out loud."

I almost hugged him. "If you think that's strange, try having an alien talk directly into your mind."

"I'll pass on that." He folded his arms. "Alright. Let's figure out our game-plan for tomorrow. And then we'll make sure Colonel Mason didn't leave any gifts behind in my store."

Taruth contacted me right on time the next afternoon. I sent a text with the gate code to Ethan, who was already on his way.

He arrived a few minutes later, and we drove to a side road near his house. He knew of an old game trail that would get us to Alder Ravine in half the time it would take from my house. And there was less risk of being seen.

To be safe, he parked the truck in the overgrown driveway of an abandoned farm a few hundred feet from the trailhead. Reluctantly, I left my phone in the truck with his. I hated being away from it in case Finley tried to contact me, but we couldn't risk a GPS history showing either of us in the ravine today.

We walked single file along the narrow trail, with a cloaked Kalyx bringing up the rear. The ground was still soft from rain a few hours before, and wet leaves slapped at us. Neither of us spoke, and I spent the time running through Taruth's instructions and worst-case scenarios on a loop in my head.

It took less than fifteen minutes to reach the ravine and another ten to climb down. One side was too steep to scale without ropes, but our side had a section where the rock had crumbled over time, forming a rough, uneven path that was slick from the rain but doable.

We made our way over the uneven ground to the crash site. Sutton had done a thorough job cleaning it up, but a furrow in the earth and a shallow indentation on the riverbank marked where the ship had hit and skidded to a stop.

Kalyx reappeared at the edge of the site, sniffing the ground. She circled the area slowly and looked back at me like she was asking, *Where is he?*

I tried to imagine what it must have been like for her after the crash, injured, confused, and alone. Taruth and I hadn't talked about the crash or how they had gotten separated, but I couldn't see her leaving him willingly. It was more likely he had sent her away to avoid her being captured, too.

Ethan stopped and turned in a slow circle, scanning the ravine. "Climbing out will take at least twenty minutes. If the military scrambles their choppers before the beacon lands, we won't have that much time."

He pointed toward the river where it snaked around a cluster of boulders. "That way's no good either. Colonel Mason's people will be all over this place, and there's no cover."

That left us with one escape route.

We headed toward a bend in the ravine wall, blocked only by a large fallen tree. On the other side, the ravine narrowed, and the trees overhead grew close, forming a canopy that would help shield us. There were a few boulders, but nothing impassable. Past that, the ravine walls gradually sloped down enough to make it easier to climb out. If we could make it behind the boulders in time, our chances of getting away were much better.

Almost forty minutes had passed since I'd last heard from Taruth. If everything was going to plan, the beacon was already on its way. There was nothing left for us to do but wait.

We sat on the fallen tree. I pulled out the small notebook where I'd copied Taruth's instructions and read through them for the hundredth time. I'd already memorized the steps, but I needed something to do. I wished I had my phone to check for updates from London.

Restless, I stood and started pacing. Kalyx trailed me silently while Ethan stayed on the log, watching. Was he always this calm, or did he just have less at stake?

"You're going to tire yourself out before it even gets here," he said.

I walked back to him. "Talk about something to help me get my mind off it."

"Like what?"

I glanced at the tactical watch he wore. "So, you were a marine?"

He nodded. "Two years. I took a bullet that tore up my shoulder, and I received a medical discharge."

"I'm sorry." I said, hearing a trace of bitterness in his voice. "Do you miss it?"

"Yeah." He watched a hawk glide overhead. "I had a great unit."

"You ever hear from them?"

"They've called a few times since I came home. Hard to stay in touch when you're deployed."

I sat next to him. "There are lots of opportunities for ex-military. What brought you back to Hudson Ridge?"

He hesitated. I almost apologized for asking before he finally answered.

"I came back for my family – mostly for Xander. Our mother died two years ago. After that, he and my dad kind of fell apart. Xander started acting out, skipping school. He needed someone to keep him in school and out of trouble." Ethan tossed a small stone into the river. "I don't know how good I'm doing. Work takes up most of my time."

"He's a nice kid. Losing his mom had to be rough for him."

"It was," Ethan said quietly. I sensed he didn't want to talk about it anymore.

I tipped my head back to look at the sky. "Just think; there could be an alien object flying toward us at this very second."

I felt him watching me. "What?"

"None of this fazes you, does it?" he asked. "Aliens, spaceships – you take it all in stride."

I laughed. "I wasn't always like this. The last few weeks have changed me. I see things differently, and I don't react the same way I would have before."

He looked at Kalyx, who was pawing at something in the river. "Is it safe for her to be out in the open like that?"

"No." I called softly to her. "Kalyx, cloak."

She looked at me and vanished.

"*That* I'm still getting used to," I said. "You wouldn't believe how many times she's snuck up on me at home."

"Does the cloaking hide sound, too?" he asked.

"No. She's naturally quiet." I checked my watch. "Ninety-seven minutes. Taruth said it will take a hundred and twenty-seven minutes, but we don't know exactly when he started his ship."

I scanned the sky. "We should start watching for the beacon when we hit that mark. It could arrive any time after that, and we need to be ready for it."

Ethan nodded. "If they send choppers, we'll hear them two miles out. If they're coming in fast, we'll have about forty seconds. If they're sweeping, maybe one to two minutes. Either way, it's going to be close."

"So, what you're saying is I better work fast," I said lightly. Inside I was like a spring ready to snap.

He quirked his lips. "No pressure."

I started pacing again. Occasionally, one of us said something, but mostly we sat in silence, waiting. At exactly the one-twenty-seven mark, he checked his watch.

"Time."

We both looked up, even though we knew it would be a few more minutes, at least. And that was if Taruth had been able to start his ship soon after they took him to it.

Three minutes passed. Then five. Then ten. At twenty minutes, my neck was starting to cramp. I rolled my head and looked up again.

By the thirty-minute mark, worry crept in. What if Taruth had miscalculated? What if something went wrong?

Kalyx suddenly popped into view, pacing like a caged animal. She sensed something.

I looked up again, but the sky was empty – until it wasn't.

A small dark object blinked into existence, growing larger by the second until I made out a black sphere. My heart lodged in my throat. It was coming fast, too fast.

The sphere slowed fifty feet from the ground, hovering silently. There was no roar of engines, no lights, and no visible propulsion. It just hung there, like an ornament at the end of an invisible string.

As it descended, the air grew charged with electricity. My body hummed, like I was standing beneath a high-voltage power line.

At twenty-feet, a soft blue light rippled over its surface. The sphere floated to the ground, landing with a soft hiss on the exact spot where Taruth's ship had crashed.

Silence filled the ravine as if every living thing here was holding its breath. I stood rooted to the spot, staring at the sphere until Kalyx started toward it. I snapped out of it and ran after her.

Taruth's images didn't do it justice. Its matte black exterior swallowed the light around it, and the glyphs etched into the surface pulsed faintly.

I stepped up to the sphere and shivered. The air around it was so cold my breath fogged, and my hand shook when I reached out. I placed my palm against the icy metal and immediately yanked it back, not from pain but from intense cold.

Ethan ran up to me. "You okay?"

"Yes. Just freezing." I squared my shoulders. "Let's do this."

I pointed to the glyph Taruth had shown me. "Kalyx, touch."

She stood on her hind legs and pressed a paw to the glyph. A pulse of energy rippled across the surface, turning it iridescent, and a six-inch square section dissolved to reveal the control panel.

I moved in front of it. Nervously, I touched it, and a soft purple screen appeared, identical to the one Taruth had shown me. Carefully, I pressed a sequence of symbols exactly as he had instructed. After the last one, a glowing orange triangle appeared in the center of the screen.

This was it, the final command. I touched it, and the control panel flashed and turned a pale yellow.

"Is it done?" Ethan asked when I dropped my hand.

The surface lost its glow, the control panel disappearing as if it had never existed. I exhaled shakily. "I think so."

"Good job," he said. "That took you less than a minute."

"Really? It felt like longer."

"You're doing great." He rested a hand on my shoulder. I was so used to going it alone, and the warm touch reminded me we were in this together.

One down.

I moved to the larger glyph that marked the core and told Kalyx to touch it. A circular opening, about four inches in diameter, formed to reveal the faint outline of a handle inside.

My hand paused at the opening. Touching the control panel was one thing. Sticking my arm into an alien sphere was another. What if the beacon recognized I wasn't Kruran, and it activated some security measure Taruth hadn't thought of?

"Do you want me to do it?" Ethan asked.

"You can't. Your hand's too big." I flexed my fingers. There was no time to give myself a pep talk. Mason could be on the way at this very moment.

Then I heard it, the distant thump of helicopter blades.

I thrust my arm into the hole as Ethan said, "They're coming."

I grabbed the cold metal handle and pulled to twist it counterclockwise as Taruth had instructed. It didn't budge.

I tried again. Nothing.

"It won't move," I grunted as I tried a third time.

"They're not coming fast. We have two minutes," Ethan said, his voice surprisingly calm.

My heart thundered. I adjusted my grip on the handle and pulled until tears pooled in my eyes. I was panting when I stopped.

"Ninety seconds." An edge had crept into his voice. "We have to leave it, Charlie."

"No!" We had come too far for me to fail now.

I gritted my teeth and pulled with everything I had in me. My muscles strained, my arm trembling with the effort. Tears poured down my cheeks, and I screamed my frustration.

There was a pop-hiss like the escape of pressurized air. I almost sobbed as I turned the handle one hundred and eighty degrees, and it released with a loud click. I pulled it out and saw the glowing core.

"One minute," Ethan said.

I reached inside again and grabbed the cylinder. It felt like cool glass, and it put up no resistance when I pulled it free. There was no time to study it. I pushed the handle into the hole and withdrew my arm. The hole disappeared.

Ethan grabbed my hand. "Come on."

"Kalyx, cloak," I shouted as we sprinted toward the bend. The beat of rotor blades was deafening.

We leaped over the fallen tree, and my foot caught, sending me to the ground. Ethan helped me up, and we sped around the bend in the wall.

I skidded to a stop. "Oh, God."

"What are you doing?" Ethan shouted.

"I dropped the notebook." I turned back. "Go. I'll catch up."

He didn't move.

If I got caught, I was not dragging him down with me. "Go," I screamed and bolted for the tree. I spotted the notebook and snatched it up.

I turned to flee, but it was too late. I'd never make it to the cover of the trees in time.

I spotted a crevice in the wall with a small overhang. I ran to it and squeezed my body in. It wasn't enough. I was hidden from above, but when someone came around that bend, they'd see me.

Ethan stood behind a boulder, waving for me to run. I motioned for him to go, and he shook his head.

The *thump-thump-thump* of blades filled the ravine, echoing off the walls and pounding against my eardrums. The rotor wash slammed into me as a Black Hawk dipped into view, soldiers in tactical gear poised at the open door.

Had they seen me?

An invisible weight pressed against my legs. *Kalyx.* At least, they wouldn't see her even if they caught me.

I looked down at the core in my hand. It no longer glowed, and it looked like a smooth crystal, but it wouldn't take Sutton long to figure out where it had come from.

Feeling around, I tucked it beneath Kalyx's collar. The fit was snug enough to hold it until she got to Ethan, and he'd figure out what to do with it.

"Kalyx, go to Ethan," I ordered, pointing at him. "Stay with Ethan."

She responded by pressing closer to me.

"No. You have to go." I shoved at her, but she refused to budge.

Kalyx's growl vibrated through me as four soldiers jogged into view, guns raised. None of them saw me, but they would the moment they turned around.

I clutched her collar, my breaths ragged. I had never been this scared in my life.

Mason and another soldier rounded the bend. He swung his arm in an arc as he spoke to the other man, who nodded and ran ahead.

Then he turned and looked right at me.

My whole being screamed for me to bolt, but I was paralyzed. He had me, and there was no escape for me this time.

His gaze moved away, sweeping past me like I wasn't even here.

What?

He stopped abruptly and spoke into his helmet mic before he spun and walked back the way he'd come.

I couldn't breathe as he disappeared around the bend. Two soldiers took up positions along the other side of the ravine. They had an unobstructed view of me, yet neither of them reacted.

What's going on?

Kalyx shifted restlessly. I looked down to see her eyes fixed on the soldiers, the metal hackles along her back fully erect. I stroked under her chin to soothe her.

My hand stilled. I could see her.

And the soldiers couldn't see me.

How was this possible? I could count at least half a dozen times when I'd touched her while she was cloaked, and it hadn't affected me. What was different now? And how long would it last?

I didn't plan to stick around and find out.

I nudged Kalyx with my knee. "Let's go."

Keeping one hand wrapped firmly around her collar, I wriggled out of the crack. The Black Hawk's blades had stopped, making it possible to hear voices coming from nearby.

"Where are my drones?" Mason demanded. "I want them in the air and a perimeter around this ravine."

Kalyx and I headed for the boulders. She moved with stealth, while I had to watch every step on the uneven ground. There was a faint shimmer in the air around us, which I'd never seen when she cloaked herself.

The distance was less than a hundred feet, but it felt like a hundred yards as we moved passed the five soldiers stationed along the sides. I was terrified the cloak would fail any second. If I appeared out of nowhere, these soldiers would probably shoot first and ask questions later.

My foot scuffed over a loose stone, sending it into a larger one with a clink. I froze.

"What was that?" A soldier's head whipped around. "I heard something."

"I didn't hear anything," said another.

The first one swung his gun in my direction. "It came from over there."

"Maybe it's the little green men," joked a third soldier.

"Not funny, Jonas," the first soldier shot back. He started toward us, his gun still raised. Kalyx let out a low growl.

"Shhh," I said under my breath.

I began walking again, placing one foot in front of the other with painstaking slowness. I didn't look back to see what the soldier was doing.

Finally, the boulder loomed before us. I rounded it and nearly collided with Ethan. He made a startled sound, and I slapped a hand over his mouth.

"It's me," I whispered. I released Kalyx's collar, and Ethan's eyes went wide.

"How –?"

I shook my head. "I don't know. It's never happened before. It must be the core."

His shoulders sagged. "I ducked out of sight, and when I looked again, you were gone. I thought they caught you."

"They almost did." I hugged Kalyx. "You are the best vestra in the whole universe."

Another helicopter approached, reminding us we weren't out of this yet. Soon these woods would be crawling with military.

"We need to get the hell out of here," Ethan said.

"You don't have to tell me twice." I grabbed the core and shoved it into my backpack. I'd figure out what to do with it once we were safe.

We stayed low and hugged the side of the wall. After a few minutes, the ravine curved, and the soldiers were out of sight.

When the sides of the ravine began to lower, we started looking for a place to climb out. The sooner we got out of these woods, the better.

Ethan pointed to a series of uneven ledges resembling giant steps. It was no more than twenty feet high and manageable.

I pointed at the wall. "Kalyx, up."

She leaped effortlessly to the first ledge. Moving quickly from one ledge to the next, she reached the top in seconds.

"I'll let you follow that performance," Ethan said.

I pulled on the hiking gloves I had in my pack and grasped the edge of the first rock, which was at eye level. I found a foothold and hoisted myself up, but it wasn't enough to pull my upper body over the top.

"Here." Ethan put his hands under my other foot and lifted, giving me the boost I needed to climb onto the ledge.

"Thanks." There wasn't enough room for both of us, so I climbed to the second one and waited for him to scale the first one. He made it look easy.

I looked up at the next ledge. It was only three feet high, but it was shallow, which didn't leave much room to maneuver.

"Need help?" he asked.

"I think I can manage it." I smiled down at him. "But be ready to catch me just in case."

The ledge had a small lip, and I held onto it, lifting myself high enough to grab a jutting rock. This one required more upper body strength, and I was breathing a little harder by the time I pulled myself up.

I rubbed my arms when a cold wind blew through the ravine. Fall had finally arrived. Why couldn't it have waited one more day to make an appearance?

"You want to borrow my jacket?" Ethan asked.

"No. I'll be warm enough once we get up there and start moving faster."

He nodded. "You're almost there. Only two more to go."

I froze when the faint mechanical whine of a drone cut through the quiet woods. It was impossible to tell how far away it was, but it was getting louder.

"Go," Ethan ordered, spurring me into action. A burst of adrenaline had me scrambling up the last two ledges and over the top, where I lay on the ground panting.

I looked down at Ethan who was on the second to last ledge. "Move your ass, Corporal," I said in my best imitation of a drill sergeant. I couldn't tell from his arched brow whether he was annoyed or amused. Maybe a little of both.

He gripped the ledge and jumped to lift himself up. The moment his weight rested on his arms, his bad one buckled, throwing him off balance. The fingers of his other hand scrabbled for the ledge, but it was too late. He fell backward.

"Ethan!"

12

His body twisted, and for one heart-stopping second, I thought he'd catch himself.

Then he dropped.

He hit the ground with a sickening thud and rolled into the river, leaving a smear of red on a flat rock when he'd landed.

My blood went cold. He came to a stop facedown in the shallow water and didn't move. If the fall hadn't killed him, he'd drown before I could reach him.

"Kalyx, get him. Get Ethan," I cried as I slid my legs over the edge.

She leaped past me, hurtling down the wall with breathtaking speed and reaching him before my feet touched the first ledge. She grabbed his hiking pack in her jaws and dragged him out of the river, laying him on the grass.

I half-slid, half-jumped down the wall, nearly falling twice. When I reached the bottom, I dropped to my knees beside Ethan. I didn't know what injuries he had, but none of it mattered if he wasn't breathing.

Yanking off my gloves, I rolled him over and felt his neck. A strong pulse thumped beneath my fingers. He was breathing okay, but his face was pale.

I tapped his cold cheek. "Ethan, can you hear me?"

He didn't respond. I said his name again and again until his eyelids flickered. "That's it, Ethan. Wake up."

His eyes opened, dazed and unfocused. A low moan escaped him before he slipped under again.

I ran my hand over the back of his head, wincing when I felt a small gash.

It wasn't deep, but he'd hit it hard enough to knock him out. I couldn't rule out a concussion – or worse.

He began to shiver. I didn't know how cold it had to be for hypothermia to happen, but the temperature was dropping fast. After dark, it would plummet. I had to get him somewhere warm.

The mine. There was an old iron mine about half a mile from here. I could make a fire there. I looked around frantically, searching for something to use as a litter to carry him. There was nothing.

My gaze landed on Kalyx, standing alert and watchful. She was strong enough to carry him, but I didn't know if she'd do it.

I hooked my arms under his shoulders and strained to lift him. Damn, he was heavy. I rolled him over and stood above him. "Kalyx, come," I panted.

She obeyed immediately, standing steady as I heaved Ethan across her back.

"Good girl." I took an emergency blanket from my pack and draped it over him, tucking it in tight. It would have to do.

We followed the river until the ravine opened enough for us to climb out. I paused to catch my bearings, checked Ethan again, and set out. It took another fifteen agonizing minutes to reach the mine, and I almost cried when I found the boarded entrance, half hidden by brush.

I easily pried one of the weathered planks loose and ducked inside. It was dark and cold and smelled of rot, but the packed dirt floor was solid, and the old beams seemed stable. I didn't plan to go far from the entrance.

I went outside for Kalyx and removed two more planks so she could fit through with Ethan slung across her back. After I cleared a spot for him, I worked fast, gathering broken timbers and the remains of an old crate. The crate was dry and brittle enough for kindling, and I soon had a small fire going.

Ethan hadn't stirred. I moved him closer to the fire, peeled off his pack, and rewrapped him in the blanket. I found another blanket in his bag and layered it on top. We were out of the wind, and the fire would ward off the worst of the cold.

I returned to the entrance and pulled the planks loosely into place. We were far enough from the ravine that I didn't think anyone would find us here. Now I just needed Ethan to wake up. I tried not to think about what would happen if he didn't.

The fire crackled louder, casting an orange glow across the shaft. I crouched by Ethan, who was still shivering violently under the two blankets. Maybe I should have removed some of his wet clothes.

Ten minutes passed, but he didn't stop shivering. I pulled back the blankets and unzipped his fleece jacket. If I thought lifting his dead weight was hard, it was nothing compared to getting him out of wet clothes. After a struggle and some colorful words, I managed to peel off the jacket along with his long-sleeve top. I left his T-shirt on. The tactical pants were loose and easier to remove, and I tried not to look when I pulled them down over his muscled thighs.

His boots were thankfully dry inside. I put them back on and wrapped him in the blankets again. I added more wood to the fire and hung his wet clothes from one of the support beams. It was the best I could do for now.

Kalyx stayed near the entrance, her eyes gleaming in the firelight. I sat beside Ethan, checking his pulse and watching the fall and rise of his chest. After thirty minutes, he stopped shivering, and color came back into his face.

Outside, it was fully dark. I hoped no one got close enough to see the fire. I also hoped we didn't have to spend the night out here.

I hadn't heard a helicopter or drone since we left the ravine. I wished I knew what was going on back there. If they hadn't seen signs of tampering, they might assume no one had been there.

Ethan let out a low moan. His eyes fluttered open, and he stared at the ceiling in confusion. I felt weak with relief when I saw his clear, focused eyes.

He turned his head toward me. "What... happened? Where are we?"

"You don't remember?" I watched his face carefully. "You fell climbing out of the ravine."

He winced. "Oh, yeah. Now I remember."

"Kalyx and I brought you to one of the old iron mines, and I made a fire," I said.

"Thanks."

"How do you feel?" I asked. "You hit your head, but it doesn't look serious."

"Okay, except for a headache." He put a hand to his head and stilled. He lifted the blanket to look beneath. "Where are my clothes?"

I smiled sheepishly. "You landed in the river, and your clothes were wet." I gestured toward them. "They haven't had time to dry."

"How long have we been here?"

"Maybe forty-five minutes," I said. "It took us half an hour to get here."

He sat up slowly. "How did you get me here?"

I pointed at Kalyx. "You can thank her. She carried you on her back."

"Something tells me to be glad I was out for that." He ran one hand through his damp hair. "Any sign of the military?"

"No. I think we're in the clear."

"Then we'll head out as soon as I get dressed," he said, pushing the blankets off him.

I busied myself folding the blankets while he dressed. I was searching my pack for my headlamp when I found the core. I'd completely forgotten about it.

I held it up. "I forgot to ask Taruth what to do with this. I don't know if it safe to bring it home with me."

He looked around. "Stash it here until you can ask him."

"Good idea." I wedged the core behind one of the beams until it was out of sight.

"You ready to go?" he asked as he laced up his boots.

"Are you sure you're okay to walk?"

"Yeah." He grimaced as he pulled on his wet jacket. "Let's get out of here."

We put on our headlamps, and he doused the fire. Outside, my teeth immediately began to chatter. The fire had made the mine shaft warmer than I'd realized. Ethan would be freezing in those wet clothes.

He led the way. Though it was dark, I made sure Kalyx was cloaked. We took a longer route, which eventually circled around to the game trail we'd used earlier.

I sagged with relief when we stepped onto the road. My body realized it was safe and decided it had had enough. I barely had the energy needed to open the truck door and climb inside. The truck shook slightly when Kalyx jumped into the back.

The first thing I did was grab my phone and check my notifications. There was nothing from Finley or my father.

Ethan slid behind the wheel with a sigh and looked over at me. "You okay?"

"I should be asking you that," I said.

"I'm good." He started the ignition and cranked up the heat.

His hand paused on the gearshift when a pair of headlights rounded a curve in the road. Neither of us moved as we waited for the vehicle to pass.

I gripped the door handle when it slowed and pulled in behind us. My first thought was that it was a police car until I made out the shape of a van.

"Kalyx," I whispered hoarsely. She was cloaked, but that wouldn't help if someone got into the back of the truck with her.

"She's good at hiding," Ethan said, his eyes fixed on the side mirror.

The van's driver-side door opened, and someone got out. My heart raced as they walked toward the truck.

Ethan turned to me. Without warning, he leaned across the center console, grabbed the front of my jacket, and tugged me toward him. Before I could ask what he was doing, his other hand cradled the back of my neck and his mouth captured mine.

For a heartbeat, my brain short-circuited. The rational part of me knew this was an act, but the soft, deliberate pressure of his lips made it impossible to think straight. His warmth chased away the cold as the world outside the cab faded.

I curled my fingers in his damp jacket, clinging to him. My stomach fluttered wildly when he pulled me closer, deepening the kiss.

A sharp knock against the window brought me back to reality. Ethan's lips lingered a few seconds longer, his warm breath mingling with mine, before he released me and rolled down his window. Cold air hit my heated face, and I looked away, trying to steady my breathing.

"Can I help you?" he asked cooly, his voice a sharp contrast to what had just happened.

"We saw you parked here and thought you might need some help," a man said.

Ethan rested his hands on the wheel. "Thanks, but as you can see we're good."

The man's laugh was forced. "Glad to hear it. You two have a good evening."

Ethan waited for the van to back out and drive away before he said, "He's from Sutton. I've seen him around town in a Sutton van."

My fingers twisted the bottom of my jacket. "Do you think they took down your plate?"

"Probably."

"Damn it." I closed my eyes and leaned back against the headrest.

He put the truck in reverse. "It could have been worse. A minute earlier and they would have seen us coming out of the woods."

"You're right." I sighed. "Let's hope he and Mason aren't sharing notes."

"Even if they are, there's nothing suspicious about parking along a road," he said. "And we already told them we're dating."

Silence stretched between us. I stared out the window, pretending to watch the trees blur by, but my thoughts kept circling back to the kiss. I could still feel the pressure of his lips against mine and his warm hand at the back of my neck.

His fingers flexed around the wheel. "I'm sorry. I shouldn't have done that without asking you first."

I kept my voice light. "There wasn't time. I think he bought it."

He kept his eyes on the road ahead. "I do, too."

We pulled into the driveway of a small yellow farmhouse, dark except for the glow from the porch light. Ethan shut off the truck and looked at me. "I'm going to change before I take you home."

"Okay." I settled back in my seat to wait.

He opened his door and paused. "Are you coming in?"

"Sure." I climbed out. "Is it okay if Kalyx comes, too?"

"Yeah. My dad and Xander are at the store." He unlocked the front door and stepped aside so Kalyx and I could enter. Once we were in, he closed the blinds. "She can uncloak now."

He disappeared upstairs, and I stood in the living room, taking it all in. The room was half the size of ours, but it had a cozy, lived-in feel. Framed family photos lined the mantle, mismatched pillows softened the worn couch, and a faded rug covered the hardwood floor.

I walked over to the mantle. Most of the photos were of Ethan and Xander, but one showed the whole family. Ethan wore a graduation cap and gown, his parents beaming on either side, with scrawny little Xander in front.

Ethan's mom had been pretty, and he looked a lot like her. Xander took after their father, who looked a decade younger in the photo.

I sank onto the couch while Kalyx sprawled out in front of the fireplace and started cleaning her paws. She seemed bigger and even more alien here than she did at my house, but her catlike mannerisms made me smile.

It also made me wonder how a planet over six light-years away had a creature so similar to an Earth feline. Kalyx was a mix of organics and engineering, but Krurans had to model her after a familiar animal. It was just one more thing I wanted to ask Taruth.

Footsteps pounded down the stairs, and I turned. "That was fast –"

The small figure coming down the stairs was most definitely not Ethan. Xander flashed a wide teasing grin. "Hey, Charlie. You getting more *help* from Ethan?"

He hit the bottom step and stopped so fast his sneaker squeaked against the wood. His eyes bugged as he stared past me.

I followed his gaze to Kalyx, who stared back at him with disinterest before she went back to her grooming. Why hadn't she hidden from him?

"Wha-what is that?" Xander's eyes bounced wildly between us.

Any other day, I might have come up with something clever. Not tonight. "Would you believe it's my school project?"

He scowled. "I'm not that dumb."

"Why aren't you at the store with Dad?" Ethan asked sharply from the top of the stairs.

Xander didn't take his eyes off Kalyx. "He didn't need me. What the hell is that thing?"

Ethan descended slowly, his face grim. He stopped one step above his brother and looked at me with quiet apology.

I opened my mouth, scrambling for something to say. "I'm starving," I blurted instead. "Who wants pizza?"

Xander's gaze snapped to me. "There's a robot panther... thing in our living room, and you want pizza?"

Ethan rescued me. "You can't expect her to explain that on an empty stomach. And I wouldn't mind some pizza."

"But..." Xander sputtered.

"Meat lovers or the works?" I asked, pulling up the app. "Never mind. I'll get both." I felt the two of them watching me as I submitted the order. When it was done, I stood. "Can I use your bathroom?"

Ethan pointed at a door past the stairs. "There."

"Thanks." I shut myself in the small bathroom and grimaced at my reflection. There were dirty smudges on my face, twigs in my tangled hair, and a cobweb stuck to one sleeve of my jacket. I took my time cleaning myself up and returned to the living room.

Ethan was at a small desk opening mail. Xander sat on the stairs watching Kalyx, who was stretched out on the rug now.

"You don't have to stay over there. She won't hurt you," I told him.

He frowned. "It's a she?"

I sank down on the couch with a sigh. "She's not an it, and her name is Kalyx."

"But what is she? Where did she come from?" he pressed.

A headache bloomed behind my eyes, and I rubbed the bridge of my nose. How many people had to know about something for it to no longer be a secret?

Finley knew because I didn't keep anything from her. Ethan knew out of necessity. Xander knew because I got sloppy. I couldn't afford to slip like that again.

"Headache?" Ethan asked.

"It's nothing." I met his concerned gaze and remembered his fall. "I should check your head."

"What's wrong with your head?" Xander asked.

"It's fine," Ethan said at the same time. "I looked at it upstairs."

Xander stood. "Are you guys going to tell me what's going on?" He pointed at Kalyx. "And what the hell is she?"

I locked my eyes with his. "Only if you swear not to tell a soul. I'm serious. This is a matter of life or death." I didn't want to scare him, but I had to make him understand the gravity of the situation.

He looked between Ethan and me and nodded solemnly. "I swear."

I patted the couch. "Why don't you come over here?"

He went to the recliner instead, never taking his eyes off Kalyx. He sat stiffly with his hands clenched on the armrests.

"Xander, this is Kalyx," I said. "She's –"

My phone buzzed. **Your order has arrived.** A few seconds later, the doorbell rang.

Saved by the bell. "Food's here."

Ethan answered the door and brought in a stack of boxes, frowning. "You paid already?"

"The least I can do is spring for dinner." I smiled at Xander. "Let's eat!"

I went to the kitchen and spread the boxes out on the counter. There were two large pizzas, cheese sticks, and two dozen hot wings. It smelled amazing, and I was suddenly ravenous.

Ethan cocked an eyebrow at me. "How many people are you planning to feed?"

"Xander can probably eat a whole pizza himself." I eyed the cabinets. "Plates?"

He took down three plates and handed me one. I put a little of everything on it and took it to the table where he had already set out sodas.

Once Xander saw the spread on the counter, he abandoned his questions and loaded his plate like he hadn't eaten in days.

"I should get you a trough," Ethan said to him.

"What's a trough?" Xander asked through a mouthful of pizza.

Snickering, I picked up a wing just as Kalyx appeared in the doorway. I tossed it to her, and she swallowed it without chewing. I'd never fed her anything besides raw meat, but she seemed to like it, so I gave her another one.

I turned back to the table to find Ethan and Xander watching us. I shrugged and bit into a slice of pizza. She deserved to take part in our little celebratory feast, too.

Xander picked up one of his wings. "Can I give her one?"

I nodded.

He hesitated a few seconds and flung it at her like she was a lion at the zoo. The wing went high, but she leaped and caught it before it struck the wall.

His eyes lit up. "She's so fast." He reached for another wing.

"No more throwing food in the house," Ethan said.

Xander pouted, but he didn't challenge his brother.

I met Ethan's eyes and mouthed, *"Sorry."*

Xander inhaled his food and went for seconds before Ethan and I finished what was on our plates. He came back to the table, but instead of eating, he turned to me with an expectant look. "Can you tell me about Kalyx now?"

I wiped my mouth with a napkin. For his safety, as well as Finley's and Ethan's, I told him the bare minimum. The ship crashed, I found Kalyx, and I was hiding her. I made no mention of my communication with Taruth or Ethan and Finley's involvement.

Xander peppered me with questions. He was too awestruck about the spaceship and Kalyx being an alien to ask how Ethan knew about her.

"What will happen when you find the other alien?" he asked.

I sipped my soda. "Hopefully, he and Kalyx can fly home."

"But how do you know if his ship can fly?" he asked. "It might have been too damaged. And the alien might be hurt." He glanced toward the living room and lowered his voice. "Or he could be dead."

"He's not," I replied. At his questioning look, I said, "Trust me. I have my sources."

He stared at me with something akin to hero worship before he turned to Ethan. "Are you going to help rescue the alien?"

Ethan carried his plate to the sink. "We haven't talked about that."

Xander turned pleading eyes on me. "Can I help? I'll do anything you want."

"That's not up to me. It's up to him." I gestured at his brother. "I have no idea yet what's going to happen, but it'll be dangerous."

Xander's face fell. "Maybe there's something not dangerous I can do."

Ethan came back to the table. "That's something we'll discuss when the time comes. For now, the best way to help Charlie is to keep your mouth shut."

"I won't tell anyone. I promise," Xander said earnestly.

"Not even your friends." Ethan fixed him with a stern look. "If this gets out, Charlie will be in serious trouble."

Xander put a hand over his heart. "I swear I won't tell a soul. You can count on me."

I hoped it was true. "I trust you."

I checked my phone. "It's after eight. I should get home."

"I'll take that," Ethan said when I stood and picked up my plate.

I nodded toward the boxes on the counter. "You guys keep the rest of it. I'm sure Xander won't mind finishing it off."

Xander grinned. "I don't mind at all."

Ethan closed the lids of the pizza boxes. "After you do your homework. And I'm going to check when I get back."

His brother's face fell, but he didn't argue as he followed us to the door. "Bye, Charlie."

"Bye, Xander."

Outside, Ethan didn't speak until we reached the truck. "I think someone has a little crush on you."

"What?" For a second, my brain misfired thinking I heard something else.

He smiled at me across the hood. "Xander. Try not to break his heart."

"Oh." I laughed, a little flustered. "Don't worry. I'm not much of a heart-breaker."

He opened his door and paused, one hand on the frame. "Sure about that?"

I stood there, caught off guard by his teasing tone. Before I could respond, he got in like it hadn't meant anything.

But it kind of felt like it had.

13

A knock came at my bedroom door while I was brushing my teeth the next morning. Hoping it wasn't my mother again, I walked into the bedroom and called, "Come in." I didn't have to look for Kalyx to know she was hidden.

My father opened the door, phone in hand, and the smile he wore sent a burst of joy through me.

"You found them?"

He stepped inside. "Jeff Miller from our Cambridge branch did. Our connection wasn't great, so he's going to call me back."

"I thought cell service wasn't working there," I said, and then it hit me. "Satellite phone."

His phone rang, and he answered. I rushed over as he put it on speaker and said, "Tom, it's great to hear your voice."

"You too, David," Mr. Bennet replied.

"Hi, Mr. Bennet," I cut in. "I'm so glad you're okay."

"Thank you, Charlie. I can't tell you how happy we are to hear from you."

"How are you, Tom?" my father asked. "How are you and the Barrows holding up?"

Mr. Bennet was quiet for a moment, and I heard the murmur of a lot of voices in the background. When he spoke, his voice was strained but steady. "We're holding on. There's no power, but we have an emergency radio. From what we're hearing, it's bad out there. Your friend Jeff had to leave his car at

Highgate Station and walk a mile to reach us because most streets are blocked."

He released a heavy breath. "The water is still running, but we don't know if it's safe to drink. We're boiling what we can on the barbecue. There are thirteen of us here and food for a few more days if we stretch it." Somewhere in the house, a baby wailed. "We have an infant who needs formula and several prescriptions that need refills."

My throat ached, making it hard to swallow. I couldn't imagine how hard the last few days had been for them. It might be another week before power was restored, and even if they could get to a store, the shelves would probably be bare.

"Whatever you need, tell Jeff, and we'll get it for you," my father said, his face lined with concern. "Anything."

"I will. Thank you, David." Mr. Bennet sounded like a huge burden had been lifted from him.

There was a pause in the conversation, so I asked, "Is Finley with you?"

"I'm here!" she burst out like she had been waiting for her turn. Just hearing her voice made me feel lighter than I'd felt in days.

My father smiled. "How are you doing, Finley?"

"Not good, sir." She let out a melodramatic sigh that drew chuckles on her end. "My backup power supply ran out of juice last night."

He laughed warmly. "Give it to Jeff. I'm sure he won't mind charging it for you."

She gave an excited "Eek" and made rustling sounds. She was doing her happy dance.

"I hate to cut this short, but we can't impose upon Jeff much longer," Mr. Bennet said. "David, we are more grateful than you know."

"There's no need for thanks," my father replied. "We're just glad you're safe."

I felt a stab of disappointment that we couldn't talk longer, but the sooner Jeff left, the sooner he could return with the supplies they needed.

"I'll talk to you soon, Finn," I said.

"Miss you," she called back.

Everyone said their goodbyes, and the call ended. The sudden quiet in my room felt unnatural after the steady hum of voices. I imagined how noisy and crowded it must be at the Barrows' with thirteen people crammed together.

My father rested a hand on my shoulder. "They'll be okay."

"Their house is gone," I said hoarsely. "Do you think they know?"

His expression turned somber. "I think they've heard enough about the flooding to guess. All they can do now is wait for the water to recede. The important thing is they're safe, and we'll make sure they have whatever they need."

Tears burned the backs of my eyes. "Thanks, Dad."

He wrapped his arms around me, and there was a tiny hitch in his breath. I would have missed it if my ear wasn't pressed against his chest.

"That you feel like you have to thank me..." His voice softened. "You never have to thank me for being here for you. You understand that?"

I nodded.

He stepped back. "This project has consumed me, and it's kept me away from home. That's no excuse, but once we complete this round of trials, I'll begin handing off more of it to my team."

I didn't know what to say to that, so I only nodded again. It was the closest he'd ever come to admitting how absent he'd been.

"You need to get ready for class, and I have to get to work," he said. "I hope talking to the Bennets has put your mind at ease."

"It helped a lot," I replied. He had come through not only for me, but for the Bennets and all those other people.

"That's good." He smiled and walked out, leaving me with a warm, unfamiliar sensation I couldn't identify.

I wasn't sure how to feel about it.

I was lying on my bed with Kalyx that night when Taruth's voice popped into my mind. Like the other times he'd contacted me, it jolted me to hear him say my name out of nowhere.

Charlie, hello.

I smiled at the ceiling. "Taruth! I'm so happy to hear from you."

I, too, am happy, he replied.

"I've been dying to tell you about the beacon," I said.

You are dying? he asked, alarmed.

I rushed to reassure him. "No. It's an expression. It means I've been excited to tell you."

I understand. Humans have many ways to express themselves. My people are more direct.

"I'll try to remember that." I used one hand to plump my pillow. "The beacon came down yesterday, just like you said it would. My friend Ethan went with Kalyx and me, and we deactivated it in time."

I am... grateful, he said. *The humans spoke of it. They do not know what it is or what it can do.*

"We'll keep it that way," I promised. "What should I do with the core? I hid it in the woods, but someone could find it eventually."

Give it to Kalyx, he said. *It will be safe in the compartment with the translators.*

"Speaking of translators, how do I remove the one attached to my ear?" I held my breath, hoping he didn't say it was permanent.

My apologies. Press your finger to it until it loosens.

"Thanks." Relieved to have one less thing to worry about, I said, "You ran your system diagnostics. Is your ship fixed?"

I have two repairs to complete, he replied. *It can fly, but the navigation does not function. I cannot go home without it.*

"Oh, no."

The navigation on Enoin's ship can be repaired, he said. *I will transfer it to mine.*

Relief washed over me. "Is that an easy job?"

No. I lack the proper tools. Earth tools are inadequate. He paused. *I must improvise.*

Sutton had some of the most advanced aerospace tech in the world, and it wasn't good enough to work on his ship. Did they honestly believe they could adapt his far superior technology to their ship?

"How long will it take to finish the repairs?" I asked.

My estimation is five solar days.

I felt a spark of hope. "When you're done, can you take your ship and escape?"

Two humans with weapons accompany me when I enter my ship, and I wear restraints, he said. *I am observed closely.*

"How did you escape the night I almost hit you with my scooter?" I couldn't believe I hadn't thought to ask him that until now.

The humans took me to make repairs on my ship and removed my restraints, he replied. *I escaped through an unguarded exit. They increased security when they brought me back.*

I remembered the lights along the river as my father drove me home that night. "Did it take them long to catch you?"

Three hours. I am faster than humans, but my flight suit was not recharged, so it became difficult to breathe.

He had been so close. "I'm sorry you didn't get away."

His next words surprised me. *I am glad I did not escape. I would have found*

Kalyx, but without my ship we are stranded. She is safer with you, and that is all that matters to me.

"I'll keep her safe until we can get you out of there," I promised.

Thank you.

"Taruth, can you show me images of the humans you see there often?" I asked, wishing I'd done it before now.

Images filled my mind of figures in white and yellow hazmat suits, their faces obscured. Then he sent me several images of people on the other side of a large observation window. I wasn't surprised to see my mother among them with Dev Malik, Colonel Mason, and Senator Jonathan Bradley. But seeing her in that group still hit like a punch.

"You can stop." I hadn't seen my father, but he could have been one of the faceless people in biohazard suits. I didn't want to believe he was involved, but the longer Taruth remained imprisoned, the harder that was to ignore.

I rubbed my eyes. "I'm sorry the only humans you've met have treated you so badly. I hope you'll believe me when I say most of us aren't like them."

I believe you. You protect Kalyx, and you have been a friend to me.

"I hope Krurans and humans can be friends someday," I said. "I'll understand if you fly away and never look back."

Human science is in its infancy, but one day you will travel the universe, he replied. *When that day comes, my people will welcome your friendship.*

I wondered if his people would be as welcoming if they knew what mine had done to him. I wouldn't want to befriend people capable of such a thing, and I certainly wouldn't trust them.

"You know what humans look like, but I have no idea what you look like," I said. "Will you show me?"

An image formed of a slender humanoid being with ashen skin. The head was oval with a high forehead and cranial ridges on top of its hairless skull. An intricate pattern of swirls covered its skull, forehead, and cheeks, and its ears were small with pointed tips.

From its large, almond-shaped eyes to its narrow jawline it had delicate androgenous features. The nose and mouth were smaller than a human's, the cheekbones high and sharp, and the neck was long and slender.

The most striking feature was their luminous silver-blue eyes. Intelligent and deep, they made it seem as though the alien was smiling, despite its neutral expression.

This is my friend Enoin. Another image followed, nearly identical, but with more serious eyes and slightly different swirls on their skin. *And this is Nylla. She is my sibling.*

"I can't send you a picture of me. You'll have to wait until we meet in person." My smile faded. "I'm still trying to find you, but it's taking longer than I hoped." I told him about Finley and the storm.

Your planet is not healthy, he said sadly. *I scanned Earth upon my approach. At the current rate of deterioration, it will be uninhabitable by the solar year two thousand, two hundred and five.*

I winced at the candid way he stated our expiration date. "I try not to think of how bad it'll be by the time I'm fifty." *If I'm lucky enough to live that long,* I added silently.

Is the human lifespan fifty solar years? he asked.

"A few decades ago, people used to live eighty and ninety years. Now it's more like seventy," I said. "Who knows what it'll be in thirty years."

What is your current age?

"Eighteen."

A few seconds passed in silence.

"Taruth, are you still there?" I asked.

Yes, he said.

I pushed aside the gloomy thoughts. "That's why they want your technology. They found a planet in Alpha Centauri that can support human life, but we can't get there without a drive like yours."

My ship's drive is not compatible with human technology.

That didn't surprise me. "How fast can your ship fly?"

It does not travel like the Earth ship does. He paused. *I am searching for the correct human words. It folds space-time to create a bridge between two points.*

"Like a wormhole?" I asked in disbelief.

Yes. I believe that is your word for it.

I tried to wrap my head around it. "Do they know your drive creates wormholes?"

No.

"And there is no way they can replicate it?" I asked.

Creating a wormhole requires anti-mass and immense energy. An image appeared of a glowing cylinder ten times the size of the beacon's core. *This is my ship's core. It holds sufficient torlacite to power a scout ship. The core for a transport ship is many times this size.*

"Torlacite?"

Torlacite is a mineral mined on an asteroid near Kruran. He showed me an image of a silver-hued rock with iridescent violet veins running through it. It was followed by an image of a silvery violet powder with the consistency of fine sand. *My analysis found no torlacite on your planet.*

"So, even if they somehow replicated your ship's drive, they can't power it," I said.

That is correct.

I stared at the ceiling. "How long does torlacite last?"

A core does not need to be replaced unless it is damaged, he said.

"Wow." I remembered the beacon's small core. "After I disabled the beacon, Kalyx cloaked me along with herself. That never happened before, and I thought maybe it was the core."

No. A vestra has that ability, but they will only do it for one they trust, he explained. *Most paired vestras trust only their Kruran. Kalyx has learned to trust you.*

I felt a rush of warmth. "What does it mean to be paired?"

He showed me an image of a wide metallic band on his forearm. *This is a tether. It is a neural link between us. It allows me to share thoughts and commands with her.*

"Are all Krurans paired with a vestra?" I asked, eager to learn more.

No. Vestras are difficult to breed. If you wish to pair with one, you must be deemed worthy of it. They are beloved among my people, and it is a great honor to be chosen.

I ran my hand along the metal on Kalyx's flank. "Are the enhancements added when they're young?"

Many vestras do not survive infancy. Those who do, receive neurofusion when they reach adolescence, he said. *Pairing is the only way to ensure their survival.*

Worry crept in. "Is she okay without you? She's so quiet and calm all the time. Is that normal behavior for her?"

I am close enough for our neural connection to remain intact, he assured me. *Paired vestras are calm by nature unless provoked. It is why they are good companions.*

"She's a great companion." I patted her side. "I'm going to miss her so much when you go home."

Taruth was quiet for a moment. *You are good to her. If you were Kruran, you would be worthy of a vestra.*

I pressed a hand to my heart. "I think that's the nicest thing anyone's ever said to me."

The humans have returned. I must end our communication, he said quickly. *I enjoy conversing with you.*

"I like talking to you, too." I didn't want him to go. There was never enough time to ask him everything I wanted to know.

I will try to communicate again soon.

Before I could say goodbye, he was gone.

My thoughts filled with the images of his sibling and friend. Krurans and humans were so different, yet strangely alike. I could imagine them as a highly evolved version of us from far into the future.

There was so much we could learn from them. Why did the government think imprisoning Taruth was better than building an alliance with him? It was incredibly short-sighted to think that venturing out into the universe with technology stolen from an advanced civilization wouldn't come back to bite them.

Maybe I would ask them – after Taruth and Kalyx were safely off the planet.

In fact, maybe the whole world should ask them. It wasn't enough to free Taruth. The only way to protect Finley, Ethan, and me was to go public and let the world know what was happening here.

I sat up. It was time to make a plan.

I set out with Kalyx the following afternoon to get the core from the mine. Knowing someone could stumble across the mine and see evidence of our fire put me on edge. If that someone was Colonel Mason, he might search the shaft and find the core.

The occasional whine of a distant drone only added to my unease. I was winded from running when we reached the shaft, and I quickly retrieved the core.

I opened the compartment with the translators and placed the core inside. My gaze fell on the small black device there, and curiosity got the better of me. I pulled it free from its slot.

The device fit perfectly in my palm, its curved grip molded like it was designed to be held one-handed. My thumb brushed over a slim control interface on the side, and it lit up. It was nothing more than an energy meter with a touch-sensitive slider.

I turned it over. Was it a tool of some kind? I gripped it again and felt a button under my fingers. Pointing the device at the floor, I pressed the button.

A thin laser shot from the tip so fast I almost didn't see it, and a small round hole appeared in the rock.

"Gah!" I fumbled with the device like it was on fire and nearly dropped it. It was an honest-to-God alien ray gun.

I shoved it back into its slot and closed the compartment. "Let's not tell anyone I did that."

Twenty minutes into our return hike, Kalyx abruptly uncloaked and went still. I froze mid-step and scanned the woods, but I couldn't see or hear anything. I trusted her senses far more than mine, so I didn't move as I waited to see what she would do.

She came to me and pressed herself against my side. I placed my hand on her back, and the woods around us took on a faint shimmer. Were we cloaked?

A low whine pierced the air. A drone came into view, flying ten feet above the ground, weaving between trees in a slow, sweeping pattern.

My eyes tracked the drone and locked onto a rectangular device mounted to its underside. I went cold all over. Was that a scanner?

I gripped Kalyx's collar, every muscle in my body taut as the drone got closer with each pass. Her dampener was working, but I had no idea if it was strong enough to mask her signal at this range.

The drone flew directly over my head. I trembled when it seemed to hover above us for a second too long. It felt like the forest was holding its breath with me.

It moved on. I didn't stir again until the whine faded into the distance.

Did they suspect Kalyx was out here? Or did they think something else came down inside the beacon? It felt like the net was tightening around us a little more every day.

"We need to get home," I whispered.

I took a step, but she blocked my path, hackles raised. I froze again, certain the drone was coming back.

The murmur of voices reached my ears, and my spine stiffened when Colonel Mason came into view. A ripple of surprise went through me at the sight of Dev Malik in jeans and a blue softshell jacket. I'd never seen him in anything but a suit. They were trailed by the bodyguard I'd seen at the party.

Dev and Mason were speaking in low voices, unintelligible until they were only fifteen feet away.

"General Stewart is concerned we still don't know what it is," Mason said. "The longer it stays in the ravine, the greater the risk."

Dev gave him an annoyed look. "Our scientists have been studying it since it landed, but there's only so much we can do without getting it into the lab."

Mason's voice sharpened. "If it's a weapon, it could destroy everything we've built. The Pentagon wants to move it to the secure site in Wyoming."

"Wyoming?" Dev stopped walking, forcing Mason to stop as well. "This object could be critical to the project. We need it here so we can study it."

"The risk outweighs the reward," Mason said. "There are nearly a million people within a hundred miles. If it's a weapon, the consequences could be catastrophic."

Dev folded his arms. "How long do we have?"

"Five days, and you're lucky General Stewart got you that much time." Mason scanned the area. I shivered when his eyes passed right over me.

"I understand," Dev replied stiffly. "Any leads on who was at the ravine?"

I swallowed a gasp. They knew? How?

Mason's jaw tensed. "We're working on it, but there's nothing identifiable about it."

"You haven't sent it to the FBI?" Dev asked.

"The second they get wind of it, we'll have them and the NSA breathing down our necks again," Mason said. "It's all they need to come in and take control."

I swallowed dryly. What did they have? I wracked my brain trying to think of something Ethan or I might have dropped?

"It could have been left there a week ago," Dev said.

Mason shook his head. "Forensics showed no sign of weathering. It rained that afternoon, which means someone dropped it after the rain stopped."

Dev didn't look convinced. "If someone was there when the sphere landed, it would be all over the internet."

"Not if it's the same person hiding the creature."

"How would they know to be at the ravine when the sphere came down?" Dev pressed.

"If I was allowed to conduct a thorough investigation, we'd get the answer to that," Mason said bitterly.

Dev frowned. "You don't have a shred of evidence she's involved. You searched her house and found nothing."

I braced a hand against a tree. They were talking about me.

"She's in this up to her ears," Mason argued. "She showed up at the store at the same time we tracked it there."

"She was with her parents at the country club while you were out following the signal." Dev's exasperated tone said this wasn't their first argument about it. "Then she went to see her boyfriend. You checked him out. He's clean with an exemplary service record."

"You don't want her to be involved because of Evelyn and David," Mason accused. "You're worried about upsetting them."

"Of course, I don't want to upset them. Where would this project be without them? Evelyn gave us some leeway, but she doesn't think the girl is involved." Dev pulled a phone from his pocket and glanced at it. "If you had solid evidence against Charlotte, I'd back you up, but you have nothing."

They resumed walking, and Dev said, "Do you honestly think a teenage girl could pull off this under our noses?"

"I think you're underestimating her," Mason said through gritted teeth.

Dev chuckled. "Maybe you're right. She is Evelyn and David's daughter."

Mason muttered something I couldn't make out.

I wanted to follow them, but it was too risky. Kalyx's cloak wouldn't hide my footsteps, and the drone might still be nearby.

Kalyx's hackles lowered, and she looked up at me as if to say *the coast is clear.*

I spent the rest of the hike obsessing over what they could have found at the ravine. Except for the notebook, everything else had been in my backpack, which had been zipped up the whole time we were at the beacon. Had Ethan lost something?

At home, I dumped my backpack contents onto my bed. Most of the items I kept in the pack were generic hiking supplies: emergency blanket, first aid kit, fire-making kit, water bottle and filter, gloves, headlamp, multi-tool, and protein bar. Nothing was missing.

I repacked it and tossed it into the closet. I turned to leave the closet and stopped. I glanced back at the pack, frowning, and picked it up again.

My padlock charm was gone.

I sat heavily on the bed. It was just a cheap little charm, the kind you could buy anywhere, and no one would know it was mine. I'd never shown it to my parents, and I doubted either of them would notice something so trivial. But still...

I rubbed the back of my neck. I had to tell Ethan. There was a chance, however small, that they might trace the charm back to me.

He didn't have Finley's encryption app, so I had to be careful what I said over the phone. I sent a simple text. **Can we talk?**

It was an hour before he replied. **In Albany. Tomorrow?**

See you then. I didn't want to wait until tomorrow, but his life didn't revolve around mine. It wasn't fair to expect him to be available whenever I needed him.

The next morning, Kalyx and I were waiting outside when Ethan pulled up to my house in a plain white cargo van. Curiosity piqued, I slid the side door open for her and saw neatly stacked boxes in the back.

"You don't have a weekend job as a drug runner, do you?" I joked as I climbed into the passenger seat. "My mother will be pissed if I can't get into an Ivy League school."

He chuckled and backed out of the driveway. "We're returning parts to the distributor."

"That was going to be my second guess." I buckled my seat belt. "I didn't know you had a van."

"I don't. I borrowed it." He glanced over his shoulder at Kalyx, who had uncloaked and was stretched out behind our seats. "But if I *was* a drug runner, she'd be the perfect guard dog... cat."

I laughed. "I'll keep that in mind if the whole college thing doesn't pan out."

Once we were out of my neighborhood, he gave me a questioning look. "So, what's the thing you couldn't say over the phone?"

I filled him in on everything. "There's nothing special about the charm that could lead back to me, but I had to warn you about it. I can't believe I was so careless."

"It's not your fault," he said. "You know what they say. There's no such thing as a perfect crime."

I let out a heavy sigh. "It's my fault Mason looked into your background."

He shook his head. "I figured he had when he called me by my rank. There's nothing for them to find."

"If they do figure out I was at the ravine, I'm going to tell them I was alone." Ethan opened his mouth to argue, but I cut him off. "I'll be fine. You have Xander to think about. Besides, implicating you doesn't help anyone."

"You told me your parents might let them disappear you for a while," he said stiffly.

"I said they might let that happen, but they won't let anyone hurt me. And I'm working on an insurance policy." I pulled a data tag from my pocket. "I made a video of Kalyx the day she came to my house. Last night, I made another one about her and Taruth, and what Sutton and the military are doing. I'm going to release it after Kalyx and Taruth are safe. It's the only way to protect us."

I held the data tag out to him. "I sent Finley a copy, and I want you to have one, too. If anything happens to me before I find Taruth, one of you can make it public."

He took the tag and put it in his pocket. "You'll go public – even if it means exposing your parents?"

I clasped my hands on my lap. "There's no way to keep them out of it. Even if I tried, everyone knows they head up the drive project at Sutton."

I'd done a lot of soul-searching last night. I loved my parents, but they were just as complicit as Sutton and the government. I still didn't know if my father was actively or passively involved, but he did know what they were doing. My mother was a different story. She would never stand back and let someone else take the lead on this.

Ethan turned onto the road that led to the small industrial park outside town. This area used to be all farmland before everyone switched to hydroponics and aeroponics. You could still find small hobby farms, but even those were slowly disappearing.

A mile or so in, the open countryside gave way to squat buildings with metal siding. Cargo vans and semis were scattered around the lot, some backed up to loading docks. Otherwise, the place was quiet.

We pulled up to a building with a sign that read ELITE CIRCUIT SUPPLY, and he backed into a space near the dock. He opened the door, letting in the hum of machinery and the low rumble of highway traffic.

I looked at the dark gray sky. "Looks like rain."

He got out. "You can stay here. This won't take long."

He approached a man on the loading ramp. They spoke briefly and shook hands. Another man joined them, and they walked to the back of the van.

"Kalyx, hide," I said before they reached us.

Ethan opened the rear doors, and they began to unload the boxes and place them on a platform cart. When the first two rows were gone, he climbed in and pushed the rest forward, keeping the other men away from Kalyx. Once they were done, Ethan closed the doors, and the three men disappeared into the building.

Raindrops began to patter against the windshield, and by the time Ethan returned, it was a steady downpour. He jumped in, shaking off water.

"That's done." He started the engine and turned on the wipers. "I'm glad we got it unloaded before this hit."

"Yeah."

"How long do you think it'll take Sutton to realize Taruth's drive won't work for their ship?" he asked as we left the industrial park.

"Not before I get Taruth out of there," I said. "Maybe I'll tell them after Taruth and Kalyx are safe."

He grew serious. "You know there's going to be a media frenzy when this goes public. Are you prepared for that?"

"I don't think anyone can prepare for something like that." I liked my anonymity, and the idea of the world prying into my life made me want to fly away with Taruth and Kalyx. "If I could do it anonymously, I would, but that won't protect us."

"And your parents? This could destroy your relationship with them."

Pain pricked my chest. My mother and I barely had a relationship now, and I hadn't expected to see much of her after I left for college. But my father... The last few days had given me hope we could work things out, but I didn't see that happening once everything went public.

I gave a hollow laugh. "There goes my spot on the colony ship."

"You don't sound too broken up about it," he said with a small smile.

"I don't think there will be a colony ship. Not in our lifetime." I thought about my last conversation with Taruth. "Taruth said one day, humans will travel the universe, but he wasn't referring to the near future."

"What if they did figure it out, and they built their colony ship?" he said. "You wouldn't want to go?"

Finley and I had talked about this many times. "Of course, I'd want to see another planet. Who wouldn't?"

"But?"

"I wouldn't go without Finley." I studied his profile. "Would you go?"

"Yeah. But people like me will never be chosen for a colony ship." His voice wasn't bitter – just matter-of-fact. I couldn't disagree with him because he was right.

"You did get to hang out with an alien," I said lightly. "How many people can say that?"

"True." He glanced at Kalyx in the mirror. "I'm looking at her, and I still don't believe it."

I laughed. "When we spring Taruth from his prison, you'll get to talk to an alien." I hesitated. "I meant Finley and I will spring him. I don't expect you to help with that."

"Why not?" he asked.

"Well... for one it's going to be –"

"Dangerous?" He raised an eyebrow. I couldn't tell if he was amused or insulted.

I rushed to explain. "I don't think it's too dangerous for you, just that it's a big risk to take for someone you barely know."

"You let me decide what's too risky for me," he said. "And I'd say I've gotten to know you pretty well in the last week. I have a feeling I already know you better than most people do."

I stared at the rain running down my window. "The last two weeks have been insane. You don't know what I'm normally like."

"You mean when you're running into people at the supermarket?" he teased.

I rolled my eyes. "You were a jerk that day. You've mellowed since, so I assume you took my advice and switched to decaf."

His laugh was low and warm. And just like that, the memory of his kiss hit me. I looked away before he saw my cheeks flush.

"You said one reason is the danger. What's the other?" he asked.

"Your family." I was grateful for a subject change. "You've got Xander to think about. And the store."

His humor fled. "Do you want to know why I returned those parts today? The owner agreed to refund us the full amount instead of the fifty cents on the dollar other retailers are offering."

I frowned. "Why?"

"The store is closing." He gripped the wheel. "I've been making deals with other retailers to buy up our stock. We'll have a clearance sale to sell off the rest."

"You're closing?" I stared at his rigid profile. "Has... this been in the works for long?"

"About a month." His voice was quiet, almost flat. "My mother died of a brain aneurysm. One minute she was fine, and the next..." He exhaled. "I thought my father was holding it together. He even told me to go back to my unit."

I stayed silent, letting him talk.

"But he wasn't," Ethan went on. "He started drinking and neglecting Xander and the store. I didn't know how bad it was until I came home in June. The store's been losing money for over a year. I tried to turn it around, but family-owned stores like ours can't compete anymore. To be honest, we should have closed it a few years ago."

"I'm sorry."

It didn't feel adequate, but it was all I could think of to say. He'd been forced to leave the marines because of an injury, only to come home to this. It was no wonder he was so angry when I met him. I would be, too, in his place.

He gave a stiff nod. "It's why I've been working so many hours, doing inventory, dealing with the creditors, and working on the books. I went to Albany yesterday to meet with the building owner. We've known him a long time, and he agreed to let us out of the lease early."

"When will you close?" I asked quietly.

"End of next month." He sighed. "I had no idea how much is involved in closing a business. I've made deals to sell off the bulk of the inventory and equipment. We should make enough to pay off the creditors."

I could feel the tension radiating from him. I wished there was something I could do for him.

"I've never worked in retail, but I can help with the clearance sale," I offered. "If I haven't been declared a threat to national security by then."

He laughed. "From anyone else, I'd take that as a joke. If you aren't locked up or on the run, I'll take you up on your offer."

I smiled back. "Have you decided what you'll do after the store is closed?"

"I've been talking to a few prospective employers." He smirked. "Would you believe I was offered a security job at Sutton three weeks ago?"

"No way. Seriously?"

He nodded. "They pay well with good benefits, but I can make more at a private security firm. They always have positions for people with my training."

"Is there a private security firm in Hudson Ridge?" I thought of Dev's bodyguard.

"No. There are a few in Albany that I spoke to when I came home. That was before I learned the store was in trouble." He gave a small shrug. "They want to meet with me once I'm free. I can make enough there to take care of Xander and Dad."

"That's... great." The pang of disappointment surprised me. I hadn't known him long, but I'd gotten used to him being here.

We dropped off the van and picked up his truck. From there, it was only ten minutes to my house.

We had barely gone a mile when flashing blue lights appeared in the side mirror. It wasn't until Ethan swore softly that I realized we were being pulled over. He slowed and eased onto the shoulder.

The police SUV stopped behind us, and two uniformed officers got out. One headed for Ethan's window, and the other moved toward the back of the truck.

Something about the measured way they moved made the hairs on my arms stand up. I twisted in my seat to check the back.

Kalyx.

14

"I'll handle this," Ethan said as he rolled down his window. Rain swept in with a blast of cold air.

"Everything okay, Officer?" he asked in a steady voice.

The policeman adjusted his hat against the rain. His nameplate said TAYLOR. "Did you know you made an illegal turn at the light?"

Ethan rested his hands on the wheel. "Did I?"

"Yes. There's no right turn on that red light," Officer Taylor said. There was an edge in his voice as if he was expecting an argument.

"I don't know how I could have missed that," Ethan replied easily.

Taylor pulled out a handheld citation unit. "I'll need to see your license and registration."

Ethan removed the registration card from the back of the visor and handed it over along with his license.

I looked for the second officer. He stood beside the tailgate, his eyes fixed on the blue tarp covering several boxes – and Kalyx. She was cloaked and tucked behind the boxes, but my heart thumped when the man laid his hand on the tailgate.

Casually, his other hand reached for the tarp.

"Ethan!" I hissed.

His eyes went to the rearview mirror, and he tensed. "Officer Taylor, what is your partner doing back there?"

Taylor didn't look up from the scanner. "He's just taking a look."

"Looking for what?" Ethan's voice sharpened.

The second officer withdrew his hand, but he didn't move away from the truck.

Taylor lifted his head, rain dripping off the brim of his hat. "Is there a reason you don't want him to look?"

Ethan held his stare. "Is there a reason you want to? A right-turn violation isn't cause for a vehicle search."

Taylor's tone changed from measured to slightly aggressive. "I know the law, Mr. Cole."

"Go ahead and look," Ethan said. It was the only way to keep this from escalating.

I held my breath as the other policeman lifted a corner of the tarp. His face was hidden from me as he said something to Officer Talyor.

"What's with all the old security drones?" Taylor asked.

"We sell them for parts in my store," Ethan said in a controlled voice. "You're welcome to look, but please keep them covered from the rain."

Taylor exchanged a look with his partner, who dropped the tarp.

"That won't be necessary." Officer Taylor pressed a button on his device and handed Ethan his license and registration. "I'm going to let you off with a warning this time. Drive safely, Mr. Cole."

"Thank you." Ethan rolled up his window as the two policemen walked back to their SUV.

"No way that was a random stop," I said as we pulled back onto the road. "We didn't run a red light."

Ethan kept his eyes on the road. "Would Colonel Mason involve the local police? Seems like the fewer people who know about it the better."

"I don't know." I sank back into my seat. "He or Sutton could have a few officers on their payroll."

"That makes more sense," Ethan said. "This means Mason could be watching us. We'll need to be more careful."

"Do you think they were following us or on the lookout for your truck?" I asked.

He thought about it. "We would have noticed them following us to the warehouse, and they would have been more likely to pull over the van. If they're working with Mason, they were probably on the lookout for my truck."

I nervously checked the mirror. "I was sure they'd notice there was an extra lump under the tarp."

"Luckily, they weren't that observant." He chuckled dryly. "I haven't seen this much action since the marines."

I smiled despite myself. "You told me to stop apologizing, so all I'll say is at least you'll never be bored around me."

This earned another laugh from him, and I liked the sound of it. He'd laughed and opened up to me more today than in all our other times together combined.

By the time we pulled into my driveway, the rain had slowed to a drizzle. We got out, and I walked around to his side. He pulled back a corner of the tarp as if he was checking something. Kalyx jumped soundlessly from the truck and pressed against my leg.

Ethan tugged the tarp back in place and turned to me with a crooked smile. "Thanks for another interesting day."

"Thanks for letting me bring her along. I hate leaving her alone." I frowned. "But if that wasn't a traffic stop, maybe it's not safe to take her out anymore."

His smile faded. "You need to assume someone is watching whenever you leave the house."

"I know." I resisted the urge to look around for spying eyes.

He reached for his door and paused. "If someone is watching, we should keep up the act."

"The... dating thing?" I asked awkwardly.

"Yes." His eyes searched mine as he stepped toward me.

I gave a small nod, and he tugged me gently into his arms. His head dipped, his mouth hovering close enough for his warm breath to caress my lips.

The air around us felt charged with electricity as I remembered the kiss in his truck. Was it just me, or did he feel it, too?

My only thought was *will he or won't he.* I didn't know what I wanted more – to kiss him, or to not risk the friendship growing between us. With everything else in my life, this was the *last* thing I needed to complicate.

I felt an odd mix of disappointment and relief when he lifted his head. Our eyes met, and for a second, something passed between us.

He stepped back, and when he looked at me again it was gone, making me think I must have imagined it.

"I should get back to the store." He smiled and raised a hand to swipe the water from his hair. I hadn't even realized it was raining again.

I nodded. "I meant what I said earlier. If you want help with the clearance sale or anything, let me know."

"I'll hold you to that." He slid behind the wheel and lowered the window. "And I meant what I said. Be careful."

"I will." I gave him a little wave and turned toward the house.

I thought about the traffic stop as I walked to the door. Had it been deliberate, or was paranoia getting the better of me?

The hair on the nape of my neck prickled. I imagined someone watching me at this very second. Kalyx pressed against my leg as if she sensed my unease.

Fumbling with my keys, I unlocked the door and we hurried inside.

My phone rang as I shut off the shower. I grabbed a towel and wrapped it around me as I ran into the bedroom. I stubbed my toe on the desk chair, but I forgot the pain the instant I saw the name on the screen.

I swiped to answer, and for a moment, the screen went dark. Then Finley's blurry, pixelated image appeared.

"Finley!" I cried. "God, I missed your face."

Four days had passed since Dad and I had talked to Finley and her father. Jeff Miller had gone twice to bring supplies for everyone in the Barrow house, but all he could tell us was that the Bennets were okay.

The news out of London wasn't good. The floodwaters had started to recede, revealing the full extent of the destruction, and finally allowing emergency crews into the hardest-hit areas. The death toll had already reached two thousand, and they expected it to double in the coming weeks.

They had begun restoring power to parts of London, but every time I tried to call or text Finley, it wouldn't go through.

Her image froze mid-smile, and her words broke up. "... happy to... connection... bad."

I turned up the volume. "You're cutting out."

The video stuttered, and her face reappeared only to go again. The next time she appeared, she was walking. Finally, it stabilized.

"Can you hear me now?" Her voice lagged a little behind the video, but I could make out her words.

"Yes."

"Oh, good. We got power and Wi-Fi back today, but it's going in and out." She leaned closer. "Are you naked?"

I laughed and showed her the towel. "I literally ran from the shower to answer the phone."

"What I wouldn't give for a hot shower." She groaned, and the image froze mid-grimace. When it came back, she was smiling, but her face was pinched, and her eyes lacked their usual sparkle. "I'm so happy to see you."

"Me too." I dropped into the desk chair. "I've been so worried. If I hadn't talked to you that one time, I would have gone out of my mind."

"Thanks for getting your dad to send Mr. Miller. When he showed up, I knew you were behind it. He's been a lifesaver. He even brought dog food for Milo." She gasped and disappeared from the frame. There was a hiss, followed by a few wheezy, ragged breaths.

"Finn?" I called.

She reappeared, held up a finger, and took a breath, "Inhaler."

Alarm shot through me. "That didn't sound good. Are you okay?"

"Yes." She smiled wanly. "You know how cold and damp it gets here in October. Mr. Miller brought me plenty of albuterol and a nebulizer. Mum's been hovering over me, making sure I'm bundled up and drinking lots of hot soup and tea."

She tried to downplay it, but I looked closer, and I didn't like what I saw. There were shadows under her eyes, and her face seemed thinner. London air wasn't great in the best of times, but most buildings had filtration systems. Those didn't work without power.

"I've been watching the news," I said. "I'm so glad you went to the Barrows that night."

She nodded, and her bottom lip quivered. "It's bad here, Charlie. The grocery stores are empty, and people are breaking into restaurants and houses for food. One of the neighbors told us his son's school cafeteria was looted, and there are people sleeping in the school."

I gasped. "In Highgate?"

"It's happening everywhere. The emergency shelters are full. People are going wherever it's not flooded, but there's nowhere for them to stay and no food. They're desperate, and some of them..." Her fingers twisted the front of her sweater. "Someone broke into the house at the end of the street. They attacked the old couple who lives there and stole all their food."

I covered my mouth. "Are they okay?"

"They have some bruises but nothing serious."

"What about the police?" I asked.

"They're overwhelmed, and they don't have anyone to send out. Mr. Barrow and some neighbors started a watch group, but they're saying it's only going to get worse." She swallowed. "The radio said people are getting sick with cholera and hepatitis from the water. The Wembley Stadium shelter has a tuberculosis outbreak."

A knot formed in my stomach. Things were even worse than the news had reported.

"The Barrows are leaving," she whispered. "Mrs. Barrow was able to reach her brother in Edinburgh this morning. They're going to stay with him as soon as the road to the A1 is clear."

"What about you and your parents?" I asked. "Where will you go?"

"I don't know." Her voice cracked. "There's nowhere in London. Mum and Dad spent hours today calling hotels as far as Birmingham. Every place is booked."

She looked so alone and scared, I wanted to reach through the phone and hug her. I had never felt so helpless.

Tears pooled in her eyes and spilled over. She put a hand over her face and let out a sob I felt in my own chest.

"It's all gone," she choked out.

"What's gone?"

"Our house – our whole street." Her voice was flat with shock. "There's nothing left."

She cried for a few minutes and dropped her hand to look at me with hollow eyes. "We're homeless. I can't believe this is happening."

"We'll figure something out." I fought back my own tears. She needed me to be strong for her. "My mom and dad have lots of connections. I'll talk to them."

Hope sparked in her eyes. "Do you think they'll help?"

"Yes," I said without hesitation. My father would for sure. And despite everything, I didn't believe my mom would turn her back on them.

Finley gave me a watery smile. The screen flickered, froze, and then went black.

I tried calling her back, but it wouldn't go through. Their Wi-Fi must have gone out again.

I called my father and got his voice mail. I didn't bother leaving a message because it might take hours for him to return my call, and this couldn't wait.

My mother was in DC again, and she never answered her phone when she was in meetings. I tried her anyway and got her voice mail.

Thirty minutes later, I rode up to the Sutton gate on my scooter. I gave the guard my name and told him I was there to see my father.

He shook his head. "Sorry, Miss, no one enters without an escort."

"This is an emergency." I pulled off my helmet. "I need to speak to my father."

"Call him," he replied, unmoved.

I glared at him. "Don't you think I tried that already? He isn't answering his phone."

He stared back impassively. "Then he's probably down in the lab. Nothing I can do about that."

We were interrupted by the low purr of an engine. I looked over my shoulder as a silver Audi pulled up beside me. Behind the wheel sat Dev Malik, who looked surprised to see me.

"Charlotte, what brings you here?"

I let my frustration show. "It's urgent that I see my dad, but I can't go in without an escort."

He smiled. "Leave your scooter here. I'll take you to him."

"Thank you." I put aside the fact that he was the enemy. If anyone could find my father, it was him.

I parked my scooter beside the guard shack and climbed into the car. Behind us idled a black SUV with tinted windows. I assumed it was Dev's bodyguard.

"I think the last time you were here was for a tour of the facility with your parents," Dev said as we waited for the gate to open.

"No, I was here three weeks ago," I said lightly. "I believe it was the night you hosted a party for Senator Bradley."

He tapped the steering wheel with his thumb. "That's right. I heard about the incident with our security. I apologize for that."

I smiled. "It was just a misunderstanding. You can bet I don't ride my scooter on that road at night anymore."

He laughed. "I imagine not."

"I guess it could have been worse," I said. "Colonel Mason could have been questioning me instead of Lydia Warren."

"Colonel Mason?" Dev's expression didn't change, but there was a note of suspicion in his voice.

"I've run into him a few times, and he's kind of... intense."

Dev nodded. "Ah, yes, Colonel Mason takes his job quite seriously. You ran into him, you say?"

I had to hand it to Dev. He was very smooth. I could see why he was the CEO of Sutton's most important division.

"I literally ran into him in the woods one day, and he scared the hell out of me," I said. "And he came to our house looking for someone on the run from the police. Dad said he was just doing his job, but would it kill the guy to smile a little?"

Dev laughed again. "Now that you mention it, I don't think I've seen him smile either."

He parked in a reserved spot near the main entrance. I saw my father's Mercedes in another reserved parking spot.

At the security desk, I was signed in and was handed a visitor badge. In the elevator, Dev pressed the button for the top floor. A small screen lit up, and he tapped his ID card against it. The car began to rise.

Somewhere in this building, Taruth was being held prisoner. The knowledge sat heavily on my chest. He was so close, and I could do nothing to help him.

The elevator doors opened to a small vestibule with a door on either side. The door on the left read PROPULSION SYSTEMS, and the one on the right read NUCLEAR RESEARCH. Both doors had a second sign that read AUTHORIZED PERSONNEL ONLY.

Dev used his card and entered a password on the security panel next to the door on the right. It opened to a corridor with a thick glass wall on our left overlooking a massive three-story lab. Metal beams crisscrossed the ceiling above a maze of workstations, monitoring stations, and high-tech machinery. At one end was a large containment unit with radiation hazard signs on the walls. Near it, a set of mechanical arms moved a large metal cylinder. People in white coats moved about the lab or sat alone or in groups at computer work stations.

At the end of the corridor was the door to the lab. The right side was lined with doors. My father's office was the last one.

Dev knocked. When there was no answer, he used his ID card to unlock the door. "Your father is most likely in his lab. I'll find him for you."

"Thank you," I said gratefully.

He left, and I took in my surroundings. The last time I'd been here, my father hadn't moved in yet.

It was a spacious office with a large window and furnished with a black desk, two chairs, a bookcase, and a couch. Above the couch hung his framed degrees, awards, and scientific journal covers bearing his image. Another wall had whiteboards and glass panels covered in complex equations. There was also a coffee station with a small fridge and another door, which led to a private bathroom.

On his desk were two large monitors, a keyboard, and a framed photo of me taken three years ago when I'd placed first at my old school's science fair.

I sat on the couch. It was comfortable, and there was a pillow and a folded blanket on one end. This must be where he slept on the nights he stayed at work. I couldn't imagine being so consumed by work that I wouldn't drive ten minutes to sleep in my own bed.

The door opened, and my father rushed in, his face wreathed in worry. "Charlie, what's wrong? Dev said it was urgent."

I stood. "It's Finley."

He came over to me. "Did something happen to her?"

"No, but it's really bad there." He sat, and I told him about my call with her. "They're homeless, Dad. There has to be something you can do."

He dragged a hand through his hair. "Jeff's kept me updated, but I admit I wasn't thinking past their immediate needs. It'll take months just to clean up the damage, let alone rebuild."

"You and Mom know people. Can you use your connections to help them get U.S. visas?" I asked.

He let out a slow breath, his expression softening. "U.S. immigration is very complicated. Even with contacts, it takes months to file the applications and personal documentation and go through background checks."

I shook my head. "They've already done all that. They've been on the immigration waiting list since last year."

That gave him pause. His brow furrowed in thought, and a spark of hope flickered in my chest.

"I can make some calls," he said. I smiled, but he held up a hand. "I can't make any promises."

"I know." It wasn't the answer I wanted, but it was something.

He reached into his pocket. "I left my phone in the lab. Stay here, and I'll be back as soon as I can."

"Is it okay if I go out to the hallway to look at the lab?" I asked.

"Of course."

I followed him out of the office, and he overrode the auto-lock on the door so I didn't get locked out.

Even inside this secure part of the building, you needed a card to go anywhere.

I stood at the glass wall and scanned the lab until I spotted my father entering a smaller glass-walled room with a drafting table and a paper-strewn desk. He picked up his phone and started dialing.

The door at the far end of the hallway swung open, and I glanced over as Lydia Warren stepped through. The head of security came up short when she saw me.

Her heels clicked sharply as she walked toward me. "How did you get in here?"

"I jumped an employee in the parking lot and stole his ID card." Her eyes narrowed, and I shrugged. "It was surprisingly easy. You really should talk to people about being distracted by their phones."

"Don't get smart with me." She stopped a few feet away. "What are you doing here?"

I met her hard gaze. "Why? Has there been another break-in you want to interrogate me about?"

Her mouth flattened.

"I'm visiting my father." I pointed at him in the office talking on the phone.

"This is a highly restricted area and no place to be wandering around," she said.

"I can't go beyond this hallway, so I'd hardly call it wandering. He said I could watch the lab from here while I wait for him."

That seemed to appease her, and she disappeared through the door to the lab. I kept my eye on the lab floor for a few minutes, but she didn't reappear.

After ten minutes of watching my father on the phone, I went back into his office and sat on the couch to read on my phone. An hour passed, and I told myself it was a good thing. If he couldn't do anything to help, he'd be back by now.

At some point, I dozed off. I woke to him gently shaking my shoulder. I couldn't tell if his smile was because he had good news or he was trying to soften the bad news.

He sat on the couch. "Your mom is going to talk to Senator Bradley about reaching out to someone in the State Department."

"Mom?" I asked surprised.

"I caught her between meetings. She said it'll likely be a day or two before he can get back to her." He exhaled. "There's a lot of red tape to get through, so it could take a while."

My heart sank.

"I do have some good news," he said. "Jeff knows of a flat in Cambridge the Bennets can use. It's only one bedroom, but it's furnished and available for the next two months."

"Really?" At his nod, I lunged forward and hugged him. The flat was only a short-term solution, but it would get Finley and her parents out of danger and give them time to figure out what to do next.

He patted my back. "Jeff is calling them to let them know about the flat."

"Thanks, Dad."

"I promise we'll do what we can," he said. "But it's too soon to know how this will go."

I pulled back. "You're saying I shouldn't tell Finley about the visa thing until you know more."

"Yes." He glanced at his phone and stood. "I have a conference call in ten minutes, and you need to get to school. Come on. I'll take you to your scooter."

We left his office. Lydia Warren was nowhere in sight, but we passed

Colonel Mason in a Jeep as we drove to the gate. I pretended not to see him, but I felt his eyes on me.

I was in much higher spirits as I rode home. Getting a visa wasn't easy, especially now, but if anyone could make it happen, it was my parents. My father had come through twice for the Bennets.

I had to believe he would again.

"Guess what I just did." Finley's face was tired and a little pale, but she wore a smile I hadn't seen since the night before the storm. "I had my first hot shower in a week... and it was amazing. I didn't want to get out."

Grinning, I plumped the pillows behind my back. "Did you leave any hot water for your mom and dad?"

"Actually, I told them to go first because I'm a wonderful daughter." She crossed the room and sat on the couch, giving me a fleeting glimpse of the bright, tidy flat they'd moved into that morning. A blanket was draped over the back of the couch, and she pulled it down to cover her legs.

"How's the flat?" I asked.

"It's small, but cozy. And safe." She cleared her throat. "It's perfect. Your dad and Jeff are miracle workers."

"Dad said the flat was all Jeff's doing."

Her phone wobbled as a white furry face filled the screen. Milo smiled adorably and settled on her lap. She scratched his head. "Milo likes it here, too."

I noticed how quiet it was there. "Where are your mom and dad?"

"They went to pick up a few things. I think they needed to get out after being cooped up for so long." Her smile wavered. "This has been so hard on them. They tried to hide it, but I could see how worried they were about me."

"You sound better than the last time we talked," I said.

She nodded. "Getting the heat back helped a lot. I don't need the nebulizer anymore, and I only used the inhaler twice today."

"That's great!"

"Yes." Her eyes shimmered with tears. I started to ask what was wrong, but she said, "I'm okay. I just can't believe we're here. When Jeff called to tell us about the flat, Mum cried, and she never cries. It's been so..."

"I know," I said softly when she couldn't finish.

She blinked the tears away. "You know what's weird? It's so quiet here. Even after the storm, there were sirens and helicopters in London. Plus, sharing a house with twelve people and one of them was a baby."

"I bet." I gave her a sympathetic smile. "Were they all still there when you left?"

"Only the Barrows. They were leaving as soon as they packed up photos and other things they didn't want to leave behind." She let out a slow breath. "At least, that's one thing we don't need to worry about. All our photos and important documents are backed up online. Everything else is just stuff that can be replaced."

My heart ached for her. "I'm so sorry about your house, Finn."

She swallowed hard. "It could have been a lot worse. We're safe and together, and that's all that matters. And we've got this flat for two months, so we don't have to worry about a place to stay for now."

I wanted so badly to tell her my parents were trying to get them visas. But I couldn't say anything until we knew it was even a possibility. Neither of them had heard back from Senator Bradley yet.

"What about school?" I asked.

"It's going to be closed for a while, so we're switching to virtual classes." She sighed. "I don't know what Mum and Dad will do about work. She took a leave from the hospital because there's no telling when we'll get back to London. Dad had to take a leave from the college, too."

I stared at her in dismay. "I didn't think about that. Will you be okay?"

"Yes." She smiled. "And if we aren't, I have a few apps I could sell."

"Not the encryption app."

She laughed. "Never that one."

"Whew." I pretended to wipe my brow. "Good thing you keep everything backed up, too. I hate that you lost your computers."

She gave me an *are you kidding* look. "You don't seriously think I left those behind."

"What was I thinking?" I said, laughing.

Kalyx walked into my room and leaped onto the bed. When it was only the two of us here, I let her have the run of the house.

"You haven't mentioned Taruth," Finley said. "Have you talked to him again? I feel like we have so much to catch up on."

"You have no idea." I spent the next thirty minutes bringing her up to speed on everything that had happened in the last week. I was saving Ethan's kiss for last, but I didn't get the chance to bring it up.

"Holy crap!" Finley's eyes went wide. "He's logged in. He's on the network."

I sat up straight. "Are you serious?"

"I just got a notification." She turned her phone toward her laptop sitting on the coffee table. "This is the first time in over a week I've been able to monitor it."

"What do we do now?"

She carried the laptop to the table and propped up her phone to face the screen. "Can you see?"

"Yes."

Her fingers flew across the keyboard. A terminal window appeared, lines of code streaming too fast for me to follow. A minute later, the screen filled with fast-scrolling text, which I recognized as a list of directories.

It stopped, and she let out a little whoop. "We're in!"

"We're in the network?" I asked.

"Not just the network. We're inside the hidden segment." She cracked her knuckles. "Okay, Sutton. Let's see what secrets you're hiding."

She navigated through the directories, expanding each one to reveal dozens of subfolders, labeled with a combination of letters and numbers. "Well played," she said as she opened the first one. It contained more folders along with documents, spreadsheets, text files, images, and videos.

"There has to be hundreds of files," I said. "Can you open one of the images?"

She did. It was a schematic, but for what I couldn't tell. She tried a text file next, and we saw what looked like computer log entries.

She tapped the edge of the keyboard. "This might take a while."

"How long do we have?" I asked.

"Only as long as he's logged in." She moved on to the next folder. "I'm piggybacked on his session, so once he's out, so am I."

I chewed on a nail. "Let's hope he's a workaholic like my parents."

The speed with which she navigated the folders made my head spin. Finding nothing of special interest, she returned to the top level and chose another directory to drill down into. This went on for almost ten minutes until she asked, "What does *Astravir* mean?"

"No idea."

She typed the command to open the folder and got a password prompt. "Hello."

I sat up straighter. This folder had to be important for them to password-protect it. "Can you get past that?"

"Yes, but it's going to take time." She began to murmur to herself as she always did when deep in thought.

I knew better than to try to talk to her when she was like this. I went to my laptop and did a search for *Astravir*. I learned it was the name of a drug, a tech company, and dozens of other things around the world.

Breaking the word into two smaller ones, I searched for *Astra* and discovered it was the Latin word for stars. I found a Latin dictionary website and typed in *vir*.

I was suddenly breathless. *Man.*

Stars plus man.

Starman.

15

I snatched up my phone. "Finn."

There was no response except for the rapid tap of her fingers on the keyboard.

"Finn," I called again.

"Hmmm," she mumbled, still typing. She was in that deep-focus place she went to when solving a problem.

I brought the phone closer. "FINN!"

"Huh?" Her hands stilled. "What?"

"We *have* to get into that folder." I stared at the name on my laptop screen. It was so... obvious. Why take all the steps to hide and secure the folder only to give it a name like that?

Finley huffed. "I know. I'm working on it."

"I know what *Astravir* means," I blurted as she started typing again.

That got her attention, and she turned her phone so she could see me. "What?"

"Starman."

For a moment, she just stared. Then she burst out laughing. "Are you serious? They called a top-secret alien project *Starman*?"

"I guess they thought no one would come across it buried this deep in their network," I said. "Clearly, they've never heard of Nightshade."

She rubbed her hands together. "Give me thirty minutes."

To her frustration, it took thirty-seven minutes. I wasn't sure which of us was more excited when she opened the *Astravir* folder. Inside were ten subfolders with names like *Species Analysis, Aircraft, Security, Communications,* and *Videos.*

She went immediately to the *Videos* folder and opened the first one. It was night, and the scene was illuminated by massive portable floodlights that cast white light over a severely damaged spaceship. The place was crawling with people in full-body biohazard suits, some gathering samples and others clustered near the ship's damaged section. There was audio, but it was impossible to make out voices over the sound of helicopters and machinery.

At the edge of the light stood a row of armed military personnel. And there was Colonel Mason, barking orders to his men.

"That can't be Taruth's ship. It's too damaged." I leaned in for a closer look. The ground was flat and sandy with low, scrubby bushes. "And that's not the ravine."

"It must be the first spaceship that came down." Finley stopped the video. "An actual spaceship," she said reverently as she started the next video. It was more footage of same site. So were the next four.

The sixth one was different.

A cold weight settled in my stomach at the sight of the alien lying on a metal table in a bright, sterile lab. There were restraints on his legs, arms, and torso, and tubes in his neck and arms. People in white biohazard suits surrounded the table, checking monitors or adjusting equipment, and the room was full of beeping machines and voices.

Finley's gasp was drowned out by a man's voice. "Subject is conscious. No visible signs of distress, but responsiveness remains limited. Restraints are holding. No signs of physical struggle. Subject's vitals remain stable. The heart rate is elevated, but that could be baseline for its species. The first subject was critically injured in its crash and lived for eighteen hours. This one appears uninjured."

Anger burned through me at the man's detached, emotionless voice. He talked about Taruth like he was a lab animal, and he mentioned Enoin with cold indifference as if he had been nothing more than a failed experiment.

At the mention of the other alien, Taruth turned his head to look directly into the camera. His unblinking gaze revealed nothing of the grief he must have felt at hearing about Enoin's death.

I gripped the edge of my desk. "Turn it off."

Finley stopped the video, and the line went quiet for a moment.

"So, that's Taruth," she said. "He looks different from your description of him."

"You try describing an alien from an image that popped into your head for thirty seconds." I pushed back my chair and went to the window. "How could my parents be a part of that?"

She sighed. "I don't know. Do you want to stop?"

"No." I went back to the desk. "This might be our only way to help Taruth. Just no more videos."

"Okay." She opened the *Aircraft* folder. Inside were research files, technical assessments, and diagrams related to the spaceship.

Next was *Security*, which contained documents about their security and containment protocols, threat assessments, incident reports, and more. There was so much data it would take days, maybe weeks, to go through it all.

"Can you open the *Oversight* folder?" I asked.

As I suspected, it held a treasure trove of executive-level documents – meeting notes, internal correspondence, briefings, and classified reports. The few we looked at linked Sutton Aerospace, the military, and high-ranking government officials and politicians in the operation. Its official name was Project G25X.

I skimmed over the list of files and folders. "Finn, is there a way to download all of this? I think we're going to need more than my videos for insurance when we go public. There's nothing to stop Sutton from wiping everything from their servers."

"We can scan some of them, but that won't work for the videos," she said. "There are gigabytes of data here. If I tried to transfer even a fraction, their security will detect it, and they'd know someone was in their system."

My shoulders slumped.

She continued. "We'd need at least an hour when their monitoring systems are down or distracted."

"So, it's possible."

"We just watched a video of an alien. Nothing is impossible." She returned to the main Astravir directory. "What do you want to look at next?"

I read the folder names. "Let's look at *Security*. That might show us where he's being held and what security measures they're taking."

"Good idea." She started typing, and the terminal window went dark.

"What happened? Did they catch us?" I asked.

She picked up her phone and gave me an apologetic look. "I have it set to kick me out when he logs off to lower the risk of detection."

I sat back in my chair. "What now?"

"Now I wait for him to log in again. Next time, I'll focus on the security files." She tilted her head. "I think Mum and Dad are back."

She turned the phone to show me her parents placing bags on the kitchen counter. "Hi, Mrs. Bennet. Hi, Mr. Bennet," I called.

"Hi, Charlie." Mrs. Bennet walked over. She was a petite woman with short curly hair and wearing a smile that couldn't hide the signs of fatigue around her eyes. "How are you?"

"I'm good. Better now that I can see all of you," I said.

Her smile widened. "It's good to see you, too."

"Hello, Charlie," called Mr. Bennet. "How's the world domination going?"

"Slowly," I replied. "It'll go faster now that Finley is back online."

He chuckled. "First, she has to eat dinner. Then she can continue with your evil plans."

"What did you get?" Finley asked. "It smells amazing."

"Lebanese," her mother said. "We found a little place near the market. They didn't have a lot of options, but we got falafel, hummus, and couscous."

"Yum." Finley turned the phone back to herself. "I'll call you back."

I hung up smiling. For the first time in days, there was no strain in their voices or faces. Instead of worrying about their safety, they were laughing and having a normal family dinner.

It had only been a day since I'd asked my father to help with their visas, so there was no word on that yet. The Bennets had the flat for two months and time to figure things out. For now, that was enough.

And maybe soon they'd have an even bigger reason to smile.

"Where are they? Are you sure they were on this flight?" I shifted from one foot to the other, scanning the faces of passengers arriving at the baggage claim area of Albany International Airport.

My dad chuckled. "I'm sure."

I had no idea how many strings my parents had pulled to make this happen so fast. Less than two weeks after I'd asked for their help, Finley and her parents got their visas. The one obstacle had been employment. My dad reached out to someone who knew the Chief of Medicine at Albany Medical Center. They were looking to hire another pulmonologist, and he put them in touch with Mrs. Bennet.

Through the flow of people, I spotted a man who might have been Mr. Bennet. I stood on tiptoe trying to get a better look at him, but he had disappeared.

The crowd parted, and there she was.

Finley's eyes met mine, and a radiant smile lit up her face as she broke into a run. I met her halfway, and we hugged so hard she nearly squeezed the air from my lungs.

"You're here," I cried.

She let out a shaky laugh. "I can't believe it."

We pulled apart, blinking away tears, and I turned to her parents, who had caught up to her with Milo. Mr. and Mrs. Bennet looked travel-weary but happy. We hugged, and my father stepped forward to greet them.

"Norah, Tom, it's so good to see you," he said warmly.

Mr. Bennet shook Dad's hand. "You too. Thanks for meeting us."

I crouched to greet Milo, who scratched at my legs in excitement, trying to climb into my arms. I scooped him up and endured an enthusiastic face-washing. "Glad to see you haven't forgotten me."

We headed to the baggage carousel. While we waited, my father handed Mr. Bennet a set of keys. "These are for the apartment. The furniture arrives in two days. I arranged for the rental car to be dropped off here."

"Thank you, David, for everything," Mrs. Bennet said, her voice edged with exhaustion.

My father smiled. "You're more than welcome to stay with us until your furniture is delivered."

"That's very kind, but there's a lot Norah and I need to do before she starts her new job next week," Mr. Bennet said. "We booked a hotel room for now."

"Finley is coming home with us." I hooked an arm through hers, and we grinned at each other like fools.

After grabbing their luggage, we stepped out into the crisp November air. A man from the rental agency was waiting, just as promised. They loaded their bags, and I reluctantly handed Milo back to Mrs. Bennet. My father took Finley's bags from her, and we walked to the parking garage where we'd left his car.

The drive from Albany to Hudson Ridge took an hour, which Finley filled with easy conversation. My father dropped us off at the house, and I grabbed one of her bags to carry inside.

"Are you ready to meet Kalyx?" I asked at the door.

"Yes! No." She gave me a nervous look. "What if she doesn't like me?"

"How could she not like you?"

Inside, Finley stayed close to me, looking around as if she expected Kalyx to jump out at her. I left her bag near the stairs and called, "Kalyx, come meet Finley."

Finley shifted beside me, bouncing lightly on the balls of her feet. I could practically feel the mix of excitement and nerves radiating off her.

Kalyx appeared at the top of the stairs, her intelligent blue eyes fixed on Finley.

Finley's mouth dropped open.

I bit back a grin. "Breathe, Finn."

She sucked in a breath, but she didn't blink.

Kalyx moved down the stairs with fluid grace. At the bottom, she paused, tail flicking, head tilted as she studied Finley. After a long moment, she padded forward until she stood directly in front of us.

"Hi," Finley squeaked.

Kalyx's ears twitched. Her eyes flicked to me before she sniffed up and down Finley's leg.

Finley shot me a panicked look.

I gave her a reassuring smile. "She must smell Milo on you."

Her curiosity satisfied, Kalyx brushed against Finley's leg, rubbing her head along it like a cat. A very big alien cat.

"I told you she'd like you," I said.

Tentatively, Finley reached down, her hand hovering above Kalyx's head. At my nod, she touched the vestra's fur.

"It's soft... like a cat," she said in wonder. She stroked Kalyx's head but jerked her hand away when a deep, gravelly sound filled the air.

I touched her arm. "Relax. She's purring."

"That's a purr?" she asked in disbelief.

"Yeah." I scratched between Kalyx's ears. "You ever hear a tiger purr? It's kind of like that."

Finley exhaled. "I've never petted a tiger."

"Well, you're only the third person to ever touch an alien cat."

Her face lit up. "You need to take a picture for me. When the world finds out about her, I can say I knew her before she was famous."

Laughing, I stepped back and held up my phone.

Finley crouched beside Kalyx, trying to look composed. I snapped a few pictures and handed her the phone.

Her mouth turned down. "I look like I'm trying not to pee."

I snickered. "Don't worry. We'll have time to take more." I picked up one of her bags. "First, let's take care of this."

I carried the bag upstairs to the guest room. There was an extra thick blanket at the foot of the bed because she got cold easily, and a pack of Oreos on the desk. She had discovered them on her first visit and lamented that they weren't available in Europe.

She spotted them as soon as she entered the room. "Oreos!" She tore open the pack and devoured one. "You are the best friend ever."

I set the bag on the floor. "I know."

She wasted no time in unpacking her toiletries, laptop, and clothes. "I've gotten used to living out of a suitcase," she said as she hung a few things in the closet.

"Not for much longer." I eyed the dark smudges under her eyes. "You look beat. Do you want to take a nap?"

"All I need right now is a shower." She groaned dramatically. "Airports and planes are gross."

"I put extra towels in the bathroom for you. Take your time." I walked out, closing the door behind me.

I went to see about dinner. I decided on soup and grilled cheese sandwiches, one of her favorite meals. By the time she came downstairs, I was plating it.

"Grilled cheese. Yum." She laid her laptop and phone on the island and pulled out a stool. Biting into her sandwich, she let out a happy moan. "You always know exactly what I need."

"I try." I took a bite of mine and tore off a piece of crust to toss to Kalyx.

Finley swiveled to look at her. "I'm eating a grilled cheese sandwich with an alien five feet away from me. Does it get more surreal than that?"

"Probably not."

She faced me again. "What do you think your parents will say when they find out they've been sharing a house with an alien?"

I smirked. "I'm sure they'll have a lot to say, especially my mother."

A soft ding came from her phone, and she dropped her sandwich onto her plate. "He's back!"

"Mr. Palmer?" I ran around the island as she opened her laptop.

"Yes, finally." She logged in and brought up the terminal window. "I was starting to worry they had canned him and we'd have to start over."

Three days after she got access to Sutton's hidden files, Mr. Palmer had stopped logging in. We had no idea if he was on vacation or had left the company. I'd staked out his house, but there'd been no sign of him.

It always amazed me how fast she was. In less than a minute, she was deep inside the Astravir project and exploring the *Security* folder.

A folder called *Containment* caught my eye. "That one."

Finley opened it, and my breath caught. "Finn, this is it." The folder had everything – Taruth's location, how they were keeping him contained, security measures, even rotation schedules.

"Jackpot." She opened a file with detailed security blueprints, including the locations of cameras and access control points for the entire building.

I leaned in and pointed at a place on the blueprint. "That's Dad's lab." I trailed my finger across the screen and tapped on another spot. "And that's Mom's lab. I don't see the lab where they're keeping Taruth."

Finley pulled up a second blueprint. It showed an underground level with a smaller lab connected to the nearest hangar by a two-hundred-foot-long tunnel. "I bet that's where your boy is."

My heart skipped. It made sense for them to have him and his ship in an area where they could come and go without being seen. "We need these blueprints and everything else about security."

"I'm way ahead of you." She opened a scanning app to capture the files. It wasn't as good as a real copy, but it wouldn't trigger a network security protocol.

We worked through the *Containment* folder, prioritizing key documents. By the end, she'd scanned nearly four dozen files, and our forgotten sandwiches were cold. We tossed them to Kalyx, and I made new ones while Finley moved to a folder called *Reports*.

"They have an incident report for the night they hauled you in for questioning." She read an excerpt from the report. "Charlotte claimed she did not see the subject's face during the encounter. She was composed and showed no visible fear or signs of distress during the interview. We believe she was telling the truth."

Finley grinned at me. "Cool as a cucumber."

I snorted and placed another sandwich in front of her. "I was pissed off."

"They also have one for that night they were tracking Kalyx in town. You and Ethan are mentioned in it," she said. "And here is one for the time Colonel Mason searched the house." She smirked at me over the top of the laptop. "You *do* get around. I wouldn't be surprised to find a whole file on you in here."

I sat to eat my sandwich. "They probably had one before this. They do background checks on new employees and their families."

Mr. Palmer was in no hurry to log off today, so we spent the next two hours snooping around. Kalyx and I went out to the woods for half an hour, and Finley was still at it when we returned.

"Here's something," she said as I removed my coat. "The Astravir project is under DARPA, but the NSA is trying to take control of it. I bet that's why Colonel Mason and Sutton are so desperate to find Kalyx. If the NSA finds out they lost an alien, they can use that to prove DARPA is mishandling the project."

"Mason said he didn't tell the FBI about the charm because the NSA would find out." I sank onto the stool beside her. "The last thing we need is the NSA and FBI sniffing around."

She didn't glance up from the screen. "They probably are already if they want it that bad."

"Don't even think that."

She closed the laptop with a sigh. "He logged out."

"What do you want to do now?" I asked.

"I just want to chill." She looked around. "I still can't believe we're here."

We settled on the couch, and Kalyx stretched out on the floor below us. As soon as we were comfortable, Finley asked, "So, when am I going to meet Ethan?"

"Tomorrow."

I hadn't seen much of him since the day we were pulled over by the police. He was working hard to get the store ready to sell. When I'd told him Finley would be here for a few days, he said he'd take time off to meet her.

I hadn't told her about the kiss. Aside from that moment in my driveway, Ethan hadn't given me any sign he wanted something more between us. Maybe he was too busy with the store to think about anything else, or maybe he just didn't feel the same attraction I did. I didn't want her making something out of nothing.

She stared off into space. "It's even quieter here than in Cambridge. I never thought I'd miss the noise."

"It was like that for me at first," I said.

She gave me a faint smile. "I remember."

"Have you talked to anyone in London?" I asked softly.

"A few friends from school. They're all doing okay. We haven't talked to anyone from our neighborhood. We don't know if they got out of London like we did or if they're in one of the shelters. I hope they got out." She hugged her knees. "I keep thinking how we could have ended up in a shelter. We were lucky."

I stayed quiet, letting her talk.

"How crazy is that?" she whispered. "We lost almost everything, and we're the lucky ones. London will never be the same. They say they'll rebuild, but it won't be the same."

"I know." London had been my home for five years, and it gutted me to see the destruction left behind by the flood. I couldn't imagine what she was feeling.

She smiled again, and it was brighter this time. "I promise I won't be such a downer all the time."

"You can be whatever you want," I said. "I'm just glad you're here."

"Me too."

Her phone dinged, and we grinned at each other.

"You feel like doing some more snooping?" I asked.

A familiar gleam entered her eyes. "Hell, yes."

I adjusted my grip on my helmet as Finley and I strolled down the sidewalk, the scent of fresh donuts from a nearby bakery mingling with the crisp afternoon air.

"That smells heavenly." She took my hand. "Let's get some for later."

Laughing, I let her tug me toward the bakery. "Aren't you full after that burrito you had for lunch?"

"I'm never too full for dessert," she declared. "Besides, Ethan might like some when he comes over."

We entered the bakery, and I checked out the window display while she ordered half a dozen donuts. Across the street, a woman stood outside a café. There was nothing about her that stood out – thirtyish with a blue coat and brown hair in a ponytail – except that this was the third time I'd seen her today.

"Got dessert," Finley said, walking over with a white paper bag.

I leaned in and whispered, "Do you see the woman across the street? Ponytail, blue coat. Don't let her see you looking."

Finley casually flicked her eyes that way. "I see her. Who is she?"

"I have no idea, but she was at the restaurant. Before that, she was at the bookstore." I snuck another peek. The woman appeared to be scrolling through her phone, but she kept sneaking glances at the bakery.

Finley's eyes widened. "You think she's following us? Do you think she works for Sutton?"

"I don't know, but who else could it be?" I motioned for her to stand with her back to the window while I pretended to take a photo. I zoomed in on the woman and got several good shots of her.

Fear crept into Finley's eyes. "What should we do?"

"Pretend we didn't notice her and keep walking," I said. "There are too many people around for her to try anything."

We exited the bakery as if nothing was wrong and continued walking toward the bookstore two streets over, where we'd left the scooter. At the corner, I crouched and pretended to tie my shoe so Finley could look back.

"She's following," Finley said when I stood. "She's by the bank now."

I kept my voice even. "Let's go."

We turned right onto the next street. As soon as we were out of sight of the woman, I grabbed Finley's hand and pulled her into the narrow gap between two shops. We ran to the back, cutting through to a small alley behind the buildings. I led her between two more building, and we emerged onto another street.

"In here." I ducked into a thrift store, weaving through racks of clothing and stopping near the back, where we had a clear view of the entrance. We didn't have to wait long before the woman passed by the window.

"What now?" Finley asked, a little out of breath.

"We get the hell out of here."

We slipped out the rear exit and moved quickly, sticking to alleys and narrow walkways until we reached the street where we'd parked the scooter. A minute later, we were riding home. I kept checking my mirrors, but saw no sign of anyone following us.

Finley's arms tightened around my middle. "What the hell was that about?"

"I don't know." I tried to calm my racing heart.

"To think I envied you for having all the excitement," she said. "I think I'll stick with my computers."

My phone chimed softly just as we stopped at a light a mile from home. It did that whenever one of my parents came home. I glanced at the screen and frowned when I saw **Cam 2 Motion.** Camera two was in the basement. Since when did my mother or father go down there?

I tapped the alert. A live feed of the basement filled the screen, and my stomach dropped like a stone.

There was a man in my house.

16

The man, dressed in black, his face hidden behind a ski mask, stood at the open door to my workshop.

My pulse pounded in my ears. "There's someone in the house."

"What?" Finley cried. "Oh my God. I'll call the police."

"No. Kalyx is there." There was only one person I trusted to call. I hit Ethan's number.

He answered on the third ring. "Hey."

"There's a man in my house," I said in a rush.

There was a beat of silence. "Get to your room and bar the door. I'm on my way."

"I'm not at home. Finley and I are coming back from lunch." My grip tightened on the handlebars. "I saw him on the basement camera. He's wearing a mask."

Ethan swore under his breath. "Can you tell if he's armed?"

"I didn't see a gun, but he could have one on him." My phone chimed again and flashed **Cam 1 Motion**. My gut twisted. "He's in the living room now."

"I'm five minutes away. Don't go into the house," Ethan said firmly. "Did you call the police?"

"I can't. Kalyx is there." I couldn't keep the note of panic out of my voice.

There was another pause. "What will she do?"

"I don't know. She hid when Mason searched the house, but she's gotten protective. If she sees him as a threat..." I swallowed, remembering how dangerous she had been when I met her.

I turned onto the road to my neighborhood. "I'm almost there."

"Stay outside, and wait for me," he said.

Finley tapped on my back. "Charlie..."

"Ethan's on his way," I told her. "It'll be okay."

"No." Her voice grew more urgent. "My laptop is in my room. It has all the files I scanned last night."

My body went cold. If the man was from Sutton, and he found those files...

I sped up. We reached the neighborhood gates, and I barely waited for them to open before racing through.

"We need to wait for Ethan," Finley said.

"He has the gate code."

I stopped a few houses away from mine to wait for him. I looked at my phone, and my heart nearly stopped.

The man was walking toward the den.

And Kalyx was behind him.

She stalked him like a predator, her body low, spiked hackles raised. He paused, turning toward the front door as if he'd heard something outside, and she vanished.

He resumed walking, and she reappeared.

I couldn't breathe as he entered the den. Kalyx followed. She stopped, her tail twitching.

And pounced.

She hit him hard, and they fell forward out of sight. There was a thud, then silence.

"Oh my God," Finley choked out. "Did she...? Is he...?"

I didn't answer. I stared at the empty doorway, trying not to imagine what was happening inside. After a minute, I couldn't stand it anymore. I pulled into the driveway and sprinted to the front door.

Finley chased me. "Ethan said to wait."

I unlocked the door and pushed it open. The house was silent, and the alarm was off.

"Stay here," I said, starting toward the den. Nauseating visions of a blood-splattered room filled my mind.

A few feet from the doorway was a booted foot. Steeling myself, I stepped into the room.

The man lay sprawled facedown on the floor, motionless. Kalyx stood over him, her body taut and her amber eyes watching me. There was no blood, but I couldn't tell if he was still alive.

"Kalyx," I said in a soothing voice. "It's okay."

Her ears twitched, but she didn't move.

I took a step forward with a hand out. "We're safe. Will you come to me?"

Her head tilted. Something flickered in her eyes, and they slowly changed from amber to blue. She looked down at the man and walked to me.

I bent to hug her neck. "Good girl."

"Is he dead?" Finley asked shakily from the doorway.

I went to the man and crouched to press two fingers to his neck. "He's alive and out cold."

The front door opened, and Ethan shouted, "Charlie?"

"In here," I called.

He stormed past Finley and into the room as if he hadn't seen her. "You were supposed to stay outside and wait. Are you okay?"

I sat back on my heels. "I'm fine."

He stared at the man. "Did you do that?"

"Kalyx did. She jumped him from behind." I stood. "And before you say anything, we weren't here when it happened. We saw it on the camera."

Ethan came to stand next to me. "Dead?"

"No."

He rolled the man over and pulled off the ski mask, revealing a white man in his late twenties, muscled, with a square jaw and a short blond crew cut. He wore gloves and a handgun in a shoulder holster beneath his jacket.

Ethan gave me a questioning look, and I shook my head. "I've never seen him before. Does he have ID?"

He searched the man's pockets, which were empty except for a black case containing six tiny cameras that made mine look they'd come out of a cereal box. He handed them to me.

"He was going to bug the house." Finley ventured closer and snapped a photo of the man. "He looks like someone you don't want to mess with."

Ethan removed the man's gun and checked for other weapons. "He looks like one of those private military contractors I saw when I was deployed. I've seen guys like him at private security firms, too."

A chill went through me, and I thought about Dev Malik's bodyguard. Could he have hired outside security to do surveillance? Maybe Mason had convinced him I was the one hiding their missing alien.

"Do you think he has anything to do with that woman who followed us downtown?" Finley asked.

I stared at her. In all the excitement, I had completely forgotten about the woman.

Ethan looked from Finley to me. "What woman?"

We told him what happened and showed him the photo I'd taken of her.

His mouth tightened. "There is no way they're not connected. Who are they working for, and why are they after you?"

"Before we have that discussion," Finley cut in. "What are we doing about the unconscious man in your house?"

"Good point," Ethan said to her.

"I'm Finley, by the way." She held out a hand. "I was hoping we would meet under more normal circumstances, but this seems to be the norm with Charlie these days."

He smiled and shook her hand. "Ethan."

I looked at the intruder and knew there was only one thing we could do. "We need to call the police."

"You said we couldn't call them because of..." She darted a look at the man. "Are you sure he's still out?"

Ethan bent and checked the man's eyes. "Yes."

To be safe, I motioned for them to go to the living room where we could keep an eye on him while we talked. Lowering my voice, I said, "We can't lock him up somewhere, but we can't just let him go. Our only option is to hand him over to the police and let them figure out who he is. We can hide Kalyx before they get here."

"You'll have police going through your house and asking a lot of questions," Ethan said.

"And you'll have to call your mum and dad," Finley added.

I grimaced. "I know, but what other choice do we have?"

Ethan removed the clip from the gun and laid them on the entry table. "We'd better get our stories straight first, and take down your hidden cameras."

I showed him where the cameras were, and I made the call while he took them down. Our story was that Ethan, Finley, and I came home and walked in on an intruder. Ethan tackled and disarmed the man, who was knocked out during the fight. I didn't mention the cameras he'd been carrying, which I'd hidden in the workshop.

Ethan wanted me to tell them about the woman following us in town, but I argued against it. We might be able to pass the man off as a burglar, but if we told them about the woman, the break-in would take on a whole new meaning. The last thing I needed were the police and my parents thinking this had anything to do with me.

After the call, I told Kalyx to cloak and hide on the roof of the shed where there was no risk of someone walking into her. Then, I called my father. He was getting better about keeping his phone with him, and he answered on the second ring. I assured him we were okay, and he said they would come home immediately.

It wasn't long before two police cars and an ambulance arrived. We gave the officers our statements as the paramedics checked the man and loaded him onto a stretcher.

Finley, who wasn't good at lying, pretended to be too shaken to talk much. Ethan told the officers his story about how the fight had gone down.

A detective arrived, and we had to repeat everything for him. We were in the living room talking to Detective Garcia when the front door burst open and my parents rushed in.

My father reached us first. His hands gripped my shoulders as he scanned my face.

"Are you okay?" he asked in a strained voice. I nodded, and he pulled me into a hug.

My mother's sharp gaze moved over me, assessing me for injury. I braced for a lecture on not setting the alarm properly or whatever else she assumed I had done wrong. I wasn't prepared when she moved in and hugged me.

It was stiff and awkward at first, and I didn't know how to respond. I couldn't remember the last time she'd hugged me.

"I'm glad you're okay," she murmured, her voice laced with worry. Taken off guard, I slid my arms around her and hugged her back.

She released me, back to her usual self – cool, sharp, and in control of the situation. "What happened?"

I gave them the same story we'd given the police, and they paled at the mention of the gun. My father praised Ethan for his brave actions.

"Do you know who he is?" my mother asked Detective Garcia.

"He has no ID on him. We'll run his prints and question him when he wakes up." The detective shook his head. "He's no amateur. He was carrying a Sig Sauer in a shoulder holster, and we found a bag of professional burglary tools near the basement door."

My father frowned. "Is it normal for a professional thief to break in during the middle of the day?"

"They might risk it if the payoff is worth it," Detective Garcia said.

My parents shared puzzled looks, and my father said, "We don't keep valuables in the house. There's some money in the safe but hardly enough to interest a professional thief."

"You both work for Sutton Industries, correct?" Detective Garcia asked.

"Is it possible he came here looking for something related to your work, maybe some files you brought home with you?"

"No," my mother answered firmly. "The work we do is classified, and we never bring it home with us."

"He might have thought you did. We won't know until we talk to him," the detective said. "There've been two other break-ins reported in this neighborhood in the last two months. They looked professional like this one, but the owners said they took only a small amount of money from the safe and left other valuables. Both owners work for Sutton."

I felt Finley's eyes on me, but I wouldn't look at her. I knew for sure those jobs had not been done by the same man.

"Half the people in this neighborhood work for Sutton," my father said.

"The three incidents might not be related, but we'll look into it." Detective Garcia closed his notebook. "We'll be here for another hour or so, and I'll have a patrol car drive around the neighborhood a few times tonight. If you think of anything else, let me know."

"Thank you," my mother said. "Please, keep us informed when you know more."

The detective nodded and left. For a moment, the house was quiet except for the squawk of a police radio in the basement.

"I should get going," Ethan said. "Work."

My father stepped forward and shook his hand. "I can't thank you enough for what you did."

"We are grateful you were here with Charlotte and Finley," my mother said.

"I'm just glad everyone is okay." Ethan looked at me. "I'll see you later."

I smiled. "Call me when you finish work."

"I like that young man," my father said, watching Ethan leave. "I don't want to think about what could have happened if he hadn't been with you."

"I bet that guy wasn't expecting to meet an ex-marine when he broke in," Finley piped in.

"We are very fortunate Ethan knew what to do," my mother said. Coming from her, it was high praise.

"Detective Garcia made a valid point," she continued. "If someone believes there is information about the drive project here, they could send someone else to search the house."

"I agree," my father said. "Maybe we should ask Lydia to put one of her people here."

I fought to hide my alarm. "I am not sharing a house with a Sutton security guard."

My father laid a hand on my arm. "It would only be for a few days."

I pulled away. "Have you forgotten the way they treated me, or that they used a drone to follow me? I don't trust them."

"We can't leave you here unprotected," he said.

"I'll activate the security drones." They were a nuisance, but one I could live with. "And Detective Garcia said he'll have police driving by."

He began to waver so I added, "Ethan can be here in five minutes if I need him."

"I'll agree to no security inside, but I want someone watching the house," my mother said in a tone that told me it was nonnegotiable.

I crossed my arms. "As long as they're only watching the house. No following me around."

My parents looked at each other, and Mom nodded. She took out her phone and walked into the den.

Relieved, I said, "I'll set up the drones after you leave."

"Leave?" My father frowned. "We can't leave you alone after what just happened."

"Dad, we're fine. No one is stupid enough to try another break-in with us at home and the police in the neighborhood."

He looked ready to argue when my mother returned. "Lydia's agreed to send someone over, and she's going to contact Detective Garcia. If this break-in was about our work, she wants to do her own investigation."

I turned to my father. "See? You have nothing to worry about."

"Okay," he conceded at last. "But if you see or hear anything suspicious, you call us immediately."

"I will." I would have agreed to almost anything to get them to leave.

After they left, Finley collapsed on the couch and let out a shaky laugh. "I thought for sure –"

I put a finger to my lips and pointed at the floor to remind her the police were still in the basement. I checked the backyard and saw an officer walking the perimeter.

I looked at the roof of the shed and wished the police would hurry up and go. I wanted to get Kalyx inside before the person from Sutton showed up.

It took almost an hour for them to finish. The moment the last police vehicle drove away, I ran to the shed and called softly for Kalyx to come inside.

I fell onto the couch, flinging an arm over my eyes. "I need a minute to have a mini freak-out."

"Only one? I've had three or four already." Finley groaned. "I'm not built for this. I think I'm getting an ulcer."

A laugh burst from me. "Remember when you used to say it would be cool if we were international spies."

"You be the spy, and I'll be the brilliant computer genius who builds you gadgets," she said. "You can bring me souvenirs whenever you come back from a mission."

I uncovered my eyes. "Deal. But for now, let's try to have a boring, uneventful night."

She laughed. "We'll watch movies and eat... Damn it! I lost them."

I lifted my head. "Lost what?"

Her expression was tragic. "My donuts."

"Don't they get bored?" Finley asked, peering out the window at the dark SUV parked in front of our lawn.

I looked up from the laptop. "Maybe they read... or knit."

She tittered and turned away from the window. "They've been watching the house for three days. I wonder who they pissed off to get stuck with that job."

"They're probably wondering the same thing." I went back to the floor plans and blueprints she'd scanned from Sutton's network. I'd looked at them so often I could probably navigate the place blindfolded.

"How long do you think they'll be out there?" she asked.

"Dad said a few days, so this should be the last one."

I hoped so. The man the police arrested had made bail yesterday and disappeared. The name he gave the police was Jason Russell, but he had no digital trail. It was all very cloak-and-dagger, and it had everyone on edge.

By day two, I realized I didn't mind Sutton's people watching the house as long as they stayed outside. I had four security drones patrolling the property, my cameras were back in place with an extra one in the backyard, and I had Kalyx. The place was as secure as it could be.

I closed the laptop with a sigh. "What do you want to do today?"

"I don't know." Finley joined me on the couch and laid her head on my shoulder. "I can't believe it's my last day here."

I rested my head against hers. "I wish you could stay."

"Me too. But at least, we're in the same time zone now." She lifted her head. "It's too bad Ethan's so busy. I really like him."

My stomach tightened a little. "You *like* like him?"

"How old are you – twelve? I think he's nice." She nudged me. "And I think he *like* likes someone else."

Heat crept up my neck. "How can you say that? You've only spent three hours with him since you got here."

"Did you see his face when he got here after the break-in?" she asked with a sly smile. "I might as well have been invisible."

I waved it off. "We're friends. Of course, he was worried."

She nodded slowly. "You keep telling yourself that."

Kalyx came over to me. Her ears were twitching, and she looked a little agitated. I stroked her head. "What is it?"

Charlie.

I startled when Taruth's voice suddenly filled my mind. I didn't think I'd ever get used to that.

"Taruth," I said surprised. It had been days since I'd last heard from him. "Is everything okay?"

I do not have long to speak, he said quickly. *The humans will return soon, and it is important I tell you this.*

Finley sat upright. "Taruth? Is he talking to you now?"

"Tell me what?" I asked, nodding.

She gaped at me. "Holy crap!"

The humans say I am to be moved, he said.

"Moved where?" Bile rose in my throat as Mason's words in the woods came back to me. *"The Pentagon is planning to move it to the secure containment area in Wyoming."*

They called it BlackReach, Taruth replied.

"BlackReach? I've never heard of that." I gave Finley a questioning look, and she reached for the laptop.

"Did they say where it is?" I asked him.

No, but I think it is far. The scientists are angry that I will be taken away. His voice wavered. *If they take me far away from here, it will sever my neural connection with Kalyx.*

His words hit me like a punch in the gut. Without the neural connection to him, Kalyx would die.

It took effort to keep my voice steady. "Did they say when you'll be moved?"

No.

"I'm going to figure out a way to get to you out of there," I promised. "I won't let anything happen to Kalyx."

I trust you, Charlie. The humans have returned. I must go.

And then he was gone.

"What's he saying?" Finley asked.

"He's gone." I stroked Kalyx's head, unable to bear the thought of losing her.

"There's nothing containing the name BlackReach in the files I have access to. I found a few mentions of it on some UFO truther sites." Finley gave me a crooked smile. "You know, the ones where people think the government is hiding aliens in secret underground bases, but no one can prove it's real."

"What are they saying about it?" I asked.

"The usual. Some guy's friend's cousin's uncle did maintenance at an underground bunker where they were working on some strange technology." She did air quotes around *strange*.

A sour taste filled my mouth. "It has to be that place in Wyoming Mason mentioned."

"If Sutton only just found out about the move, they might not have had time to update their files." She typed something and nodded. "Wait. There are some new ones in the *Internal Directives* folder."

She lifted her eyes to mine, and I leaned over to look at the monitor. The header of the document on the screen made my body go cold.

CLASSIFIED MEMORANDUM – NSA DIRECTIVE: TRANSFER OF PROJECT G25X

I skipped to the body of the memo.

Per directive from the National Security Agency, Project G25X and all associated assets will be placed under NSA jurisdiction. NSA field teams will be onsite to oversee the preparation of all project assets for transport, and to ensure data is backed up and encrypted in accordance with NSA protocols.

I gripped the edge of the cushion. "The NSA is taking over."

"Why would they move everything?" Finley asked. "Why not just put their people at Sutton?"

I skimmed the rest of the document and felt the blood drain from my face. "Six days."

In six days, they were taking Taruth away, and I'd never find him again. *And Kalyx will die.*

"We have to get to him before they move him."

Finley furrowed her brow. "How?"

"I don't know." I clenched my jaw so tightly my teeth ached. "If I have to, I'll steal a bloody tank and drive it through their front door."

"Whoa." She raised her hands. "Let's hold off on the grand theft tank. We need to sit down and talk about what we know and don't know. Then we'll try to come up with a plan that doesn't end with us in some government black site."

I began to pace. "What if Kalyx and I snuck into the building? She could cloak us until we got to Taruth."

"How are you going to get past all those locked doors?" Finley asked.

"We could steal someone's card," I suggested weakly.

She raised her eyebrows. "And the password?"

"I have my code reader."

"You'll need a much better one for Sutton's security," she said. "Too bad we didn't look for Jason Russell's tools before we called the police."

I slumped onto the couch. "There has to be a way. Help me, Finn."

"We know where they're keeping Taruth and his ship. We also know the location of all the doors and cameras and how many security people they have on a shift." Her gaze drifted as she mulled it over. "Even if we had an access card, someone would notice doors opening by themselves. There's also the lab, which has added security and people there around the clock to monitor Taruth."

I lifted my head. "Tell me something I don't know."

She closed her laptop. "Call Ethan. We'll show him what we have and maybe he can help."

I couldn't tell him anything over the phone, so I asked if we could meet up. He said he could meet us at his house in half an hour.

"You're taking Kalyx?" Finley asked when I told the vestra to come with us.

"I can't leave her here. What if Taruth tries to contact me again?"

Finley stuffed her laptop into her backpack. "You're not afraid of losing her in traffic?"

I scratched Kalyx's head. "She can outrun my scooter, so she'll have no problem keeping up."

I took a back road to Ethan's house, and he was waiting by the door when we got there. I forgot to tell him Kalyx was with us, and she nearly bowled him over when he tried to shut the door.

"Sorry," I said after he closed the door. "I should have told you."

He waved us into the living room. "Don't worry about it."

The three of us sat, and Kalyx lay at my feet as if she knew I needed her to stay close. Ethan's questioning gaze flicked between Finley and me as he waited for one of us to speak.

I took a steadying breath. "Taruth's being moved in six days."

"Where?"

"The NSA is taking the project from DARPA," I said. "They're moving Taruth and his ship to a secure location called BlackReach. We don't know where that is."

"If it's an NSA facility, I doubt even the president knows where it is." His face softened. "I'm sorry, Charlie."

I clutched my hands in my lap. "I'm going to get Taruth out of there before they move him."

Ethan stared at me like I'd begun speaking in Kruran.

I continued. "I know what you're thinking, but –"

"I'm thinking you've lost your damn mind." He looked at Finley. "Is she serious?"

At her nod, he dragged a hand down his face. "Let me get this straight. You're going to break into a secure, military-protected site crawling with NSA operatives, rescue an alien... and escape."

"With his ship," I said.

He exhaled hard. "You have no team, no weapons, and zero experience in infiltration. This is the kind of job SEAL teams train for. Do you even know where they're holding him or what containment measures they have in place?"

"Yes."

His mouth opened slightly. "You do?"

Finley took out her laptop and set it on the coffee table. She opened one of the blueprints and spun the laptop toward him.

"That is a security blueprint of the building, showing the location of the labs and the camera and access points," I said when he came over for a closer look. "We also have a detailed floorplan that shows the layout of the lab where Taruth is being held and the containment procedures document – among other things."

"How?" he asked, his eyes riveted on the screen.

"These are scans of the originals," Finley explained. "Those are in a secure directory on a hidden server deep inside the Sutton network."

His gaze snapped to her, and she smiled innocently.

"Remember when I told you Finley is a computer genius?" I asked. "I wasn't exaggerating."

"Aww, thanks!" she turned the laptop toward her again. Mr. Palmer was logged in, so she navigated to the project folder and played him some of the first video from the crash site.

Ethan watched in stunned silence for a minute. "You're telling me you are inside Sutton's network right now?"

"Yes." She stopped the video and showed him the directory contents. Then she opened the classified NSA memo and let him read it.

He raked a hand through his hair. "Okay, I'm convinced."

"We have all the intel we need about the facility," I said. "But that doesn't do us any good without a security card."

He returned to his chair. "It wouldn't matter if you had ten cards. There's no way you could get past all the security to that lab without someone realizing you don't belong there. If you did reach it, how would you and Taruth get out? And if you somehow pulled that off, how far do you think you'll get with the military and NSA on your heels? You'd need a full extraction team with air support to pull off something like this."

I met his eyes. "I have air support. Taruth can fly us out in his ship."

Ethan barked a laugh. "I honestly can't tell if you're serious or not."

The front door swung open, making us all jump. Xander strode in with his backpack slung over one shoulder. "Hey, Ethan –" He broke off, his eyes bugging out like they had the first time he met Kalyx. "Wha–? How did you do that?"

"Do what?" I asked.

He continued to gawk at me. "You disappeared for a second."

"I did?" I shot Ethan and Finley confused looks before my gaze dropped to Kalyx, who lay across my feet. "She cloaked me again," I said in a soft scolding tone. She looked innocently up at me, and I sighed. I was going to have to explain to her why suddenly cloaking me like that could get us into a lot of trouble.

"That is so cool!" Xander tossed his backpack on the floor and started for the other chair when he noticed Finley.

"Xander, this is my friend Finley," I said.

She smiled at him. "Nice to meet you, Xander."

"Hi... uh... you too," he said shyly. "Cool accent."

"Thanks," she replied as if she hadn't noticed his sudden awkwardness. "So, you're Ethan's brother."

"Yeah." He gave her a goofy smile – and walked into the coffee table. He managed to catch himself and turned bright red as he dropped down into the chair.

I pressed my lips together and saw Ethan trying to keep a straight face. Finley pretended to look at something on her laptop.

"So, what are you guys up to?" Xander asked.

"Nothing." Ethan looked at his watch. "Did you cut school?"

Xander scowled at him. "We have a half day, remember? They sent out an email about it on Monday."

Ethan nodded. "That's right. Sorry, it completely slipped my mind."

"I suppose you also forgot to sign the permission form for the class field trip on Friday?" Xander said.

"Field trip?" Ethan asked, frowning.

Xander huffed. "The Sutton field trip? I told you and Dad about it yesterday, and there was a link in the email."

"A Sutton field trip?" Finley and I asked at the same time.

"Yeah." He absently picked at the fabric on the arm of his chair. "It's probably gonna be boring, but it's better than sitting in class all afternoon."

Finley and I shared a look, and I said, "Are they going to show you the labs?"

He shrugged. "Maybe. Our teacher said we might get to see a mini fusion reactor."

My heart jumped. If he was right, they were going to my father's lab in the restricted area of the building.

"No," Ethan said sharply.

I gave him a puzzled look that didn't fool him one bit.

"I know what's going on in that head of yours." His eyes moved from me to Finley. "In both your heads."

I pulled Finley's laptop to me and opened the blueprint. "They're taking a group of students to my father's lab." I traced my finger to the lab where they had Taruth. "I'll never get another chance like it."

He rested his elbows on his knees. "It's impossible."

"What are you guys talking about?" Xander asked.

"A rescue mission," I said, my gaze still locked with Ethan's.

"Who are you rescuing?" Xander shot to his feet. "Holy shit! The alien is in that building?"

"Yes," Ethan said. "And he might as well be inside the Pentagon. It would take a small army to get him out."

Xander's face fell. "So, no rescue?"

"No." Ethan shook his head. "I'm sorry, Charlie. It can't be done."

Finley murmured something unintelligible. She stared off into space, nodding as if she was having a conversation with someone. I was used to it, but Ethan and Xander stared at her in confusion.

"Wait." I held up a hand when Ethan started to speak. "Give her a minute."

His expression was skeptical, but he did as I asked.

Finley came out of her trance, and there was a gleam in her eyes. "I have it."

"What?" I asked.

She smiled. "A plan."

17

I reviewed my mental checklist as I went through the contents of the small backpack for one last time. Had I thought of everything? What if I needed something I'd forgotten?

I zipped it up with hands that shook from nervous energy. There was so much riding on today and too many things that could go wrong. One mistake and everything would fall apart.

My phone rang, and Finley's name appeared on the screen. I answered as I pulled on a hoodie. "I'm almost ready –"

"They know," she burst out, her voice high and frantic. "They know you have Kalyx."

I froze. "What?"

"They're coming for you," she shouted. "You need to get out of there. *Now.*"

"Going now. Warn Ethan."

I hung up and removed the SIM card from my phone.

Grabbing a heavy pan from the cabinet, I smashed the phone on the counter. I threw the pieces into the garbage disposal with the card and turned it on for five seconds. I'd wiped it last night, but I couldn't risk the NSA finding a trace of Finley's encryption app.

"Let's go," I said to Kalyx as I grabbed the backpack and ran to the back door. Taking hold of her collar, I said, "Cloak us."

I opened the door, half expecting to find the yard full of armed soldiers. I didn't bother to lock the door before we took off for the woods. The plan had been for me to ride my scooter to Ethan's, but that was out.

Holding onto Kalyx's collar made running awkward and slow, and we barely made it past the shed when I heard the roar of engines. A cold sweat broke out all over me. If Finley had called a minute later, it would have been too late.

We reached the tree line, but instead of entering the woods, we skirted around Cathy's yard. At the far corner, I slowed and looked back.

Six armed figures in black tactical gear swarmed my yard. They moved with military precision, but there were no Sutton logos or other identifying markings on their clothing. *NSA.*

One of the men caught my eye, and I nearly stumbled. It was the man who had broken into our house. He was NSA? Did that mean the woman who had followed Finley and me was also NSA? I shoved the thought aside. There was no time to think about that now.

Five houses down from mine, we emerged onto my street, and I stared at the chaos before me. It looked like a scene from an action movie.

The once-quiet street was packed with vehicles. In front of my house were two black military trucks, three dark SUVs, two vans, and something that looked like a large armored truck. My stomach lurched when I realized it was a mobile containment unit. For Kalyx.

Soldiers and more operatives in tactical gear stood on my driveway and lawn. I crossed the street for a better view and saw a man and woman in black suits arguing with Mason in front of the open door. On either side of the street, my neighbors stood in their driveways, craning their necks to see what was going on. A few held phones, but it looked like they were being ordered to stop recording.

Kalyx and I turned away and walked toward the military truck blocking the end of the street. Two armed soldiers stood beside it, their rifles held ready, scanning the area with practiced discipline.

We had to cut across the leaf-strewn lawn of the last house to go around them, and I clenched my jaw as I stepped over the dry leaves with agonizing slowness.

The door of the house opened, and a man came out holding the leashes of two Golden Retrievers, who immediately started barking at the soldiers.

One of the dogs broke free from him and ran straight at us. It stopped a few feet from us and went into a barking fit, drawing the attention of the soldiers.

"Gracie, no," called the man hurrying toward us. He grabbed the end of her leash and tried to pull her back. "I'm sorry," he called to the soldiers. "It's all the excitement."

He might have succeeded in restraining Gracie if the second dog hadn't joined the frenzy. The two dogs pulled him toward us. I tensed to make a run for it.

Kalyx growled so quietly I could only feel the vibration. The dogs froze, whimpered, and sped back toward the house, yanking the man off his feet. He yelled for them to stop as they dragged him across the ground.

I gave Kalyx's collar a quick tug, and we hurried past the truck where the soldiers were trying not to laugh at the spectacle.

My heart was still racing when we approached the gates. They swung open before we reached them, and my father's Mercedes came through them. His hands gripped the wheel, his face a mask of fear and worry. My mother sat in the passenger seat, but I couldn't make out her expression.

The gates started to close, and we sprinted to them, slipping through just in time. I didn't look back as they clanked shut on the life I used to know. Whatever happened from here on, it would never be the same. I didn't know what that meant for my parents and me, but there was no going back now.

Kalyx and I set off at a run. We didn't stop until we reached the same convenience store parking lot where I had dropped Xander off the night we met.

Still cloaked, I opened the backpack and took out one of the two burner phones I'd programmed with the numbers for Finley, Ethan, and Xander's new burner phones.

The first person I called was Finley. "We're out," I said between pants.

"Oh, thank God," she cried. "Where are you?"

"About a mile from home. Did you warn Ethan?"

"Yes. He's safe," she said, her voice shaking. "I was so scared I was too late. Did they pass you on the road?"

"We made it out just in time, thanks to you." I caught my breath. "And guess who was with them. The man who broke into my house."

She gasped. "No way. He's from Sutton?"

"I think he's NSA."

"This is nuts," she sputtered. "Why was the NSA bugging your house?"

"Your guess is as good as mine. Maybe I'll ask them when this is over." I tried to joke, but it landed flat. "How did you know they were coming? And how did they find out about me?"

She huffed in disgust. "It was a trail camera. Some guy had one set up near the ravine, and a drone spotted it. They tracked down the owner and saw a video of you and Kalyx. Luckily, the man wasn't keeping up with it, or he would have seen you sooner."

I let my head fall back to stare up at the sky. A trail camera. The thought of passing one had never crossed my mind. "How did you find out?"

"It was sheer luck." She let out a nervous laugh. "I was checking to see if they had made changes to security in the lab when a new document popped into the folder."

"What kind of document?" I asked.

"It was an emergency authorization for them to bring you in and capture Kalyx," she said. "I guess even NSA operatives need to file paperwork."

A new fear gnawed at me. "Finn, they could come for you, too. My parents know you're who I would go to for help."

She chuckled. "That's why we create contingency plans. I'm somewhere safe."

I released a breath. "What did you tell your parents?"

"I left them a note. I told them not to worry, and I'll explain everything later."

I scanned my surroundings, but there was no unusual activity on the road. It wouldn't stay that way for long. "I need to call Ethan. I was supposed to meet him at his house."

"Keep me posted," she said. "I'll keep my eye on this for as long as I can."

I hung up and called Ethan. As I expected, he tried to talk me out of going through with the plan.

"Too many things can go wrong." He had been repeating that ever since Finley had come up with the idea. I knew he was right, but there was no alternative. I could go to the media with what I knew, but the government would have Taruth moved before anyone got inside Sutton to confirm my story.

"Where are you now?" I asked.

"There's an abandoned homestead just outside town. It's off a dirt road, and most people have forgotten it's there," he said. "I'll hang low there until I hear from you or Finley. But this means I won't be able to pick you up."

"Don't worry. I'll find another ride."

It was Xander who saved the day. I called him to explain my dilemma, and fifteen minutes later, he arrived on a scooter he'd borrowed from a friend at school.

"I thought you wouldn't be caught dead on one of these," I teased when he pulled up beside the dumpster Kalyx and I hid behind.

"Except during alien rescue missions." He grinned and passed me the spare helmet. "Were you serious about the soldiers and S.W.A.T. team at your house?"

I donned the helmet. "It wasn't a S.W.A.T. team. I think they were Black Ops or something like that."

"That is so cool!"

"You wouldn't say that if it was your house." I secured my pack to the dog harness I'd gotten for Kalyx. She hadn't liked it at first, but she was tolerating it.

"Cloak," I said to her as I sat behind Xander. I put my arms around his waist, feeling very exposed. I hoped the helmet was enough to hide my identity.

There was no sign of my pursuers as we pulled out of the parking lot and drove to his school. It was lunch time, and the school grounds were bustling with students, all wearing the uniform of dark pants, a white shirt or polo shirt, and a burgundy sweater. Some, like Xander and me, wore a burgundy hoodie with the words *Ridgeview Academy* across the front.

We parked in the student lot and walked toward the sprawling brick building. Xander practically bounced with energy, and someone was going to notice if he didn't calm down.

"You need to act normal," I said in a low voice. "You look like you just drank a six-pack of energy drinks."

"Sorry." He took a deep breath. "How are you so calm?"

I slowed to avoid two boys crossing our path. "This is the easy part. You didn't see me half an hour ago."

Most of the students were in the courtyard, sitting at picnic tables or on the low brick walls bordering the courtyard. We walked to a small group of boys standing off by themselves, wearing matching hoodies and caps bearing the school's name.

"Charlie, this is Caleb, Jayden, Luca, and Asher," Xander said. "Guys, this is Charlie."

Jayden, a lanky Black boy with a big smile, said, "Xander told us about the prank, and we're all in."

I smiled back. "Thanks."

All they knew was that they were helping me sneak into Sutton as part of a prank on my parents who worked there. Once the truth came out, they could tell everyone about their part in it.

"If you can pull this off, you'll be a legend," said Asher, who was the closest to my size with shaggy brown hair. He handed me his school ID and baseball cap.

"Are you sure none of the other students will know I don't go to this school?" I asked.

Asher looked around us. "We have three grade eight homerooms. No one knows everyone who goes here."

I tried on the cap and fixed my hair so it fell into my face like his did. "How's this?"

"Pretty good as long as no one gets too close," he said.

When the bell rang, all of us except Asher headed for a row of parked school buses. Two of the buses were running, but I didn't see any teachers herding students onto them.

Five minutes passed and people began shifting restlessly. I exchanged an anxious look with Xander. What if Sutton had cancelled the tour because of what was going on there today? The whole plan hinged on this field trip.

Two harried-looking teachers ran up, and one of them called for everyone to stop talking. "We're running a little behind, so we'll need to hustle," she said in a voice that carried well. "Form two lines, and have your ID ready to scan. Let's go."

"Just stick with us," Xander whispered. He leaned in close. "Is she with us?"

"Yes." I couldn't see or hear Kalyx, but she was close enough for me to feel her warm breath on my hand.

When we approached the lineup for the first bus, I crouched, pretending to tie my shoe lace. "Kalyx," I whispered, pointing as discreetly as I could at the bus. "Get on top of the bus."

We got in line with Xander and Jayden in front of me, and Caleb and Luca behind me. I gripped Asher's ID as the line quickly moved forward.

Xander and Jayden scanned their cards, and then it was my turn. I didn't look at the teacher as I held the card above the screen and waited for the tablet to beep.

At that exact moment, Caleb stumbled into Luca, who yelled, "Watch it." The teacher's head swung toward them as the tablet beeped, and I climbed onto the bus.

Xander and Jayden were waiting for me, and we grabbed two seats with me near the window. Grinning, Caleb and Luca took the seat in front of us, boxing me in.

"So far, so good," Xander whispered.

The ride to Sutton was short. Our bus stopped near the guard shack, and a guard walked over to speak to one of the teachers. He stepped back and waved us through the gate to where another guard waited. My fingers curled tightly in my hoodie when he boarded the bus, but he stood up front, never glancing back.

When the tall glass building came into view, my nerves kicked in. This was it, where it would all begin.

Xander laid a hand on my thigh, and I stilled the foot that had been bouncing against the floor. I placed my hand over his and gave it a quick squeeze to let him know I was okay.

The buses rolled up to the front entrance, and we filed off. Xander and I moved to the edge of the crowd, and a minute later, I felt the brush of Kalyx's nose against my hand.

The glass doors opened, and a woman stepped out. She was in her mid-thirties with short, dark hair and dressed in a tailored gray pantsuit. She smiled and raised a hand. "Welcome, everyone. My name is Monica, and I'll be taking you on your tour today."

Raising her other hand, she showed us a bunch of disposable wristbands. "Each of you will get one of these visitor passes for the duration of your visit." She gave the wristbands to the teachers, who proceeded to hand them out. They were thin and plastic with RFID chips like the kind given out at concerts. I made sure not to fasten mine too tightly around my wrist.

"One more thing before we start," Monica called. A man had joined her, carrying a plastic bin.

"Cell phones are not permitted in the lab areas, so I'll ask you to place them in this bin." She passed it to one of the teachers. "They'll be returned to you at the end of your tour."

There were groans and muttered protests, but everyone grudgingly complied. I hadn't considered this possibility, and I reluctantly added my burner phone to the bin. I had a backup, but I didn't like the idea of leaving this one behind.

"I'll take it when we leave," Xander whispered as if he'd read my mind.

"Excellent," Monica said when the bin was handed off to the man with her. "Follow me."

Everyone surged forward. I reached back and felt Kalyx's head. "Stay close, and try not to touch anyone," I said under my breath.

Xander, Kalyx, and I entered last. The lobby was too crowded for my comfort, so we moved to the nearest corner. I kept my head low enough for the baseball cap to hide my face from the security cameras. I doubted anyone would think to look for me here, but I couldn't risk someone like Lydia Warren recognizing me.

The security guard from the desk walked over to join Monica, who stood at the entrance of a hallway to the right of the elevators. "Your attention, please," she called, and the buzz of conversation in the lobby quieted.

She smiled, her voice warm and polished. "Here at Sutton, we take security very seriously. Let me give you a small demonstration." She turned to one of the teachers. "Would you mind stepping forward?"

The teacher walked toward the hallway entrance. The moment she passed Monica, lights flashed overhead and a small alarm chimed. Murmurs spread through the students as the guard punched a code into a panel on the wall to turn off the alarm.

I shifted my weight from one foot to the other. I'd read about the sensor in the security files, but now that I was here, I couldn't help being nervous.

"This is called an Advanced Human Presence Scanner or AHPS," Monica said. "It detects human bioelectric fields. Any person who passes it without an authorized ID card or an activated visitor pass will trigger the alarm. It also logs the activity of every ID and visitor pass in our system."

The guard held up a device and scanned the teacher's wristband. He motioned for her to go through again, and this time the alarm didn't go off.

"Cool," said someone as the murmurs started up again.

One by one, the students stepped up to the guard, had their wristbands scanned, and passed through the sensor. Xander and I were last, and I was glad the sensor didn't detect elevated heart rate because mine was going at the speed of an Olympic sprinter.

"Whew," Xander said under his breath after we made it through the scanner. I gave his hand a quick squeeze as we followed the group down the hallway. We had cleared the first checkpoint.

At the end of the hallway, double doors led to a small auditorium with curved rows of seats bolted to the floor. A giant screen displayed the Sutton Industries logo. Monica stood next to a podium slightly off to one side as a young man handed us booklets about the colony ship.

Jayden, Caleb, and Luca waved from the back row. We joined them, and Xander gave me the outside seat so I could be near Kalyx.

"So far, so good," Jayden said.

Caleb leaned across Xander and whispered loudly, "When are you going to make your move?"

"Keep it down," Xander hissed, elbowing his friend in the ribs. "You better not screw this up."

Caleb winced. "Sorry."

The lights dimmed, and the Sutton logo on the screen was replaced by an image of stars. It zoomed out to show a ship moving through space, and a narrator began talking about Sutton's role in the development of the colony ship that would take humans to Alcea.

I quickly zoned out, my mind going to what was happening at my house. At this very moment, strangers were going through my bedroom, my workshop, digging through my life.

They wouldn't find much. I'd expected them to come, just not this soon, and I'd prepared for it.

They'd find my laptop – but not the one I used for sharing files with Finley. I'd disposed of that one yesterday. My cloud storage and email were clean, too. For everything secret, I used the accounts Finley had created and accessed them only from the second laptop.

I thought about my parents, wondering what was going through their minds right now. I'd considered writing them a letter or recording a video, but nothing I came up with felt right. Maybe when this was all over, I'd get the chance to tell them in person.

Applause pulled me from my thoughts as the lights came on. At the front of the room, Monica wore the same smile as earlier, and I was starting to wonder if she had any other expressions.

"I never get tired of seeing that," she said. "Now, who wants to see a scale model of the actual colony ship being constructed in space?"

The room stirred with excitement, and everyone stood. We followed Monica out of the auditorium and down another hallway. She held her ID to a scanner and opened the door to a large, well-lit exhibition room. Aware of the camera in the far corner, I pretended to study my booklet as I entered.

At the center of the room was the colony ship model. It was massive, even at this scale, with sleek curves and four enormous propulsion units at the rear. Habitat rings extended outward, designed to house five-hundred people comfortably for the voyage.

Avoiding the models would draw attention, so I told Kalyx to stay by the wall while I went for a closer look at a cross-section model of the ship. It showed the inner structure of the ship, with cutaway floors revealing the various sections such as the bridge and command center, the living areas, agricultural area, and engine rooms.

"Good afternoon. You must be our visitors from Ridgeview Academy," said a male voice that froze me in place.

"Hello, sir," Monica chirped. "Everyone, this is our CEO, Dev Malik. Mr. Malik runs the aerospace division of Sutton Industries, including the FTL drive project you just learned about."

When Dev spoke again, his voice came from somewhere to the right. "I hope you're all enjoying your visit."

There was a chorus of yeses. I risked a look in his direction and caught a glimpse of him walking through the crowd. I shifted my stance slightly, pretending to be engrossed in the cross-section. The urge to duck behind the model was strong, but that would only look suspicious.

"Impressive, isn't it?" he asked, and I almost jumped at how close he was.

"Yes, sir," gushed one of the girls standing between us. "Have you been to the real ship?"

He chuckled. "Not yet. Every section you see here is still under construction. They'll bring them in pieces to the space dock for assembly."

"Will you go on the first colony ship?" asked another girl.

"I hope I'm one of the lucky ones," he said conspiratorially. "Anyone could be chosen to go."

If I wasn't close to hyperventilating, I might have snorted. He and his family already had their spots secured, as did mine and many other powerful people. Unless you were needed to run or maintain the ship, the closest you would get to it was a model like this.

"What jobs would you all like to have on a ship like this?" Dev asked, and I realized with a jolt he was speaking to me, too.

Forcing myself to breathe quietly, I scanned the room for an escape route and locked eyes with Xander. The moment he saw my face, his mouth parted slightly, and his eyes widened in understanding.

He rushed over, placing himself between Dev and me. "Mr. Malik, how big will the drive need to be for such a huge ship?"

I didn't hear Dev's answer as I moved away as casually as possible. Spotting Xander's friends, I walked to them and whispered, "That's my parents' boss."

The three boys immediately shifted until they blocked me from Dev's view. They were enjoying their part in this. They thought the most that would happen to me if I was caught was a slap on the wrist.

"He's walking away," Luca whispered. "He's talking to Miss Allen."

I let out a breath. "Where are they now?"

He tilted his head to my left. "Over there."

I scanned the crowd until I found them standing near the wall – mere feet from where I'd left Kalyx. I forced myself not to react. She was smart, and she could move through this whole room without touching anyone. The only one in danger of getting caught here was me.

Dev shook the teacher's hand and headed toward the door. He spoke to a woman standing there and turned to the room. "I'm needed elsewhere. I hope you all enjoy the rest of your visit."

Even after he left the room, I couldn't relax. My heart was still racing when I walked over to where Kalyx waited for me. That had been too close.

I was growing impatient by the time Monica called for us to follow her again. She led us to a door and used her card to open it.

"This connects us to the aerospace building." She gestured to the door-frame. "Sensors monitor all movement between buildings. Only authorized personnel can access the aerospace wing, and all traffic is logged."

We entered an enclosed walkway with plain white walls and industrial tiles. It was more crowded than the hallway, so Xander had to walk directly behind me with Kalyx between us and the wall. One of the teachers had dropped back to take up the rear, making it even harder to avoid contact.

Monica used her card and entered a code to unlock the far door, and we filed into a wide, modern hallway with white walls, recessed LED lighting, and a faint hum from the air filtration system. Doors lined either side, each labeled with engineering department names or individual names.

"This is the administrative wing of the aerospace building," she said. "Offices for engineers, project managers, and other key personnel are located here."

We continued down the hallway, past a breakroom with vending machines, a coffee station, and four tables. A few people in lab coats sat together at a table, and they barely glanced our way as we passed.

At the end of the hallway was a set of double doors marked AUTHO-RIZED PERSONNEL ONLY.

Monica stopped at the doors and turned to us. "Behind these doors is where our research takes place." She paused for effect. "Including the FTL project."

Excitement rippled through the hallway, and my pulse picked up again.

"The FTL project is highly classified, so we can't visit that lab," she continued. "But I have been given clearance to show you the Nuclear Research lab. That is where they are developing the power source for not only the drive but the entire ship."

The doors swung outward, revealing yet another wide hallway, but it had a different feel than the others we'd seen. It was colder here, and the steady whir of machinery filled the air.

The hallway was a T-shape. The sign on the left said PROPULSION SYSTEMS, and the one on the right said NUCLEAR RESEARCH. The hall straight ahead led to the main aerospace lab.

Monica turned down the right hallway and stopped in front of the doors to the lab. "This is an active research lab. You must stay with the group, and do not touch anything."

A hand shot up. "What about radiation?"

"It's completely safe," she assured them. "Nuclear materials are housed in a specialized containment area inside the lab. It's basically a lab within a lab."

She unlocked the doors, and they slid open, revealing the massive three-story lab. The group surged forward eagerly, and I had to nudge Kalyx to one side with my leg when a boy got too close to us. We had to get away from this crowd before our luck ran out.

I'd only seen my father's lab from the hallway outside his office, and it looked so much bigger down here. And louder.

The loud hum of machines filled the air along with the steady buzz of voices and the whir of a pair of robotic arms that were maneuvering a metal cylinder into position. The ceiling looked impossibly high, and I suddenly felt very small.

At the far end of the lab was the glass-walled office I'd seen my father in. It was empty now. Was he upstairs in his office? Or was he still at our house, trying to figure out what I had done and where I was now?

Monica stopped to speak to a woman in a lab coat, and I used the opportunity to scan the lab for a place to hide. There were a lot of workstations, but they were too exposed. The bank of storage lockers would have been an option if they weren't so far away. I doubted Monica would take us over there. The large work benches had plenty of space underneath if we could get close enough, but that was the busiest area. I needed a spot easy to access and where no one was likely to go.

The group started walking again. The woman in the lab coat spoke, and she had to almost shout to be heard. I was too distracted to listen. There had to be somewhere I could duck out of sight.

I looked ahead to where we were going. My gaze landed on the stairs to the upper floors. The space beneath was wide open, but that wouldn't matter if I timed it right. If we stayed on our current path, we were going to walk right past them.

I leaned in to whisper to Xander. "I'm going to do it here."

His eyes lit with nervous excitement. "Where?"

"The stairs." I looked around for Jadyen, Caleb, and Luca and easily spotted Jayden's head on the other side of the group. "You and your friends ready to create a little distraction?"

He grinned. "Hell, yeah."

"You'll need to get out front so everyone is looking that way. Do it just as we reach the stairs." I yanked off my wristband and shoved it into his hand along with Asher's ID. "Thank you."

"Good luck." He grabbed my hand and squeezed it, and then he was weaving through the other students toward his friends.

We drew closer to the stairs, and my muscles coiled as adrenaline surged in me. I glanced back and saw no one. I was ready. All I needed was the distraction.

On the other side of the group, someone yelped.

18

A body thudded against the floor, followed by a second. The group stopped so suddenly, I almost ran into the boy ahead of me. All heads swiveled toward the noise.

Now.

We ducked under the stairs, and I whispered, "Cloak me."

I pressed myself against the wall, pulling Kalyx close as I waited for a shout, a sign I'd been seen. It didn't come. I was counting on anyone monitoring the security feeds not to notice one person missing from a group of students all wearing burgundy and white.

A teacher was scolding the boys, and some of the other students snickered. My legs wobbled, but I didn't dare budge until the group moved on.

I hugged Kalyx, burying my face in her neck. It took me a few seconds to notice she was trembling.

I pulled back to look at her. "What is it?" I whispered. I'd never seen her afraid of anything. Could she sense Taruth nearby?

"You'll see him soon," I promised.

People moved around the lab, going about their work and oblivious to our presence. I couldn't believe we were here. If not for the field trip, we never would have made it past all those locks and sensors.

I shifted uncomfortably in my hunched position. We couldn't stay here for hours. I had to find a better hiding place, somewhere I could contact Finley and let her know we were in.

Kalyx made a soft noise. I followed her gaze through the gaps in the stairs to two security guards walking this way with quick purposeful strides, their eyes locked on the stairs.

Someone had seen me.

We barely had time to creep out from under the stairs and press flat against the wall five feet away before they reached the stairs. They leaned down to look underneath, and one said, "It makes no sense. You saw the monitor. One of those kids went under the stairs and didn't come out."

They straightened, and the second guard touched his earpiece. "All clear." There was a short pause, and he said, "Copy that." He looked at his partner. "Brian said there's been no activity here since we left Control."

The first guard didn't look convinced. "Then where did they go?"

"Maybe what we saw was a kid picking up something they dropped." Guard Two swept the area with his hand. "Look how open this is. There's no way anyone got past the cameras."

They turned away, and Guard One said, "Brian wants us to do a quick sweep just to say we did."

I sagged against the wall. That was too close. We needed to move from here.

Tugging lightly on Kalyx's collar, I stepped away from the wall. The lab was busy but spacious enough to navigate without bumping into anyone. We could stay here as long as we kept on the move, but there was nowhere private to talk to Finley.

We caught up to Xander's group, staying behind them until they left by the same door we'd entered. Every now and then, he glanced around furtively as if he expected to catch sight of me. Kalyx and I couldn't have made it this far without him. I'd make sure to let him know that.

For the next hour, Kalyx and I circled the lab looking for a place to lie low. No one came looking for a missing student, so I figured they hadn't noticed the group was down by one when they left.

My eyes lit on the glass-walled office, and I steered us toward it. Before we reached the open door, I knew we couldn't use it, even cloaked. There wasn't a lot of room to move around inside, and if anyone came in, we'd be trapped.

I stopped in front of the door and looked inside at the complex equations covering the whiteboards and the schematics spread across the drafting table. This was my father's world, and I knew as little about it as he knew about me.

I turned away and stifled a yelp when I almost ran into a large cart being pushed by two men in white coveralls. On top of the cart was a large metal cylinder secured with straps.

"That was supposed to be in Propulsion an hour ago," called a woman in a lab coat walking toward them.

The cart slowed, and the man at the back said, "We're running behind without Dr. Ross."

Propulsion? They were taking it to my mother's lab, which was closer to where Taruth was being held.

The woman nodded and waved them on.

Kalyx and I followed them to a set of extra wide doors where they stopped while the man in front scanned his card. I didn't hesitate. Dropping into a crouch, I grabbed the lower frame with one hand and pulled myself up onto the two metal bars that ran the length of the cart. It wasn't an easy feat with one hand wrapped around Kalyx's collar, and I was glad for the noise of nearby equipment that muffled any sound I made.

Kalyx had no such trouble. She climbed on silently and easily got her footing on the narrow bars.

The cart lurched forward, and the man at the back grunted. "Jesus, did this thing get heavier in the last thirty seconds?"

The other man laughed, and the cart rolled through the doorway.

An alarm chimed, and a red light flashed.

"What the hell?" said the man in front as the cart stopped moving. "Did you forget your card?"

"No, and it can't be me," the other man replied. "I haven't reached the sensor yet."

I stiffened. The AHPS sensor. How could I have forgotten about that?

"What's wrong?" asked the same woman they had spoken to a few minutes ago.

"No idea," said the man in front. "It went off when I walked through, but I have my card. It's never done that before."

The woman walked over and shut off the alarm. "Come back in, and try again."

I clung to the frame as they backed the cart up and pushed it through the door again. The alarm went off for the second time.

"Strange." She crouched to look beneath the cart. If I were visible, she would have been looking me square in eye. She straightened. "It could be a problem with your badge. Let someone in security know when you get back."

I let out a slow breath as the cart rolled out of the lab and down a short hallway to another set of doors. As I expected, an alarm sounded when they pushed the cart through.

A man came over. "There a problem, Elliot?"

"It's my card," the one in front said. "I need to call security about it."

"Okay," the other man said without hesitation. "Take it to bay two."

From my position under the cart, I had a limited view of the Propulsion lab, but my ears were assailed by the noise from the machinery and cooling systems, which grew louder the deeper we went. It was punctuated by the hiss of compressed air, the clang of metal, and beeping machines.

The cart stopped near a loud machine, and the two men had to shout to be heard. Kalyx and I used the opportunity to climb off the cart and slip away. It was a lot busier here, and we had to weave between people and equipment to reach a safe spot near the wall. From there, I got my first real view of the lab.

Like my father's lab, this one was three stories high with thick metal beams crisscrossing the ceiling and a glass walled viewing area on the third floor. Massive thruster assemblies dominated one end, and near them was the large reinforced chamber used for engine testing. Robotic arms hovered above workstations, and a crane was lifting the metal cylinder we'd arrived with. I'd spent hours studying the floorplan, blueprints, and photos, but nothing compared to seeing it in person.

Our position had zero traffic, but it also didn't offer a solution to our bigger problem. We couldn't leave the lab with all those security measures in place, and I didn't want to stand here for the next ten hours.

We made our way around the lab, hugging the edges of the room. After a few close calls, I began looking for another place to stop. My gaze caught on a workstation partly concealed by an idle crane. A lab coat hung over the chair, but I didn't see anyone nearby. I almost walked past until I noticed an ID card clipped to the coat pocket.

I moved before I could second-guess myself. Glancing around, I unclipped the card and slipped away. Small items I held were cloaked, too, so I didn't have to worry about someone seeing a floating ID card as we hurried away from the workstation.

Back in our corner, I turned the card over in my hands. I couldn't use it to unlock a door without a passcode, but I could use it to fool the AHPS sensors if I slipped out behind someone else.

I didn't want to go back the way I'd come, so I decided to stake out the other exits. One led to the offices upstairs, and the other led deeper into the building toward the third lab.

I watched them for almost an hour, but not a single person came or went. I looked around, deflated. If the card's owner hadn't noticed yet it was gone, they would soon. Every time an ID was scanned or went through a sensor, it was logged so they could easily track its last location.

"I'll be there as soon as I take these files to Dr. Ross's office."

I spun toward the voice. A slim man of about thirty in a lab coat with neat blond hair and a thin, serious face walked briskly past. He wore a Bluetooth earpiece and had a file folder under one arm.

Kalyx and I followed him as he threaded through the lab like a man on a mission. He started up the stairs, and I hesitated at the bottom. They weren't that wide, and if we met someone coming down, it would be disastrous.

He reached the first landing before I moved. I might not get another chance like this. We went after him, our footsteps quiet on the stairs. He was too absorbed in his call to notice what was happening around him.

At the top, he opened the door, and we ran to catch it before it shut. I pushed it open and slipped through, relieved when no alarms went off. Before it closed, I dropped the stolen card on the stairs.

The man was talking animatedly as he stopped at the first door and unlocked it. He entered, and we crept up to the door just as he reached the desk. We were in the room before he turned to leave. He walked out, shutting the door with a soft click.

I let go of Kalyx's collar and rolled my aching shoulder as I looked around my mother's office. It was the same size as my father's and exactly what I'd expected – comfortable but efficient with everything in its place.

The metal-and-glass desk was as neat as a surgeon's tray. There was no bookcase, only several shelves filled with more awards than books. One of the books had her name on it.

I was surprised to see a photo of the three of us. It was a few years old, from before I'd cut my hair, and I was smiling. I couldn't remember when it was taken.

A digital whiteboard glowed faintly on one wall, covered in equations written in her precise handwriting. Beneath it sat her laptop bag, the one she never came home without. She must have left in a rush.

The sitting area had a gray couch, a matching chair, a small glass table, and a compact fridge. Above the couch hung a gallery of degrees and awards, just like my father's office.

I opened the bathroom door and peeked inside. It was nearly identical to the one in my father's office with the addition of a small closet containing several changes of clothing, a pillow, and a blanket.

I walked over and sank down on the couch, taking what felt like my first full breath since I'd run out of my house two hours ago. We weren't much safer in here – my mother or someone else could come in at any time – but it was better than being out there in the lab. And it gave me the privacy to finally call Finley.

I called Kalyx over. "Stay near me in case someone comes in," I said, unzipping the pack strapped to her harness. I pulled out the second burner phone and connected it to my earpiece.

Finley sounded like she had been running when she answered. "Charlie? Are you okay? Are you in?"

"I'm in."

She made a noise that was half sob, half laugh. "I've been losing my mind waiting for you to call. I can't believe it worked."

"Of course, it worked. It was your idea." I smiled at the far wall. "Why are you out of breath?"

"I was doing yoga to help me stay calm."

I did a double take. She hated any form of exercise. "Yoga?"

"Power yoga. I started doing it in Cambridge." She let out a slow breath. "You should try it."

I shook my head. "Where are you?"

"Cheap motel," she said, and I could almost hear the shudder in her voice. "They don't really care about ID as long as you pay."

"What about cameras?" I asked.

She scoffed. "Their security is a joke. Where are you?"

I smiled. "I'm relaxing on the couch in my mother's office."

"You made it all the way to her office?" she asked, incredulous. "How?"

"Used my secret ninja skills." I rubbed my face. "Honestly, it was sheer luck and good timing. I'll tell you all about it if we make it out of here."

Her voice sharpened. "Oh, you're making it out. You do your thing, and I'll take care of the rest."

I leaned back into the couch cushions. "Everything is good to go?"

"All set," she said. "I'll text you when it's time."

"Will you let Ethan and Xander know I'm good so far?" We'd agreed that while I was in here, only she would communicate with Ethan, Xander, and me and pass messages between us.

"Will do." She made a *hmmm* sound. "There's not a single news report about the raid at your house. The NSA must be working overtime to bury it. I found a few posts from your neighbors but no photos or video."

I remembered the men ordering my neighbors to stop filming. "I bet the NSA confiscated the phones and deleted the videos."

"It's scary how much power the government has," she said.

"That's why we have to get all of this out to the world."

"You leave that to me," she replied. "We're going to flood the world with so much information they won't dare touch you. They'll be too busy dealing with the fallout."

Thinking about what was going to happen after we went public did nothing to help my nerves. I knew it was the only way, but imagining myself at the center of a media storm made me want to throw up.

"Where's your mum?" Finley asked. "Aren't you worried she'll walk in on you?"

"I don't know if she's still at home or here somewhere. Kalyx is staying close in case we need to disappear." I glanced toward the door. "I don't want to go, but I think we should hang up so I can hear anyone coming."

"You're right. We have another" – she paused – "eight hours and thirty-seven minutes until phase two of *Mission: Impossible(ish)* commences."

I groaned. "That's the name you went with?"

"You said I could name it, and that's the one I like." I heard the grin in her voice. "Anyway, stay safe."

"You stay safe, too. Talk to you soon."

The first thing I did was pull off the bulky hoodie and stuff it behind the couch. From my backpack, I took out the thin black coat I used to wear during my brief career as a burglar. I ate two protein bars, drank from my small water bottle, and used the toilet. Then I sat on the couch with Kalyx pressed to my legs and waited.

I didn't realize I'd dozed off until Kalyx growled. I jolted awake and grabbed her collar as the lock clicked. "Cloak us," I whispered, getting to my feet.

We moved to stand near the bathroom as the office door opened. Expecting my mother, I was surprised when a Korean woman in a dark suit entered, followed by Dev and Mason. Dev wore a serious expression, but the other two radiated anger. My mother's office suddenly felt very small.

"We can talk in here while we wait for them," Dev said.

The door had barely shut when the woman spoke in a clipped tone. "Someone please explain how a teenage girl can cover her tracks so well she might as well have vanished into thin air."

"This was your operation, Leah. You tell us," Mason replied, arms crossed.

The glare she shot him could have peeled the paint off the walls. "You're the one who didn't see what was right under your nose this whole time."

Her barb bounced off him. "And *you're* the one who lost her. Wasn't it you who said your superior team would have apprehended her on day one?"

"She clearly isn't working alone," Leah retorted. "She's getting inside help. It's the only way she could have known we were coming."

"This arguing is getting us nowhere," Dev said. "If you're implying Evelyn or David are involved, you're wrong. No one is more dedicated to their work. If either of them had suspected Charlotte, they would have confronted her."

Leah gave a derisive laugh. "You believe they'd turn in their daughter?"

"No," he said, surprising me. "They would've convinced her to give up the creature or tell them who she was working with."

The woman walked over to study the contents of the shelves. "We're past that now. Charlotte Ross not only knows about the aliens, she hid one of them from us. Her parents can't protect her from the consequences of that."

Ice filled my veins, and my knees felt weak. Kalyx pressed harder against me, her chest vibrating. I stroked her neck to calm her.

Alarm crossed Dev's face. "What are you saying?"

Leah faced him. "The girl and whomever she's working with know things that could threaten national security. We cannot let that happen."

"She's a teenager," he said, appalled.

"She's eighteen, technically an adult," Leah countered.

Dev looked ready to argue again, but the door opened, and my mother walked in. She set her handbag on her desk, her face unreadable to anyone who didn't know her as well as I did.

In eighth grade, another parent tried to have my science fair project disqualified, insisting my parents had helped me build it. My mother wore this same expression right before she eviscerated the man. My project won first place.

"You wanted to speak to me, Ms. Kim," she said.

Leah Kim's mouth formed a thin line. "I wanted to talk to you and your husband. Where is he?"

My mother sat in her chair. "David is out looking for our daughter. I can speak for both of us."

"If either of you have an idea of where Charlotte is, you need to tell me." Leah Kim's voice was hard and authoritative. I suspected she was used to being in control.

My mother's expression didn't flicker. "Once we find her and know she's unharmed, we will let you know."

The NSA operative straightened and took a step forward. "Dr. Ross, I need to question your daughter. If you or your husband think to obstruct me, you would do well to remember who I work for."

"Ms. Kim, why did the NSA send a man to break into my home last week?" my mother asked abruptly. "If you suspected Charlotte then, why did you wait until today to do anything?"

Dev frowned. "That man was from the NSA?"

My mother clasped her hands on the desk. "The police showed us his picture, and I saw him this morning at my house."

Leah Kim didn't deny it. "He's one of our private contractors. And no, we didn't know about Charlotte's involvement. We sent people to the homes of all the Sutton executives and scientists connected to Project G25X to ensure no classified information had been removed from the lab."

"You entered our homes without our knowledge?" Dev's voice was stiff with outrage.

"Yes," Kim said unapologetically. "Jason said he didn't know what knocked him out. It must have been that alien creature." She looked at my mother. "About your –"

My mother cut her off. "Why didn't you inform us before you sent your people to my house today?"

Kim blinked. "It wasn't necessary."

"You sent an armed assault team to our home after our child," my mother said with deadly calm. "And you didn't think it was necessary to tell us?"

"Charlotte is not a child, and your presence on the scene would only have impeded us," the other woman replied.

My mother's eyebrows arched. "If you had come to us first, David and I could have gone home to talk to her. There would have been no need for a raid, and we wouldn't be searching for her now."

Kim's jaw flexed. "You arrived less than ten minutes after we did. Someone told you about it. Someone also warned Charlotte we were coming."

"I told Evelyn," Dev said. "She and David had a right to know."

His admission surprised Mason and the NSA operative, and neither was happy about it. She rounded on him. "Did you also warn Charlotte?"

"No."

She swung her accusing gaze to my mother. "Did you?"

My mother didn't blink. "No."

"*Someone* did," Kim said, not backing down. "Whoever that was obstructed a federal operation."

My throat went dry. I couldn't let them ever learn about Finley's and Ethan's parts in this.

Leah Kim clearly hadn't spent much time with my mother. When her veiled threat didn't provoke a reaction, she said, "We're going to find her and the asset. The longer she makes us search, the worse it will be for her."

"When we find her, you can question her," my mother agreed. "But that is all you will do to her."

For the first time, a crack appeared in Kim's composure.

"Dr. Ross, you seem to think you have some say in this. Charlotte is not a minor, and she'll be taken into our custody when we find her."

My mother stood. "I don't like to repeat myself, so I'll only say this once.

No law exists for alien lifeforms. Charlotte will answer to us for her actions, but she broke no law. She won't be taken into anyone's custody."

She walked around the desk to stand in front of the other woman. She was a good four inches taller, and I could feel the cold rolling off her from across the room.

Her voice was quiet but razor-sharp. "I'm sure you are very good at your job to have reached your current position. But if you ever threaten my family again, you'll find yourself monitoring radio chatter from a bunker in Greenland."

The room fell so quiet I finally understood what it meant to hear a pin drop.

Mason looked at my mother like he'd never seen her before. Leah Kim went rigid. She tried to stare her down, but my mother turned her back and walked to her chair.

I could only stare at them. I knew my mother loved me in her own way, and she would protect me from real harm. I also knew she was formidable. But this was something else entirely. She left no doubt in my mind that she would make good on her threat. The look on Kim's face said she was slowly coming to that same realization.

"If that is all," my mother said coolly. "I need to check on a few things before I return to my husband and continue searching for my daughter."

Kim didn't move at first. She squared her shoulders and adjusted her jacket. "If you or your husband hear from Charlotte, I expect you to let me know."

My mother smiled thinly. "I'm always happy to cooperate with our friends at the NSA." She turned to Dev. "I'd like to speak to you if you wouldn't mind staying for a few minutes."

Dev looked startled but nodded. "Of course."

Mason opened the door, and Kim swept out of the office like a storm cloud. The icy tension in the air left with her.

"I want to thank you for telling us about the raid," my mother told Dev once the door closed. "You didn't say how you knew."

"One of Mason's men told Lydia." He took the visitor chair. "How was it at your house?"

"Chaotic. They're still going through it, but I don't believe they'll find anything."

I pictured strangers combing my room, touching everything I owned. Grimacing, I made a mental note to throw away everything in my underwear drawer.

"Charlotte was thorough. They found nothing on her laptop or in her email, and she destroyed her phone." My mother leaned back in her chair, a thoughtful look on her face. "It would have been impossible for her to do all that in the twenty minutes it took them to get there. It's like she knew they were coming before they did."

Dev's mouth parted in surprise. "What about her friends? Could any of them be in this with her?"

"The only two we know of are her friend Finley and the young man she started seeing a few weeks ago," she said. "They've disappeared too, so we can assume they're involved, although I don't know how. Neither of them could have known about the raid, so there has to be someone else."

"I agree." Dev paused. "Have you seen the video?"

She nodded. "Mason showed it to us."

"The creature is exactly like the dead one from the first crash." He leaned forward. "It walked beside her like a dog, and she looked so at ease. How do you think it happened?"

"That's a question David and I have been asking ourselves all day," she said. "We think she found it in the woods after the crash and kept it in the basement. She knows we rarely go down there."

"Do you think she knows it's an extraterrestrial? Or about the ship and the pilot?" he asked.

"Yes," she said without hesitation. "Charlotte has above-average intelligence, and she's gifted with technology. She'd know something that advanced wasn't human-made. She would logically conclude it arrived on a ship, and if there's a ship, there's a pilot."

She said it in the same logical way she spoke about most things, stating the facts without embellishment. But there was something else. If I hadn't been looking at her face, I would have missed the gleam of pride in her eyes.

It caught me so off guard, my fingers slipped from Kalyx's collar. Luckily, she was pressed against me, or I would have given us away.

Dev sobered. "They're no longer interested in bringing in the creature alone. If she has formed some kind of bond with it, they'll want her, too."

His words sent a shaft of fear through me. I imagined being trapped in a lab like Taruth, surrounded by scientists wanting to study me.

"I know," my mother said, and there was actual worry in her eyes. "I called Martínez before I came in. She'll intervene, but if the NSA finds Charlotte before we do, they'll take her away and drag it out for months."

I swallowed. If the NSA could give the run around to the Vice President, what hope did anyone have against them? I had to get Taruth out of here tonight before they hid him away in some secret bunker where he'd never see the light of day again.

Her phone rang, and she answered. "Yes." Her eyes went to the folder on her desk. "I haven't had time to look them over. No. I told them not to start the test until I've reviewed the numbers." There was a pause, and she said, "I'm coming down."

She hung up and returned the phone to her handbag. "I need to take care of that before I leave."

Dev stood and walked to the door. "Let me know if there is anything I can do to help."

"Thank you." She pulled the folder toward her and opened it. Her brow creased in a slight frown. Then she stood and walked around the desk.

I didn't breathe as she passed less than a foot away from me and entered the bathroom. The toilet flushed, and water ran in the sink. She came out and walked straight to the desk to pick up the folder and her handbag. I didn't move until she left and the door clicked shut.

I waited a few minutes before I told Kalyx to uncloak. Checking my phone, I was surprised to see it was close to seven-thirty. We had been at Sutton for almost six hours.

We still had hours to go until phase two of our plan began. I wanted to drop down onto the couch, but I didn't trust myself not to fall asleep again. I sat in the chair with Kalyx pressed to my legs, ready to vanish at a moment's notice.

I wanted to talk to Finley, but I couldn't risk being heard if my mother came back. I texted her instead.

Is there a way you can get a message to my parents without the NSA tracing you? I asked.

She responded right away. **Yes. What's the message?**

Tell them I'm ok and we'll talk soon. An idea came to me. **And send me an email from my PETA contact in Syracuse asking if we're still meeting up today.**

What contact? She wrote. **Oh! hahaha. Why didn't I think of that?!**

I smiled. **Because you're not as devious as I am.**

That's true.

Ok. Going radio silent until the main event, I said. **Talk soon.**

I stuffed the phone into my pocket and scratched Kalyx's head. "Just a few more hours. Won't Taruth be surprised to see us?"

I hadn't heard from him since he told me they were moving him. I wished I could have told him we were coming, and to let him know we hadn't abandoned him.

The hours crawled by. I imagined the building emptying as most employees went home for the day. Sutton had employees working around the clock on the drive project, but there were fewer people here late at night. The only department that didn't reduce the number of staff overnight was security.

I occupied my time going through the floor plans over and over, visualizing every corridor, every turn, every locked door between us and Taruth. The NSA's involvement meant additional security on site for the move, but we had the element of surprise on our side. No one would see this coming.

At 2:00 a.m., I ate another protein bar, drank some water, and used the bathroom. Fifteen minutes later, I began pacing the office to release the nervous tension building up in my body. Ten minutes after that, I began checking my phone once a minute.

At 2:30 a.m. I stopped pacing to stare at my phone. *Any second now.*

2:31 a.m. *Give her a minute.*

2:34 a.m. *She's just being extra careful.*

2:36 a.m. *Come on, Finn. Where are you?*

2:40 a.m.

Cold dread uncoiled in my stomach. Something was wrong. What if it had failed? What if the NSA had found her? What if –?

My phone vibrated, and the screen flickered.

An image formed of a purple flower, its petals unfurling like a star against a dark background. Beneath it appeared the words NIGHTSHADE IS BLOOMING.

I let out a breathless laugh. "The girl has style."

Kalyx looked up at me.

I smiled. "It's time."

19

I hit the button to call Finley.

Her voice, calm and controlled filled my earpiece. "You ready?"

A thrill went through me. "Yes."

"My troops are engaging the enemy now," she said. "It's a go."

By troops, she meant dozens of the best hackers in the world, currently executing a coordinated cyberattack on Sutton. When Nightshade sent out a call to arms, people answered. They didn't need to know why, only that if they succeeded, they'd be part of something historic. For most, that was just a bonus. The real reward was being able to say they'd worked with Nightshade.

Why had she waited until 2:30 a.m. to launch the attack? Two reasons. A scheduled system-wide update was running, and this was when the security shift changed. They wouldn't be more vulnerable.

"Do you have the stun gun?" Finley asked as I walked to the door.

"Crap." I pulled it from the pack and stuck it in my coat pocket. It was the only weapon I had – except for Kalyx – and I hoped I wouldn't get close enough to someone to use it.

"Remember, we don't know how long we have, so to go as fast as possible," she said. "And I can't see inside the underground lab, so you'll be going in blind. They're on a closed system."

"Got it." I took a deep breath and wrapped my fingers around Kalyx's collar. "Cloak us."

I opened the door, and we stepped into the hallway. I looked down into the lab. Most of the workstations were empty, and only a handful of engineers and maintenance staff remained.

My eyes locked on a monitor, which was dark except for the Nightshade symbol. A woman sat ramrod straight at the workstation, jabbing uselessly at her keyboard. She reached over and picked up the phone.

I faced the door to the lab. "I'm at door eleven."

"Five seconds," Finley said. "Four, three, two..."

The panel turned green, and the door clicked. I pushed it open, and Kalyx and I descended the stairs into the eerily quiet lab. Most of the machinery was idle, and the constant noise from this afternoon was reduced to a hum.

"I think the network's been hacked," a man called out.

Finley's warning echoed in my head. I moved quickly, passing the woman now speaking angrily into the phone and two men rushing to another station.

We neared the door I'd scoped earlier. "Door thirteen."

"Anyone in sight?" she asked.

I scanned the area. "Don't see anyone. You have the cameras, right?"

"For now, so get moving. It's clear on the other side."

The door lock clicked, and I had to pull hard to open the heavy door. "What is this, a blast door?"

"Why is that door open?" a woman called. Footsteps hurried toward me.

The opening was barely wide enough to squeeze through. I went first, twisting to keep my hold on Kalyx's collar. As soon as I was out, she followed, nearly bowling me over.

"Are you out?" Finley asked.

I caught myself and backed away just as a woman reached the door. She looked about my parents' age with graying hair and wearing a white lab coat. She grabbed the edge of the door, swung it wider, and peered into the hallway, her eyes sweeping the space.

Another set of footsteps approached. "What's going on?"

My knees locked when a security guard arrived. The woman gestured at the door. "It was open, but I don't see anyone."

The guard's eyes narrowed, looking past her into the hall.

"Do you think it has anything to do with the hack?" she asked.

"A hacker can't open a door." He touched his earpiece. "Control, we have an open door in the Propulsion lab. Do you have eyes on P3?" His eyes widened. "All the cameras?"

He grabbed the door. "Roger that. Locking it down now." He swung the door shut. Seconds later, the scanner on this side of the door went a solid red. That couldn't be good.

"Charlie, are you okay?" Finley asked. "I hate not being able to see you."

"I'm out. They're locking down the lab," I whispered. "You think they know someone is inside?"

"Maybe. They –" She broke off, typing furiously. "Where do you think you're going? Gotcha."

"They're putting up a fight," she said. "Keep moving."

Kalyx and I set off down the hallway at a run, and I was glad for my lightweight, flexible shoes that made no sound on the tile. At the end of the hall, we turned left. I nearly tripped over my feet when a restroom door opened halfway down the hall.

A security guard stepped out.

"Frick!" Finley cried as I flattened against the wall.

The guard touched his earpiece. "I'm on my way now," he said, hurrying toward us.

I watched it unfold in slow motion. As he pulled his hand away, he knocked the earpiece loose. It hit the floor and skidded across the tile to rest against my foot.

He swore and bent down to grab it – and his hand brushed my shoe.

He jerked back. "What the hell?"

I had no choice. I pocketed my phone, pulled out the stun gun, and lunged at him. But I miscalculated the distance.

The momentum tore my fingers from around Kalyx's collar. I stumbled and appeared in front of him.

"Shit!" Finley yelled in my ear.

The guard staggered back, his eyes wide with shock.

I regained my footing and struck again, but he was fast, and he caught my wrist in an iron grip. I kicked out at his knee, and he twisted away to avoid my foot.

He spun me, wrenching my arm as he pulled me against his chest.

Kalyx's growl filled the hallway a second before she uncloaked. She stood before us, her fangs bared, hackles up, and eyes glowing like hellfire.

"Wha–" the guard choked out. His hold loosened.

I broke free and drove the stun gun into his stomach. Electricity crackled in the air as his body locked up, and he dropped.

Breathing hard, I stood over him, dimly hearing Finley in my ear. It felt like someone had plunged a needle full of adrenaline straight into my chest.

"Charlie," she shouted.

I straightened. "Yeah."

"Listen to me," she ordered. "You need to get him out of sight before someone comes. Pull him into the restroom."

Grabbing him under the arms, I dragged him to the single-occupancy restroom. I turned to leave, and he groaned. I couldn't risk him calling for backup.

"I need to tie him up," I told Finley.

I ran to Kalyx, opened the pack, and took out the roll of duct tape I'd brought. You never know when duct tape will come in handy – though this wasn't exactly what I'd had in mind.

I wrapped his wrists and ankles and covered his mouth before I unclipped his ID card.

"His earpiece is still in the hallway," Finley said.

I found the small device and tossed it into the bathroom before I locked the door. I took hold of Kalyx's collar. "Cloak us."

"She can be kind of terrifying," Finley said. "Glad she's on our side."

I hurried to the next door. A sign said LEVEL 4 ACCESS ONLY. We were getting close.

"Hold on." Finley sounded like she was gritting her teeth. "That's not good."

"What's not good?"

It was a long ten seconds before she answered. "Two of my people just got booted out. I think the NSA joined the fight."

My stomach pitched. "Can you beat them?"

"I could, but I need to get you in... there!" The panel turned green.

"Wait," she said as I pushed the door open. "I can see two security guards posted at the elevator. They weren't listed on the roster."

The only way to the underground lab was the service elevator or the stairs. If Sutton was beefing up security, they had to suspect someone was inside.

"This is the only way in," I whispered, easing the door shut.

"I know. Give me a minute to think," she said.

Kalyx and I crept down the hall. As we neared the end, I heard a man and woman talking. We rounded the corner, and I spotted the elevator at the other end. A security guard stood on either side.

"You ever wonder what's down there?" the male guard asked as we crept closer.

"Yeah. But good luck finding out," she said. "My own brother's in Black Division, and he won't tell me a thing."

Black Division was Sutton's advanced security team made up of ex-military. I was pretty sure I'd run into some of them the night I'd almost hit

Taruth with my scooter. They handled security for the underground level, and I wasn't looking forward to seeing them up close again.

"Where are you?" Finley asked.

"I'm there," I said under my breath.

"Get close to the stairs," she said. "Hurry."

I moved silently toward the door to the left of the male guard. We were almost there when an alarm blared behind us.

The guards snapped to attention, and the female touched her earpiece. "Control, we have a door alarm in Sector Five," she yelled over the alarm. Her other hand went to her gun. "Roger."

"Come on," she called to her partner as she took off toward the noise.

I reached the door and stopped cold. The sign read LEVEL 5 ACCESS ONLY, and the access panel required a card, a passcode, *and* a fingerprint.

"This one is different," I whispered. "It needs a fingerprint."

"I know. I'm working it," Finley said. "Damn it."

The alarm cut off.

My heart sped up. "Finley..."

"It's not the same as the others." Her voice was strained as she typed. "I can't get around the fingerprint."

The guards' voices drifted to me. "They're coming back."

"If I had more time..." Finley's voice cracked. "I'm sorry, Charlie. I'm so sorry."

"He's sending reinforcements," the female guard said, her voice growing louder. "He said not to move from that spot."

Angry tears burned behind my eyes. *This can't be it.*

Kalyx moved forward, stood on her hind legs, and pressed a paw to the panel. The light turned green, and the door unlocked.

I stared at her, stunned.

She dropped back to all fours, and I snapped out of it. I shoved the door open, nearly falling through. Catching myself, I let go of her collar and spun to ease the door closed behind us. The guards arrived just as the lock clicked.

I put a hand to my heaving chest and forced myself to breathe slowly before meeting Kalyx's calm eyes.

"You waited until now to show me that?" I whispered hoarsely.

"Show you what?" Finley asked. "What happened?"

I let out a ragged breath. "We're in."

"What? How?"

I descended the stairs and stopped on the landing. "Kalyx has been holding out on us." I told her what she'd done.

"Holy –" She broke off. "Damn it! I lost two more. They're dropping like flies."

"Is it the NSA?" I asked. "Can you hold them off?"

She made a frustrated sound. "They're trying to do a system reboot."

I looked at the door below. "Wouldn't that disable all the locks? Would they risk that if they think someone is inside?"

"They would to get back control of the system." She resumed typing. "Once you're on the bottom level, it won't matter because I can only see as far as the elevators down there. We need to get you past that before they get the cameras back."

I rested my hand on the stair rail and took a deep breath. "Let's go."

I started down the stairs. Finley's voice crackled in my ear. "Kalyx will have to... door."

"You're breaking up." I stopped a few steps from the bottom and heard nothing but static. I returned to the landing. "Can you hear me?"

"Yes. I was afraid of this," she said. "They must be blocking signals down there."

I grimaced. "I should have thought of that. They're using a dampener to block the alien signal."

She went quiet for several seconds. "I'll hold them off as long as I can. When you enter that level, there are no guards by the door."

"Anything else?"

"Yes," she said softly. "Promise me you'll be careful. You're invisible, not invincible."

"I will." I couldn't promise her nothing would go wrong because we both knew it was only going to get harder from here. But we'd come too far to turn back, even if we could.

"Remember I have Kalyx. We're going to do this." I tried to inject confidence into my voice. "See you on the other side."

"I'll be waiting. Love you, Charlie."

"Love you too, Finn." I hung up and pocketed the phone.

Kalyx and I cloaked, and she unlocked the door. I grasped the handle with shaky fingers and cracked the door to peek out. All clear.

We entered a bare white elevator lobby with a set of double doors on the other side. Above them, a security camera faced the elevator. It seemed odd that with all their security measures to keep people out of this level, they didn't have guards posted here.

I took a cautious step forward, and another before I realized Kalyx wasn't walking with me. I tugged on her collar and whispered, "Let's go."

Her ears flicked, and she moved in front of me, blocking my way.

The skin on the back of my neck prickled. "What is it? Do you hear something?"

She shifted slightly, and the small section between her shoulders opened to reveal her control panel. Her hologram appeared, spreading outward to include the space around us – and a crisscrossing web of thin red laser beams a few feet away. If she hadn't stopped me, I would have walked straight through them.

"That explains why they don't need guards here."

I looked around for a panel but found nothing. Authorized personnel must carry a device to deactivate them.

"Great," I muttered. Lasers hadn't been on the security blueprints for this level, so they had to be new. How the hell were we getting through them?

"I don't suppose you can disable lasers, too," I said with a sigh.

She swished her tail, and the compartment containing the core and translators opened. The only other thing inside was the small black device that shot laser beams. I stared at it and hesitantly picked it up.

Charlie.

Taruth's voice in my head startled me into almost dropping the device. Relief flooded me, and tears blurred my vision.

"Taruth," I whispered. "Can you hear me?"

Yes. It is good to hear your voice. He sounded different, weaker.

"You too. I was so worried when I didn't hear from you."

I do not have much time. The humans are preparing to sedate me for transport.

I jerked back. "Transport? They're not supposed to move you for two more days." Then it hit me. The cyberattack and the possible breach had spooked them into pushing up their schedule.

My words came out in a rush. "We're coming for you. Just hold on a little longer."

I can feel Kalyx is near. Our neural link is stronger, and I can see what she sees. He paused. *The tool you hold is a –* My translator clicked as it searched for a word. *– energy disruptor. At half strength, it will disable a Kruran. At one third strength, it will disable a human.*

I looked at the meter on the device. "By disable, do you mean kill?" I didn't think I could take a life, even to get us out of here.

It will render them temporarily unconscious. Do not use it above that strength, or it will cause permanent harm.

"Good to know." I adjusted the setting to one third. "What does it do below that strength?"

The lowest setting will temporarily disrupt electronics. At one quarter strength it permanently disables them, he explained.

A thrill ran through me. It was an EMP. "Anything else?"

There is no time. I must go.

"We'll see you soon," I said. But he was gone.

They were moving him, which meant we had hours, maybe less. If they sedated him before we reached him, how would we get out of here?

Tightening my grip on Kalyx's collar, I set the disruptor to its lowest setting and fired at the lasers. The device gave a short hum, and instead of a beam, it emitted a quick pulse of energy. The lasers disappeared, and no alarms went off. We ran to the double doors, and when I looked behind me, the lasers were back.

"You waited until now to give me this?" I whispered, thinking of all the ways I could have used an EMP today.

I faced the doors. According to the security roster, there should be two armed guards between us and the lab. But if they suspected a breach, there could be more. There might also be more lasers we didn't know about.

"Kalyx, can you extend your hologram beyond these doors without anyone on that side seeing it?"

Her ears twitched, and the hologram expanded to reveal the large space on the other side of the doors. The lab took up two thirds of the space, and there was an armed man on either side of the lab door. Both guards carried a handgun in a holster and held a semi-automatic rifle.

I zoomed in on their body armor. There was an insignia above the Sutton logo that contained the letters B and D. Black Division.

The lab sat in one corner, leaving an L-shaped space around it. On the left was a massive, boxy machine with pressure gauges and ribbed hoses snaking across the floor to the lab wall.

To the right was a row of storage lockers and a small glass-walled room containing biohazard suits. Past that, there was a door I didn't remember from the blueprints. Two cameras faced the lab and another faced the doors in front of us. I'd have to take those out, too.

The lab itself was a large blank space. Whatever was in the walls blocked her hologram from seeing past them. That meant we had no idea how many people or weapons were in there. I had the disruptor, but I couldn't take on multiple skilled shooters. Even two was pushing it.

We'd deal with that when the time came. First, we had to get through these doors.

Beside the scanner was a large flat button used to hold the doors open. That could work. The guards would see the doors open on their own and come to investigate.

Or they could be trigger-happy and shoot first. All I could do was hope it wasn't the latter.

I readied the disruptor and took a steadying breath. There was no going back. Our only way out of here was on the other side of these doors – with Taruth.

I fired an EMP pulse at the camera. The air rippled, and the green light on the camera went dark.

"Kalyx, unlock the doors."

The second the lock clicked, I hit the button, and we ran to press ourselves against the opposite wall before the doors swung open.

No bullets whizzed past, so I peeked out. The lab door was twenty feet away. In front of it, the two guards stood rigid, rifles raised, their eyes locked on the open doors.

One of them touched his earpiece, saying something I couldn't hear. Shit. I hadn't thought about them calling for backup right away. We had to move before reinforcements arrived.

Guard One said something to his partner, who nodded and trained his gun on the doorway. Then Guard One started forward, his gun up.

He reached the doors and swept his gun side to side as he stepped through. For a split second, I was staring down the barrel before he swung it in the other direction.

"Clear," he called. He lowered his gun and walked to the access panel.

I gave Kalyx's collar a quick tug, and we slipped through the doorway. We moved to the left of the doors and stopped.

I took aim at the closest camera and fired. The light went out. I shot the last two, but they were too far away to know if I hit them. I fired several times to be sure.

My pulse thundered in my ears as I changed the weapon's setting to one third strength and turned to the man beside the lab. I planted my feet shoulder-width apart and aimed at him with trembling hands.

Behind me, the other guard said, "Everything looks normal."

I fired. The pulse hit the door with a soft thump.

The guard whipped around to stare at the door, but the pulse hadn't left a mark. I didn't give him a chance to make another move. I lined up my shot and fired again. He seized like he'd been tased and collapsed in a heap.

I spun toward the doorway. The first guard was talking on his radio and hadn't heard his partner fall.

"It must be the hackers because it's quiet here," he said. He lowered his hand and turned. He spotted the other guard on the floor, and his gun came up.

At this range, I couldn't miss. My shot hit him squarely in the chest. He jerked as his muscles locked up, and he dropped to his knees before he fell forward.

I stared at the disruptor. This thing was way better than the stun gun I'd used on the guard upstairs.

We ran to the man, and I felt for a pulse. It was strong and steady. I checked the first one. They were alive and out cold. I didn't know how long they would be out, but there was no time to tie them up.

I looked at the lab door, my body trembling with a mix of nerves and adrenaline. Taruth was behind that door, but I had no idea what else waited for us.

The access panel was different from the last few I'd seen. Instead of a fingerprint, it required voice authorization – something else that hadn't been in the security files. I wondered if it was new and if there were other security measures Sutton hadn't documented. Either way, it was too late to worry about that now.

"Let's go find our boy," I said.

Kalyx unlocked the door, and I pulled the handle. The door was heavier than I expected, and it opened with the hiss of pressurized air. Cold sterile air greeted us as we stepped into a decontamination chamber with a door at the other end.

I closed the outer door and held my breath as thin jets of cool mist sprayed from the walls and ceiling. The jets stopped, and a blue light swept over us from head to toe. A low chime sounded, and the inner door opened with a soft hiss.

We hurried inside before anyone came to investigate the open door. I froze mid-step when an alarm went off. It sounded like the AHPS alarm, but I still had the guard's ID card.

A man in a black tactical vest strode toward us, his hand on the gun at his hip. Kalyx and I scurried into an empty glass-walled workstation seconds before he reached the door.

"What is it?" A harried-looking woman rushed over to him. She wore a white lab coat, and the ID card clipped to her pocket said *Dr. Yvonne Andrews.*

"Nothing. No one's there," he answered gruffly.

She reached past him and swiped her card to silence the alarm. "You're sure no one came in?"

He shot her a look. "I saw the door open, and no one came in."

Another man in a tactical vest joined them, and I noticed neither man had the Sutton logo on their clothes. They had to be NSA.

"Is there a problem?" the second man asked, and the first one told him what had happened.

"It has to be a malfunction," Dr. Andrews said. "Even if someone had entered, the sensor only detects nonhuman bio-signatures."

"Has this happened before?" asked the second man.

"Not that I know of," she replied.

The first man shook his head. "I don't like it. First, their system is hacked. Then they suspect there was a breach, but they can't find them. Now this."

I bit my lip. From here, I could probably take down all three with the disruptor before they knew what hit them. But there were two lab techs on the other side of the glass partition between the workstations who could sound an alarm before I got to them.

"Close this door and don't let anyone in," the second man said. "I'm going to check in and see if they know anything." He turned to the doctor. "How long is it going to take to finish packing up this lab?"

She scowled. "We're packing up what we can, but we're half-staffed at this hour. As I told your boss, we were supposed to have two more days to get it ready for transport."

"Then bring in all your people. Just get it done." he ordered and stalked off.

Dr. Andrews glared at the other man and hurried away. He shut the door and stood in front of it with his arms crossed.

I shifted my gaze away from him and took in the lab. I was in one of two rows of enclosed workstations, separated by glass partitions. The stations around were empty except for the one with the two lab techs.

Along the nearest wall were shelving and storage units and three wide refrigerators. One cabinet was open, and a female technician carefully loaded boxes onto a rolling cart.

At the center of the lab was a large enclosed room, and most of the activity seemed to be happening around it. It had to be where they were keeping Taruth.

Coming here, my only plan had been for Kalyx to cloak all three of us for the escape. Our odds were a little better with Taruth's disruptor. But first, we had to get to him without bringing every armed soldier, security guard, and NSA operative in the building down on us.

Kalyx and I left the workstation and carefully made our way down this side of the lab. It wasn't as busy as I'd expected, just people packing up equipment and supplies.

We passed the refrigeration units that held neatly organized racks of test tubes and canisters. I didn't look too closely because I didn't want to know what was in them.

We made it to the end and turned left. I stopped short and almost cried out.

Two large specimen tanks loomed ahead, filled with a pink-tinted fluid. In the first tank, the preserved corpse of an alien was suspended in the viscous fluid, its face so much like Taruth's that for one horrific moment, I thought it was him.

Rational thought took over. *You talked to him ten minutes ago. It's not him.*

Relief mingled with sorrow for the dead alien. Curiosity had brought him here, and for that, he'd ended up as a science exhibit. He deserved better.

The second tank contained his vestra. It had been so badly damaged in the crash its body had nearly been shorn in two. One of the back legs was missing, and the right side of its head was burned beyond recognition.

The thought of Kalyx in a tank like this made me want to throw up. I turned to get away from it and walked straight into a loaded cart, sending two containers crashing to the floor.

The male tech pushing the cart yelled and jumped back as glass shattered. The lid came off one and broken test tubes spilled across the tiles along with a pool of yellowish liquid.

I backed away as Dr. Andrews stormed over. She took one look at the mess and let out an aggravated sound.

"I don't know what happened," the tech stammered. "They just fell."

The NSA operative came running. "What's going on over here?"

The doctor rounded on him. "This is what happens when you rush a job that requires more time."

"If you can't do the job –" he began.

"Get the hell out of my lab," she ground out as more people gathered. "You have no reason to be in here."

I tugged on Kalyx's collar, and we slipped away before it got too crowded. Raised voices trailed us as we passed machines, empty glass tanks, and a glass-walled room filled with another refrigerator and a microscopic analysis station.

We slowed when we saw a technician pushing a wheeled metal container toward a wide door ahead of us. He opened the door and rolled the container inside.

I picked up speed again and got there as the door sealed shut. He was visible through the window in the door standing in a large decontamination chamber. The door on the other end of the chamber opened, revealing a long white hallway.

This was it. The tunnel to the hangar.

I caught sight of two armed men in the tunnel ten feet from the door. There'd be more on the other end, but I could only deal with one obstacle at a time.

Right now, it was time to finally meet Taruth face-to-face.

I turned to the door of the containment room at the center of the lab. I knew from the blueprints that the room was thirty feet wide and long, with thick reinforced walls and a tinted viewing window. A row of vents ran along the top of the walls, and a rack of pressurized Xenon tanks sat on one side.

I wasn't surprised to see an access panel beside the door and a camera above it. The lock was no problem, but we had no idea who would be waiting inside.

We moved to the side with the window, but it was dark. I had no choice but to wait near the door until someone went in or out. But time wasn't on our side. Someone was going to find those guards I'd taken down.

I crouched beside Kalyx and whispered. "Can you use your hologram to show me what's inside this room?"

Her hologram appeared, and I held my breath as it expanded toward the room. I was afraid it couldn't get through the walls, but they were no match for her.

My eyes locked on the chair bolted to the floor at the center of the room. It resembled a dentist chair with the addition of thick metal restraints, and a scary-looking robotic arm hanging from the ceiling above it.

In the chair lay Taruth, his legs, arms, chest, midsection, and head secured by wide metal bands. Around his throat was what looked like a metal collar, and he wore a mask connected to a machine. He wore his flight suit, but his feet were bare.

Kalyx made a soft, plaintive sound, and I stroked her head. "Shhh."

Near the head of the chair, machines monitored his vitals, and an IV ran to his arm. The rest of the floor around the chair was clear. Medical equipment and data terminals took up most of the space along the walls.

There were three people inside. A man in a lab coat and a female tech stood next to a cart holding an assortment of vials, syringes, and instruments I didn't recognize.

In the far corner stood an armed man. I had expected to find at least one guard inside, so his presence was no surprise. I'd take him out first.

The bigger problem was the cameras. There was one in each corner, covering every inch of the room. The second I made a move, security would know.

I looked at the disruptor. Could I take out all four cameras and knock out the three people inside before anyone raised the alarm?

I was weighing my options when Dr. Andrews approached the door. Her face was still flushed from her argument, and I almost felt a little bad that her night was about to get worse. Almost.

Kalyx and I got into position behind her as she opened the door. The moment she crossed the threshold, I fired an EMP at the doorway in case there was a sensor.

Then I lunged forward and shoved her hard.

She yelped and flailed as she crashed to the floor. I darted in behind her, firing EMP pulses in every direction before I'd even shut the door. The others were too distracted by her fall to notice the lights on the cameras blinking out and the machines dying around them.

I adjusted the disruptor and aimed at the armed man. It took two shots before I hit him. He dropped, and I fired at the doctor, who was trying to get up. She slumped, motionless.

"Dr. Andrews?" the other doctor called, starting toward her.

Kalyx broke free of my hold on her collar, and we uncloaked. The man froze, stunned, and the lab tech screamed.

I lifted the weapon and shot him. The woman cowered with her arms over her head when I swung the weapon in her direction.

"Please," she whimpered as I fired.

The room fell silent. I lowered my hand and turned to the chair.

Kalyx stood on her hind legs, her front paws resting on the chair as she nuzzled Taruth's face. I walked around to the other side of the chair, my chest tight with emotion as I met his eyes for the first time.

"Hi, Taruth."

20

His lips moved behind the mask, struggling to form words.

"Hel-lo, Char-lie."

I smiled. "There's so much I want to say, but we don't have time."

Tucking the disruptor into my pocket, I studied the band across his legs and found a clamp beneath the chair. One by one, I released the restraints.

"Can you sit up?" I asked. I'd fried the chair motor, so there was no way to incline it.

He removed the mask and tried to sit up but fell back into the chair. I slipped an arm under his shoulders and helped him up, surprised by how light he was.

"Thank... you," he said weakly.

I released him. "Did they drug you?"

He paused before answering. "Yes. Their sedative is less effective for me. It will pass."

"I wish we had more time for you to get your strength back, but we need to get out of here before they realize what happened," I said. "Can you make it to your ship?"

"Yes." He stood on unsteady legs, one hand resting on Kalyx for support.

I moved to his other side. "Can Kalyx cloak all three of us?" I hadn't even considered that she might not be able to.

He took a cautious step. "As long as we maintain contact."

We walked to the door, and I had Kalyx show us the situation outside. It was a straight shot to the tunnel door, but there was more activity around it now. Two lab techs had arrived with carts, and the NSA operative from earlier stood nearby talking on his radio. No one gave any sign they knew what had happened in here, but that could change any second.

One of the techs opened the containment chamber door and pushed his cart inside. The door closed, and the second tech rolled her cart over to wait her turn.

An idea came to me. It was risky, but there was no time to come up with a better one.

"Do you trust me?" I asked.

"Yes."

"I need you to get on my back," I said. "You're light enough to carry, and we can move faster that way."

He didn't hesitate, wrapping his legs around my waist so I didn't need to hold him. He had to be half my weight, if that.

I took hold of Kalyx's collar. "Cloak us."

If anyone noticed the door opening and closing, they didn't react. Disruptor in hand, I watched the female tech waiting by the decontamination room door. I made sure no one was coming and closed the distance between us.

The door swung open, and she rolled her cart into the chamber. I disabled the door sensor and followed her in.

I pressed the weapon between her shoulder blades before she could turn to shut the door. "Say a word and you're dead."

Her body went rigid.

I kept my voice low and cold. "Good. Now close the door. Try anything else and you're dead. Got it?"

She nodded frantically and pulled the door shut.

"There are NSA people in the tunnel," she whispered. "You'll never get past them."

"Don't worry about them. You just worry about yourself." I jabbed her with the weapon. "Remember, not a word. I can kill you before they can reach for their guns. Understand?"

"Yes." She sounded ready to hyperventilate.

"Calm down. You'll be fine as long as you do as I say."

There was no decontamination on the way out. The outer door began to open as soon as the inner one locked, revealing the long, white tunnel and the armed men stationed there. The male tech was already thirty or forty feet ahead, pushing his cart at a light run.

I stayed glued to the tech's back as she pushed the cart outside and hit the button to close the door. The NSA operatives gave her a quick look and waved her on. I felt her sharp intake of breath when they didn't even glance at me. I gave her another little jab, and she kept walking as if nothing was wrong.

Taruth hadn't moved a muscle since we left the containment room. I wanted to ask how he was doing, but it was safer for the woman to think I was alone.

We were a quarter of the way down the long tunnel when she spoke. "They acted like they didn't even see you."

"Because they didn't," I replied. "Stop, and look behind you, like you thought you dropped something."

She did, and her eyes went wide. "You're... That's not possible."

"Face front and keep going," I said. "You have aliens and a spaceship here, and you think being invisible is impossible?"

She didn't respond.

"What's your name?" I asked brusquely.

Her voice was almost a whisper. "Jenny."

"How many people are in the hangar, Jenny? How many soldiers and security guards?"

She shook her head. "I don't know. It keeps changing."

I prodded her with the disruptor. "Guess."

"Last time I was there, they had six or eight people loading the trucks," she said. "None of Sutton's security are there – just NSA. I think there are six of them, plus two at the tunnel door."

Only six operatives and no guards? That didn't sound right.

"And the soldiers?"

"They're outside the hangar. I heard they have it surrounded and the doors locked down. There's no way out." She hesitated. "How... did you get in?"

"If I tell you that, I'll have to kill you." She started shaking. "That was a joke. I'll only shoot you if you don't do what I say."

We were about forty feet from the end when the tunnel began to slope upward. At the same time, one of the double doors burst open.

Three people in black came out. They sprinted toward us, joined by the two stationed outside. My heart kicked hard against my ribs. They knew.

I pressed closer to Jenny with Kalyx pulled tight against me. Kalyx growled, low and dangerous.

Jenny jumped. "What was that?"

"Quiet," I hissed. "Not a word to them."

One of the men slowed as they passed, but the other four charged ahead.

He barely glanced at Jenny as he gave her cart a quick once-over. Without a word, he sped after the other men.

She and I released a breath at the same time.

I took a step back. "Go. Faster."

The NSA wasn't stupid. Even if they hadn't seen Taruth leave through the tunnel door, they'd lock down this whole facility.

She picked up speed, grunting as she pushed the cart up the incline. We reached the doors just as a faint alarm came from the far end of the tunnel.

Instead of using the access panel, she pressed a buzzer. One of the doors opened, and sound spilled into the quiet tunnel.

A woman in black tactical gear stood there, her dark hair in a tight ponytail that added a sharpness to her features. I recognized her immediately. It was the woman who had followed Finley and me in town.

The woman's eyes swept the tunnel before she pulled both doors open and barked, "Hurry."

Jenny pushed the cart inside. I pressed close again, careful not to brush against the other woman. The doors closed, and I felt a tiny burst of elation. I couldn't believe we had made it this far.

My shoes didn't make a sound on the polished concrete floor as I followed Jenny to two white semi-trucks being loaded with lab equipment and supplies. One of the trucks had a refrigeration unit for whatever was in the lab refrigerators. A flurry of activity surrounded the trucks as people transferred items from the carts into larger transport containers.

"You're doing well," I said close to her ear. "Keep acting normal, and this will all be over soon."

We reached the trucks, and she stopped behind the male tech impatiently waiting for his cart to be unloaded. His fingers tapped on a box as he looked at her. "I hope you're not in a hurry. These guys seem to think we have all the time in the world."

She replied with a simple, "Oh."

It was time for us to part ways. Looking around, I spotted some large coolers near the wall. "Leave your cart, and go sit on one of those coolers," I whispered.

Jenny obeyed. Once she was seated, I said, "Put a hand to your head like you're not feeling well."

"W-what are you going to do?" she stammered.

"I promised I wouldn't kill you, and I won't if you do as I say." I couldn't see her face, but she was probably as white as a sheet.

She raised a shaky hand to her head. I waited a few seconds and fired the disruptor. Catching her before she fell forward, I eased her back against the wall. The least I could do was keep her from cracking her head and waking up with a concussion.

I moved away before anyone noticed her. When I'd put at least fifteen feet between us I said, "How are you doing, Taruth?"

"I am well." The hangar was noisy, and I almost couldn't hear him. It was strange hearing his voice outside my head. "You sounded sincere, but I do not believe you would have taken her life if she did not cooperate."

I smiled. "No. I just had to make her think I would."

It was the male tech who saw Jenny and rushed over to her. He tapped her cheek, and when she didn't respond, he called, "I need some help here."

Our view was blocked by the semis, so I moved around the front of them for a better look. The hangar was enormous, cavernous enough to easily swallow a four-story building. It had a high retractable ceiling and elevated platforms and catwalks at the far end.

Ahead of us, near the center of the hangar, sat two massive flatbeds. One held the scorched, twisted wreckage of the ship that had belonged to Taruth's friend, Enoin. Three soldiers were securing the ship with steel cables and clamps.

On the second flatbed, a heavy-duty military tarp covered an object fifty feet long and twenty-five feet wide. My pulse quickened. Taruth's ship.

I counted five black-clad NSA people, including the woman who had let us in. Two paced the catwalk with rifles, keeping watch on everything below. The woman stood by the tunnel door, and the last two patrolled the floor.

I focused on Taruth's ship again. My brilliant plan was to remove the clamps on one side, sneak inside the ship, and fly out of here.

The problem was that both sides of the flatbed were too exposed. On one side, a soldier worked on securing the other ship. The outer side faced the hangar wall, but it was visible from the catwalk whenever someone walked to that end. There were also the men walking the floor to consider. They wouldn't see us, but they might notice the unlocked clamps.

I was about to move when a male voice came over the intercom system.

"Charlie, it's Dad."

I froze.

"If you can hear me, please, stop what you're doing." His voice was strained. "They know you're in the building and what you came for."

My eyes darted left and right, but nothing looked out of place. The hangar had gone still as everyone stopped to listen.

"They have the building locked down, and it's only a matter of time before they find you. There's no way out." His voice grew pleading. "Mom and I don't want you to get hurt. Please, let them bring you in before things get worse. We can work this out."

I closed my eyes, steeling myself against the worry and fear in his voice. We were past the point of no return. Giving myself up would doom Taruth and Kalyx, and I would never do that to them. No matter the cost.

I placed a hand against one of the arms around my neck. "We're in this together, and we'll make it out of here together."

A different voice filled the hangar. "This is Leah Kim with the National Security Agency. Listen to your father, Charlotte. We can work this out. You won't be in any trouble if you give yourself up."

Angry heat flushed my body. This woman had called me a threat to national security and wanted me disappeared. If I surrendered, I'd be whisked away to some black site before I knew what hit me. And Taruth and Kalyx would spend the rest of their lives as little more than lab animals.

Leah Kim continued in that smooth, reassuring tone. "I know you think you're doing the right thing, but you don't understand the full picture. Come out, and talk to us." She paused. "This doesn't have to go any further. No one here wants it to escalate. I don't think you do either."

Did she think she was talking to a ten-year-old? Scratch that. Even a ten-year-old could understand the "full picture" here. And they wouldn't trust someone who had come after them with guns the day before.

"I'll give you five minutes to think it over," she said kindly. I could imagine her face trying to hold up the charade.

My parents might not know me as well as they thought, but they had to know I was too smart to fall for her BS. Would they tell her that?

They thought we were in the building. I doubted they considered the hangar as part of the building. If they had the slightest suspicion we were out here, they wouldn't have pulled their people away.

Activity resumed in the hangar. Grateful for the noise to drown out our voices, I said, "We can get to the truck where your ship is, but we'll have to figure out how to release the clamps without anyone noticing. The ship is fixed, right?"

"Not all systems are at full capacity, but it will fly," he replied.

I checked for the men patrolling the floor and found them near the door talking to the woman. Tightening my grip on Kalyx's collar, I headed for the flatbed.

Up close, I felt dwarfed by the flatbed. I'd never seen a truck this size. The top of the closest wheel came almost to my chin, and I had to stand on tiptoe to see over the bed.

Taruth's ship was secured to the flatbed by eight two-inch thick steel cables. I studied the clamp on the first one and saw it could only be unlocked with a special key. Of course, they wouldn't use standard clamps for something this important.

"I don't suppose Kalyx has a gadget that can unlock these," I whispered.

"No," he replied. "But the energy disruptor can sever the cables."

"I didn't even think of that." I touched the taut cable. "Won't the cables snap when we cut them?"

"We will not sever them completely," he said. "If we cut halfway, it will weaken them enough for my ship to break free."

I took the disruptor from my pocket, remembering the hole I'd burned in the floor of the mine shaft. "What strength do I use for that?"

He loosened his legs from around my waist and stood, keeping one hand on my shoulder. I hadn't been carrying him that long, but it was a relief to let the weight go.

"I will do it," he said.

I gladly relinquished the disruptor. To free both of his hands, I placed one of mine on his back.

He adjusted the setting to three-quarter strength and positioned himself in front of the cable. I kept an eye on the catwalk while he made the cut. The sharp, acrid smell of burnt metal filled my nose, and I grimaced. It wasn't overpowering, but I hoped no one working on the other flatbed had a sensitive nose.

"It is done," he said.

I glanced at the cable, which had a thin slice halfway through it. No one would see the cut unless they were standing this close to it.

We moved on to the second one and the third. At this pace, he'd be done in another minute or two.

A loud metallic clatter came from the other side of the truck as Taruth started on the fifth cable. Something hit the concrete floor, bounced once, and skidded beneath our flatbed, stopping near the rear tire. It looked like a misshapen monkey wrench, probably used to tighten the clamps.

One of the men swore, and boots thudded against the floor coming toward us. I went rigid, and I felt Taruth tense.

The soldier came around the rear of the truck and stooped as he searched for the tool. Spotting it, he dropped to one knee and reached for it. His fingers closed around it, and he grabbed the edge of the flatbed with his other hand as he stood. I stared at the hand inches from one of the cut cables.

I began to reach for the disruptor. I didn't want to use it out in the open, but it might be our only option. It could give us enough time to cut the last four cables before anyone came looking for him.

I stilled when one of the men on the catwalk walked into view. He stopped at the end, and his gaze landed on the soldier.

The soldier turned his head toward the cable. My body went cold.

A thump came from the other side of the flatbed, followed by a loud, "Damn it."

The soldier let go of the bed and disappeared around the back of the truck.

I watched the NSA operative on the catwalk. He wasn't looking our way, but he wasn't leaving either. We couldn't resume cutting the cables while he lingered there.

Several minutes dragged by before he turned and walked away. I exhaled shakily as Taruth finished cutting the cable. If he was rattled by the close call, he didn't show it.

He was cutting the seventh cable when there was a commotion on the other side of the hangar. We crept to the front of the truck to see what was going on, and it felt like someone had dumped a bucket of ice water over my head.

The tunnel door stood open, and two NSA operatives had entered along with six Sutton security guards. They weren't rushing in with their weapons raised, but their expressions were hard and focused as they began to spread out. They had extended their search beyond the building.

We hurried to the final cable, and Taruth made the cut.

I took the disruptor, stuffed it in my pocket, and looked at Taruth. "You go first."

He started to speak, and I cut him off. "No time for chivalry."

Bending, I wrapped my arms around his knees, easily lifting him up to sit on the bed. I had to break contact with Kalyx to do it, but being invisible wouldn't matter if we didn't get into the ship.

"Kalyx, up," I whispered, and she leaped effortlessly to stand beside Taruth.

I grabbed the edge of the bed and jumped, planting one foot on the wheel hub. But I couldn't gain purchase and dropped down. A second later, the disruptor clattered against the floor.

Shit. I snatched it up and stuffed it back in my pocket.

"Who's over there?" a soldier called.

My eyes met Taruth's as I reached for the bed again and launched myself upward. My foot landed on the wheel hub, but I lost my balance again and started to fall backward.

A surprisingly strong hand wrapped around my wrist and hauled me up over the edge.

"You there, stop," a man shouted from above. "They're on the flatbed."

Boots pounded the floor as I scrambled to my feet. I yanked the disruptor out of my pocket and sliced through the first strap holding down the tarp.

"Go!" I shoved Taruth under it and ducked in after him.

CRACK!

A bullet slammed into the ship's hull inches from me. Another shot rang out, followed by a shout. "Stop shooting. You'll hit the assets."

More shouts came from much closer. A man grunted as he hoisted himself up onto the bed.

A low mechanical hum came from the ship as the door retracted. I looked behind me as a man's face appeared beneath the tarp.

"Stop," he barked, lunging after us.

Kalyx whipped around, her tail slashing as a chilling, guttural growl filled the air. The man's face blanched, and he fell backward trying to get away.

I shoved Taruth into the ship, tumbling in after him. Kalyx leaped in beside us.

"Door, close," Taruth said.

There was another low hum, and the door sealed shut, muting the noise outside.

I landed on my hands and knees, my breath coming in ragged gasps. My heart pounded so hard I could feel it inside my skull.

We made it. We actually made it.

My arms trembled, my body wired and exhausted at the same time. I tried to take a deep breath, but the air felt too thin like I'd just run five miles. My lungs started to burn, and dizziness crept in at the edges of my vision. Something was wrong.

"Charlie," Taruth said, but it sounded hollow. "It is the air. There is too much carbon dioxide."

"My pack," I gasped, fighting to stay conscious.

Taruth moved away, and I couldn't hear what he was doing over the roaring in my ears. A minute later, an oxygen mask was fitted over my nose and mouth. The attached cannister was good for forty-five minutes if I wasn't breathing heavily. I'd brought two of them just in case.

The first breath was like ice. The second one came easier. The third one was deep, and my lungs stopped burning. The dizziness receded, but my arms and legs still felt too weak to move, so I stayed where I was until they stopped shaking.

"Are you well, Charlie?" Taruth asked.

I nodded and sat up. He was kneeling beside me, one arm wrapped around Kalyx, who was glued to his side, her body tense, and her tail flicking. The sight of them together at last made my heart squeeze.

"She missed you," I said hoarsely, tucking the oxygen cannister inside my jacket.

"And I her." He didn't smile exactly, but his face softened into what felt like the equivalent of one. He had the most expressive eyes I'd ever seen, and they were a little brighter than when I found him.

Something wet glistened on Kalyx's fur. My gaze jumped to a purple streak on Taruth's flight suit and then to a small pool on the floor.

"Oh, God! She's been shot." I scrambled toward them. We had gone through so much to get here. We couldn't lose her now.

I felt her fur, and my fingers came away coated in blood. She was pressed tightly to him, so I couldn't check her side. "Let me see, Kalyx."

"She is unhurt," Taruth said calmly. "Do not be alarmed."

I pointed at the pool on the floor. Had it grown? "Look at all the blood. How can you say –?"

My eyes snapped back to his as realization dawned. "You were shot?"

He held up a hand. "It is not serious. I will tend to it once we are away from this place."

"Has anyone ever told you you're a terrible liar?" I asked, pushing Kalyx aside to see his wound.

"No." He held up his arm, so I could examine him. "Thank you for the compliment."

It was difficult to see the wound in his side through the small hole in his suit. He was bleeding profusely, and that couldn't be good. And there was no exit wound.

"We need to stop the bleeding, and the bullet's still in there." I met his gaze. Were his eyes a little glazed? "I don't know what to do. You'll have to tell me."

"I require the MedSpray," he said. There was a split-second lag as my translator found an English word for it. "It is in the medical locker." He pointed to a smooth panel on the wall. "There."

I stood and took in the cockpit for the first time. I'd seen pictures and videos on Sutton's network, but they didn't do it justice.

The pilot's seat sat in a circular well, surrounded on three sides by a curved control console glowing with soft blue and white lights. One screen showed a star chart, and another displayed a ship schematic with system diagnostics. There were at least a dozen different displays, but the alien symbols were gibberish to me because my translator worked only for spoken language.

There were no windows, and I wondered if the large screen at the center of the console projected an outside view. That was a question for later, after I made sure Taruth didn't bleed to death.

The panel he had pointed at had no visible button, so I pressed my hand against it. A drawer slid out, revealing four identical silver cylinders fitted into slots. "Which one is it?"

"It is the first one," he said.

I picked it up. It fit neatly in my palm, with a button on top and a small hole on the side where the spray must come out. I hurried back to Taruth and dropped to my knees. Alarm filled me at the sight of his pale skin. His breathing was shallower, and his eyes were full of pain.

He held out a hand, and I placed the MedSpray in it. He pressed the nozzle to the wound and sprayed. A fine white mist hissed out and thickened on contact, forming a foam that hardened instantly.

"What does it do?" I asked, worried about the bullet still inside him.

"It sterilizes and seals the wound and relieves pain," he said, handing me the device.

I frowned. "Don't you need to get the bullet out first?"

"I will use the MedPod to perform the surgery when we are away from here." He tried to stand and swayed.

I helped him up and supported him as he walked to the pilot's seat. Kalyx sat at his side, and I stood just behind him, watching in fascination as he touched the controls, activating holographic interfaces.

"I powered down most of the systems after I completed repairs," he explained. "They will require three minutes to come online."

"Can we see what's going on outside?" I asked.

The wide screen in front of us came to life, and instead of the tarp I expected to see, it showed us the view over the top of the truck's cab. They had removed the tarp.

We were facing the hangar door which now partially open. Outside, a row of armored military vehicles waited, weapons aimed directly at us. I wasn't an expert, but I knew a missile launcher when I saw one.

"Can those weapons hurt the ship?" I asked, thinking of what the military had used to shoot him down when he arrived.

He touched the controls, and alien text scrolled down the holographic display. "No. The shield will activate shortly. It is not at full strength, but it will protect us unless they use a more powerful missile."

I rubbed my arms. "Is that what they used to shoot you down?"

"Yes. My weapons system was malfunctioning. I could not cloak or erect the shield," he explained. "I was able to perform repairs, but new components are required for it to be at full strength."

"Let's hope they don't want to destroy their shiny new toy."

He touched the controls again, and the viewscreen split into six separate displays, showing us everything around and above us. The hangar had gotten a lot more crowded since we entered the ship. The workers and techs were gone, replaced by dozens of soldiers, security guards, and NSA operatives. Some watched the ship, and others looked deep in discussion. Leah Kim stood with Mason and Lydia Warren, and none of them looked happy.

I pointed at them "Can we hear what they're saying?"

"Certainly." Taruth touched a control, and a cacophony of sounds flooded the ship. He adjusted something, and the noise became distinct voices.

"It's no coincidence she broke in exactly when Nightshade launched a coordinated attack on the network," Kim said.

"You've heard of this Nightshade?" Warren asked.

Kim scowled. "Every intelligence agency in the world has heard of them."

"Them?" Mason said.

"Analysis suggests Nightshade is a decentralized global collective of hackers," Kim replied. "No one has been able to identify them. They aren't known for malicious attacks, though, which makes us think this was engineered to help Charlotte by compromising security."

Warren looked incredulous. "How would she know where to find a group of hackers so elusive that no intelligence agency in the world can find them?"

"Maybe they found her," Kim said. "That's one of the questions we'll ask when we bring her in."

"If you can bring her in." Mason looked at the ship. "There's no way into the ship short of blasting our way in."

"We won't have to," Kim said confidently. She walked toward the ship, stopping twenty feet away. "Charlotte, if you can hear me, I need to talk to you."

"Do you wish to speak to her?" Taruth asked.

I tucked my hair behind my ears. "Yes."

He touched a control, and the split screens vanished as the panels around the cockpit became one long window. His seat rotated to the right, and I moved with it to face the window. Below, a dozen stunned faces looked up at us.

"They can see and hear us," he said.

I laid a hand on his shoulder and raised my voice so they could hear me through the mask. "I'm here. Talk."

It took Kim a few seconds to respond. "Hello, Charlotte, my name is Leah

248

Kim. I spoke to you over the intercom."

"I know who you are." I looked at Mason and Warren. "There's no need for introductions."

Mason's face was stony, and Warren folded her arms.

Kim wore a forced smile. "A lot has happened tonight, and tensions are high. Look around you. If this continues, people are going to get hurt. You don't want that on your conscience."

"The only people shooting here are you." I swiped my hand across Taruth's suit and held it up to show them the blood. "You should have thought about that before you shot Taruth."

Alarm flashed across their faces, and Kim took another step forward. "The doctors here can help him. Just open the door, and let them in."

I let out a humorless laugh. "I've seen what your doctors can do. No, thanks."

"You're willing to let him die?" Her tone was still easy, but her frustration leaked through.

"I would choose death over a life of captivity," Taruth said.

I squeezed his shoulder. "Don't say that. You and Kalyx are going home."

As I spoke, lights and more displays flared to life around the cockpit, and a low vibration began beneath my feet.

"You can talk to it?" Mason asked in disbelief. "How?"

Fury spread through me. "His name is Taruth, and he is NOT an *it*. If you people weren't so blinded by your greed and selfishness, you'd know that."

Kim's face hardened. "Charlotte, the attack on Sutton tonight could be classified as an act of terrorism. The only way you'll see any leniency is by coming out of that ship."

I swallowed. "You might want to work on your negotiation skills."

"Anyone who helped you is complicit," she bit out. "Your parents, your friends, your boyfriend. Are you willing to let them take the fall for you?"

The door to the tunnel burst open, and my father ran in, followed by my mother and Dev. They came up short when they saw us.

"Charlie..." my father began at a loss for words.

I waved at them. "Hi, Mom. Hi, Dad."

He lifted a hand and let it drop.

My mother recovered faster. She fixed me with a sharp look. "Charlotte, explain yourself."

"I'll give you the condensed version," I said. "Taruth came here to find his missing friend, the one you have on display in your lab. After you shot down his ship and locked him up like a lab animal, I found Kalyx in the woods. She's been living with us ever since."

I paused to take a breath. "Taruth contacted me through her. He told me you were going to move him, and we came up with a plan for me to sneak in and break him out. And here we are."

My father scrubbed his hand over the stubble on his jaw. "I don't understand. You've been talking to him all this time? How can you speak his language?"

I turned my head and pointed at my ear. "You can't see it from there, but I'm wearing a translator I got from Kalyx. Taruth has one, too."

"You say he told you he was being moved?" Kim asked.

"He understood every word you said around him. That's how I know you were trying to steal his drive for the colony ship. You should know his drive is powered by a mineral that isn't available on earth, so it never would have worked."

I hoped that by telling them, they'd realize the futility of their efforts, but I wasn't going to hold my breath.

"How did you get past all the security and know where to go?" My mother asked. She looked more fascinated than angry now.

"I used some of that cool alien tech." I grimaced. "That reminds me. Can you tell Jenny from the lab I'm sorry for knocking her out? And I hope there's no hard feelings?"

"Charlie," Taruth said, and his voice sounded off. I looked at him, and I drew back at the sight of his pale, almost gray skin.

"Oh my God, Taruth." I grabbed his arm. "We need to get you into that medical pod."

He laid his slender hand over mine. "It will take too long. I must fly us safely away from here."

"First, we need to get off this flatbed," I said. "Are you sure the ship can break the cables?"

"Yes."

I looked at the two dozen soldiers, security guards, and NSA people surrounding the flatbed. When those cables snapped, anyone within thirty feet was in danger.

"We're about to break the cables holding down the ship," I called. "Pull your people away from the truck if you don't want them to get hurt."

Warren looked ready to comply. Kim and Mason didn't move.

"I will not do that," Mason said.

"Then whatever happens to them is on you," I warned, praying they wouldn't call my bluff.

They did.

Kim folded her arms, smug. "You're not going to hurt innocent people."

I scoffed. "You have a loose definition of innocent. And I think we've established you don't know me or what I'm capable of – especially after you shot my friend."

I hardened my voice. "You have ten seconds before those cables start breaking. This is your last warning."

No one spoke or moved.

"Taruth," I said in a low voice. "Rev the engine."

"I do not know what that means," he said.

I leaned in. "Pretend we're taking off."

Understanding filled his eyes. He moved his hands, and the vibration under my feet increased. Outside, a hum rolled through the hangar.

It took a few seconds for anyone to react. Then they all moved at once, shouting and scattering to the sides of the hangar.

"Do it," I said.

A sharp metallic crack split the air. One of the cables whipped free and slammed into the floor with bone-shattering force. The others followed, one by one.

The floor dropped away as we rose into the air to hover fifteen feet above the truck. I looked at the stunned faces below, and it hit me. *I'm flying in a spaceship.*

Kalyx stood on her hind legs to nuzzle Taruth's chin. He leaned toward her, and for a moment, I thought he was passing out.

"Do not worry," he told her softly. "I will be well."

If she could sense he was in trouble, it had to be worse than he was letting on. We needed to get out of here.

I turned to the row of armed vehicles blocking the hangar door. "We can't go through that without shooting our way out."

"I do not wish to harm your people," he said.

"Me either." I looked around. "Can you go through the wall?"

"Jex, what is the composition of the walls in this structure?" he asked.

A holographic image of a cross-section of the wall appeared, and a voice answered, polite and slightly robotic. "The walls are composed of high-density concrete, reinforced with steel plating and composite armor panels."

Taruth studied the image. "Will it harm the humans if I use the ship's weapon to penetrate the wall?"

"At this range, the concussive force will be fatal to the humans inside the structure," the ship answered.

"Can we go through the roof?" he asked.

The image changed. "It is constructed of steel plating and composite armor. Firing the weapon at it would also result in a lethal concussive force."

"Well, shit," I muttered.

Taruth gave me a puzzled look. "Excrement?"

I let out a small laugh. "It's an expression that means this is bad. I'll explain it later."

I faced the crowd below. "We have two options here. You can back off and let us go, or we can blast our way out. Taruth doesn't want to shoot anyone, but he wants to be a lab rat even less."

Mason crossed his arms. "We are not removing the barricade. We are prepared to use deadly force if necessary."

Leah Kim turned on him. "What?"

"That's our daughter in there," my father shouted, closing the distance between them. "You will not hurt her."

Mason's voice was hard and unwavering. "I'm sorry, David, but I have my orders."

"Orders?" my father and Kim said together.

"If we can't contain the ship, we have to bring it down," Mason said. "We can't risk it falling into someone else's hands."

"Are you *frigging* kidding me?" I yelled. "You can't have the toy, so no one gets it? You'd rather kill Taruth and Kalyx than let them go home."

"My orders come from the top," he said flatly. "Did you think the Pentagon would let you fly out of here?"

I gripped the back of Taruth's seat. "That's it. We're going through them."

"I cannot kill them," he said weakly.

"Then I will," I bit out. "It's us or them."

"Don't do it," Mason ordered just as my father shouted, "Charlie, no. Your mom and I will figure this out."

I realized then that my mother hadn't said a word about Mason's threats to kill me. Why wasn't she standing up for me like she had with Leah Kim in her office?

Scanning the crowd, I found her off to the side with Dev, tapping on her phone. Her *phone*?

Dev leaned in and said something. She shook her head. And then she looked up at me. Our eyes met, and she wore a cool, controlled expression, not a flicker of emotion. Something sharp pricked my heart as I held her gaze.

She glanced down at her phone, touched the screen, and looked up again. But not at me.

The harsh grind of machinery cut through the hangar. Everyone stopped speaking at once as faces turned upward.

The retractable ceiling was opening.

21

I didn't breathe as a sliver of the night sky appeared. It widened, and stars flickered like distant embers. I'd never been into astronomy, but nothing had ever looked so beautiful.

Taruth's eyes were fixed on the screen. He'd been locked away underground for over a month, thinking he'd never see the stars or his home again. He didn't need to speak to tell me what he was feeling. His face said it all.

"Taruth," I said softly. His gaze shifted to me, and I smiled. "Let's get out of here."

He barely moved his fingers. The ship responded instantly, rising toward the opening. I glanced down at my parents, standing together, watching us as chaos erupted around them.

The ship jolted, and I stumbled, grabbing onto the seat for support. Below us, everyone had been knocked off their feet by the blast.

I searched frantically for my parents and found them on the floor, my father's body shielding my mother. They moved to get up as the ship accelerated through the open roof.

Outside the hangar, soldiers ran for military vehicles, some aiming guns at the sky, trying to lock onto us. Two Black Hawks waited, blades spinning, as people scrambled aboard.

The ship shot forward, and the coil of tension I'd had in my gut all day loosened. I still couldn't believe we'd done it. Even with Finley's help, Kalyx and I never would have made it through all those sensors without a serious dose of luck.

We didn't go far before the ship slowed and lost altitude. My heart leaped into my throat. Had the blast in the hangar caused damage?

The ship rocked from side to side, and the ground rushed up to meet us. I grabbed the seat with both hands and squeezed my eyes shut.

We touched down with a slight wobble. I opened my eyes to see we were on an empty stretch of road. I turned to Taruth and found him half slumped in his chair.

"Taruth!"

"I cannot... I am sorry, Charlie," he said weakly.

"This is not your fault." I took his hand. "What can I do?"

He lifted pain-filled eyes to mine. "You must fly the ship."

"Me?" I stared in horror at the holographic controls covered in alien symbols. Any other time I'd be thrilled to fly a spaceship. Maybe when the military wasn't trying to shoot us down.

"Can't you tell the ship to fly itself?"

"The auto-pilot could not be repaired," he said faintly. "It is not difficult. I will teach you."

He walked me through the basics of how to steer, accelerate, slow, change altitude, and land. We went over it three times, and I would have asked for a few more if not for the oncoming lights of two Black Hawks.

I helped him lie down on the floor, and Kalyx curled protectively beside him. I slid into the seat, praying I wouldn't throw up.

I positioned my hands in front of the controls and felt the strange thrum of energy. I let out a breath and touched one of the symbols. The ship lifted off the ground.

"Okay... I've got this."

We rose above the trees, and I touched the symbol to accelerate. The ship blasted forward, skimming the treetops. I tried to go higher, and it banked left instead. I tried turning right, and it shot straight up, ripping a small scream from me. I corrected it and managed to level off at fifty feet.

I was going to set two new Guinness World Records tonight. I'd be the first person to fly an alien spaceship. And the first person to die in an alien spaceship.

In the viewscreen, the landscape was bathed in crisp, pale light – like infrared but with washed out colors. I could make out trees, roads, and fields, but nothing looked familiar. The only good news was I might have lost the Black Hawks.

I looked down at Taruth's closed eyes, and panic surged.

"Taruth," I called sharply.

His eyes fluttered open.

"You stay with me," I said firmly. "We didn't go through all of this for you to check out on me."

I had to get him into that pod before he passed out completely. I searched for a place to land, and spotted a small hill with a meadow on top. Two dark buildings sat at one side, but there were no lights. It didn't matter. I had to land.

Descending proved to be less exciting than my other maneuvers, and I somehow managed to set us down in the grass without crashing. My hands trembled when I pulled them back from the controls, and my oxygen mask was foggy from my rapid breathing.

I dropped to my knees beside Taruth. He was so still and pale, and I was terrified I'd lost him. I tapped his face and nearly cried when his eyes opened.

"Taruth, it's time to get you into the medical pod," I said. "I need you to tell me what to do."

He blinked and weakly lifted his hand. I helped him sit up, slipping my arm around him as he struggled to stand. He sagged against me, murmuring something I couldn't make out. I draped his arm over my shoulders, grateful again for his lighter weight as we walked to the back of the cabin.

We stopped in front of one of the two doors. It slid open, revealing a small room with a bunk built into the wall and several closed compartments. Crossing the room, we entered a smaller one with no furnishings. He directed me to touch a wall panel, and a white pod slid out, its curved glass top reflecting the pale overhead lights.

He sagged against me, and I shook him gently. "You're almost there. How do we turn it on?"

"Jex, activate the MedPod for surgery," he whispered.

The interior of the pod lit up, and the top opened with a soft hiss. I picked him up and laid him in the molded interior.

"You'll be good as new in no time." I smiled, but his eyes were closed again.

I stepped back as the lid lowered, sealing with a hiss. A white mist sprayed until the glass was completely fogged over.

"He's going to be just fine," I said to Kalyx, who had followed us. I scratched her head, praying I was right.

I walked back to the main cabin on unsteady legs and spotted the disruptor on the floor. I picked it up and laid it on the console before I collapsed into the pilot's seat.

The only sound was the barely perceptible hum of the ship's systems. The stillness was disorienting after all the noise and chaos. My body felt jittery as if it thought it should still be running, but it was heavy and tired at the same time. It was a strange, unsettling sensation.

I stared blankly at the viewscreen. We'd made it. My mind hadn't fully processed it yet.

Taruth was going be okay – I refused to believe anything else – and he and Kalyx would go home. The last thought caused a pang of sadness, but it also made me smile.

My phone vibrated in my pocket, startling me. I fumbled for it and smiled when I saw Ethan's name on the screen. "Hi."

"Charlie, is that you?" he asked hesitantly.

"Who else?" I laughed. "Sorry. The oxygen mask makes me sound weird."

A car door closed on his end. "Does that mean you're on the spaceship that just landed?"

I sat up straight. "How did you –?"

Movement on the viewscreen caught my eye. Someone walked from behind a dilapidated barn and waved a flashlight.

"Look out the window if you have any in that thing," he said.

"No way!" I spun the seat and leaped out of it, nearly tripping over Kalyx. I gave her a quick hug and ran to the door, but I couldn't see the panel to open it. Remembering Taruth's earlier command, I said, "Door, open."

The door slid up, and the cold night air rushed in. In two strides, I was down the small ramp and sprinting through the grass. Moonlight bathed the meadow in silver light, making it easy to see Ethan walking toward me.

I didn't slow down. Meeting him halfway, I tore off my mask and threw myself into his arms, hugging him like there was no tomorrow.

He chuckled in my ear. "That's one hell of a greeting. You should do this spy stuff more often."

Laughing, I pulled away and looked up at him. His face was shadowed, but his smile set off butterflies in my stomach. Aside from our one kiss weeks ago, there'd been moments where I'd felt like there was something more between us. But there had been too much going on to think about romance.

Without thinking, I stood on my toes, pulled his head down, and kissed him.

He hesitated for only a heartbeat before he responded, his arms tightening around me. The kiss was short and breathless, fueled by adrenaline and raw feeling.

I pulled back, suddenly self-conscious. "Sorry."

His voice was low and rough. "Don't be."

He lowered his head and kissed me again, one hand cradling the back of my head, the other holding me against him. This kiss was slow and deep, and it left no doubt that I wasn't the only one feeling something more between us. When we finally parted, his forehead rested against mine, our mingled breaths forming steamy puffs in the cold air.

"It worked," he said in disbelief. "Your crazy plan actually worked."

"Yeah," was all I could say.

He held me at arm's length. "I've been going crazy. Finley called half an hour ago and said she lost contact with you. We had no idea if you were caught – or worse."

"I'm not going to lie. It was close. And scary." My lips quivered. "Taruth got shot."

"Is it bad?"

I nodded. "He's in his medical pod now. I think we got him into it in time."

"Jesus." Ethan pulled me back into his arms. "How long will it take him to heal?"

I closed my eyes, feeling safe for the first time tonight. "He didn't say, but I hope it's not long. I managed to give them the slip, but they'll be combing this whole area soon."

He went still. "*You* gave them the slip? You flew the ship?"

"Yes. And we're lucky we made it here in one piece. I'm surprised I didn't use up all my oxygen – shit." I pulled away and reached inside my coat. "I only have one cannister left."

"I have the extras in the truck." He pointed a thumb toward the barn. "It's parked back there."

"Oh, good." I closed the cannister valve. "Where are we? I was zipping all over the place. I couldn't tell if we were close to town or halfway to Albany."

"Hope's Rise. This is the old homestead I told you about." He looked over at the ship. "When the ship landed, I didn't know if you somehow found me or more aliens had arrived."

I looked around. The meadow was wide and open, surrounded by dense trees where the ground began to slope down. I couldn't see anything beyond the trees, which meant no one could see us unless they were in the air. The ship's external lights were off, and its black hull seemed to absorb the moonlight, blending itself into the dark. I had no idea if the ship could be detected by radar or thermal imaging.

I stuck my cold hands in my armpits. "I need to check on Taruth. You want to see inside a spaceship?"

"Hell, yes. I'll grab the stuff from the truck." He jogged off toward the barn, and I called Finley as I walked back to the ship.

She answered on the first ring. "You're out?"

"All present and accounted for." I held the phone away from my ear when she squealed.

"I want to hear everything," she said. "This is... epic. They'll be talking about it for years. I wonder who'll play you in the movie."

I snorted. "Slow down. We aren't out of this yet." I told her about Taruth getting shot and where we were. "All we can do now is hope the medical pod finishes before they find us."

I neared the door of the ship where Kalyx stood like a sentry. It hit me hard again that she and Taruth would soon be gone from my life. I wished Taruth and I had more time to talk before he left.

"Can't the ship cloak like Kalyx?" Finley asked.

I stopped at the ramp. "Taruth said it was malfunctioning before he crashed. Even if he fixed it, I wouldn't know how to turn it on."

Her voice brightened. "Well, I have good news. My troops were able to keep Sutton busy long enough for me to grab a ton of files. I'm ready for Phase Two when you are."

Phase Two of our plan had been for Taruth to land us somewhere safe where I could record him, Kalyx, and the ship. After he and Kalyx left, Finley and I would upload everything to the internet before anyone realized what we were up to.

What was that saying? *No plan survives first contact with the enemy.*

"Are you still at that motel?" I asked.

She groaned. "Yes, and I can't wait to get out of here. The people in the room next door have been arguing on and off all night."

"That sucks," I said sympathetically. "Have you talked to your mom and dad since you left?"

"I sent Dad an email from a dummy account on one of the university servers. He wrote back that the FBI came to the apartment looking for me." She heaved a sigh. "Needless to say. I have a *lot* of explaining to do."

"Your parents are cool. They'll understand." I hesitated. "You're not going to tell them about the hacking, are you?"

"God, no."

I laughed. "By the way, every intelligence agency in the world believes Nightshade is a global collective of hackers."

She snickered. "I know."

"Of course, you do." I spotted Ethan jogging toward me. "I'm going to check on Taruth and show Ethan the ship. I'll talk to you soon."

"I'm so jealous," she whined playfully. "I want to see the spaceship."

"Next time," I said, even though we both knew there wouldn't be one. "I'll call you when it's time."

"I'll be waiting," she replied in a singsong voice.

Ethan reached me, carrying a backpack in one hand and a dark blue fleece pullover in the other. He passed the pullover to me. "Put this on so you don't freeze."

"Thanks." It was at least three sizes too big, but I instantly felt warmer in it. It smelled like him, and I discreetly sniffed it.

He took a mask and an oxygen cylinder from his backpack. "I talked to Xander. He said the FBI questioned him and Dad for a few hours. They left, but they probably have someone watching the house."

I was sorry to bring this down on his family, but he'd known it would happen whether or not he and Xander participated in the rescue. His connection to me had guaranteed it.

I pictured Mr. Cole's reaction to the FBI showing up at his door. "This isn't going to improve your father's opinion of me."

"He doesn't have a high opinion of most people these days." Ethan fitted a mask on his face. "Now, give me the grand tour."

"Come on in." I led him into the ship, smiling at his wide-eyed expression when he saw the cockpit. I'd been too panicked about Taruth getting shot to enjoy my first sight of it.

He stared at the console. "You actually flew this thing?"

"One of my many talents." I grinned behind my mask.

"You're the first human to ride in an alien spaceship," he said.

"Remind me to call Guiness when this is over."

"I think Guiness will be calling you." He turned in a circle. "It's like looking at a movie set. It doesn't feel real."

"I know what you mean." I headed toward the back. "Come with me to check on Taruth."

We passed through Taruth's quarters and entered what I was calling the medical bay. The MedPod's glass was still fogged, so I had no idea how he was doing.

Back in the main cabin, I suggested we go outside to conserve our oxygen. We had extra cannisters, but we might need them later.

Kalyx stood in the doorway. It was like she was torn between staying near Taruth and keeping us in her sight.

It was too cold to sit on the ground. Ethan wrapped his arms around me from behind and leaned back against the ship.

"Is this okay?" he asked softly, his voice doing funny things to my insides.

"Mm-hmm."

Quiet settled over us. There were things to say, but neither of us was in any hurry to say them. For now, I was content to stay like this, wrapped in his solid warmth. After everything that had happened tonight, just being held was enough.

"Charlie," he said softly in my ear.

I blinked open my heavy eyes, disoriented until I remembered where I was. I was shocked to see the sky was no longer black, but a deep blue, and the silhouettes of the trees were visible.

"I fell asleep," I said groggily. "I'm sorry."

He kept his arms around me. "You needed it. You were out in minutes."

I yawned. "What about you?"

"I spent most of yesterday sitting in my truck," he said. "I was well rested."

I turned in his arms. "It'll be light soon. You should go before anyone shows up. They have no proof you or Finley were involved in this."

"You're crazy if you think I'm leaving you to deal with this alone. He lowered his head and pressed a sweet kiss to my lips. "We're in this together."

Reluctantly, I stepped out of his embrace. "I need to check on Taruth. I hoped the medical pod would be finished by now."

Kalyx lay just inside the doorway, and she stood when we came in. I scratched her head just as a beep came from the cockpit.

Ethan pointed at the viewscreen where two lights were visible in the sky a quarter of a mile away. "Black Hawks."

It was too soon. Without Taruth to operate the ship and activate the shield, we were sitting ducks.

"What should we do?" I scanned the console as if the answer would pop out at me. "I wish the translator could help me read this."

"A ship this advanced must take voice commands," he said. "Maybe it has a built-in translator like Kalyx does."

I gripped his arm. "Ship, can you understand me?"

"I am Jex. I am programmed to learn and translate over one thousand languages," it replied.

I wanted to jump up and down. "Can I give you voice commands?"

"Yes, Charlie. Taruth gave you full authorization."

I shot Ethan a surprised look. I couldn't remember Taruth doing that. "Jex, please, activate the shield."

A light blinked on the console. "Shield activated. It is currently operating at ninety percent."

I hugged Ethan. "The shield is up."

"Just in time," he said.

I turned back to the viewscreen as the harsh glare of vehicle headlights swept across the meadow. It was followed by another and another as a line of vehicles poured onto the meadow from the road. Instead of approaching the ship, they fanned out along the perimeter.

"Shit." I ran to the door and looked for the panel to close it. "Jex, close the door."

Back at the console, I asked, "Jex, does the shield block more than weapons? Will it stop people from getting near the ship?"

"The shield prevents all matter from passing through," Jex replied. "Would you like me to extend the shield?"

"You can do that?" I asked.

"At current power, it can be extended to a radius of thirty feet. Would you like it extended?"

"Yes."

On the viewscreen, vehicles continued to flow into the meadow. There were military trucks, jeeps, SUVs, and vans. Three helicopters circled above us, high enough that their engines were a dull thrum rather than a roar. Mason must have called in reinforcements from Fort Drum because there weren't a quarter of this many soldiers stationed at Sutton.

Soldiers, NSA operatives, and private contractors spilled from the vehicles. The soldiers moved with speed and efficiency setting up floodlights at intervals until the clearing was bathed in harsh white light. The viewscreen blocked the glare, making it possible to see past the lights.

A black vehicle that resembled an armored RV rolled in and parked directly across from us. The satellite dish and thick antennae on the roof marked it as a mobile command center.

A small group gathered beside it. I asked Jex to zoom in, and I wasn't surprised to see Mason and Leah Kim.

An older man with a graying buzz cut stood with his hands behind his back, posture rigid. His dark uniform was decorated with more medals than I'd ever seen, and his hard, angular face radiated authority.

"That's a four-star general," Ethan said.

I squinted at the man's name tag. "It's General Stewart. Mason mentioned him, and we saw his name in the project files."

Ethan rested a hand on my shoulder. "You stirred up enough trouble to pull a top general out of bed. I'm impressed."

"Another one of my talents," I joked.

"Who's the woman with them?"

I let out a derisive snort. "That is Leah Kim from the NSA. Nice lady. She basically called me a terrorist and threatened to lock up my parents and friends if I didn't give myself up."

He gave my shoulder a light squeeze. "I hate that you had to go through that alone."

"I wasn't alone." I glanced toward the back of the cabin, worry creeping in again. "Jex, how long until the medical pod finishes healing Taruth?"

"Estimated time remaining is thirty-one minutes," it said.

I dropped down into the pilot's seat. All we could do now was wait and hope the general wasn't impatient or trigger-happy.

"What did it say?" Ethan asked.

"Crap. I forgot you don't have a translator." I turned to Kalyx. "I need a translator for Ethan."

The compartment opened, and I picked up one of the small translucent devices. I grabbed a second one and tucked it away for Finley. A souvenir.

I showed Ethan how to put it on, and he jumped when it molded itself to his ear.

"In a few minutes, you won't even notice it." I glanced at the console. "Jex, say something."

"What do you want me to say?" it asked.

Ethan grinned behind his mask. "This is amazing."

I glanced at the viewscreen where Mason, Kim, and the general were deep in conversation. "Jex, can we hear what they're saying?"

"Not at this distance."

General Stewart fixed his razor-sharp stare on the ship, and it felt like he was looking right at me. "Jex, can they see us?" I asked uneasily.

"No," it replied. "Do you want them to see you?"

"No."

Ethan's warm hand covered mine. I turned my palm up, lacing my fingers with his like we'd done it a hundred times before. His thumb stroked mine in a gentle, reassuring motion.

"What do you think they're planning?" I asked him.

"First, they'll lock down this area. They won't want anyone getting close enough to see what's going on here."

I watched a group of soldiers erecting tarp fencing behind the vehicles. "And then?"

"They'll try to make contact and talk you out," he said.

I shifted my gaze to his. "And when I don't go out?"

His expression told me all I needed to know.

We silently watched the scene unfolding outside. In under ten minutes, they had us surrounded, and three-quarters of the field was fenced in. I counted fourteen armored trucks with mounted weapons trained on us, three of them missile launchers.

"Jex, what will happen if they fire one of those missiles at us?" I asked.

"The shield will hold against them," it said. "The missiles on the aircraft are more powerful and they could penetrate the shield at its current capacity. However, that would be a tactical error."

"Why?" Ethan and I asked at the same time.

"The shield will absorb the initial strike to minimize damage to the ship," Jex explained. "When the shield collapses, the energy will be released with the force of... one third of a kiloton."

I looked at Ethan, who said, "It'll destroy everything on top of this hill."

"Not everything," Jex said. "The ship will be damaged, and you may sustain severe injuries, but you will not be destroyed."

I shivered. "Thanks. I feel so much better now."

"You are welcome."

Ethan's eyes flicked to the viewscreen. "Something's happening."

A jeep drove slowly across the meadow toward us, its occupants hidden from view. What were they up to?

Unease crawled over me as the jeep drew closer. Jex had said the shield's radius was thirty feet. Was it wrong? What if the shield wasn't working at all?

The jeep suddenly jolted like it had run into a wall. The air shimmered, and a ripple of light spread out from the point of impact, revealing the invisible dome around the ship.

Two soldiers climbed out. The passenger rubbed his forehead where he'd bumped it, and the driver glanced around like he was dazed. Slowly, they walked forward, stopping before they reached the front of the jeep.

The driver reached out cautiously and recoiled. He said something to the other man as he shook out his fingers. They got back into the jeep, and a minute later, they turned toward the perimeter.

I watched Leah Kim and General Stewart, who appeared to be arguing. "I really wish I could hear what they're saying."

"I think you're about to find out," Ethan said when the general stepped forward.

He raised a megaphone. "Charlotte, this is General Benjamin Stewart. A lot has happened in the last twenty-four hours, and it's understandable that you're frightened and confused. I just want to talk to you." His voice held a touch of warmth, but his rigid posture said something else.

"That's what they all say right before the threats begin," I said.

He continued. "You're an intelligent, resourceful young woman, and I'm impressed by what you pulled off last night. It's clear you've developed a close bond with the creature, and I understand how that could drive you to act as you did. I have two daughters a little older than you, so I know how emotions can cloud your judgement."

I looked sideways at Ethan. "Did he just say I'm too emotional to think clearly because I'm a girl?"

His eyes lit with amusement. "Pretty much."

General Stewart went on. "You're not a criminal, Charlotte. You got swept up in this, and you thought you were doing the right thing. You made a few bad choices, but there's no reason to let them destroy your future."

"There's the first threat right on schedule." I met Kalyx's intelligent blue eyes. "And you are one of the best choices I've ever made. I'd do it all over again to save Taruth – except maybe not get him shot next time."

She leaned against the chair, and I scratched under her chin, rewarded by a low purr. Knowing this might be one of the last times I heard that sound created a hollow ache in my chest. How was it possible to feel happiness and heartache at the same time?

"Why don't you come outside so we can talk face-to-face? Just you and me," General Stewart said. "Your parents are worried, and everyone wants to know you're okay."

Where *were* my parents? I scanned the faces around him, but I didn't see either of them. Were they in trouble because of what I did? Or because of what my mother did at the hangar? I hadn't even begun to unpack my feelings about that.

General Stewart lowered the megaphone to speak to Mason, and the two men walked a short distance away to talk privately. Leah Kim's sour expression said she didn't appreciate being left out. I had a feeling the blame for losing the "assets" was about to fall squarely on her. I couldn't say I was sorry.

A tiny ding came from inside my jacket. I opened it and saw the gauge on my oxygen tank was almost on empty. I switched it out with a fresh one from my pack and returned to the seat as a female soldier emerged from the mobile command center and walked over to the two men.

She saluted crisply and handed the general a small tablet. His jaw locked as he looked at whatever was on the screen and passed the tablet to Mason. The colonel read it and returned it to the soldier with a sharp gesture. She saluted again and disappeared into the command center.

"What do you suppose that was about?" I asked.

Before Ethan could answer, the general raised the megaphone again.

"Charlotte, I know you believe you're doing the right thing, but you've placed a lot of trust in a creature you barely know. Are you willing to risk your life – and the lives of others – for it?" His voice was still measured, but it had an edge to it.

"He's not a thing," I bit out.

General Stewart wasn't done. "The lives of everyone here are my responsibility, and I need to do what's necessary to protect them. That's why I'm hoping you'll end this before it turns into something neither of us can walk back."

Ethan's phone rang, the sound sharp and jarring inside the ship. He took it from his pocket and answered without checking the screen. There were only two people who could be calling him.

"Hi," he said. "We're good. Yeah, hold on." He handed the phone to me, and I saw Finley's name.

"Hey, what's up?" I asked.

"Why aren't you answering your phone?" she scolded. "I've been trying to call for five minutes."

"It didn't ring." I pulled it out and groaned at the dark screen. "The battery is dead."

Ethan reached for it. "Let me have it. I brought a charger."

"Everything okay on your end?" I asked Finley, putting her on speaker.

"Thought you should know the media's starting to show up," she said. "There's a military blockade about a quarter of a mile away from you, and two local news vans are already there. More are on the way from Albany."

Ethan rooted through his bag for the charger. "With this much military activity and Black Hawks overhead, it was bound to happen."

I bit the inside of my cheek. This was what we wanted, but now that it was happening, the nerves were kicking in.

I almost laughed. I had missiles aimed at me, and I was more worried about going on camera.

"That must be what the soldier told General Stewart," Ethan said. "He wants to shut this down before it gets out."

As if on cue, the general spoke again, all pretense gone. "Charlotte, I've given you every opportunity to do the right thing and come out on your own terms. Do not make me use force. That's not what I want, and it's not what you want either." He paused. "You have nowhere to go. If that ship lifts off, my men have orders to fire on it."

Finley's panicked voice filled the cabin. "He's going to fire on you? Like actual missiles?"

"He won't," I assured her.

"Damn right, he won't," she declared. "I'm going to make sure every news van and chopper within fifty miles is there. And we need to do our broadcast ASAP."

"You handle the media, and I'll let you know when we're ready," I said, ending the call.

I puffed out my cheeks. "I guess it's time to talk to the general. You sure you want to be seen in here with me."

Ethan returned to my side. "Yes."

"Jex, please let them see and hear us," I said.

Nothing changed for us, but the shocked faces outside said they could now see us. The general raised his megaphone, but I spoke first.

"I have just a few things to say." My voice trembled, and I steadied it. "You're right. I don't want anyone to get hurt. And we're not going to use the ship's weapons, which are far superior to yours." I had no idea if that was true, but it sounded good.

"We'll come out when we're ready, and we have no intention of taking off before then," I said. "You've figured out the ship is shielded. You should know that if one of those Black Hawks fires a missile, the shield will absorb the blast and send it back. It'll be the same strength as a..."

"One third of a kiloton," Ethan said.

I shot him a grateful smile.

General Stewart nodded slowly. I had to give him credit – he barely reacted to the news. But a look at Mason told me they hadn't seen that coming. If they wanted to launch a missile, they'd need to get everyone off the hill first.

"If you aren't taking off, why wait to come out?" the general asked.

I decided to tell the truth. "Taruth was shot at the hangar, and he's recovering. That's why he's not the one sitting in this seat."

A calculating gleam entered his eyes. "You can't take off because he is not able to fly the ship."

"I flew us here after he was shot." Barely, but he didn't need to know that.

"You can operate the ship?" he asked, dubiously.

"I'm a fast learner."

His gaze shifted to Ethan. "And what's your role in this, Corporal Cole?" he asked sharply like he was addressing one of his men.

"I'm here to support my girl, sir," Ethan said lightly.

His girl. I was glad the mask hid the silly smile tugging at my lips. Leave it to him to give me butterflies in the middle of a military standoff.

The general's mouth flattened. "You didn't help her break into Sutton's lab and steal classified technology?"

"No. And I didn't steal anything either," I cut in. "Taruth and his ship don't belong to you."

"The moment that ship crashed on U.S. soil, it became a matter of national security," he said. "This isn't about ownership. It's about containment and safety. That ship isn't just a vehicle. It's a weapon, and your friend is an extraterrestrial organism. It could be carrying pathogens dangerous to all biological life on this planet."

My knuckles turned white on the arms of the seat. "He crashed because you shot him down, and he's as much a person as you are. How would you like to be called an organism and locked up in a lab?"

The door at the back of the cabin slid open. I spun the seat in time to see Taruth step out.

He was a little unsteady on his feet, but his skin had more color, and his eyes were clear. Kalyx was at his side in an instant.

"Jex, turn off the viewscreen." I jumped out of the chair and ran to Taruth, throwing my arms around his shoulders.

He froze like he wasn't sure what to do, and then his slender arms gently wrapped around me.

I pulled back. "I'm sorry. I didn't even ask... do your people hug?"

"It is done among family and friends." His eyes softened. "You are a friend, Charlie."

Warmth blossomed in my chest. "I'm so happy you're awake. How do you feel?"

"The surgery was successful. My strength will return soon."

Smiling, I said, "Taruth, this is Ethan. He's one of the people who's been helping me."

Taruth stepped forward, using Kalyx for support. "Hello, E-than. I am happy to meet you."

Ethan looked a little dazed. Not that I could blame him. If I'd met Taruth under different circumstances, I would have reacted the same way.

He shook himself out of it. "It's nice to meet you, too."

"You have a translator," Taruth said. "That is good."

He swayed, and I helped him to his seat. As soon as he sat, Kalyx rose on her hind legs to nuzzle his face. He scratched under her chin, making her purr.

"I have missed you too," he said softly.

Ethan and I stood back, letting them have their reunion. Everything I'd done, every risk I'd taken, had been for this moment. He took my hand, lacing his fingers with mine, and I rested my head against his shoulder.

Taruth looked up at me. "I do not know the words to express my gratitude."

I smiled. "You just did."

He murmured something to Kalyx, who dropped back to all fours. Turning the seat, he reactivated the viewscreen.

Outside, dawn had arrived, washing everything in soft color. No one moved, except General Stewart, who was shouting into the megaphone, his face several shades redder than before. The sound was off, but I could imagine what he was saying.

"The human is agitated," Taruth said.

I walked over to him. "He's angry at me. Ignore him."

He looked up at me. "I do not want your people to have anger for you."

I chuckled. "Too late for that. If they hadn't locked you up, I wouldn't have had to rescue you, and they'd have no reason to be mad at me."

"That is true, but I do not think they will agree." His eyes grew troubled. "Will you be punished when I am gone?"

"Not if we tell the whole world what they did. Once it's public, they won't be able to do anything to us."

He tried to stand. "Then we must tell your people."

I gently pushed him back into the seat. "Let me talk to them first, and then I'll introduce you and Kalyx. Ethan brought a camera, and my friend Finley will make sure the whole world sees us."

Taruth relaxed. "What must I do?"

"Nothing yet." I called Finley, and she answered on the first ring.

"Is it time?" she asked, her voice high with excitement.

"Yes. Taruth is healed, and we're about to set up."

"I'm set to livestream to every major platform, and I've got mirrors on dozens of private servers. No way they're killing this," she said. "All the files are uploaded and ready to dump. Just say the –"

The line went dead.

I frowned at the blinking red bar at the top of the screen. "I don't have a signal anymore."

Ethan checked his camera. "Me either. They must be jamming it."

My stomach sank. "I didn't think of that."

"Jex, isolate the signals from Charlie and Ethan's communication devices and amplify them," Taruth said.

"Signal amplified," Jex replied, and five bars appeared on my phone.

"It's back!" I said just as the phone rang.

"They'll realize you bypassed the jam, if they haven't already," Finley warned when I explained what happened. "We need to start before they figure out how to block it again."

"I'm ready when you are," Ethan said.

I connected my earpiece and tucked the phone into my pocket. Ethan handed me a small mic, which I clipped to my collar. Turning to Taruth, I said, "You rest. I'll let you know when it's time."

"Yes."

"Okay, let's do this." I sucked in a nervous breath and stepped up to the door.

"Door, open."

22

The door slid up, and cool morning air rushed in. I stepped out first, my eyes downcast as I pulled off my mask. I expected to hear shouts, but all that greeted me was the chorus of morning birdsong.

I lifted my gaze to the soldiers standing silently at the edge of the meadow, watching me like I might morph into an alien any second. I located General Stewart with the megaphone frozen halfway to his mouth. I couldn't make out his expression without the viewscreen's zoom, but I had a pretty good idea.

Ethan stepped up beside me. "Your parents are here."

I swung my gaze away from the general and spotted my mother standing near the front of the mobile command center, her pale blonde hair gleaming in the dawn light. Beside her stood my father. What was going through their minds? Were they worried? Angry? A bit of both?

"I've tagged every major news outlet in the U.S., Canada, and the UK," Finley said in my ear. "I'm adding Europe and Asia now. I'm promising them the story of the century – and Nightshade is a man of his word."

"Give me one minute." I looked at Ethan. "I'll stand here so you can zoom out and get the whole ship. Make sure to get General Stewart and Mason in the shot. Wouldn't want to leave them out."

He chuckled. "Let me know when you're ready."

A ripple of noise went through the spectators, and General Stewart's voice boomed from the megaphone. "Any attempt to broadcast from this location will be blocked."

I glanced toward my parents, who had moved forward. I flashed a smile at them and faced Ethan. "I'm ready."

"You're live," Finley said.

I swallowed hard and looked into the camera. "Hi. My name is Charlie Ross." My voice wavered, and I gave a small, apologetic smile. "It's been a really long twenty-four hours, so bear with me."

Ethan smiled from behind the camera and mouthed, *"You've got this."*

I squared my shoulders. "I live in Hudson Ridge, New York where Sutton Aerospace is building the drive for the North American Coalition's colony ship. Six weeks ago, an alien spaceship crashed in a ravine outside town. This spaceship." I turned slightly and gestured at the ship behind me. "The official story is that one of Sutton's test planes crashed."

I looked back at the camera. "That's a lie."

"Oooh, nice shot of the ship and the military," Finley said. "That general looks ready to blow."

I took another steadying breath. "You're probably wondering where I come in. A few days after the crash, I found an injured creature in the woods. At first, I thought she was some illegal lab experiment." I let out a shaky laugh. "Imagine my shock when I realized she was an alien. Her name is Kalyx."

I let that hang there for a moment.

"Then I found out the spaceship's pilot was being held in a secret lab at Sutton." I gave a wry smile. "I know how crazy this all sounds. It was hard for me to believe, and I was there."

Finley whooped. "The networks are picking it up. They're showing the files."

I resisted the urge to wipe my palms on my clothes. "The pilot's name is Taruth. He's from a planet called Kruran, and he came to Earth looking for his friend who crashed here two years ago. Taruth was shot down by the U.S. military and locked up in the lab at Sutton, where they have his friend's body and ship."

Anger hardened my voice. "When they weren't treating Taruth like a lab animal, they were making him repair his ship. They want his drive for their colony ship.

"You're probably thinking this is some kind of deep fake, and I don't blame you," I said. "But there's proof. Hundreds of photos, videos, and documents have just been shared online. Search for Project Astravir, and see for yourself."

The invisible dome surrounding the ship shimmered like heat off pavement, distorting the world beyond it for half a second.

I scanned the perimeter, heart thudding. Had they fired at us?

I hurried into the ship, holding my mask over my face. "What happened to the shield?"

"It was struck by a weak electromagnetic pulse," Taruth said. "The shield was not compromised."

Relief swept through me. "How do you feel?"

"I am stronger."

"Great! I'm going to ask you to come outside in a few minutes." I turned to go and hesitated. "You don't have to do this if you don't want to."

"I wish to do it for you," he said.

I went outside and faced the camera again. "The military has us surrounded, and they're trying to stop this broadcast. They can't kill the signal, so they fired an EMP at us. But they can't get through the ship's shield. And they can't stop the truth from coming out."

Finley laughed in my ear. "You're trending. Everyone's asking how to spell Taruth and Kalyx."

Another bout of nerves hit me, and I glanced away from the camera for a second. "Last night, Kalyx and I snuck into Sutton to rescue Taruth. We found him and escaped in his ship. But he got shot. We landed here so he could heal."

"Taruth's gone viral!" Finley said. "His face is everywhere."

I smiled. "Taruth agreed to let me introduce him and Kalyx to you before they leave. He understands English, but he can't speak it, so I'll translate for him."

Ethan pointed to his ear, and it took me a second to catch on.

I pulled back my hair. "I don't know if you can see it, but I'm wearing a translator. It's how I'm able to talk to him."

I went to the door and said, "Taruth, are you ready?"

"Yes."

A hush settled over the meadow as Taruth and Kalyx appeared in the doorway and descended the ramp. He was calm and graceful; she was alert at his side.

The three of us stood together, and I said, "Everyone, this is Taruth and Kalyx."

"Hello, humans," he said in his gentle voice. "I am Taruth from Kruran."

I translated for him.

"I came to your world to find my friend, Enoin. I was saddened to learn his ship crashed and he did not survive. I was alone in captivity and afraid for Kalyx."

He paused, and I translated.

"My friend Charlie found Kalyx and protected her," he continued. "It gave me comfort to know Kalyx was safe, and I no longer felt alone."

I reached down and clasped his hand. My voice was a little rough when I translated for the camera.

"Charlie found me as well," he said. "She is a brave friend. I will miss her when I return to my home."

"Taruth…" My voice broke, but I would *not* ugly cry in front of millions of people. I took a moment to compose myself before I translated his words.

He looked at me. "That is all I wish to say."

Finley squealed. "You just broke the internet – literally. Sites are crashing from the traffic. People are losing their minds."

"That's all," I said to the camera. I switched off the mic and turned to him, emotion crowding my chest. "I guess this is it. It's time for you to go."

"First, I wish to show you something," he said.

"Ah, hell," Finley groaned. "I just lost my internet connection. I need to go fix this. Don't do anything interesting until I come back."

Curious, I followed Taruth and Kalyx into the ship. He settled into the pilot's seat and activated the hologram, his fingers moving deftly over the controls. A star map appeared in front of us. He touched a cluster of stars, zooming in to show seven planets orbiting a sun.

He pointed to one of the planets, wrapped in a soft amber glow. Its surface was a mix of deep violet forests, rust-colored mountains, and shadowy blue-black seas.

"That is Kruran."

"Wow," I breathed.

He selected the planet farthest from Kruran. The image zoomed in, and for a moment, I thought I was looking at Earth. Swaths of green and blue covered the surface, part of it obscured by cloud cover.

"This is Velas."

"Who lives there?" We hadn't talked about other civilizations in his system.

"It is uninhabited," he said.

"Why?"

He rotated the planet three-hundred-and-sixty degrees. "The oxygen levels are very high."

A spark lit behind my ribs. "As high as they are here?"

"They are higher on Velas because there is no industry releasing carbon into the atmosphere." He looked up at me. "Do you wish to see it?"

"Yes! How close can you zoom in?"

"Jex, calculate a viable surface coordinate for an anchor," he said.

The holographic Velas expanded, rotating in every direction as Jex scanned the terrain. Blurred colors swirled across the screen until it abruptly stopped over a plain covered in tall, waving grasses.

"Coordinates calculated," Jex said.

Taruth touched the console. "Open a wormhole."

I gaped at him. "Wait – what?"

A deep, low hum vibrated beneath my feet, subtle at first but growing. The air pressed in around me, my ears tightening, and a pulsing thud began, like the ship had developed a heartbeat.

The viewscreen activated, and I gripped the back of Taruth's seat when a small circle of blue light, no bigger than a basketball, appeared twenty feet from the ship. It spiraled outward, a kaleidoscope of color folding in on itself with dizzying speed.

The circle expanded to ten feet across, the edges solidifying into a ring of rippling blue light. Beyond it stretched an undulating tunnel of swirling light, like a path carved straight through the Milky Way. The tunnel stilled and the view became a distorted blur of color, as if I was staring through frosted glass.

I didn't realize I was holding my breath until Taruth's hand touched mine. I gasped, oxygen rushing back into my lungs.

"Is... is that Velas?"

"Yes. Do you wish to see it?" he asked.

My mind reeled, and I felt lightheaded. I was looking at a planet trillions of miles away. It couldn't be real.

His words sank in, and my legs wobbled. "You mean... go there?"

"The wormhole is temporary," he said. "The visit would be less than five minutes."

I couldn't speak, so I nodded.

He stood, and I followed him to the door like I was in a dream.

Outside, the air felt electric. The first thing I saw was Ethan frozen in place, his mouth open as he stared at the wormhole. The camera dangled from his hand.

Along the perimeter, soldiers stood with their weapons half-raised, eyes locked on the glowing blue ring. No one moved, no one spoke. Even the birds were silent. It was eerie, like time had stopped for everyone but Taruth, Kalyx, and me.

We walked to the ring. Up close, it was less distorted, and I could make out a sea of golden grass and the silhouette of a mountain against a soft blue sky. The wormhole itself was silent.

Taruth turned to me. "You are safe with me, Charlie."

My pulse jackhammered as I took his outstretched hand.

We stepped up to the entrance, and shouts erupted around us. Over the noise, my parents' voice rang out, and my father shouted, "Charlie, no!"

Together, Taruth, Kalyx, and I entered the wormhole.

It felt like I had plunged into the deep end of a pool. Pressure tightened across my chest, and sound was muffled and distant. For several fearful seconds, I couldn't breathe.

When we emerged from the wormhole, the light was blinding after the pale dawn I'd left behind. Shielding my eyes, I drank in the view before me.

We stood in a grassy valley. Ahead, mountains rose into the sky, white-peaked and jagged, their slopes tinged with lavender shadows. At their base, short leafy trees mingled with tall, slender ones. Some gleamed with silver tones, while others were hues of soft bronze, pale violet, or deep jade – their colors shifting subtly in the light. From high branches hung long, ribbon-like fronds that cascaded in soft arcs, waving in the breeze.

The grass beneath my feet was green with a lavender-silver hue. Scattered throughout were small, coiled flowers with fan-shaped petals in shades of coral and electric blue. With my first few steps, dozens of butterfly-like insects rose into the air, their delicate, gold wings shaped like elongated teardrops, each pair tapering into a shimmering tail.

I began walking and stopped. Something felt off.

I took a few more steps and felt a slight spring in my step that had nothing to do with my mood. The gravity here was lighter, not by much but enough to notice.

Kalyx ran past me, tail swishing. She darted through the grass after the insects, swiping playfully at the air. She missed every time, but she seemed more delighted with the chase than catching them.

Smiling, I took a deep breath. The air smelled clean and warm, carrying the scents of grass, exotic flowers, and a faint tang that was oddly familiar. I'd been in environmentally controlled greenhouses where the air and water were clean and the soil free of contaminants. They couldn't compare to this.

I turned, and a quiet gasp slipped out.

The valley sloped gently to a cliff, and beyond it, an ocean stretched to the horizon. The water shifted color as it rolled. One moment it was deep teal, the next muted violet, fading into a cool, blue-gray where the sunlight struck at an angle. Above it, two moons hung in the cloudless blue sky – one pale and sharp, the other smaller and more distant.

I walked to the edge and saw waves lapping at a white sandy beach that gleamed like pearls under the sun. The water was so clear, I could see a school of small silver fish moving in a tight, fluid pattern. I had never seen an ocean so clear, and without a single piece of garbage.

Overhead, a large bird glided in slow circles. Its wings spanned ten feet, its white feathers streaked with iridescent color. It had the curved beak of a bird of prey, taloned feet, and a forked tail that fanned out behind it.

Without a sound, it tucked its wings and dived. It skimmed the water and rose with a wriggling fish in its talons.

A quarter of a mile away, a huge dark shape broke the surface. The body was long and eel-like with a tapered head and fins along its length, and larger fins on its sides that fanned out like wings. It arced through the air and vanished beneath the surface again without a splash.

Taruth had said the planet was uninhabited. He must've meant no civilization, because it was teeming with life.

"Is this real?" I whispered.

"Do you like it?" he asked.

"How could I not like it?" My gaze met his. "Thank you for showing me this. It's the best gift I've ever received."

His eyes darkened in concern. "Why do you cry?"

I reached up, surprised to feel wetness on my cheek. I let out a shaky laugh. "Humans can cry when we're happy. Your people don't do that?"

"No." He studied my face. "You are happy?"

"More than I can say." I looked up at the haze-free sky, and I had to shield my eyes again. "I never dreamed I'd see something like this in my lifetime."

He didn't speak for a moment. "It will be many years before humans develop the technology to travel across the universe to a new planet."

I sighed. "I know."

"I want you to have this in your lifetime," he said softly.

My breath caught. "Are you going to show us how to build a drive for the colony ship?"

"Humans are not ready for that technology," he replied. "It is better for your civilization to advance at its own pace."

I deflated, but I understood. If his people treated me the way mine had treated him, the last thing I'd want would be to unleash them on the universe.

"I can place an anchor here and another on Earth," he said. "It will allow you to open a wormhole between the planets."

I stared at him. "What? You mean like a physical anchor? You can do that?"

"Yes. First, I must return to my planet to request permission from the

Council and assemble the materials to construct the anchors. They will require a torlacite power source and anti-mass." He didn't seem to notice my shocked expression as he continued. "Jex will do an analysis to determine the best geographic location on Earth."

"Taruth." His name came out as a hoarse whisper. "Why would you do this for us?"

His voice grew quieter. "I want you to have a long lifespan."

"But after everything we did to you..."

He took my hand. "There are bad people in my civilization too, but they are far outnumbered by the good. You showed me kindness and friendship, and you took a great risk to free me. In you, I see the good of your people."

I didn't know what to say. I looked out at the ocean, blinking away fresh tears.

"You do not want the anchors?" he asked.

"Yes!" I threw my arms around him. "Thank you."

He patted my back. "You are welcome, my friend."

I pulled back. "You said we aren't ready for your technology, but you're willing to give us the ability to create wormholes?"

"Humans cannot open or replicate the anchors," he explained. "They will not impact your technological evolution."

It all seemed too good to be true. "What about your people? Will they be okay with you giving us the anchors?"

"I believe the Council will grant me permission when I show them the data I collected on Earth," he said. "Your planet is dying, and my people would not allow your species to go extinct if we could prevent it."

"And they'll be okay with humans colonizing a planet in your system?"

He nodded. "Velas is the farthest planet in our system, and it is uninhabitable for us. It holds no value for Kruran, but it can offer your people a chance to survive."

I was trying to think of a response when a deep, echoing roar rolled out from the trees. I spun toward the sound. "What was that?"

"A surnek," he said, unconcerned.

I scanned the trees, but saw nothing moving. "What's a surnek?"

"It is a predator." He moved to my side. "You are in no danger. It is not hunting."

"How do you know?"

"If it was hunting, you would not hear it coming," he said. "It is warning another surnek to leave its territory."

A chill crept up my spine. "Are there a lot of predators here?"

"Yes. Like Earth, Velas has many dangers. It resembles your planet, but its evolution was different. It has never known civilization, and life here survives by instinct, not invention." He met my eyes. "There is much your people must learn to thrive here. It will not be easy."

I nodded. "They've been talking about colonizing Alpha-C-A1 for years. They know there are risks and challenges."

"My people have surveyed the planet you call Alpha-C-A1," he said. "It can sustain human life, but it is a hostile world. Humans would struggle to survive there."

I shivered. "Good to know. I'll be sure to pass that along to them."

He extended his hand. "It is time to return to Earth." He called for Kalyx, who bounded happily back to his side as we walked to the wormhole.

"Wait." I took out my phone and hit record. Slowly, I swept the lens across the valley from the jagged mountains to the glittering ocean, just as another serpentine creature breached the surface. This was for Finley and Ethan.

"Okay, I'm ready." I curled my fingers around his. Together, we stepped into the wormhole.

Seconds later, we were back in the meadow. Everything was the same – but also different. The air was heavier, acrid, and the world seemed dull and colorless despite the sun peeking over the horizon. It was familiar but changed in ways I couldn't explain.

Or maybe the world hadn't changed at all. Maybe I had.

My gaze found Ethan, standing exactly where I'd left him, his camera now aimed at us. Our eyes met, and the relief in his was almost palpable. I managed a small smile to let him know I was okay.

The unnatural hush shattered when a phone rang. The sound seemed to break the spell, and noise swelled around us.

Two voices rose above the rest, drawing my eyes to where my mother and father stood holding on to each other. We had a lot to talk about when this was over, more than a single conversation could fix. Something heavy settled on my chest. So much had happened, and I didn't know where we'd go from here, or if we could move past it at all.

Taruth touched his armband. "Jex, close the wormhole."

I looked back as the space inside the ring folded in on itself, rapidly shrinking and disappearing as if it had never existed.

The phone was still ringing, and I realized it was mine. I answered, and Finley babbled incoherently before blurting, "Don't you ever do that to me again!"

"I'm sorry. I didn't know that was going to happen," I said as Taruth and I walked back to the ship.

"That was a wormhole! Where did you go?" Her voice cracked. "I've never been so scared in my life."

"It's called Velas, and I'll tell you all about it." I sent her the video. "You can be the first to show it to the world."

She fell silent, Seconds later, she made a squawking noise. "This can't be real. Oh my God! What is that thing in the water?"

Taruth and I reached the spot where we'd stood before. Ethan nodded to let me know the camera was still on.

I turned on the mic. "What you just saw was a wormhole. Taruth's ship travels by creating wormholes through space, but he can also create them directly from one planet to another. This one went to a planet called Velas in his home system.

"His planet Kruran has a much higher level of carbon dioxide than Earth, which is why I need an oxygen mask inside his ship. But Velas is high in oxygen, even more than here. I can't describe it." Vivid imagery filled my mind. "It's like something out of a dream."

I cleared my throat. "Taruth can't give us his drive technology. But he can ask his people for permission to give us a way to build a stable wormhole between Earth and Velas."

I let those words sink in. Ethan's face had gone slack. Millions of people watching likely had that same expression.

"You're probably wondering why he'd help us after everything he went through here," I said. "He knows most of us aren't like the people who held him captive. And he sees how bad it is here. We're running out of time, and he wants to give us a chance to start over."

I wished it could be that simple. But this wouldn't magically solve all our problems. Billions of people couldn't just pack up and move to Velas like pioneers claiming land on the old frontier. If anything, this was going to cause a firestorm of new problems before it got better.

I could already picture the bureaucracy, politics, and global arguments. Every government would try to stake a claim, while every person with a platform weighed in on how it should be managed.

I turned to Taruth. "Do you have anything you want to say?"

"I will return in fifteen Earth days to inform you of the Council's decision. If they allow it, I will bring the materials to build the anchor. When I return, I wish to take Enoin and his vestra home to his family. I also wish to see his ship."

"Do you need something from his ship?" I asked.

"I cannot leave it intact," he said. "I will use autonomous molecular deconstructors to disassemble its materials until nothing remains but inert matter."

"It sounds like nanotech."

He nodded. "That is the closest equivalent in your world."

I translated for the camera, omitting his reason for seeing the ship. "One more thing. It would be great if no one tries to shoot him down when he comes back. That's all for now."

Ethan still looked dazed when he walked over to us. I stepped into him, wrapping my arms around his waist. He held me tightly, and for a moment, everything else faded into the background.

"It was incredible," I whispered. "I wish you could've been there with me."

"Next time," he murmured.

Taruth's voice pulled me back to reality. "It is time for us to leave."

His words hit me square in the chest. I'd known this was coming, but that didn't make it easier.

I dropped to my knees in front of Kalyx, wrapping my arms around her neck. "I'm going to miss you so much."

She leaned into me, nuzzling my head like she did with Taruth. Then she rested her head on my shoulder, a soft, resonant purr vibrating through her chest. I stayed like that for a moment, trying to memorize everything about her, before I reluctantly let her go.

Tears blurred my vision when I stood to face Taruth. "I know you have to go, but I wish we had more time."

"I will return." He stepped forward and lifted his hand, palm facing me. I slowly raised my hand to mirror his. He pressed his palm to mine, drew it back, and pressed it to his chest. I did the same.

"This is how we say goodbye to family," he said quietly. "I will carry you with me."

I gave him a watery smile. "I'll carry you with me, too."

He inclined his head to Ethan, and turned away without another word. Kalyx fell in beside him, and they disappeared into the ship, the door closing behind them.

I wiped my eyes as Ethan and I retreated to a safe distance. We turned at the low hum of the engines, and saw Taruth on the viewscreen watching us from his seat. I waved, and he waved back.

The viewscreen vanished. Seconds later, the ship lifted off. It barely made a sound as it rose above the trees and hovered for several heartbeats. It angled skyward and shot into the sky so fast it was as if it had never been there at all.

Ethan took my hand and gave it a gentle squeeze. "I hope you weren't attached to your backpack. We left our bags on the ship."

A small laugh burst from me, and I felt lighter – until I saw the group of people making a beeline for us. I gripped Ethan's hand like a lifeline.

"Well, this is going to be fun."

23

———

"Odds are up to a thousand to one now."

I lifted my head from Ethan's shoulder to look at him. "Seriously?"

He angled his phone to show me a live thread tracking the odds on the hottest betting event in the world. The biggest question on everyone's mind was: Would the alien return?

"They've been going up all day." He smiled playfully. "Think I should place a bet? I could win enough to put Xander through college."

"Go for it." Laughing, I sat up and glanced at Finley, asleep against the RV's window, earbuds in and her laptop open on the table.

All the blinds were drawn so I stood and went to the door to peer out at the meadow. Not much had changed since we got here at 5:00 a.m. The military presence at the perimeter resembled the one there the day Taruth left, except there were no guns pointed at us. Now, they were just keeping people away.

Near the mobile command center, a large military tent had been set up for the VIPs, which included top military brass, high-ranking Pentagon officials, several Cabinet members, the head of NASA, scientists, and a bunch of other people in suits. UN observers and select foreign ambassadors had also been invited to witness the event of the century.

A few people were conspicuously absent. General Stewart was facing Senate hearings and likely to be stripped of command. Colonel Mason had been under Stewart's orders, so he'd avoided a court-martial. My father said he'd been deployed to Myanmar for flood relief.

Leah Kim had quietly disappeared after testifying at a Senate hearing. I thought she'd ended up in some black site until Finley found out she had been reassigned to a base in Antarctica. Someone had to take the fall for the NSA, and it wasn't going to be anyone at the top.

Senator Bradley was under congressional investigation, and Sutton Industries was facing a barrage of investigations and lawsuits. I think Sutton took the brunt of the public backlash because the lab was one of theirs.

I checked the time as I walked back to the couch. It was almost 1:00 p.m. Taruth had said he'd return in fifteen days, but he hadn't specified a time.

I sank down beside Ethan again, and he slipped an arm around me. We'd talked on the phone, but today was the first time I'd seen him in fifteen days. I was soaking up every second. What we had was so new I hadn't known if it would still be there when I saw him again. The kiss he'd given me when he got here this morning erased any doubt.

I closed my eyes, thinking about our last day together, and everything that had followed.

After Taruth left, my mother and father had reached us first. There'd been no time to talk before everyone descended, speaking over each other, and firing questions at us from every direction. It quickly devolved into a shouting match over who was taking us where. My parents made it clear I wasn't going anywhere without them, daring anyone to try separating us.

Hours later, I was in a classified facility outside D.C., sitting in a room with a team of lawyers and a dozen people in suits who all acted like I owed them something.

I told them Ethan had nothing to do with any of it, and he'd only shown up after the fact. After some questioning, they'd let him go. As for Finley, no one could connect her to what had happened. She was too good to leave a trail.

I lost track of how many agencies, scientists, and doctors I met with. They called it a debriefing, but it felt more like an interrogation. By the sixth day, the stress and exhaustion caught up with me, and I shut down, refusing to say another word.

It was worse when we left the facility. My face was everywhere, and the media was relentless. The video had been viewed over twenty billion times by then, and everyone wanted to talk to me. Most didn't ask. They demanded. It was like my life wasn't mine anymore, like the world had claimed owner-ship of my thoughts, emotions, and every waking moment.

I couldn't go home, so I'd been hiding out at a private estate in

Connecticut where I contemplated my life between an endless stream of interviews. I'd already turned down six book deals, four movie offers, and three endorsement contracts.

Finley had stayed with me for a few days, but Ethan had his family and the store to worry about. If there was a silver lining to his brush with fame, it was that the store clearance sale had been a smashing success.

A shout came from outside.

Ethan and I shot to our feet and ran past Finley, who jolted awake, eyes wide. Ethan threw open the door, and my heart kicked when I saw people pointing up at the sky.

It took only a few seconds to spot the black object high above us. It grew larger, and a wide grin split my face when I recognized the familiar shape. I grabbed an oxygen mask and bolted from the RV.

The ship touched down in the center of the meadow, a rush of wind rippling the grass as the landing thrusters hissed softly and fell silent.

I paid no attention to the shouts as I sprinted for the ship. The door slid up before I reached it, and I stopped long enough to strap the mask over my face before running inside.

"You're here," I said breathlessly as Taruth walked toward me.

My steps faltered. The person standing before me wore a flight suit and looked a lot like Taruth, but they were smaller than he was, and there were subtle differences in their features. Their expression held curiosity, not recognition.

"Hello, Charlie," said a familiar voice from the cockpit.

I looked past the stranger as Taruth stood. Beside him was Kalyx.

Kalyx came to me, and I crouched to hug her. She nuzzled my face, her whiskers tickling my nose.

"You have no idea how much I missed you," I said.

Taruth joined us. "This is my sibling, Nylla. I told her much about my human friend, and she wished to meet you."

She took a step toward me. "Hello, Char-lie. I am Nylla. I am... happy to meet you."

I smiled. "I'm happy to meet you, too. I'm so glad you came with Taruth."

"I will assist Taruth in constructing the Earth anchor," she said. "We constructed the anchor on Velas before we travelled here."

My heart fluttered. "Your Council gave permission?"

"Yes," he said. "Some are hesitant, but they agree your people will not survive without intervention."

I thought I would burst with joy. "Did you put the Velas anchor in the same place you took me?"

He shook his head. "That location was not suitable for a human colony. We chose a region with a reliable source of fresh water and rich soil for agriculture. It has an abundance of native species humans can consume."

My excitement grew. "I can't wait to see it."

His face softened. "I am eager to show it to you."

"Is it okay to come aboard?" Ethan called.

"You may enter," Taruth said.

Ethan appeared in the doorway and stopped short when he saw Nylla. After Taruth introduced them, I asked, "Where's Finley?"

I walked around him and found her standing ten feet away, clutching her oxygen mask. I went to her, ignoring the people at the edge of the meadow.

"I thought you were excited to meet Taruth," I teased.

She gave a small nod. "I am. It's just that... that's an actual spaceship."

"And it's way cooler inside." I hooked my arm through hers. "Are you wearing your translator?"

"Yes." Her hand went to her ear. It had taken her two hours this morning to work up the nerve to attach the device.

"Come on," I said.

Her eyes went wide when she stepped through the entrance and saw Taruth and Nylla. I gave her arm a reassuring squeeze. "Finley, this is Taruth and his sister, Nylla."

"Fin-ley, I am happy to meet you," Taruth said. "I wish to thank you for assisting Charlie in my rescue."

"You're welcome," she replied shyly.

"How long can you stay?" I asked him. There was so much I wanted to learn about him and his planet.

"We will stay for four kels," he said.

Two days was less than I'd hoped for, but better than a few hours. "How long does it take to set up the anchor?"

"It will take two hours."

"Only two?" I thought it would take the whole two days to build it.

"We constructed the components on Kruran. All we must do is assemble them," he explained. "Do you wish to accompany us to the site?"

I frowned. "You're not building it here?"

"This region is unsuitable. Jex performed a geological and climate analysis of your planet to locate the most stable sites." He went to the cockpit and brought up a holographical model of Earth. He rotated it slowly and pointed to a spot. "This is where we will build it."

The world looked different without boundary lines, but it wasn't hard to recognize North America.

"Is that Quebec?" Ethan asked.

I leaned in. "I think it's Ontario."

Taruth highlighted a wide swath of Northern Canada. "The anchor can be built anywhere within this region. The bedrock is old and stable, and there is minimal seismic risk."

"The Canadian Shield," Finley said. Ethan and I looked at her, and she smiled. "We studied Precambrian rock in Earth Science two years ago. They call that area the Canadian Shield."

The government wasn't going to be happy about this. The rest of the world would be ecstatic. No one outside the U.S. was happy about the anchor being placed on American soil, especially after learning about the cover-up. We'd be dealing with the international fallout for a long time.

"That's a different country, so we'll have to talk to someone first," I told Taruth. Not that I expected Canada to say no.

I went to the door and looked out. The VIP tent had emptied, and every pair of eyes locked onto me as I walked toward them. I was acutely aware of the cameras tracking my every move, but I kept my gaze on the group of officials.

I stopped ten feet away and cleared my throat. "Taruth's people gave him permission to build the anchor."

Smiles spread across every face, and suddenly, everyone was talking to me at once.

I held up a hand to silence them. "However, he can't build it here. He said this area is not stable enough for the anchor."

A flurry of murmurs broke out, and the Secretary of Defense spoke up. "He created the wormhole here the last time."

"That was a temporary wormhole created by his ship," I said as if I hadn't explained this a hundred times during my debriefing. "The anchor is permanent."

Her nostrils flared. "Where does he want to put it?"

"Northern Canada."

Chaos erupted as dozens of people started talking at once. A man with a Canadian flag pin on his lapel hurried toward me.

"I'm André Rousseau, the Canadian Ambassador to the U.S.," he said with a French accent. "What do you need?"

"How long will it take to get permission to put the anchor in Canada?" I asked him. "Taruth can only stay for two days."

He smiled and pulled out his phone. "It won't take long. Did he give you a specific location?"

"Just that it has to be inside the Canadian Shield."

As soon as he walked away, I noticed a small group heading toward me. Seeing no way to avoid them without being rude, I resigned myself to answering their questions.

"Charlie."

I turned toward my father's voice and found my parents a short distance away. His smile was warm, his expression slightly tentative.

Her face was harder to read. Her expression wasn't warm, but it wasn't the cool, detached one I was used to either.

I went to them, and we walked a little farther from the others. I could feel eyes on us, everyone wondering what I was sharing with my parents.

"So, Northern Canada," I said, curious about their reaction.

My mother didn't look surprised. "It's a logical choice."

"Geographically, it's one of the most stable regions on the planet," my father added. "Has he said what's involved in building the anchor?"

"No, but he said it'll only take them two hours."

"Them?" My mother's eyebrows shot up. "There's more than one."

I nodded. "His sister came to help."

It felt strange talking openly to them about Taruth. I was still getting used to all the changes in my life, not the least of which was my relationship with my parents.

In the last fifteen days, I'd spent more time with them than I had in the past year. They'd gone with me to DC, stayed at the same facility, and made sure I was treated well the entire time I was there. I knew my mother was formidable, but I'd never seen her like that. One day, she walked in when a group of doctors were trying to force me into undergoing invasive neurological tests. One of them left the room in tears, and I never saw any of them again.

She'd been questioned too, about her role in the project, but I wasn't all that surprised when she ended up with nothing more than a slap on the wrist. I still wasn't sure how I felt about that.

After we left the facility, they took me to the estate owned by none other than Vice President Martinez. Her family wasn't in residence, but you wouldn't have known that with all the security. My parents handled all the media requests and shut down anyone I didn't want to talk to, which was almost everyone.

We weren't together constantly, but we ate meals and spent time in the same rooms for more than five minutes. That's not to say we were a happy little family. Meals were awkward and conversations were cautious. Our problems had started long before Taruth's arrival, and they wouldn't go away overnight.

My father had already begun trying to repair our relationship, so it was a little easier with him. I had trust issues to work through, but I believed we could fix it with time.

My mother was more complicated. She'd never been the affectionate type, and she didn't talk about feelings. I wasn't sure she knew how, and I couldn't see that changing. But there was something different in the way she looked at me now. Like she finally saw who I was instead of who she thought I should be.

"Only two hours?" my father asked.

"They built all the components at home so all they have to do is put them together." I was sure it was a lot more complicated than it sounded. "They placed the anchor on Velas before they came here."

Mr. Rousseau came over. It had barely been five minutes since I spoke to him. Either Canada had the most efficient government in the world, or they were afraid Taruth would change his mind and go somewhere else. I was betting on the second one.

"You have permission," he said. "I'm just disappointed I won't be there for it."

He wouldn't be the only one. It was supposed to be televised to the whole world, and over a billion people were expected to watch the historic event.

"I'll take pictures," I said.

My father inhaled sharply. "You're going with him?"

"Yes."

He and my mother exchanged a look, and I braced for an argument. He surprised me when he shrugged off his long wool overcoat and held it out to me.

"Here. It'll be a lot colder up there."

"Thanks." I took it and draped it over my arm. "I'd better go."

My mother pulled a pair of leather gloves from her coat pocket. "Take these, too."

I had a sudden flashback of them dressing six-year-old me to play in the snow. Where had that come from?

"Thanks. I'll see you later." I smiled and hurried back to the ship.

Taruth sat in his seat and touched something on the console. A soft whir filled the cabin, and three small seats emerged from the walls. "It is safe to stand, but you may sit if you wish," he said.

We opted to stand with Nylla around his seat. I wasn't sure who was more excited when we lifted off. The night we'd escaped from Sutton, I'd been too worried about Taruth and crashing the ship to enjoy the ride.

The nose of the ship tilted upward, and Hudson Ridge fell behind us. We climbed higher and higher until the sky turned a clear blue, and the world blurred beneath a dirty veil of pollution.

The change happened so fast it was startling. One moment, the sky was blue. The next, it was black, and the earth was a giant blue and green sphere below us.

"Oh my God," Finley and I said in unison.

Ethan's voice trembled slightly. "That's something I never thought I'd see."

"It's beautiful." That was all I could manage. Maybe tomorrow, after I'd had time to process it, I'd find the words to describe what I was feeling now.

"You do not need to wear your masks," Taruth said. "I have adjusted the environmental controls to increase the oxygen level for you."

My eyes never left the screen as I pulled down my mask. I was flying in an alien spaceship with my boyfriend and best friend. I couldn't imagine anything ever topping this.

The ship tilted toward the earth, and my stomach lurched even though nothing inside the cabin moved. We plunged through the blue haze of the atmosphere, descending so fast it felt like we were in freefall. Then we dropped below the clouds, staring down at a world of muted greens and browns growing bigger by the second.

Below us stretched the tundra, an expanse of bare rock, small lakes, and low, patchy terrain. Snow clung to the shaded spots, and a few lakes were iced over. Everything looked cold, wet, and remote, and it felt more like Siberia than Canada.

We flew south over a forest of spruce and pine trees. As we descended, I caught sight of a small town and a narrow two-lane road winding south through the woods. It was remote, but at least, it wasn't the frozen tundra.

Taruth landed the ship on a patch of flat, gray rock, surrounded by spindly trees and scrubby brush. Snow covered the ground in places, and the sky hung low and dull, a washed-out gray that matched the rock beneath us.

The door slid up, and I walked over to look out. A blast of icy air slammed into me, slicing through my jacket. I gasped and stepped back as Kalyx darted past me, unfazed by the cold.

"It's freezing out there!" I said, teeth chattering.

Taruth joined me. "You will stay inside the ship while Nylla and I build the anchor."

"Won't you be cold?" I asked.

"Our flight suits regulate our body temperature," Nylla said, walking past me to the second door at the back of the cabin. Behind it was a storage bay filled with long metal boxes. She picked up one and carried it outside like it weighed nothing.

"Do you need help carrying those?" Ethan asked when Taruth came out with a box.

Taruth paused in the doorway. "Thank you, but these are too heavy for a human to carry."

That surprised me. He and Nylla were slender and much lighter than us, and he hadn't seemed that strong the night we escaped from Sutton. The gunshot wound and sedative must have weakened him more than I'd realized.

We watched from the cockpit as Taruth and Nylla made four trips, lining up the boxes about thirty feet from the ship. He came back one more time for a shorter box, which he placed beside the others. Nylla had already begun opening them, revealing sections of what looked like square metal columns.

Kalyx wandered over to investigate, but quickly lost interest. With a flick of her tail, she vanished into the trees beyond the clearing. She was livelier and playful, and seeing her like that made my heart lift.

Taruth and Nylla began fitting the sections together into two columns, each piece snapping and locking into place. Where two pieces joined, they wrapped a strip of flexible metal around the seam. As soon as the strip touched the surface, it melted in, sealing it until there wasn't a trace of the seam left.

Ethan let out a low whistle. "You won't find those at Home Depot."

Once the columns were assembled, Taruth opened the last box and took out a tool that looked like a drill. Instead of a bit, it emitted a laser that burned deep narrow holes in the rock. Into these, he inserted metal rods that fused with the rock. He walked fifteen feet and repeated the process.

"How the heck are they going to lift those things into place?" Finley asked.

Taruth returned to the box and removed a flat, round object. He attached it to one of the columns like a magnet, and the column floated off the ground.

"Anti-gravity device," I breathed. "They have a tool for everything."

Taruth and Nylla lifted the sixteen-foot column upright, aligning it with the rods. When they let go, the column stayed locked in place. They did the same with the second column, and stepped back to check their work.

Taruth came back to the ship. "Jex, verify the anchor alignment."

"Verified," Jex replied.

"I will now teach you how to operate the anchor," Taruth said to me.

"Me? Shouldn't we wait for the professionals?" This was the most advanced technology on the planet. There were supposed to be scientists and engineers here. People who had at least graduated from high school.

Taruth glanced at the viewscreen where Nylla was stacking the empty boxes. "I will teach you, and you will teach them."

"Okay. If you think that's best."

I pulled on my father's heavy coat and my mother's gloves. When I'd dressed this morning, a trip to Northern Canada hadn't been on the agenda.

Outside, the wind whipped my hair into my face, making me grateful for the extra layers.

Up close, the columns seemed much bigger. The surface looked more like obsidian than metal, and on one column was a single large glyph like the one on the beacon. Taruth touched it, and it pulsed with blue light before a circle of nine smaller glyphs appeared around it. He touched them in a sequence and pressed the center one again. A control panel appeared.

He closed the panel, and all but the center glyph vanished. He pointed at it. "You will do it now."

I had to remove a glove to touch the glyph. The smaller ones lit up again, and he walked me through the sequence several times. Each time, the glyphs appeared in different locations. Sneaky.

My fingers were starting to go numb, so I recorded the sequence on my phone to memorize later.

We opened the panel again, and he pointed to a glyph shaped like two overlapping waves. "I have modified this panel to accept voice commands. You can speak to it as you do with Jex."

"Does that mean only someone wearing a translator can create a wormhole?"

"Yes. I have brought more translators," he said. "You will give them to the people you trust to activate the anchor."

I opened my mouth to protest. I had no idea who to entrust with something this important, and I didn't want that kind of responsibility. But I was the only one here he trusted, so it had to be me.

I touched the glyph and jumped when Jex's voice spoke directly into my ear. "State your command."

I looked at Taruth, who gave a single nod. My insides quivered, and I forgot the cold as I said, "Open a wormhole."

A sharp point of light, so bright I had to squint, flared between the two columns. It twisted outward, not in neat spirals, but in wide, powerful arcs, like the air itself was being torn open.

The pressure dropped, and my ears popped. The space between the columns crackled with static, raising the hairs on my arms.

The light expanded, ribbons of blue, silver, and violet streaming outward as the circle grew larger, and the edges pulsed with restrained energy. When it was as wide as the gate, the tunnel formed, its walls bending and twisting the light in slow motion. It stabilized into a silent curtain that blurred the green and blue shapes beyond it.

I stared at the wormhole that was big enough for a semi-truck to drive through. A wormhole *I'd* created.

"Do you wish to see your new home?" Taruth asked.

My heart skipped. "Yes!"

I turned toward the ship and motioned for Finley and Ethan to join us. They jogged over, their excitement and awe mirroring mine.

"You guys want to see Velas?" I asked with a grin.

Finley shifted her weight uncertainly, and I bumped her shoulder with mine. "You just flew into outer space. This'll be a piece of cake."

She brightened and hooked her arm through mine. "Let's do it."

I glanced around. "Is Nylla coming with us?"

"She will remain here with the ship," Taruth said.

I didn't need to ask why. Taruth trusted me but not everyone else here. Not enough to leave his ship unattended.

"Kalyx," he called.

She emerged from the trees, loping toward us, a few small feathers clinging to her fur. She licked her chops and took her place at his side. Together, they stepped into the wormhole.

Finley and I followed, and her hold on my arm tightened when we stopped in front of the entrance. In my best British accent, I said, "Mind the gap."

She snorted a laugh as we stepped into the wormhole. Her hold turned into a death grip when the disorienting underwater sensation hit us.

Warm air wrapped around us like a blanket when we emerged on the other side. A brilliant blue sky had replaced the dull gray we'd left behind, and we had to shield our eyes against the sun.

I shrugged out of my father's coat and slung it over my arm, already sweating from the sudden change in temperature. The air smelled clean and faintly sweet, like new grass after rain.

We stood on a low rise, overlooking a vast plain that stretched for miles toward the foothills of a distant mountain range. The land was open, covered in knee-high grass and dotted with the occasional tree or low thicket. It reminded me of a savanna – only greener and cooler.

A wide river wound down from the mountains and emptied into the sea, where the land sloped gradually toward the coastline. The ocean wasn't the same teal blue as on my first visit. It looked more like Earth oceans had before they became polluted.

In the distance, a herd of gray and white animals moved slowly through the grass beside the river. They grazed like the hoofed animals on Earth, but they were too far away to make out more than their silhouettes.

This place wasn't as lush or exotic as the valley, but it felt less alien. At first glance, you could pretend you were on Earth – until you looked up at the two moons in the sky.

"We're on another planet, Charlie," Finley whispered as if she was afraid it would all disappear.

I smiled at Taruth, who stood nearby watching us while Kalyx rolled around in the grass at his feet.

Finley took two steps and stopped abruptly. "Whoa. Did I just bounce?"

"Remember gravity's a little lower here. We'll need to get used to that."

She lifted her foot and bounced on her toes like she was testing a trampoline. "This is so weird. I feel like I could run a marathon or accidentally launch myself into a tree."

"Try not to do either," I said, laughing.

Ethan let out a low whistle behind us. "Wow."

I turned to see him standing just beyond the wormhole gate, which was an exact replica of the one on Earth. His gaze swept across the landscape, his expression one of pure wonder, like a kid seeing Disney World for the first time.

I felt a rush of warmth. We were the first humans to stand here. No scientists or governments, no cameras or reporters. In this moment, the whole planet was ours, pristine and untouched, and I was so glad we got to have this before the rest of the world came rushing in.

"It's incredible." He inhaled deeply. "The air is so clean."

"Bye-bye inhalers," called Finley, skipping oddly through the grass.

Ethan shielded his eyes. "How far away do you think the ocean is?"

"Half a mile maybe."

"Let's walk down to it." He looked at Taruth. "If we have time."

Taruth nodded. "We do."

We strolled leisurely in that direction. A warm breeze carried the faint tang of the sea, and overhead, a flock of brown birds circled in wide, restless arcs, reminding me of seagulls.

"How long is a day here?" Ethan asked.

Taruth glanced up at the sky. "One day on Velas is equal to twenty-three-point-two Earth hours."

"That's a lot better than the twenty-eight-hour-days on Alcea," I said.

For years, scientists had been researching how to manage the disruption to our circadian rhythms and the mental and physiological effects it would have on our bodies. Twenty-three-hour days would still cause problems, but we could adapt over time.

"What about climate and seasons?" Finley asked. "Is this summer, or is it like this all year?"

"It depends on the region," Taruth replied. "Some are hot and humid year-round, and others are extremely cold. This region has a long, mild warm season. The cold season is short but extreme."

I frowned. "How extreme?"

"It is very cold, and there are many blizzards. Your people have the technology and knowledge to survive the cold season."

"There's a lot we'll need to learn about this planet," I said.

He nodded. "I will provide you with the data my people have collected."

We reached the embankment above the rocky shore, where we had a better view of the coastline sweeping out in a wide arc. Below us, waves crashed loudly against the rocks in bursts of white spray. A mile or so away, the jagged shore gave way to a stretch of pale gray sand. There, the waves softened, rolling in with a gentler rhythm.

For a moment, I imagined the shoreline lined with houses and buildings, the beach crowed and noisy, and I felt a pang of sadness. Velas was a clean slate, a chance for us to get it right this time. Had we learned from our mistakes, or would we make the same ones all over again?

I looked at Taruth, who stood beside me. "The air here isn't bothering you, is it? We can leave if it is."

"I am well."

I drew in a breath to ask him the question I'd been holding in since he left. "Now that you've built the anchors for us... I was wondering... Will I see you again?"

"Yes, if that is what you wish."

Relief crashed over me like a wave. "Of course, I do."

His eyes softened. "I am glad."

A small green bird shot past us toward the beach. A second later, Kalyx was at the edge of the embankment, launching herself into the air. She twisted midair and landed lightly on a boulder below, the bird dangling limply between her teeth. With one swallow it was gone.

"Did you see that?" Finley cried.

I laughed. "I think Kalyx likes it here, too."

"Night will come soon," Taruth said. "It is time to return."

Reluctantly, we turned to head back to the gate. The sun was low in the sky, and as it dipped behind the foothills, it set the sky ablaze in deep amber and gold. The light spilled across the plain, washing every tree and blade of grass in a warm, golden glow. My first sunset on an alien planet, and it was breathtaking.

By the time we reached the top of the rise, night had fallen. The only light came from the wormhole and the moons in a black sky blanketed with more stars than I'd ever seen.

"I've only ever seen stars like this in pictures," I whispered.

"Me, too." Finley said softly. "Do you realize we're the first humans to see this sky?"

"And the first to watch a sunset on Velas." I met her gaze. "Just think of how many firsts there'll be here."

She nodded. "Like the first baby and the first wedding."

Ethan took my hand and pulled me close. "And the first of these," he murmured before he kissed me. It was soft and unhurried, and it felt like a promise of more to come.

No one knew what the future would look like, but for the first time, there *was* a future and a whole new world opening up before us.

And it couldn't belong only to the privileged. Not this time. Everyone deserved a chance to start over, to breathe clean air, to look up and see stars like this.

We stepped up to the gate. On the other side of the wormhole, it was still daylight. I could make out the familiar shapes of trees through the curtain, but everything looked gray, washed out, and tired.

In the distance, a low, rasping howl rose into the night air, long and raw, like something ancient had woken in the dark. A second answered, then a third and fourth. The calls weren't wolf-like, but sharper, more guttural, with a rising screech that set the hairs on my arms on end.

I remembered Taruth's warning about the predators and dangers here. Velas was paradise compared to Earth, but it wasn't going to welcome us with open arms. We were going to have to earn our place here.

Kalyx let out a deep, rumbling roar in response, low at first then rising into something fierce and primal that rolled across the plain.

The howling stopped.

"Glad you're on our side, Kalyx," I said.

If she'd made that sound when I found her, I'd never have gone back. And things would've turned out so differently. Mason would have captured her, and I wouldn't have met Taruth or freed him. Maybe I still would have met Ethan, but we wouldn't have become friends. Or more.

And none of us would be standing here now, beneath this beautiful alien sky, with a future full of endless possibilities ahead of us.

Kalyx loped over and shoved between Ethan and me, nuzzling my hand impatiently as if to ask, *What are you waiting for?*

Laughing, I scratched her head. "Something tells me we haven't had our last adventure together."

She let out a soft chuff of agreement.

And, together, we stepped into the wormhole.

~The End~

ABOUT THE AUTHOR

When she is not writing, Karen Lynch can be found reading, baking, or gardening. A native of Newfoundland, Canada, she currently lives in Maine with her dogs Kenya, Dax, and Des.

www.ingramcontent.com/pod-product-compliance
Lightning Source LLC
Chambersburg PA
CBHW061645190726
48289CB00006B/1745